Mr. Bridges

A Novel

Jessie Thorpe

Mountain Lake Press
Mountain Lake Park, Maryland

Also by Jessie Thorpe

Bolton Roper: A Novel
Small Wonders: Reviews & Commentary

Mr. Bridges: A Novel

ISBN: 978-1-959307-20-4

Published in the United States of America
By Mountain Lake Press

Cover design by Jutta Medina

Backward, turn backward,
O Time, in your flight,
Make me a child again just for tonight!

"Rock Me to Sleep"
Elizabeth Akers Allen

Prologue

August 1978, Northern Virginia

Will You Be Ready?

Two weeks before the start of fall semester, Jack Bridges surveys the grounds of Great Forest Elementary. The building itself is situated on a crested oval rising like a great grassy egg, with the front property spreading to a distant half-circle of houses. A low fence separates the parking lot from a small courtyard with trees. Play equipment clumps outside the fenced area but close to the school. An empty flagpole stands without casting a shadow. Jack grins.

It needs a lot, but I'll make it work.

He walks onto a blacktopped basketball court. The asphalt warms his shoes. He jogs in place a few seconds then takes off for the playing fields farthest away. Twice he dances around, running backwards, shading his eyes. Heat shimmers off the school's flat tar roof, blurring the bushy crown of trees in the woods behind the building, making them appear to float a little.

Jack passes the houses where the schoolyard ends, counting half a dozen gates leading to empty patios and gardens. He runs back up the gently sloping property, puffing slightly, toward the organized playground. He stops and breathes deeply while assessing the equipment. Three metal jungle gyms, two monkey bars, and a swing set stand forlornly rooted in gravel and uncut weeds like shaggy socks. Jack kicks at the packed dirt base, raising dust that settles in streaks on his sweaty legs. He makes a mental note to get this cleaned up and spread with soft mulch.

He glances back over the distance he ran. A moving van is parked at the side of one of the houses. Furniture and boxes lie scattered. Now a small girl leans on a gate staring at him, her long braids falling forward. Jack reaches up and grabs one end of a ladder bar and walks himself hand under hand. He hangs with one arm and scratches his armpit, bounding up and down until he falls to the ground, crouching. He spins around, but the child has disappeared. Laughing, he saunters toward the building's entrance. Dropping onto the grass in a shady spot, he pulls out his T-shirt to mop his dripping face then leans against a scarred maple and begins making more mental notes.

The building's boxy structure, squatting blank and lazy, is of a color orange seen nowhere in nature. Unpopulated and inanimate, its appearance is that of a child's crudely drawn picture of a school, not a school itself. Jack frames the entrance with his hands. His mind adds a thin squiggle of black smoke curling up from the cylindrical chimney and two flags on the pole: the green safety flag and above it a square American standing straight out and stiff in a perpetual breeze, the way kids draw it.

The drone of late-summer insects fuzzes the warm, stagnant air. Jack moves as if shrugging off a blanket and begins to circle the school. Parting shrubbery, he peers in a window. Manila cards of stenciled alphabet letters march above the chalkboard around the room. Uneven stacks of yellow plastic chairs surround heaped desks in the center. Crumpled paper and debris have been swept into a pile and left to gather dust.

Jack looks in more windows and frowns at the disarray. He reaches a tall windowless block at the end of the building, newer and of a different color brick. The gymnasium, he decides, standing a minute where an irregular corner creates a well of shade. The grass is tramped away there, and words and initials are chalked or scratched on the wall. He reads a few of them.

Behind the school, only fifty feet of property extend before the ground drops abruptly to the floor of a thick woods. Jack walks along the shelf at the edge. Dead limbs and vines knot in dense tangles where the embankment ends. Trash and bits of litter dot the area and cling in leafless branches. At some point, steps were dug into the steep slope and planked with rough boards. At bottom, the steps meet a wandering path that looks infrequently used as far as Jack's eyes follow it. He starts down then climbs back up and walks a few yards to a fallen tree hanging below the rim of the drop-off.

The old sycamore, massive and silvery, shoots outward at a crazy angle, like a bridge arching into the forest then broken off. There is something dramatic about its appearance and sad. Jack stares at it as one would a shipwreck. Roots, wrenched from the earth and exposed, snake lifeless from the solid dirt ball. A few strong tendrils crawl up the bank, as if the tree had plunged by mistake and now wanted to drag itself back. Jack places a foot at the base of the trunk and pushes. He pushes harder, rocking.

"You got some business here, fella?"

Jack smiles hugely at the sound of the rough challenging voice. "I sure hope so." He sticks out his hand. "Jack Bridges. I'm the new principal."

"Clem Brody. Head maintenance."

6

The man in dark green work clothes, belt sagging from a clip of two dozen keys, evaluates Jack's hair, his damp shirt, and wrinkled shorts. "Thought I saw you sneaking along the front."

"A boyhood habit. In summer, you want to look in the schoolhouse windows."

Brody shifts his chewy cigar and shakes hands. "We got to be careful." Jack's forceful grip sways him.

"Hey, I'm glad you're keeping an eye out."

"That Jeep yours?"

"Yeah."

"Well. So, Mrs. Randolph's not coming back."

"Nope. She decided a few weeks back, kind of spur of the moment, she'd retire along with her husband. They're moving to Phoenix."

Brody shakes his head, jangles keys. "She's a fine lady. We think a lot of her."

"How about showing me around?"

The two men start toward the school. Jack jerks a thumb over his shoulder. "Why do they let that thing hang out there, d'you know?"

"What thing?"

"That tree. The busted one."

"Slid down like that years ago. Storm tore up half the forest. I guess it's all right."

"It's about dead. Maybe should be taken out."

"Not my job. Not even on school property. No one pays attention to it."

"Uh-huh. Just wondered." *So it's starting already---not in* my *job description.*

"No one comes back here much. Kids aren't allowed."

"Why is that?"

"Just aren't. That's all I know. Been the rule as long as I've been here."

"How long is that, Mr. Brody?"

"Since I retired from the service," he answers proudly. "Fourteen years. Almost as long as Mrs. Randolph."

"Then you will be a big help."

And for a couple of hours, Clem Brody does help Jack, reluctantly, sparingly. He unlocks doors, pretends to listen, and once says, "Tell me your name again." Brody is no pushover. Jack is amused.

Along with Jack, Brody carries cartons of papers to the Jeep, shoving them in, wiping his forehead, saying, "You got all you need?"

7

"For now. You come in at what time?"

"Ten or thereabouts."

"Okay. Let's start at eight tomorrow. Secretary arrives day after. Teachers next week. Lots to do."

"Labor Day's still more'n two weeks off."

"I'm sure we'll make it." Jack grabs Brody's upper arm and squeezes. Friendly but not too familiar. "Thanks. See you, Clem."

Brody does not answer. Jack drives off. From superintendent to janitor in a few hours. Both a bit tough to handle. But he'll get it. He knows where he is now.

On his drive home, Jack reviews his interview that morning with the superintendent of schools for Courtland County, Virginia. Dr. Phineas Porter had extended his hand as Jack entered the vast, dim office.

"Nice to see you again, Jack."

He had met Porter twice at large meetings and once when Porter visited Miller's Corner where Jack is assistant principal. Porter earned his reputation as a money man, not an educator. His focus is budgets, always. On his desk a brass plaque read, "I have time to spend but not to waste." Jack's personnel folder also lay on the desk, closed.

"Thanks for coming in on short notice."

"Not a problem."

"These late-summer retirements leave us scrambling." Porter laughed a little.

Jack smiled but said nothing. The man was direct and thorough. Not the slightest hint of "scrambling."

Porter tapped the beige file before him. "I've been acquainting myself with your background and record." He paused. "I'm interested in why you applied for this position and what you know about Great Forest."

Jack gave himself a few seconds then spoke firmly. "I know the school by reputation only." Porter was silent so he went on. "A friend informed me of the opening and advised me to try for it."

"A friend?"

"Neal Bannerman. He's principal at…"

"I know Bannerman." Porter acknowledged the name without

revealing anything.

"He sort of got me started years ago, and I rely on his advice." Jack did not like the way that came out, but it was true. Neal was his oldest friend in the system.

"Your training is not particularly in the field of education, and you lack advanced degrees."

"That's right."

"I don't consider that a disadvantage. Not always."

"I've had fantastic on-the-job training." Jack grinned.

"I spoke with your boss, of course. He said he'd be reluctant to lose you."

Jack was silent. *I do his job for him. Naturally he's reluctant.*

"You seem sure of yourself."

"I have the experience. I love the work. I can run a school."

"I expect the person I choose to run it." Porter leaned back, his manner less formal. "I'm talking to some other people about this."

"Of course."

"I'll make a decision soon. Thanks for coming."

And that was all, until a couple of hours later, at home and building a treehouse with his sons, he got the call that the job was his.

Then he dashed out in his sweaty shorts and T-shirt to see it—his new life. And now, driving home, he thinks of how his days will be spent with the messy chaos of children, the careful management of teachers and their classrooms, and a guy like Brody—all of whom will need attention.

He will thrive during those days, far removed from the hushed boardroom atmosphere of Porter's domain, even when those days will be exhausting at times.

Jack enjoys driving along the soothing backroads that are the defining landscape of Courtland County. Raw, new Colonial-style homes, impressive in size, coexist with older, smaller cottages and farm houses—vestiges of the county's rural, yeoman history.

He pulls into his driveway and stops by the mailbox, idling the engine. He looks at his watch. *Not bad. This will be easy. Long in bad weather but a good drive with time to think and plan.*

He continues to sit, cool now under the trees, and thinks about his new routine. In essence, he will have two homes: this one and a school that at last will be truly his.

He can barely see his house down the drive in this leafy season. He loves the house, a cut above what he could afford on his salary alone. He bought it as a surprise for his wife three years earlier after his dad died. A confusing and painful time, with Greta pregnant again. She does not like the house; it is too remote. But that makes it perfect for Jack. He loves coming home, away from it all and quiet—if you could ever be quiet in a house with three boys.

He allows himself a precious few seconds to exult in private. He is happy and satisfied that he tried for this job. He always likes reaching for something more. His dad raised him that way. Try it. Try everything then choose.

That's how he'd chosen teaching. After college, he left his small Michigan town for Washington, D.C., to work in the Department of the Interior. He loved the outdoors and thought it would be a noble and rewarding effort—preserving the country for future generations. But the actual work was numbingly dull. He could never understand what he was supposed to do. The routine never matched the goals. It was important to look busy all the time, even when he had nothing particular to work on. And lunches. There was always some intrigue about whom you ate with. And guys like Porter were all over the place, assured and careful. Jack lacked the ambition to get ahead, so he had to get out. He drifted from job to job for a while.

But when you're married with a baby and your wife is working, you don't have months to spare fooling around with career choices. Jack signed up as a substitute teacher in the Virginia suburbs—to bring in a paycheck while he looked for a real job, he told Greta.

He discovered he liked it out there. Being a young father he was not worried about being drafted to Vietnam. If he felt restless at times, it was in longing to find something to do, something that mattered. After a few months of teaching, it was clear what he wanted. He had instincts and energy for the work. He felt good, not tired at the end of the day but filled with ideas for tomorrow.

A gift was handed to him in the form of a lengthy eight-week assignment with a sixth-grade class while their teacher recovered from surgery. He was so happy. And the kids! They cried when he left.

"Simple problems," he told Greta. "Simple problems easily solved." It became his creed.

At first she was appalled. She hated the idea. "Jack, you're wasting yourself." But she gave in because he was not going to quit. She helped him get the credits he needed for certification, typed his papers, and kept working during her second pregnancy. He really owed her for that. And for managing on his pitiful salary. He had wanted this promotion for her, to finally give her something she would like.

Jack sits a few minutes more, savoring this day, banking it in his memory, the way he'd learned to do as a boy. He is able to recall moments of his life with crystal clarity—and not just dates or occasions but scenes of lived experience with every flash of light and color and intensity of initial feeling. And this rare gift will enrich his long and interesting life. But he does not know that as he slips the gears and bumps along the solid ruts of the unpaved driveway toward Chris and Buddy who are spilling over the railing and rushing to him, climbing over the sides of his stubborn Jeep and falling into the back seat. His boys.

Chris stares at him, silent and accusing. Buddy, younger and less severe, throws his arms about Jack's neck. "Where were you, Daddy? You promised!"

Jack reaches back to rough his hair.

"It's almost school! We won't have time to play in it!"

"Summer's not over just 'cause school starts."

"But you promised!"

"Yeah, well. Where's Mom?"

He goes looking for her and pauses by the open sliding door leading from their bedroom out to the rear deck. She is calling to Chris and Buddy as they run to their half-finished house in the pin oak tree at the back of the yard. Her pale hair, usually knotted into a bun, hangs in a thin tail to her waist. She wears a pair of Jack's shorts, their bagginess accentuating her lithe, tanned legs. From the back, she looks wispy and vulnerable and jumps when Jack puts his arms around her.

"My God! Don't do that!"

Her sweeps away her hair and kisses the back of her neck. "What?"

"Scare me."

"Sorry about the boys. I got involved."

"They won't hold it against you."

"Where's Sammy?"

"On the pot. Forever. Today was a real setback." She tries to move away. "I'd better check on him."

Jack holds her. "Another minute." His hands drift over the thin fabric of her blouse. She tenses. "I love it when you don't wear a bra. Is this special for me?"

"I'm behind on the laundry, Jack."

"Say it's just for me."

"You're in a good mood."

"Getting promoted makes me horny."

She crosses her arms over her chest. "You've been getting calls."

"Yeah? Who?"

"Oh, people. Neal was the only one I recognized."

"I called him from the school." Neal! He had shouted into the phone. I got it! "He was thrilled."

"Then so am I." She smiles nervously. "Really. Let me get Sam, and you go monitor the boys."

"One nice kiss before I let you go."

"Above the neck."

"Deal."

They eat dinner by the large kitchen window, open to the calm evening, the table a circle of boisterous spirits gathered together by Jack's terrific mood.

"Tomorrow while I'm at work, Chris, you and Bud clear up the mess around the tree. I'll stop and get tar paper on the way home, and we'll finish even if it gets dark, even if we have to use flashlights."

Greta declines Jack's urging to join him in a celebratory glass of wine. She seldom drinks and never in front of the boys. So Jack sips beer from a tall glass because it looks and tastes cooler that way. Greta feeds Sammy a bowl of mushed soup and crackers.

"Can't he do that himself?" Jack watches her. "He's almost three."

"He could, but he won't."

Jack lets it drop.

Above Sammy's helicopter noises, Buddy asks, "Are you the *real* principal now?" And Jack hugs him. "Yes. The real one. The only one."

"Is it bigger than my school, Dad?" Chris asks seriously.

Jack, relaxing, suddenly realizes why Chris sounds so odd to him lately. He is trying to talk like an adult, so he answers in kind, enjoying inside sweet and tender feelings for the boy.

"No. A lot smaller. Maybe three hundred, three fifty kids. Lots to do there, of course, but the best I could hope for."

He tells them the school is rather secluded, that he almost could not find it. But that is good, as he hates schools that face a main road, like a bank or factory. "And even the parking lot is on the side, so there's a lawn and play area right in front. Oh, and behind there's a woods or kind of park. In the classrooms along the back, you look out on trees. It's all you see. I sat in a room and thought how a kid might think better, looking at trees." He smiles. "I'm talking too much."

Anyway, it was nice to be alone and see that. Maybe I should have waited for Paula Randolph to introduce me. Maybe I shouldn't have run over there in my shorts. But I liked it alone for just a while.

"What's dessert?"

"You didn't finish what's on your plate, Bud." Greta is strict about this. "Eat up."

The boy turns to his father. "Do I have to?"

"Eat half." Jack does not look at Greta.

Buddy studies his plate. "Where's the finish line?"

Greta moves around, closing doors and windows. She does not look at Jack. "It's so hot we'll never get to sleep without the air conditioning."

"You think?" Jack asks dubiously. He feels stifled in closed rooms. "We could use the fan."

"It has not cooled off a bit. And the ragweed. Sam's allergies."

He shrugs. He wants to be nice to her. "I'll get Sammy in."

"Would you?" She radiates gratitude. "He's all set except for stories."

"All set" is a relative term to a toddler. Jack reads and rocks and cuddles, but Sam is a handful, climbing out of his crib, screaming for Mommy, running out to clinch on Greta's back as she plays checkers with Chris. "Maybe I'd better do it," she says softly.

"He's gotta learn." Jack laughs. "You have quite a mouth for a runt." He scoops the boy up and swings him onto his shoulders. "Come on. This is the last round."

After getting him back in bed, Jack holds one hand on the child's chest, exerting slight pressure and talking in a low voice. Sam falls asleep with his head turned as though talking to a bird perched on his shoulder.

Jack kisses his thumb and places it on his son's cheek. Sam does not stir. "Sometimes you are so lovable," he tells him.

Jack leans in the doorway of the room Buddy shares with Chris. "Ready for lights out?" The boy frowns darkly from the lower bunk.

"What's up?"

"I don't want to go back to school, Daddy. I really don't." Buddy has an unusually deep voice that Jack finds interesting. He hears tears lurking in it somewhere.

"Hey, Bud." Jack kneels by him.

"I hate it."

"Let's see. Going into fourth. Yeah. Gets tougher."

The boy sniffles.

"Teachers get serious. Stop putting all those smiley faces and stickers on your papers."

Jack's hands sweep under the sheet, removing bits of nondescript plastic, brushing crumbs. "I won't try to fake you out. You gotta do real work."

Buddy groans and turns toward the wall. "Can I go to your school?"

"Sure. I'll take you later this week."

"But can I *go* there?"

"Oh. I get it. No. We're not in the district."

Buddy sighs.

"Besides, you'd hate being the principal's kid. Everyone'd expect you to be perfect, and you'd have to call me Mr. Bridges."

"Mr. Britches." He smiles faintly.

"Big smile." Jack grabs him. "Bigger! And I just thought of something. In fourth, you get an extra hour of PE every week."

"Big deal."

"Well, it's something!" Jack punches him. "Hey, you're pretty solid. You got real muscles. Look at that!" He kneads the boy's upper arms.

"Want to wrestle?"

"Maybe. While I can still bust you." Jack kisses him. "First thing in the morning. Wake me."

He showers quickly and noisily, his energy reviving under the hot then cold water. He wipes steam off the mirror and glances at his smeary image. He shakes his head, and his hair, thickened from the moist air, explodes. He combs it down, but it curls up on his neck. He needs a trim—but when? Tomorrow is jammed. Maybe Greta could, if she would. She used to do all his haircuts. God, it was sweet. She'd drag a kitchen stool into the tiny bathroom in their apartment and stand there in her bra and underpants for about an hour snipping, patting, and frowning at her work. She'd put her hands on his cheeks and stare across the top of his head into the mirror, checking the length and if the sides were even. If he leaned back against her breasts, she'd straighten him up and say, quietly, "Sit up. Let me get it right."

God, it was wonderful to see a woman concentrate with that detached look, almost like a doctor performing some intimate act in an impersonal way. And afterward, she'd take a small, soft towel and dust all the hair chips off him. Then do the same for herself, taking off all her clothes and dropping them into the hamper. He always jumped her, right there, one foot in the bathtub. But not for years. She has enough heads to cut now, she says. She does the boys on the deck but in the utility room in cold weather. Businesslike, professional.

Wearing nothing but his shorts, Jack wanders into the living room. The house is cool now and has lost its sticky touch. He sprawls in a chair watching Chris and Greta play, moving their kings back and forth, two pale heads almost touching over the board. The discs slide and click. Jack clears his throat, coughs. They don't look up. His wife and their first. So alike. Quiet, serious—even play is work for them.

He breaks the silence. "Hey, Chris. Your grandfather used to say that if you let a girl win sometimes, she might play with you again."

The boy looks up blankly.

Greta flashes a smile of genuine interest and warmth. "Did Samuel really say that?"

"Yeah." He touches her cheek, her lips. He wants to take that smile in his bare hands.

"It sounds like him." She moves one king then whispers, "I was thinking earlier that I wish we could call him with the news. It's the kind of thing he always liked to hear." She pauses. "Do you mind me saying that?"

"I love you saying that." He kisses her shoulder. "Isn't this about over?"

Greta turns away slightly. She is uncomfortable with what she calls "physical displays" in front of the boys. "Let me concentrate." But Jack continues to distract her with subtle caresses.

Gradually, she places her three remaining kings where Chris can snatch them and win. Jack admires the way she submits her men to defeat, not obviously giving up the game.

"Don't feel bad, Mom." Chris, the gracious winner.

"I was outplayed."

Chris kisses Greta and flips his hand at Jack as he leaves the room.

"Eleven must be the cut-off."

"For what?"

"Good-night kiss for your dad."

"He's almost twelve." Greta frowned thoughtfully. "It's probably a phase. He feels pretty big tonight."

"So do I."

She feels around for the checkers and becomes busy putting them away. "The new job?"

"Among other things."

"I don't think he noticed what you were doing. He's not all that aware yet."

"He probably knows more than I do."

"He's not like that."

"Some of them sure are. You should see what's on the walls of the school. Got to get that cleaned up."

"Reminds me. Will you please talk to Bud about bathing? I think it's been a week now."

"He's got some other problems."

"I tried to get him with the hose today, but he ducked me."

They walk arm in arm to the bedroom.

"I need a bath."

"Let me watch."

"What I need is two minutes to myself, Jack. Please."

"Two minutes. Promise!" he growls. "Don't fall asleep."

He lets her go and wanders onto the deck. The air is thick; he thinks he could mold it like putty. Even so, he likes it and lies in a plastic lounge chair, letting the night press down on him, wanting another beer but not moving to get it. After a while, through the glass door, he sees Greta in the bedroom, moving between the closet and the dresser. Her flat stomach and hipless figure thrill him, so childish compared to her heavy, matronly bosom. He cannot remember her pregnant. The boys appeared, leaving no trace on her. Only those absent gray eyes at times.

He calls softly through the screen, "I'm out here."

She comes out and lies with him on the lounge, not talking. He holds her between his legs, the way he'd held Sam earlier. The lights are out in the house, and it is very dark. Jack senses things alive around them in the night as he rakes his hand gently through his wife's long hair, which is not heavy but has a nice smooth liquid feeling around his fingers in the dark.

He piles her hair in his cupped hands and kisses it. "I'm getting you a new car. Or almost new."

"What about yours?"

"Those guys run forever. If you treat 'em right."

"I can't remember what color it was. When you got it."

"Army green. I don't know what to call it now."

She is quiet for a while then says, "Thanks."

He draws a large question mark on her back, tapping the dot for emphasis. She says nothing. He draws it again. "What's wrong?"

"It seems I should feel more a part of it. And I just don't."

"You helped me get here."

"But not for years. It's all you."

"Be happy for me."

"I am."

"It's okay to show it."

"You always want people to be happy because you are."

He laughs. "Is that bad?" She is so serious. "Baby, baby." He opens her robe. She is wearing a cotton nightshirt. "Why get dressed when you know we're going to do it?"

"It was cold inside."

"Let's sleep out here."

"Never."

"Come on. I'll cover us with a blanket or something. Let me drag out the mattress."

She rises. "It's too buggy. Besides, I couldn't hear if Sam cries."

He makes gentle love to her, waiting a long time, and she says, "That was nice." It would have been better if she'd said it only once and not added, "Really, nice," as she pulled away. But the first part had been wonderful, and now, with her back to him and his cheek against her shoulder blades and an arm going under her breasts and the warm gluey sensation below and feeling still together.

He is keyed up and not sleepy. He jerks Greta with wakeful spasms.

"What?" she says. "I crave sleep."

"Can't turn it off. I keep thinking of everything. Pack up my office. Move it. Teachers. They'll know it's my first shot."

"You'll woo them."

"And kids, kids, kids. Names, faces."

"Mmm."

"I think I lost one today. I did my hanging gorilla act and scared her away." *Maybe I shouldn't horse around so much now.*

"She'll come back."

"I don't know. There was a moving truck. Couldn't tell if they were arriving or leaving. She might be gone." He rolled onto his back. "This day! So much to do!"

"Will you be ready?"

"I've *been* ready."

Two weeks later, in the house with cartons and boxes still piled around, Nina Talbott brushes her daughter's hair, but its coarse texture snarls and resists her efforts. Nina struggles. "I'm going to cut out this one rat's nest."

The girl does not answer.

"Okay, Polly? Then it won't hurt so much." She rummages in a drawer for scissors. "I don't want you to be late."

Polly keeps her head immobile while her mother snips. Nina peers at the girl's pale face and works faster. She parts the hair equally from the forehead to the nape of the neck then divides each side into three strands. She weaves one long braid, fastens it with a red band and starts on the second. "Don't worry, darling. Mommy's going to walk you over."

A tiny voice shivers. "Elaine says kindergarten babies need their mommies. She says I'm not a big girl."

"Honey! Elaine's in junior high. She doesn't remember all this stuff." Nina talks around a barrette in her mouth. Now she removes it and clips it on stray ends. "Besides, new house, new school. Everything's different."

No answer. Nina slows her braiding, caressing the plaits, her voice soothing and rhythmic. "Elaine's bus left early. She'll never know if I take you or not."

Polly bows her head. "I don't know anyone."

"By the end of the day, you'll know lots of kids." Nina puts a hand over her mouth. *Wrong. Too cheerful; too false.* She hands a new pink lunchbox to her daughter. Together they strap on a red backpack crammed with tablets of paper, erasers, paste, blunt scissors, crayons, and lead pencils sharply, perfectly pointed.

They walk to the back of the house and through the yard to the gate. In the distance, the great yellow buses unload children. Polly lags, new sneakers scraping the ground. Nina watches buses pulling away. Most of the children have entered the school.

"What's in my lunch?" Polly stalls.

"Peanut butter, orange, Twinkie, juice." Nina kneels beside her daughter. She puts her ear to the child's stomach and says, in a deep voice, "What's going on in there? Any frogs jumping up and down?"

Polly smiles.

"Remember Mrs. Sawyer, the nice lady who showed us your room last week?"

Polly nods.

"If you can't find it, go to the office. She'll be there. She's the secretary."

"'kay."

"And your teacher is Miss Moss." Nina stops herself from reminding Polly to speak up. When the little girl is nervous, her slight lisp is more noticeable.

They stand at the gate. The summer heat has spared a few blooms on the rose bushes there. "Would you like to take one to Miss Moss? They're so pretty."

Polly's eyes answer "yes," so Nina runs for her garden shears. "Pick the nicest one."

Polly points to a pink rose, beautifully shaped and just opening from the bud. Nina wraps damp cotton around the stem. "She'll love it, darling."

Nina opens the gate. A bell rings. The morning is hot, but the front of the school is shady. Fewer than a dozen children linger on the playground. Nina holds onto Polly. "I should have made you wear shorts." But Polly wanted to wear her new dress to feel more grown up and ready for kindergarten. "I'll be right here waiting when you get out." Nina lets go, and Polly begins a slow trudge across the field to the school, her body shrinking smaller and smaller.

A man stands by the flagpole. Nina has not seen him before in the crowd of children.

He wears a light blue shirt and tie but no coat. Looking into the morning sun hurts Nina's eyes, and she puts on dark glasses. Heat already rises in waves from the blacktop. Through a watery haze, Nina sees the man greet Polly. Polly hands him the rose. Nina clenches her hands, smiling.

Typical of Polly to give her flower to the wrong teacher.

Almost as if in slow motion, she sees the man pantomime "For me?" and strip the thorns from the stem and snap off a few inches. He bows to Polly and tucks the rose into the bosom of his shirt. Then he takes her daughter's hand, and together they walk into the school.

Chapter One

They Think They Own Him

Jack Bridges sat in his office, a small room where four people could be a crowd. Four people sitting still. This morning, Mrs. Oliver was speaking to him about cafeteria manners. She had eaten lunch with two of her children last week and found the noise and disorder appalling. She wanted something done. Mrs. Oliver had brought a younger child with her, a girl about eighteen months old who crawled under Jack's desk and sat on his shoes.

The first two years, Jack had kept a log of appointments—names and subjects of discussion. He averaged twelve conferences a week with parents, mostly mothers. This year, his third, he was trying a different scheme, an attempt to organize his fragmented days better. He saw parents on Wednesday mornings only, except for emergencies. But he allowed many emergency visits.

He listened with deep courtesy to Mrs. Oliver, a heavy woman who sat fully in her chair. Her legs were bare, and her thick-soled sandals showed fat toes. Jack liked her earnest, respectful manner.

"Tell me what you found so objectionable," he said thoughtfully. "I eat in there several times a week myself."

"The children did terrible things to the food and wasted half of it."

"What was the menu that day?"

"Grilled cheese, green beans, and canned peaches."

"Ah." The Olivers were new to the school this year. He was glad she had not visited on turkey croquette day. "We cannot force them to eat. Many parents think the children must decide for themselves. They'll eat if they're hungry."

"It doesn't seem right. Mine are taught to eat what's put before them." She paused. "The language. And so loud."

"The children are restricted and monitored in the classrooms. We think lunch and recess are the natural times for them to enjoy more freedom."

"But so much?"

Jack gave a smooth glass paperweight to the toddler. He watched her try to roll it like a ball. "Do you have any suggestions, Mrs. Oliver? We always have room for improvement."

"Perhaps the teachers could sit with their classes and make them mind."

Jack laughed. "That's the one real break they get. If I even proposed such a thing, they'd all quit on me. We have a cafeteria supervisor. Most days, she does a good job keeping order."

"Yes, I know Mrs. Jennings. It seems too much for her to handle."

He threw up his hands, smiling. "The budget only allows one person in that position."

He looked at his watch under the desk. Ten-thirty. He'd been in the school for three hours.

Years ago, Neal Bannerman had briefed him on three types of problems and how you dealt with them. They were shit, real shit, and good shit. You might be offended if you didn't know Neal and know this was his way of keeping things simple. The real shit mostly involved angry parents, incompetent teachers, repeat discipline cases, and the superintendent on your ass. There wasn't much of it, but you had to take action on real shit, and it was always unpleasant. Good shit was the stuff you had to do but wanted to anyway, so it was okay: taking over classes, giving neat programs for the kids, handing out awards, kidding the teachers, keeping them happy.

Right now, he was dealing with shit: things that are always with you, like spitballs and chewing gum—and cafeteria disruptions. You can't change the basic situation, so you move it along and try to make everyone like it. That was what Neal said, and Jack thought he was right.

He cleared his throat. "I'll mention this to the PTA and see if they have any thoughts. Perhaps the art teacher could work on some posters with the children, something to remind them of good manners."

Mrs. Oliver smiled beautifully at him. "Why, that's a lovely idea!" She picked up her child and handed Jack his paperweight, dripping with saliva. "Thank you."

He touched the baby's nose. "See you in a couple of years, cutie." He walked them out through the main office. "And maybe discuss this with your kids. Andy and Lisa might come up with something."

"Yes." Then, "I wasn't criticizing *you*, Mr. Bridges."

It was quiet in the office for a change. Irene Sawyer raised her eyebrows at him. He gestured. "Piece of cake."

"She sounded annoyed on the phone."

"Most of them, once they say their piece, run out of steam."

"Uh-huh. I'm sure that's it."

"They just want someone to listen." He took several squares of yellow paper she handed him. "Any urgent?"

"Maybe one or two."

"Okay. Back in a minute."

The phone rang. She waved him away. "I'm sorry. He's out of the office."

He walked down the hall and up the stairs toward the library, moving swiftly. He stopped a few students wandering aimlessly and watched them return to class. He refastened a fallen artwork to the wall—string dipped in paint and dragged into ragged patterns on tissue. He made a mental note to tell Brody the halls looked better in general.

Couple of years and still working on it.

He passed Charlotte Brown's room and saw her sitting at her desk, surveying twenty-eight quiet bodies, heads bent over identical writing tablets. She held up a flash card of the word "beat," and the children copied it. She nodded to Jack as she changed to the "bent" card. Silence and order were the rule in Charlotte's class. She taught with no interference. When parents came in for a conference, she made them sit in a little chair. In her view, she put up with a great deal from the students and saw no reason to put up with nonsense from parents also. They were all children to her, anyway, and indeed she could have taught many of them. Mrs. Brown often expressed dissatisfaction with Ms. Preen across the hall.

Ms. Preen, who allowed the children to call her "Ms. Prune," taught fourth grade. The window in her door was covered with brown wrapping paper, and no one could see the activities inside, only hear the noise and scraping of chairs and desks being often moved. Jack had had calls from parents about Laura Preen, but he didn't want to curtail her. Some of her experiments were interesting. In certain moods, he thought he could learn in either room and kids could, also.

He had to keep a watch on them. Some strict teachers produced anxiety; some innovators created nothing but confusion.

On the library door hung a black velvet cat with silver paws and orange sequin eyes, swaying a little, trembling. This was Jack's third time to cycle through the librarian's decorative monthly motifs. Rowena Castle had made them all by hand, and she preserved them season after season. In September, a huge calico apple with a green felt stem appeared. Jack couldn't remember them all. The cat was his favorite— startling and sinister and beautiful. And it meant October, a nice month in school, a relaxing month. The opening was hectic. Changes every day, classes shuffled around, books and supplies not arrived, nothing quite in place. Reports were due, accurate numbers were demanded, frantic calls, parents questioning class assignments. But October was smooth usually; easy warm outdoor days and happy teachers.

He caught Rowena's eye as she sat reading to the morning kindergarten. He pointed to the cat and circled his thumb and finger in a sign of approval. She gestured to her office, knowing what he wanted. She kept a coffee setup and always had a pot going. Jack thought it was the best he'd ever had and told her so often. She let teachers come in, too, if they brought their own mugs. She reserved a special one for Jack and even washed it for him.

A glass wall separated the librarian's office from the main library. Jack stood watching Rowena in the story corner, which included several large plants and a rocking chair. Sometimes when she read to the younger children, she wore a shawl and shoved her glasses way down on her nose. Jack had listened to her many times, her voice deep and musical, slightly Southern, a calming and gently controlling voice. It went with her great height. She was taller than Jack—at least six feet—majestic and maternal, especially as she was now with the little ones, hushed and expectant, gathered around her.

Jack was comfortable with Rowena. She managed children well. She knew a lot about what went on in the school also, and he could pump her if he needed to know something badly enough. He tried not to take advantage. She had two traits he admired in co-workers: She was consistent, and he absolutely trusted her.

She came into the office, pushing her glasses back on her head, picking up papers, looking for a particular one.

Jack pulled a folded note from his pocket. "What's this about?"

Rowena peered at the blue slip. "Just what it says. I need more money."

"Everybody does."

"But I deserve it."

Jack smiled. "I respect your spirit, Rowena. But, c'mon. Aren't you being arrogant?"

"Yes."

They smiled at each other.

"Okay. I don't expect to get everything I request. Could you at least sign an order while you're here? That much? Then you can decide later if the budget will allow the expense."

"Sure." As principal, Jack was responsible for every book in the library. He never questioned Rowena's lists; her judgment was impeccable. But today he lingered, reading the titles, killing time a little. Then, "Have you seen Tim this week?"

"Two days ago."

"How did he seem?"

"As usual. More or less."

"He's been sent down three times. Serena won't deal with it." Serena Rudd taught fifth grade with no humor or patience. At the slightest whiff of misbehavior, she sent kids to Jack's office with a snotty note or no explanation at all. Jack had a policy about suspension. Three times to the office and that was it.

But he made an exception for Serena's class. They'd miss too much school. When he first came to Great Forest, he had tried to make her smile. He succeeded once and had not tried since. It was worse, really, that smile.

He poured more coffee, half a cup. "I'm addicted to this stuff."

She waited.

"I don't want to switch him to a different class. That other fifth grade is a split."

"That boy is so…"

"Yeah. He's got something. Those eyes…" Jack gestured vaguely.

"He wants to trust people. He's just not sure."

"Exactly."

"Well."

"Serena says he won't do anything she assigns in class."

"Tell her she can send him here. I can usually get him to work."

"Okay, thanks. I don't want to see this one slip through the cracks."
He handed her his mug and left.

Rowena stood quietly for a minute then set the cup firmly on her
desk. She grabbed a stack of cards and began filing them rapidly.

Amy Ellen Webber hurried into the office. "I need to change the
movie for next Thursday. I had the wrong unit in mind."

Rowena passed her a form. "Fill this in. I'll see what I can do."

Amy Ellen sat down to write. "My class has a worksheet. Usually, I
don't dare leave." She wrote furiously, scratched out, rewrote. "I'm so
mixed up. I always forget how to fill out these requests." She held the
form on her lap and sat awkwardly, her knees pressed together and her
toes pointing inward.

Rowena murmured, "And after only twenty years teaching."

"Do you think I'm experiencing burnout or menopause or
something?"

Rowena laughed. Amy Ellen looked at the sand-colored mug on the
desk. "Was he here?"

"Left a few minutes before you came."

Amy Ellen ran one finger around the rim of the cup, lightly, delicately.
She barely touched it. "He's the only one I've never minded coming
into my class to observe. I've dreaded the others, even Paula."

"Why? Did the others seem critical, and he just tries to be helpful?"

"I guess." She picked up Jack's cup and held it in both hands. "I think
I'll have coffee."

"You didn't bring your mug."

"I'll use this."

"Honey, forget menopause. You've gone straight to senility."

"Do I talk about him too much? Am I too old for this?"

"Your *daughter's* too old for this."

Amy Ellen pouted. "It's different for you. You've never been married, so you don't know what it's like. I can't help it, Rowena. I miss having a man. I like them."

"Honey." Rowena looked at Amy Ellen, her youthful clothes, her fluffy perm. "I'm sure you're not the only one."

"Well, what is it about him?" She flounced. "I mean, he's not exactly good looking."

"Isn't he?"

"It isn't why we like him!"

"Oh?" Rowena moved papers. There was that art teacher, Miss Boot, the blonde who left after one year and no one was sorry. She came into the teachers' lounge the morning after Jack's first faculty meeting with them, looked around brightly and significantly, and said one word. "Yum!"

"Rowena, I hate it when you talk that way. I never know what you mean."

"I mean nothing."

Amy Ellen made one final scribble and signed her name. "You know what I wonder? I wonder if his wife appreciates him."

Rowena studied the paper Amy handed her. Jack's wife was rarely seen at Great Forest. Some liked that; some didn't. Rowena had sat with her once at a school program. Afterward they had watched the women ease up to Jack and engage his attention. Rowena had said mildly, "We all admire him so much."

"I suppose so," Greta had answered. "They think they own him."

Rowena often thought of that remark. She didn't respond to Amy's question, but she knew one thing: Greta Bridges was no dummy about her husband.

"I can see you're not into it today." Amy Ellen looked at her watch. "I've been gone fifteen minutes already." She sighed and hugged Rowena. "See you."

Rowena lit a cigarette and stood by the open window, watching the children go out for recess. She wasn't supposed to smoke in here and didn't when classes were present. It was the one perk she allowed herself for the arduous duty of being Mother Goose to every child in school. No one ever said anything.

She smoked infrequently, so little that it caused her to drift dizzily for a moment. Amy's question, over and over.

What is it about him? The sweet idiotic yearnings from a widow in four-inch heels. Before he came, what did we talk about? Perhaps we needed this. A definite man. But isn't there something … the boy in him jumps out, picks up your spirits so you are not so tired or bored. When he smiles, you have to smile back.

Rowena tried to picture Jack at a conference table, keeping his mouth shut, being serious. Opening a briefcase and passing papers along a row of business suits?

No. He never pushes you away. Lively but unhurried, he has the time. The attention he gives you. There is power in it. And then the teasing, personal things. Innocuous, aren't they? How many women does he have some private thing with?

Rowena closed her eyes and imagined someone older, taller, and single. She thought up a hard obscenity, whispered it to herself.

Rowena saw Tim come into the library. He slouched to a corner table, threw down some books, and slumped in a chair. She waited for him to begin work, but he didn't move. He stared at Rowena through the glass partition with an expression of I'm here so what? She stared back.

You and I've put in a lot of time together, kid. I'm not about to let it go to hell.

In a cabinet in the school office, the boy's fat, bulging file contained test results, teacher evaluations, interviews with specialists. But to Rowena, the entire story could be read on one file card: Timoko Wells. Ten years old. Father deceased. Mother deceased.

Over time, Rowena had become aware of Tim's sad and confusing personal history. His father, Branch Wells, in Japan on business for six months, fell in love with a Japanese woman. He returned to his wife in the States not knowing about the child. Only when the boy was five, and his mother killed in an industrial accident, did Branch learn about him. Divorced now, Branch went over right away and brought his son back.

Rowena remembered Timoko starting first grade. Small and quiet in strange surroundings, he didn't work. No one could get him to use much English. Charlotte Brown let him spend his days cutting geometric shapes out of colored paper. During library periods, Rowena offered enticing picture books. He sat, folding and refolding paper blocks.

A field trip changed things. Charlotte Brown banged into the library, demanding to know what books Timoko had been looking at. Rowena told her to calm down because he never looked at any. But it seemed he was kind of wild, babbling about "eyes like the picture." They couldn't figure it out until Rowena patiently drew out of him that Mrs. Brown's eyes were like the eyes in the portrait of Abraham Lincoln, the one the class had seen in the museum. The eyes followed you all around the room. No matter where you were, the eyes watched you. The guide had made all the children try it.

Although Rowena found this amusing, she didn't say so, telling the boy only that she was glad he understood so much English. She called him Tim, and he seemed to like that. Pulling out a book, she read him a short, simple story about Abraham Lincoln and his son Tad, to show what a nice man he was.

After that, for about a month, when the first grade came in, she read something extra, just to him. Then she would get busy, too busy to finish the story, so he'd have to do it on his own. And then it became a game. She pretended she couldn't keep up with him. He was going too fast, couldn't possibly be reading *all* those books he checked out. She let him read brand new books that no one had touched. He misbehaved in class sometimes, Rowena suspected on purpose, and was sent to the library to work alone—not a problem for her. She told his teachers that he knew plenty; he just didn't let on.

And all that time, there was stuff at home. His dad remarried a much younger woman. Then the worst crisis, right after Jack started at Great Forest. Branch Wells died of a heart attack. All contact with Japanese relatives had been lost. Tim was left to the care of an immature stepmother. Eight years old and he came to school with a house key hanging on a shoelace around his neck. He never looked quite clean or smelled it. Notes went home; no replies.

Rowena was grateful that Jack took a kind, personal interest in him, letting him hang around after school and even taking him home sometimes. Tim loved riding in that beat-up Jeep. Things got better. Just last June, getting out of fourth grade, Tim had brought his report card to Rowena, pointing to Jack's initials and his scrawling "Great!"

Now what?

Tim rocked back in his chair, smacking a pencil on his knee. Rowena wandered into the large room, shelving books and straightening stacks, gradually moving toward the corner where Tim sat.

"What are you working on?" she asked, her voice bland.

"Nothin'."

She picked a book off the stack. Social studies. "Fifth grade is explorers, right?"

"I'm not doin' it."

"Why?"

He shrugged, silent, concentrating on his jeans. "No point. I might be leaving here." Then, "I hate this dumb school."

"Any particular reason?"

"Nah. I just hate it. I hate everything."

"Are you moving, Tim? Is your mother moving away?"

"She's not my mother. And he's not my father." He turned his back on Rowena. He would not look at her.

"He?"

"The new one. He lives there now."

"Do you like him?"

Tim shrugged again.

"If your mother wants to marry…"

"They're not getting married. He's not divorced."

Rowena lowered her eyes briefly. Timoko Wells. Knowing too much. TV wise and hip. Now an all-American kid. "Tim, why did you say you were moving?"

"She wants to go somewhere with him."

"And you would go along?"

"Nah. They're putting me in a place. Those places for kids."

"A foster home?"

Now he looked at her. Hard, his eyes so hard. "I don't know what they call it."

"Tim, I want you to complete this assignment before lunch. Bring it to me when you're done." She didn't move her eyes from his. "I'll be in my office. Do not leave before showing me your work."

She walked away, not looking at him. Gave him the order and trusted him to follow it. She stood at the window. The early lunch periods were all out on the playground. Jack was playing Red Rover with the second grade. Every other call was "…let Mr. Bridges come over!" He ran hard, giving it a lot but somehow he never broke the line. Polly Talbott ran smack into him and then caught his hand, staying close. The teachers on duty grouped to watch. It was the highlight of recess, that glorious game.

Now some girls from the upper classes came over, tugging at him. Rowena knew they were collecting and pressing autumn leaves. The science unit was cycles of nature. Several girls had folders and gave them to Jack to look over. They gestured, begging Jack to take them to the woods in back. It was inviting there now. Jack had badgered the county to spread paths of wood chips. He'd organized the Student Council kids to do a cleanup. They had worked long hours getting rid of debris. Jack encouraged the faculty to plan outings there. He had a few rules. No kid back there without a teacher. No climbing trees unless he was watching. The big fallen tree was off limits, period. No exceptions. Jack was still working on an order for the county to remove it.

Rowena saw the group start to walk, talking all at once, drifting out of sight at the end of the building. Enjoy yourself, Rowena told Jack silently. She'd have to talk to him soon about Tim. The cracks were widening. She smiled at the interlude of laughter and play, turned slightly to look at the boy. He flipped pages and wrote rapidly. For a while, he was just a kid, his biggest problem was racing through his homework so he could get outside, get free. Rowena thought that was good.

"If we can just keep him going," Jack told Rowena later, when he heard about it, "Keep him focused."

He would talk to Serena Rudd and try to get her to understand the sullen behavior, that it was fear, a terrible fear. Then he'd try to get to the stepmother, but he didn't have much hope. She never showed interest, and the last time he'd spoken to her on the phone about some of the boy's problems, she said, "You people do what you can. I have enough problems of my own. Tim will have to adjust, whatever it is." It was cold but honest, and Jack had told himself at least he knew what he was dealing with.

He had little time at the moment to dwell on Tim. He was due to take the last hour of Millie Wagner's fourth grade, as he'd released her early for an in-service on the new reading series. The class had been alone for a few minutes when he got there. They were restless. He ran them through some exercises, let them stretch their tireless bodies then made them settle down.

"What's the lesson?" he asked, knowing anyway. Millie hated math and put it off until the last period. *Which is probably why she never teaches it well.*

"Fractions," they grumbled.

"Great! I love fractions."

They hooted.

"Now, this is easy. We're all going to get this. Someone name a favorite food."

"Peanut butter."

"No, something else."

"Chocolate shake."

"Uh-uh. Fractions are not milkshakes. C'mon, help me out."

"Pizza."

"Okay! This is all you have to remember. Fractions are pizza." He drew a huge diagram with chalk and began the lesson. He moved around the room, divided the kids into groups, held their interest. Then he had them take out paper and fold it into four columns while he wrote a dozen simple problems on the board.

"Okay. Take your time. This is not a test. I just want to see if we're still together on this. When you're done, turn your paper over. We'll see who finishes first. Girls or boys."

He went to the window. The room was second floor on the front, overlooking the playground. No classes out now. Couple of jackets hanging on the fence where kids had forgotten them. The only person he saw was Mrs. Talbott, way off, stretched out on a patio lounge in her yard at the end of the school property. She didn't look asleep, just resting. But he couldn't tell; she was so far away.

Polly's mother. They should all be like her. Well, maybe not; he didn't really know her. She made a good impression, though, every time he saw her. She'd come in late for a parents' get-acquainted coffee his first month here. Kind of messed up, as though she'd remembered about it in the middle of digging dirt, dropped her shovel, and run over. He'd discovered later that was basically true. Everyone else was clean and neat. She had sat in the back, hiding almost. He'd introduced the new teachers then told about himself, his so-called philosophy of education, some of which he actually believed. The parents there were smart and asked good questions.

Several mothers had brought toddlers. That was expected. The staff had prepared for them with coloring books and small toys. One, however, screeched constantly. The mother casually plunked him down to wander around the room. Jack tried to talk over the noise, sensing irritation in the group. Then he saw this lady, this lady with the odd appearance, kind of scoop up the screamer and begin to play with him. She let him paint her fingers and hands with a purple marker, even slashing color on her face. Jack had made a point of going over afterward to thank her, and she was so embarrassed, wanted to thank *him* for being so nice to her daughter. Then he connected her to the little girl with the flower.

Now, he watched her idly, thinking about her. Cheerful, that's what she was. A lot of the children's mothers worked now, but this one was always around. She didn't come to the school much, only to walk Polly home. He'd seen her in her yard. She was unusually active, working endlessly or walking her dog, a big spaniel. "What's your dog's name?" he'd asked Polly once. "He's Mommy's dog," she said. The dog lay beside her now but jumped up and barked a moment before a man came around the corner of the house, his jacket hooked on a finger and hanging down his back, a piece of soft luggage in his other hand. The two kissed upside down, he so tall leaning over her and she stretching back, one arm up, pulling him down toward her.

Jack knew he shouldn't look. Guy coming home from a trip, greeting his wife. Needs a little privacy. But he was, well, interested. The man sat at the foot of the lounge, loosening his tic, tugging a little on his wife's leg. She reached for her husband's arm to look at his watch. Then she glanced at the school. Jack drew back and checked the wall clock. Not much time, guys.

God, he loved to do it in daytime. When was it? The last one? He tried to think. Probably on vacation. Ages ago. Greta wouldn't if the boys were in the house. He'd have to take a day off. A day when Sam had nursery school and Greta's schedule was clear. No appointments or anything. He'd have to plan it. Soon.

"Mr. Bridges, why are you smiling?"

"Oh. Hey. I like to see people having a good time. And you guys sure look like you're having fun!"

Groans.

"Looks like the boys finished first."

Protests from the girls.

"Now don't give up. We've got to check the answers. What counts is not being first but being right!"

He moved to the head of the class, shooting a quick look back over the schoolyard to the Talbott's. The patio was empty, and the dog stood at the sliding door into the house, wagging his tail, peering in.

Chapter Two

Everyone Sleeping But Me

A tropical Christmas! Love it! Anne Masters stood on the patio and called to her sister. "Nina! Get out here!"

The large spaniel appearing in the sliding door with Nina galloped to the fence and back again. Nina giggled. She wore a patchwork hostess apron and held a wine glass, half full. "Don't you want to talk about something else? Three days, Annie—weather."

"But compared with Minnesota—it's amazing. Christmas night and I'm standing outside with no coat! Look at me."

"It's not always like this. You got lucky." Nina put an arm around her. "Is Tom coming?"

Nina glanced toward the house. "I don't think so. He flopped in his chair."

"Let's sit out a while." The women pulled two lounges together and lay facing the night. The Christmas lights beaming through the wall of glass drew a rectangle on the bricks and bathed them in rosy color. Almost one thousand lights decorated the ten-foot spruce that Tom had cut, made a special stand for, and spent two days trimming; that tower of evergreen they all called "Daddy's tree." Nina sipped her wine.

"Bowser staying out?"

"Suitor. His name is Suitor. Is he bothering you?"

"As long as he doesn't jump on me. I have to save this outfit."

"He won't." Nina called the dog over and made him lie by her chair. She trailed a hand down to pat him. "Good baby. You're good, aren't you, baby?"

"I hate it when people talk to dogs." Anne made a face.

"Don't make fun. Take a deep breath. Can you smell it?"

"Him?"

"The earth, honey. Christmas night and it smells like spring."

"Paradise," Anne murmured.

"It's throwing the whole garden off. My tulips are showing." Nina waved her glass dreamily. "Christmas night. How pretty that sounds. When we were little, do you remember how Christmas Eve was everything? Now I kind of like it after. Everything done." She offered her glass. "Want a sip?"

"I'm still full from dinner."

"Was it okay?"

"Honey, great."

"I hope everyone liked it, 'cause I'm serving leftovers for the next several days."

"Your seconds are better than anyone else's firsts."

"Does that tempt you to stay over?"

"If anything would. No, tomorrow I check into the hotel."

"You could stay here."

"No. I wouldn't be close enough to the convention." Anne gestured gracefully. She wore many rings, some with tiny stones in clusters. Her nails were perfectly shaped and polished. "The meetings, seminars take place at God knows all hours. I'd miss too much trying to go back and forth, especially at times when traffic is terrible."

"Well, it's not far, so if you get bored..."

"Won't be time. All that going on, and still I have to interview. We need to pick up a new member for the department. I hate it. All so eager. Perhaps a few of them competent. And you have to say thanks we'll let you know. And send them off to try for an inferior university or even a high school position. They'd be better off going to Madison Avenue."

Nina was looking at her sister with thoughtful interest. "Annie, what if you hadn't been given that ... what did you tell me ... that pension thing?"

"Tenure."

"Yes. What if you hadn't? What would you have done?"

"Left Minnesota. Gone somewhere else. I've published just enough, I'm sure someone would take me. Being a woman is ... well. English departments are conservative and male. It's changing but not for my generation." She stopped. "I could probably do well at a women's college but, dammit, I have to have some social life."

"But if you didn't get the promotion, could you stay? Do you have to go?"

"Absolutely. It's up or out."

Nina shook her head. "I've never understood that. If you're happy, even if you're not the top person..."

Anne laughed. "It doesn't work that way." She said softly, "Tom?"

Nina twisted her head to check the house. She sat up. Anne also sat up, and the two faced each other, knees touching, holding hands.

"It wasn't what you said—up or out. He retired from the Navy. He wasn't pushed out or anything." She lowered her voice. "But it still nags him. He never got a sea command."

"I remember when you married. Said he wanted to 'drive ships.'" Anne sighed. "God, I thought he was arrogant."

"You didn't like him."

"Oh, I didn't know him. Now I do."

"He thinks the main reason was he was ROTC and not Academy."

"What?"

"About the command," Nina whispered. "Not getting it."

"Was it? Are they that snobbish?"

"Maybe it was some other thing."

"Something about him? His personality?"

"I don't think they go by that. Well, he jokes about it now. Says he navigates a 'paper ocean.' But I hate the way he says it."

"What exactly does he do?" Anne said gently. "I asked him how work was going, and he kind of dismissed me. Said he was on leave."

"It's a big company. Defense contractor. He's vice president in charge of contracts. Not the legal stuff, but he makes sure they are producing what it says on paper. PR, customer service."

"But what does he actually do?"

"You would ask me that. I only have the vaguest notion."

"Money?"

"Yes. And constant travel. You've seen. He has to check a lot of things personally. But mostly, lots of paper. It's really kind of important, and he is good at it." She paused. "But I think he hates it."

"Nina! All those years of scrambling and striving for promotion! He should relax. He's an extremely successful man."

"It was more to him than that. It wasn't the rank. He wanted the ship." Nina finished her wine. "I understand that part of it."

"You do?" Anne raised her eyebrows, pressing one finger into a hollow place in her cheek. "Understand the complexities of a man's ambitions and his personal accounting of success and failure?"

Nina was silent.

"Did I sound condescending?"

"I don't know. I guess not." Nina jumped up. "I'll be right back. Want anything?"

"Just to lie here forever." Anne lay back and closed her eyes.

Nina patted her head. "You cold?"

"I'm fine." Anne pointed to her slacks and sweater. "Time is it?"

"I don't know. After nine." Nina slid the door open quietly and crept through the family room. Her husband's head leaned into the corner wing of his chair, his eyes shut. Nina moved up the stairs and down the corridor to Polly's room. The light was on. Polly sat on the floor, dressing dolls and plush animals in her own new Christmas clothes.

"You didn't come down to kiss Aunt Anne." Nina smiled. "Pretty busy?"

Polly pointed to her doll family. "It's not fair. They didn't get presents."

"Grandma's fault. I'm not very good to them." Nina made a neat stack of clothing, new books, and toys still in boxes. "I'll put all your stuff here, and you can play first thing when you wake up."

She coaxed the little girl into bed. "Which baby do you want to sleep with?"

Polly indicated a tired, flattened Koala bear dressed in a brand new pink quilted jacket. "I let him wear the prettiest thing."

"Maybe you could wear it tomorrow, so Daddy will see how much you like it."

"How many days 'til I go back to school?"

"About a week."

Polly snuggled down, and Nina kissed and hugged her. "You made me happy today," she whispered to her daughter.

"Is Santa back at his house?"

"Of course. He's asleep in his big feather bed, and all the reindeer have their blankets on. The elves are passing around buckets of carrots and maple sugar." Nina loved the dreamy expression on Polly's face. She hoped it wouldn't be the last year for Santa. "Lights out."

Polly shook her head.

"Mom's ready." Nina carefully untangled herself from Polly's arms and left, looking back and blowing kisses.

She went to the kitchen, opened the freezer, and cracked ice cubes into a bowl. She searched the refrigerator, moving covered dishes around until she found a bottle. A few minutes later, carrying a tray with two glasses and the other things, she went back to the patio. Elaine sat on the lounge with Anne, her head hanging sideways at a funny angle. Anne squinted and fiddled with Elaine's hair.

"I had to get help with the new earrings, Mom. The hooks kept going into my flesh instead of through the hole."

"Let me see." Nina set everything on a low table.

"I can manage." Anne spoke crisply. "This is a perfect job for an old maid aunt. Useful and requires no experience with kids." She worked another few seconds. "There. Okay?"

Elaine sat still until the second ear was done. Then she clipped back her hair and shook her head to make the earrings dance.

"How do you like them?" Nina asked.

"Great! I can hardly feel them." She kissed Anne. "I want to show Daddy."

"Don't wake him," Nina called, but Elaine was gone. "Oh, well."

"When we were kids, pierced ears were considered trashy."

"It wasn't my idea. She asked Tom, and he took her and had it done."

"He's so generous with them. Those earrings!" Anne rolled her eyes. "For thirteen! Of course, the stuff he gives you is..."

"It's too much, isn't it? I don't do it justice."

"You're very pretty, Nina. When you try. Your hair, dear."

"Don't start."

"It's exactly the way you wore it in college." She gestured toward the door where Elaine disappeared. "Is she the most beautiful thing, or are they all like that now?"

Nina laughed and poured champagne. "It's hard not to be impressed. Even if I am her mother."

"She's unreal. I felt so honored. She sought my help."

"She does that. Sort of bestows herself on you. If you'd seen her struggling and offered, she might have refused. I can't approach her— only when she allows me."

"It's the age, isn't it?"

"Mmm. Did you notice when I asked her to play carols last night how she wouldn't? Kind of snippy. And then this afternoon, no prompting, that ... that concert she put on!"

"Nina, she's talented."

"I know. But you have to wait. She's skimpy with favors."

"Artistic people are not exactly easy. But worth it. That one."

Nina sipped her wine.

"This is fantastic stuff," Anne sighed.

"Tom gets it somewhere. This was supposed to be for New Years, but since you won't be here, let's enjoy." She filled the glasses.

"Hey, whoa."

"It doesn't make you high if you drink it with ice."

"Where did you hear that?"

"I made it up. But I think it's true."

They laughed. "To you, baby sister."

Nina answered, "To you visiting more often."

"I really should. I miss a lot with the girls. Elaine will be touring the world's concert stages."

"Do you think she's that good?"

"Nina, believe me. She needs training, of course. But why resist it?"

"I just don't want it to take over everything. She's domineering enough already. Tom bought her that huge grand, and she doesn't want Polly to touch it."

"Yesterday Polly got peanut butter or something on the keys. Elaine had a fit. Said Polly had 'music dyslexia.' I thought it was funny."

"Sometimes she's not so amusing. When she calls Polly difficult. 'Mother, she's so awkward.' It's insane, the way she goes after her. And Polly's defenseless. If Tom's away I go out of my mind." She paused. "She's so superior to Pol about the music. Polly wants to do everything Elaine does. Bangs away every chance she gets."

"Tell Polly to try something else."

"I can't. She'd think it's because she's not as good as Elaine."

"She's not."

"But you can't tell her that. I'm hoping she'll come to that conclusion herself." She sighed. "I go crazy listening to her stumble on the C-scale."

"What might she be good at?"

"So far, nothing. Oh, what am I saying? She doesn't have to be good at anything. It's not a contest."

Anne studied her.

"She still wears corrective shoes, did you notice? Her speech is improved. And I think getting rid of all that hair helped. Her sweet little face shows now."

"Honey, I had a really nice conversation with her. The other night when she let me put her to bed? Have you heard about her Heaven dream?"

"Not that one."

"She told me Heaven is on a big cloud. All the angels sit on kindergarten chairs, around a piano. And the teacher plays music for them."

Nina laughed, tried to stop but couldn't.

"Well, she likes school, obviously."

"If Heaven is her classroom, then I know who the face of God looks like."

"So?"

Nina waved a relaxed hand in the air. She lowered her voice. "Polly has a crush, I guess you'd call it, on the principal. I mean, it's a real thing. She does this bit where every year, first day of school, she gives him a flower."

"That's healthy, isn't it? At that age?"

"I'm sure. I think it's adorable. And he is nice to her." She was quiet a moment. "She must get it from me. I was always in love with all my teachers. Remember?"

Anne did not respond.

"Hand me your glass."

"Nina!"

"Oh, come on. It's a holiday."

"Okay, you talked me into it." She sipped. "Are we done?"

"There's more."

"Honey, watch it. We don't have the greatest history."

40

"You mean Dad? He's all over that now."

"I'm sorry I mentioned it. Let's not start."

"We won't. But he's good now, really." She was quiet awhile. "It was just seeing Mama go like that. It was hard."

Anne exploded. "Seeing her! He never saw her. You kept her, and then in the home you went to see her. Never him. Even I have the decency to feel guilty about leaving so much of it to you. I was very involved with my thesis. But him!"

"Shh. He couldn't do it. Some people can't. I think he tried."

"He had that woman before Mama even died. He wasn't trying hard enough."

Nina sat up and reached over to slide a hand along her sister's beautiful palm, turning it over to hide her own, rough and brown. "I understand it more now. He lived with the idea of death a long time. After a point, he chose life. I don't blame him. After all this time."

"Let's stop this. It's Christmas. You sound preachy, and I have an entire week of lectures ahead of me."

Nina carefully set her empty glass on the table. She put her arms around Anne awkwardly. "Can I tell you something?"

"May I?"

Nina blinked, confused.

"*May* I? Your grammar is sloppy."

Nina hugged her again. "Mama couldn't talk much the last months. She wasn't connected when she did. It was hard to understand her. I'd sit with her, doing things the nurses never got around to. Mama had a radio and played music. Have I told you this?"

Anne did not answer.

"She liked this oldies station. One day a song came on. Tony Bennett. 'I Don't Know Why I Love You Like I Do.' She perked up, seemed more aware. I watched her listening, and when it was over she said, very clearly, 'Dedicated to Harold Masters.'"

"You're maudlin, Nina. Do not cry."

"She loved him. He knew that, and he just couldn't go."

Anne was stiff and silent.

"I always think of that, how much she loved him."

Anne moved away.

"I'm having Dad next summer. He promised to visit."

"Her, too?"

"I hope so. Try to come."

"No."

"He's getting old."

"Never."

"Don't say that. Say, 'not yet.'" Nina could not see her sister's face. The patio was suddenly dark. "Tom!" she called.

The glass door was pushed open. "I wanted to give them a rest. I didn't know you guys were still out here. I'll turn 'em back on."

"No. Come here, baby. Did you have a nap?"

"Reading." He smiled at the empty bottle. "Girl talk?"

"Sit."

"I'm turning in. You guys?"

"In a bit. Anne's leaving tomorrow."

"Oh. I'll see you in the morning then. Before you go."

"I've enjoyed it, Tom."

"Yeah. Me, too." He surveyed the yard, the night. "I'd better turn on the spotlight. If you're going to sit out."

Nina rose. "No. It's nice in the dark. We'll be all right. I'm getting more ice."

Tom followed her. "For what? I thought you drank it all."

"I'm getting the other one. Want to share?"

"I'll leave you to it." He kissed her, a dry peck. "I'll probably be asleep when you come."

She kissed him warmly. "Are you upset?"

He hugged her. "I know you don't see her much."

Nina picked an afghan off the sofa and took it back to the patio with her. "Budge over." She lay next to Anne, drawing the table close by with the champagne and fresh ice. They stayed under the blanket except for the hands holding their glasses. The glasses sweated icy drops on their wrists and chins when they drank. Suitor squeezed under the lounge, and the straps sagged almost to his back, making it warm underneath. "Isn't this nice?" Nina sighed.

"Was Tom irked? Did he want you to go up?"

"Oh, no. He doesn't mind."

"I never know how he feels about me."

"He likes you, Annie."

"Now, maybe. I like him. I think."

"I never can remember why you two used to go at one another."

Anne spoke precisely, as though wanting to get it right. "He took you out of school and married you. And he didn't let you finish."

"I didn't want to finish."

"You liked school."

"Only when I was little. Not college."

"He left you alone. All the time."

"He had sea duty, honey."

"You were twenty years old, Nina. He was thirty, and I was twenty-five. I felt like your mother, and there he was—demanding and self-centered."

Nina squirmed. The old words. She knew exactly why she married Tom, remembered the moment she decided. He had picked her up from school for the weekend and taken her to his apartment. She was sitting on his lap while he talked on the phone. She was reading papers on his desk, and he kept taking them from her and putting them back in order. One page was titled: Goals for the Year. The list included: stick to schedule, run 10 (crossed out) 7 miles per week, save additional $1000, try to laugh more.

She had never told Anne about it. But she knew right then she had to marry him. Try to laugh more.

"You like him now."

"I've become used to him over the years." Anne filled her glass then Nina's. "I know his game."

Nina giggled. "He doesn't play games."

Anne ignored her. "His game is he does exactly what he wants."

"No, Annie. He doesn't have what he wants." She spoke softly.

Anne went on talking. "He plunks you and the girls down here, then off he goes. You hang around waiting for him. You cater to him. How can you stand it! I just couldn't live so … on call."

"He chose this for us especially. It's nice, so safe, near the school."

"He says, 'Here, baby, here's a playhouse. Buy stuff, fix it up, have a ball.'"

"Don't make fun."

"It's confined, Nina."

Nina sat up and stared into the dark, across the yard. "I wish you could see it when it's blooming. It's so pretty. You'd like it. Come sometime. We'll sit and drink iced tea. Then I'll disappear, and you can read under the umbrella." She patted her sister's leg under the blanket, kept patting her. "You just can't question everything, dear, when you're married. You'd go crazy."

"Honey, are you happy?"

"I'm busy and happy."

"Well." Anne shook her head. "Don't let me be so bossy." She was quiet then started to giggle. "I'll tell you something. I'll tell you. One thing." She stopped.

"What?"

Anne leaned back. "Oh, God, forgive me. I'm tipsy, not in control." She paused, a long time. "I think he's cute. I mean, no, not cute. Handsome. Truly. He really keeps up. Gray in the right places."

Nina giggled and whispered. "He has the teeniest, tiniest bald spot right on top, did you notice? About the size of a nickel, well maybe a quarter. He's so *sensitive* about it. Thinks people are looking at it." She sighed. "It's that nutty stuff about him I like. I think about it when he's ... you know, when he's being overbearing and humorless."

"Well, you said it." Anne picked up the champagne bottle and peered at it. "Shall we bury it?"

"If we're that close."

"I haven't done this in forever."

"Me neither."

"I wish I hadn't quit smoking. I'd like to smoke."

"You're better off not."

"Let's go slowly, this last one."

They held their glasses.

"What am I talking about men for? There are no men for intellectual women."

"I thought you were seeing someone."

"I'm always seeing someone, more or less. Mostly men I work with. And you can't be really relaxed and natural. We're in competition."

"But you've been in love."

"Always with a lid on. Never all out. Never *me*. Stuff myself back in the box."

"I wish I were as thin as you."

"Doesn't matter, Nina. Keep your shape, so what, do they care? I swear I don't know what men want."

Nina pondered. "They want food."

"Anyway, my next paper, I'm doing ... *trying* to do ... theory of what women want ... in literature." She stopped. "Can't make sense of it now. God, I'm in bad shape." She put down her glass, unfinished. "That's it. I'm done. How come I'm worse off than you, baby?"

"I eat more."

"I should do this from time to time. It's fun. Makes you not care." Anne jabbed a finger at Nina. "Seriously, do you like my paper? Important. Do you?"

"Tell me again."

"I take women writers back, way back to ... Sands, Eliot, everybody. On the theory that ... women write about what they don't speak about. I get to the bottom of it—what they want."

Nina said nothing.

"It's something ... I need to publish outside the ... the..." she enunciated slowly, "ac-a-dem-ic community. Would you read it?" She stared intently at Nina.

"Maybe. I guess."

"Nina! You make me so mad! You do not read. Why don't you read?"

"Shh. There's always so much to do."

"You haven't developed yourself."

"I try to. I try to read. Things come up." *Children, friends, flowers, everything intrudes. Real things. Much better, more interesting than in books.* "Don't be mad. Lots of people would want to read it, I think."

"I'm not mad," Anne said, lying back and closing her eyes.

"I don't watch soap operas, either. Does that make you feel better?"

"Nice." Anne took Nina's hand and held it, but she didn't open her eyes.

Nina spoke dreamily. "I wish I knew as much as you. You're so smart. I don't think about things so much. Maybe if I did, I could figure out Polly and Elaine and what's fair." She sipped the last wine in her glass. "There." She put the glass down. "We should smash them. She giggled. "No." She reached down and patted Suitor. "Not on your soft paws, baby. Oh, Annie, everyone I love, I want you to love each other." She looked at her sister. "Are you asleep?"

No answer.

She picked up Anne's glass and began to drink the last champagne. "What do women want?" She sang it, softly, tunelessly. "I want to love. Sometimes, after Tom and I ... I lie so drained, so tired, I think I'll never do it again. It's all gone. And after babies too. You can't imagine.

But even with all of it, something in me, I feel it. Never been touched. Never. Something so strong, deep and wide. It's open, I want to fill it up. It's everything I feel for life." She stopped. "It could hurt me." She set the empty glass on the table next to the other. "Don't listen to me."

She inched down and put her head on her sister's shoulder. In a little while, she would waken Anne. She was happy and warm, keeping her eyes wide open in the dark.

Christmas night and everyone sleeping but me.

Chapter Three

Polly's Boyfriend

Nina Talbott liked every aspect about her bedroom. Its rosy peach and gray tones were restful, with yellow here and there like fallen tulip petals. In the store, before they bought the carpet, she had kicked off her shoes and walked on it to make certain of its depth and softness. On winter mornings, she often brought coffee here and drank it hot among the pretty mirrors and flower prints. In warm weather, she worked outside early, before the girls awoke, going back to the room later. On summer afternoons, she turned the slats in the blinds upward so light slanted on the ceiling. She would lie crosswise on the bed, sometimes undressed, feeling cool and dry with breeze on her skin, watching the diverted sun ripple above her creating a pleasing, underwater sensation. She hid away for hours, alone in her room.

When Tom was home, everything was different. After he went away again, she would leave the bed unmade for days, sleeping in its careless mess.

Tonight, Nina sat in her bedroom, listening. Music played very low on a small stereo. Nina did not particularly hear the song. Lounging in her cushioned rocking chair, she cuddled Suitor. A heavy book lay on Nina's lap. Her fingers tangled in the dog's thick fur as she watched the light from a floor lamp move shadows back and forth across a page. The window behind her was open slightly, and tree branches cracked in a rising wind. She listened to the silence of the house.

Tom walked into the room. He snapped off the music, turned on the TV, and stretched out on the bed. He flipped open a newspaper and spread some sections around on the quilt.

Nina frowned at her book.

"What are you reading?"

"*Middlemarch.* Anne gave it to me when she left."

"Looks long. For you, I mean."

She didn't speak. In a kinder tone, he said, "Any good?"

"I just started. It's about Miss Brooke. Miss Brooke is admirable, Anne says." She paused. "I think she spends half the book deciding whether to have sex and the other half deciding whether she likes it. It happens over a hundred years ago."

Tom laughed. "That sounds like something Anne would pick." He looked at his paper. "Why bother?"

"It will make her happy." She turned a page. "Are you watching that?"

"Habit, I guess. Too many hotel rooms." He gestured absently. "But leave it on. I want to catch the news."

They read awhile. "I hope it's going to change," Nina said.

"Mmm."

"The weather. Doesn't feel like winter. Not satisfying to miss a season."

"Do you want to read or talk?"

"Is Polly in bed?"

He nodded.

Nina watched him a minute then said, "Did you work it out with her?"

He shrugged. "I suppose."

"Does she know why she was sent to her room?"

He looked at her over the top of his reading glasses. "I've already been through this twice. Is three a magic number or something?"

She hesitated. "Well, I'm not sure I understand why you punished her."

"I did not punish her. It was not a punishment. I merely sent her away because she kept contradicting me."

"About what?"

"Maybe not contradicting. That's not the right word. She just wouldn't drop the subject."

"What subject?"

"Nina!"

"I want to know what you were talking about."

He dropped his head back on the pillow and closed his eyes. "I think I can discipline my own daughter without interference."

Nina was silent. When she spoke again, her voice was soft. "You're away so much, Tom, and Polly's..."

"You're too protective of her."

Nina petted Suitor between his sleepy eyes. "She's afraid of so many things."

"Afraid!" He exploded, laughing. Suitor slid off the chair and began barking wildly. Tom raised his voice. "She's not afraid of *me*! You should have heard me afterward. I was so ... meek!"

"You sounded annoyed to me." Still she was soft-spoken, almost distant.

"Maybe at first. A little. Can't you shut him up?" He paused. "Okay, I was pissed."

Nina held the dog's muzzle and roughed his ears. "Back to the original question," she murmured. "What did she say?"

"It's going to sound idiotic." He sat up on the side of the bed. "After dinner, she brought her thermos bottle to me—from her lunch box. She couldn't get the top unscrewed."

"She never can. She has horrible small-muscle control."

"Let me finish. I looked at it and saw it was all rusted. I took it to the sink, to disassemble and clean it. Well, I couldn't get the damn thing apart."

"That's not her fault."

"Nina!"

"Sorry."

"God, I know where she gets it!"

"Are you mad at me?"

He ignored that. "I'm struggling with this thing, and she says, 'If Mr. Bridges was here, Daddy, he'd open it.'" He imitated Polly's lisp.

Nina smiled. She knew he liked to hear her talk.

"She kept saying it. 'Mr. Bridges could do it, Daddy.' Jesus! Finally, I put it in the trash and said too bad about Mr. Bridges; we'll just throw it out. She still wouldn't quit, so I sent her to her room. She cried."

49

He gathered the sections of newspaper together and stacked them neatly on the floor. "I went in to see her, of course. Told her I'd buy her a new one."

Nina went to the bed and lay beside him. Suitor followed and nestled between them. Tom put an arm around both of them. "God, you feel so helpless. You're not in charge when they cry."

Nina gently removed his glasses and kissed him. "That was a nice story."

"Mmm."

"Inept fathers make perfect husbands."

"Where'd you hear that?"

"I just read it. In that book."

He raised his head to look at her face and smiled. "What is Polly now—she's six?"

"Nearly seven."

"Why does this guy…?"

"He's the principal. He's nice to her. He helps her with little things." She tried again. "He's … I don't know … he's fun. He's Mr. Bridges, that's all."

Tom grumbled. "I don't remember Elaine doing this."

Nina punched him playfully. "With Elaine it was a woman. Miss Donna Cordray. You never noticed." She stretched.

"You think it's a phase?"

"Hmm."

"I guess if Elaine got through it."

"Don't compare the two of them."

"Elaine is not as difficult as Polly."

"Oh, Tom." She rolled over and sat up. "I'm going back to improving my mind."

He grabbed her. "Your mind is fine."

"Not according to Anne."

"She putting you down again?"

"Not too bad. She can't help it." She tugged at the arm that held her. "Suitor needs to go out. Come with me."

"I don't feel like it."

"It's not cold tonight. Let's take a walk."

"No. Just let him out back."

"I beseech you … pray, accompany me. I'm talking like Miss Brooke."

50

Tom looked at her, unsmiling. "I'll walk him alone."

"It's too late."

"It's perfectly safe."

"I don't want you out alone at night, Nina." He put on his glasses and picked up a financial magazine.

Nina led Suitor downstairs and opened the front door. She held him by the collar and stared seriously into his eyes. "Not on Mrs. Cooley's property," she said. "Not." The dog strained away and leaped into the night. She closed the screen door and stood in the hall. The stirring breeze made a nice rushing sound in the trees. She stepped onto the porch and whistled, but there was no response. Hearing music from the open window above, she went inside, up the stairs, and tapped at Elaine's door. There was no answer, so she peeked in.

Elaine lay in bed, gazing at the ceiling, her boom box beside her. She held one finger toward her mother in a gesture both elegant and forbidding. Nina waited. After a moment, Elaine smiled. "It's the Top Ten at Ten. I wanted to hear Moon Goose."

"Should I ask?"

"Listen. What do you think?"

"I can't understand the words. But it sounds, at least, like they're all playing the same song." Nina listened another minute. "Please turn it down."

"I can barely hear it now."

"How you can play Kabalevsky as easily as tying ribbons and still like that!"

"Mom, I'm a teenager. I'm supposed to be inconsistent!"

Nina laughed. "Just barely!"

Elaine rolled her eyes upward. "You want me to have friends, don't you? People don't talk about classical music."

Nina moved around the room, picking up clothes.

"Mom, when you put my stuff away, I can never *find* anything."

"I think you will find these in the clothes hamper. They're filthy, Elaine. You must take care of this more than once a week."

Her daughter tossed her head with lovely disregard. "I always forget." Her mussed hair landed in charming waves on the pillow. She asked, curiously, "What was Dad yelling at Polly for?"

"Nothing that concerns you. She misbehaved a little." Nina sat on the edge of the bed. "Honey, do you remember your second-grade teacher? Miss Cordray?"

"No. Mom, is this going to take long? They're doing the countdown."

"You missed her for a long time after we moved from Norfolk?" *When Daddy was away for months? And you and I talked every night and you told me everything?*

"That was about a thousand years ago."

"At least!" Nina began to straighten the bedclothes, but Elaine squirmed impatiently. "You chattered about her all the time. You were going to run away and live with her. I almost felt jealous about it."

Elaine giggled. "I do remember her. I wrote letters to her. But then she got married and had a baby, so I quit."

Nina drew up her knees, hugging them. "I had this special teacher once. Every spring he came around the neighborhood and painted flowers on all the kids' windows. You'd go out one morning and daffodils and violets were..."

Elaine's eyes pleaded, "Go."

"He would never admit doing it."

Elaine turned up the volume. "It's my favorite."

Nina took her hand. "Your nails need a trim. Want me to?"

Her daughter folded her hands together silently. Nina kissed the side of her head. "I have to let Suitor in."

Elaine sank beneath the blanket. She kissed a finger and wiggled it at her mother as Nina closed the door.

Suitor scratched at the screen. "What misery did you commit out there?" He bounded in and followed her gratefully back to the bedroom, pulled himself into the rocker and flopped, motionless and content. "That took a while." Tom was still watching TV.

"I went in to say goodnight to Elaine. Tom, did I ever tell you about Mr. Keener? Fred Keener?"

Tom showed mild interest.

"He was my science teacher in grade school. His classroom had this greenhouse attached—he called it the conservatory. Lots of pots and things growing and fermenting. He had the blackest dirt ever. Smelled so good."

Tom looked back at the screen. Nina sat on the bed to block his view. "He made up a contest for us to learn the parts of the body. He'd call out a part, and we had to race each other grabbing that part. Watch." She touched his knee. "Patella." She held his hand. "Upper phalanges."

She stroked his thigh. "Biggest bone in the body."

He laughed. "Still cute." He rested a hand on her head.

"Still?" She kissed his bald spot. "Cranium. Pate. Skull."

"Enough." He pushed her away.

"No, no. Wait. He let me water his plants, and one time, after I sprayed the leaves, Mr. Keener came in and said, 'Poor plants. Don't make them cry, Nina. Just a little damp. A sprinkle.'"

Tom stood up. "Good idea." Suitor yawned and stretched. Tom frowned and said sternly, "Nina, I found dog hairs in my shower."

"I washed him in there last time. It was such a cold day, and I didn't want to do it outdoors. That special nozzle is great. He loved it!"

Tom opened his mouth then shut it. After a moment, he said quietly. "Never again, I mean it. And he can't sleep in here."

"But he's used to it."

"Not when I'm here." He began to undress.

"Do you want anything? From the kitchen?"

"No thanks."

"Ice cream? I have walnut fudge."

"No."

"Cake? I'll slice it so thin you can't even see it."

"Holiday's over, Nina."

Nina dragged the dog down to the family room and patted and cajoled him into his proper bed. "Just a few more days, pal. And he's right. You're very intrusive." She shook a few biscuits into his red bowl. She took another bowl from the cabinet, opened the freezer and reached to the back for a small carton of coffee ice cream. She dug in a spoon and scraped it over the smooth surface, as though she were shaving wood. She licked the creamy curls. She did it again. Then all at once, she returned the carton to the shelf and quickly slammed the door. *See, you can do it if you want to.*

She went into Polly's room on her way back. The little girl had fallen asleep with the light on. She wore a dirty T-shirt and sucked her thumb in a tightly clenched fist—a sign of stress Nina hadn't seen in months.

She should probably tell Polly not to talk about Mr. Bridges so much. But she was reluctant to start something. One more no-no. Nina gently removed the thumb from Polly's mouth. She blotted the hand with the edge of a quilt and held it quietly. Polly worried so about being a good girl.

Next week, when Tom is gone, I'll bring her into the bed, maybe Suitor too, and listen to her read and not get impatient when she stumbles over words.

"Polly," she whispered. "I knew this wonderful man once. He taught me about the world. He was an artist, the truest ever. Every fall, he covered a wall with sheets of white paper and drew murals of bird migrations." She closed her eyes. "I can see them still. All down the hemispheres. Streams of color cascading over the continents. The birds flowed like rivers." She opened her eyes. "I forgot to give you a pretty dream."

She tucked in the quilt very carefully then drew the curtains, not closing them tight but leaving a narrow slit for the beam of the schoolyard light to shine in, the only nitelite Polly wanted. Many nights, Nina would look out the window and see Mr. Bridges' odd Jeep standing alone by the entrance. He must come back to work in the quiet. It was hard not to think of him when she heard about him daily, like the weather.

Polly's agitation bothered her. *Don't think about her now. Remember rivers of color. You had forgotten that. Tell her in the morning.*

She turned off the TV in her own room. The wind blew the curtains out then sucked them back against the blinds. She closed the window to stop the rattling. The room filled with steam and a tangy odor from Tom's citrine soap. The shower was running, and he always left the bathroom door open.

Nina picked up her book. Miss Brooke again. Miss Brooke has put aside some worthy cause and is examining her deceased mother's jewelry. Anne had told her, "The jewels are significant." The younger sister is entranced by their beauty. But not Miss Brooke. She is indifferent to worldly goods unless they can be used for the improvement of mankind. She is also indifferent to the sensual pleasure of objects. The sister wants Miss Brooke to touch, to try on her mother's ring. But Miss Brooke rejects this and closes the jewel box.

Nina tried to think what she had from her own mother. She and Anne had given away most of the things—some clothes and a little furniture—they were worn but still useful. And Nina was glad. She didn't want to keep them. When she and Tom had bought their first tiny bungalow in Norfolk, Mama had given her a rose cutting. She called it "Autumn" and said it would bloom in the fall when the others were gone. It never did much. Only once, after Mama died at the end of summer, in October the rose put out new shoots, turned a healthy dark red on the leaves, and Nina had gathered more than a dozen perfect blushing-pink rosy roses from that bush. It was a thing you remember, but they never have things like that in books. She thought they must not be interesting enough, or sound true. Everything in books must be made up to sound true.

Nina tucked a light cashmere blanket around her legs. Across the room and through the bathroom door, she watched Tom step out of the shower and begin to dry off. He looked lean and hard. Ten years. Nina felt under the cover and squeezed the soft skin of her upper thighs. She put a hand on her midriff and pressed down flat. Not fat but spreading. *In ten years, you'll be all over, honey. But not yet. Not quite.*

Tom rubbed his head vigorously, burying it in the towel. He emerged wild and kinky, and rubbed his body dry with thorough, deliberate movements. He swung the towel between his legs, patted his pubic area then, leaning his feet alternately against the commode, he inspected and carefully dried between each toe. There's a right way and a wrong way to do everything, he always told the girls. Let me show you. Watch while I attach the string to your kite. Do it just like this. Nina, this is the way to fold my shirts. Put them here in the suitcase. Socks over there. Nina, relax. Let me love you—like this. Can you feel it now? Good?

Nina kept her eyes on the book, as though Tom could see what she was thinking. She squirmed a little. *This isn't nice. He is so good and competent. And more than that. He is unfailingly competent.*

Tom snipped off about a yard of dental floss and wound it around his fingers then began doing his teeth. His teeth were beautiful. He told the girls it was because he never smoked or drank soda. Nina suspected he was right. The twine snapped in and out of his mouth, efficiently. He massaged his gums, and Nina admired the way he did it, so thoroughly. You can depend on me because I take care of my body. How many times had he said that?

She noticed he had a partial erection. He stood back from the sink and combed his hair then inspected his skin. His erection grew. The color of rose wine, it would darken, she knew. But it was nice to see it like this. A whispery flutter tensed inside her. She pulled her soft blanket higher in her lap. She folded and tucked herself in, relaxing. *Men don't care. They want you to see, or anyway don't care if you do. But on me, nothing shows. And it's nice to hide things.* Even her body in loose clothing.

Tom hung in the doorway, one hand slapping at his mid-section. "I met this guy, right?"

She turned a page. "What guy?"

"Polly's boyfriend. Short guy."

She continued to read. "He's shorter than you, but he's not ... short."

"I don't see how he can run a school if he's so busy playing with the kids. He's okay, though? You don't think there's anything funny about him?"

She waited a full minute. "I'm not even going to comment on that."

Tom straightened towels, put the bathroom in order, and got into bed. He picked up a magazine and studied it.

Nina quietly turned pages.

"Are you trying to finish that tonight?"

Borrowing Elaine's elegant gesture, Nina held up one finger for silence. Miss Brooke at last has put on a ring and a bracelet. She admires the flash of an emerald as it catches fire in the candlelight. Nina sent her an unuttered, throbbing message: *Open the casket again. Sift your hand through that chunky rubble of warm color!*

"I guess I'm at a stopping place." She riffled the three inches of pages remaining in the book. "I probably won't finish this until next summer." She turned off her small reading lamp.

She rose from her chair, dropped her clothes in an untidy puddle, and wrapped a robe of navy silk over her naked skin. She sat in front of the mirror at her dressing table and rubbed cream on her hands and throat. She bent and brushed her hair down then threw her head back, making her hair fat and her neck long and slender. She changed her earrings from jade buttons to long gold threads that dangled almost to her shoulders.

"Should I let my hair grow—or leave it?"

"Either way."

"I'm starting a diet." She held her cheeks in, turning her head this way and that.

Tom looked up. "I'm going to Hong Kong next month. Do you need anything?"

"You buy me too many things."

"Women need things."

"How do you know?" She sounded vague, dreamy, pulling back her hair, swishing the gold earrings.

"I'm observant."

She sat on the foot of the bed, letting the silk slide off her skin a little. "I was a shit, Nina."

"When?"

"All the time."

"You only act humble when you want something."

"Try to fool you?"

"I can't resist fake humility. Better than the real thing." She stroked his leg under the sheet. "Do you know what I told Anne? She asked how I could stand your being away so much. I told her that a few days before you go, I start to pick on you. Then it doesn't hurt so much when you leave."

"Come here."

She crawled slowly along his body and reached her arm over his head. "Lights out."

He took her hand, kissed it and moved it back. "Lights on. I have something for you."

"And I," she said, "have something for you."

"Tell me."

"Pearls," she whispered. "Rubies."

Chapter Four

I Think They Made a Bad Call

"Nothing." Jack put down the phone, breaking its frustrating busy signal. "Turn the radio on. They have to announce it by noon. If not, we stay open."

"End of January and we haven't had a snow closing yet. So odd." Irene Sawyer pulled a small portable from the bottom desk drawer. "They usually call us directly, don't they?"

"There's a new guy in the transportation office. Or maybe they just can't get through." Jack stood in the doorway. "I've got to check something with Brody. Heating plant's off again. Keep listening. Get one of the aides in here if you have to. To do the phones."

"I've got the station." Irene looked at her watch. "The announcement should come in a few minutes."

Jack walked down the stairs toward the heat and petroleum stench of the boiler room, rolling up his sleeves as he went. He knew Clem Brody was there, probably smoking and daydreaming. Jack didn't care, as long as things kept running. Brody's territorial pride in the school's equipment made him hate to admit failure or breakdowns. When Jack called for repair people, Brody would complain to himself or anyone who would listen, "Jumped the gun on me. Just needed a little time to work on it. But he gets itchy."

Jack played along with him, gave him extra days to fiddle with his ladders, wrenches, and tape until he'd say, "Clem, I think what we need is parts. You've done all you can. That thing needs new parts." "Parts" was a magic word that absolved Brody from further tinkering. Then he'd shrug and say, "I guess I can't fix what can't be fixed without *parts*."

Today, Jack couldn't fool with it. The temperature outside had been dropping slowly for a week. The building needed heat. Besides, he had concerns other than Brody's ego. He was certain they'd have to close early.

He'd been out for morning recess with a class when the snow began falling around ten o'clock. The winter had been mild so far. Only the past week had the ground frozen. The kids cheered when the first lazy flakes appeared, and he'd had fun seeing them dance around, chasing and catching them on their tongues. But the snow changed rapidly to tiny, driven needles, sticking to the hard grass and pavement. The sky was dark to the northwest, and there was an icy coating on the air. The children kept looking over their shoulders as if watching something. Jack didn't like it.

Some of the children had not switched to heavier winter gear, and they shivered in light sweaters or jackets, sneakers but no socks. He blew the whistle. A few die-hards wanted to stay out, arguing and talking back. Tim gave him a bad time. He was excited about the snow, and it made him crazy. Jack never labeled any of his students as problem kids. But he thought of Tim as troubled, and he went easy on him. Things had been more upbeat lately. The foster home crisis appeared to be over. The stepmother had dropped the boyfriend or the other way around. Tim was working again, and Jack kept him busy any way he could.

Just now he was annoyed to see Tim in the boiler room with Brody. The boy hung around constantly after school. Jack encouraged Brody to be helpful with Tim but not during school hours. He shot a thumb toward the stairwell. "Back to class."

"Mrs. Rudd said to find out what's wrong with the heat."

"You go to the office and ask. You don't goof off down here."

"But..."

"Out."

Tim kicked each riser as he climbed the stairs.

"Tim." The boy stopped. "I'm going to watch while you tie those shoelaces. Leading cause of death for kids under twelve is floppy laces."

"Who says?" Tim smiled. He bent over.

"Everybody knows that. C'mon! I haven't got all day."

"Boy wasn't doing any harm." Brody lifted a heavy black wrench and banged it on a pipe.

"This is not his classroom." Jack was irked with Brody's interference. He knew he should act interested in the janitor's clanging exertions, stroke him on his efforts, but when Brody began to discuss the boiler problem, Jack said he'd already called county maintenance. "Irene'll buzz you when they get here. Practically the whole second floor has no heat." Before he left he added, "Hey, the PTA wants to thank you, the way you set up for that program Monday night. Looked great."

Brody turned his back and shut his tool box noisily.

Let him resist. He's a resister and a mutterer. Forget it.

In the office, Irene had the phone to her ear. Two students stood by her desk, one sucking a thermometer. With the clinic aide out, Irene was filling that position. Jack looked at her. She shook her head.

He called Lucy Taylor, principal at Bush Street, the school closest to Great Forest. "What are we, closing or what?"

"I've had no word. I guess not." Lucy's voice was calm.

"Have you been outside?"

"I've had meetings all morning."

"Well, I don't know. I think they made a bad call on this one."

"Maybe they're predicting a let-up." Lucy sounded cheerful, hopeful.

"Yeah, maybe. I sure thought we'd close. We've shut down for far less."

"I know what you mean. Two inches panics this county."

He talked another minute then hung up. He stood in the main office by the copier and stared at the playground. He could clearly see the flagpole and the fence, but the houses in the distance were shadowy. It looked like at least a couple of inches on the cars in the parking lot. Jack glanced at his watch. Three and a half hours to go. At this rate, it would be bad news by closing time. But maybe it wouldn't keep up.

He walked outside and stood at the entrance, looking to the northwest, scraping his shoes on the gritty snow. The sky was blue-black. He turned to go in. Although it was midday, all the lights were on. *Damn!* He wished they were getting ready to go. He hated waiting, inactivity.

Even blindfolded, he could read the sounds and smells of the school. He recognized that restless pulse, a certain pitch to the voices. Excitement, anticipation balanced on the very edge of control. Jack sighed. It would be a long, difficult afternoon, wearing out the teachers. Maybe he should bring everyone into the gym for some kind of program. *No. Better to keep them in smaller groups. Easier to manage.*

Several teachers milled around his office. They were cold. Could he dismiss everyone because of lack of heat? He knew they didn't understand the complications of such a procedure. He doubted the repair guys would show up but assured the teachers that everything was okay. He managed a few jokes. Jack turned on the PA and announced that school would close at the usual time in spite of what seemed to be bad weather conditions. He spoke to the children about cooperation and continuing to work normally.

He called Roland Parkman, his administrative superior at the superintendent's office, and tried to find out the rationale for staying open—without appearing to question the decision. With more than five hundred buses on the roads carrying thousands of students in staggered schedules, he knew decisions concerning transportation and safety were never made lightly.

"We get so much flack over these things." Parkman's voice on the phone sounded unconcerned. "Porter really takes heat from parents when we close, and it turns out to be nothing."

"This is not nothing. Trust me."

"His information is pretty good. Word is it'll blow over quickly. Sort of a snow squall." Parkman's tone changed to busy, bored.

I'm looking at the sky, fella, not listening to a damn weather report.

Jack tried to sound casual. "I guess it feels like a real blizzard 'cause I've been in a few."

"Around here?"

"Midwest. When I was a kid."

"Well, no problem. I thought weather didn't scare anyone out there."

"It scares them—so much they know what to do about it. Here, they never learn."

"This is Virginia, man. Those things never get past the mountains."

"Right!" Jack hung up. *Hope you're right, jerk.* He didn't know. Maybe *he* was being the jerk. Still, he would have Brody look for the shovels. They'd have to clean walks before dismissal. No point doing it now, the snow was falling so fast. He would visit classrooms and spend the afternoon diverting attention from the storm. He went to the window to look for signs of a thinning sky. It was so dark the lights from the school fell on the snow, casting shadows on the ground outside. Now he couldn't see to the end of the playground. The houses beyond were lost in blank, silent snow.

Nina sat in her kitchen sipping coffee and cutting apples for a pie. She perched on a high stool at the counter, watching the snow paint over her garden, filling first the lines between the bricks and the little hollows in the flower beds. Now each blade of grass wore its own white sheath, and the snow swirled to the back fence and whipped peaks by the posts. In the far corner, the surface of the fish pond silvered as the snow froze on the murky black water. Her golden pets had gone under last week and stayed there.

Across the way, the school appeared to be moving in the shifting snow, like a ship in and out of a fog bank. Now the lights fixed it in place, and Nina smiled at its luminous presence anchored in the gauzy snow. She was drifting, not quite concentrating. The house all around her was polished and shining. She tried to think if there was something she should do. Tom had brought in wood before he left town, and it was dry and ready if she wanted a fire. She had candles, matches. Lots of food. The storm made her feel closed in and protected. They would have a cozy afternoon and evening. And maybe it would last for days. Nothing to do for days.

Elaine wandered in, wrapped in her mother's best velour robe, rubbing her eyes and yawning. She'd been home for two days with a slight cold. "I feel much better."

Nina felt her forehead. "Fever's gone, honey."

"I think I could eat something."

"Soup? Tea? Toasted cheese? What sounds good?"

"Everything, I guess."

"Sit still. I'll fix it." Nina liked fussing over Elaine. There was so little this daughter required anymore. She filled the kettle, opened the refrigerator, and sliced bread. "I'm glad, really glad you're home. I'd worry if you were in school."

"I'm way behind. I know I missed at least one test."

"No matter. You always do so well."

Elaine snorted. "Only when I keep up."

"Don't be too hard on yourself." Nina carried a bowl of fragrant beef vegetable soup to the table. "Here, now. Try this."

"Mother! You don't have to feed me!"

Nina giggled and blushed. "I'm terrible, aren't I? Forget I did that." She backed over to the stove and stuck a sandwich under the broiler.

Elaine blew across her spoon, delicately. "You don't want me to grow up."

"Oh, I really do. It's only the snow or something. Makes me feel all maternal. Like when you were little and I'd make you cocoa and help you dip graham crackers in it." She paused. "Makes you want to be together with someone."

Elaine rolled her eyes, but she was smiling. She stirred her soup, lifted another spoonful. "I feel old around you, Mom. Sometimes."

"I hope not. But you can be mature if you like."

Nina opened the back door and called to Suitor. The dog lunged into the kitchen and raced around, wet and sloppy, leaping on Nina. She sat down, peeled and sliced more apples. Elaine ate slowly. "How come the pie? Dad coming home?"

"It's for us. Snow makes me hungry." Nina filled her coffee mug. "Daddy won't be back 'til Friday. He wouldn't fly in this anyway."

"He's not afraid to."

"Your *father*? I should hope not." Nina laughed. "But it would be stupid and risky. And he doesn't take risks." She shook spices into a cup of flour then tossed it all with the apples to give them a speckled sugary coating. She popped one in her mouth and fed one to Elaine. "Mmm." They sat in the warm kitchen. Nina began to roll a piecrust. Suitor's nails clicked on the floor as he roamed to the door and back.

"Mom, shouldn't you dry him off? He's all muddy."

"It's all right," Nina said dreamily.

"But you had it all so nice."

"It's okay. It reminds me..."

"What?"

"I was thinking it reminds me of Daddy."

"Daddy's not messy."

63

"Yes." Nina stooped down, hugged the dog, let him put his paws on her chest. "He's a very organized person. But this reminds me of him just the same."

"You're weird, Mom." Elaine stared at her mother. "You look so..."

"I've been busy. Really busy."

"Still, Mom, you shouldn't let yourself..."

"When Dad's not here, there's no one to look at me anyway."

Elaine swiped an apple from the pie. "I don't care how old I get I'm always going to look wonderful. Like Aunt Anne."

"I'm sure you will." Nina laid the top crust over the mounded apples and pinched a ruffle around the edge. "Well! Maybe you could put makeup on me this afternoon. You used to like that. Practice on me." *And you thought I was beautiful. My eyes glued shut with mascara. My bloated and glossy lips.*

Elaine yawned. "I'm going back to bed." She rose to leave.

Nina looked away from her.

"I'll do it if that's what you want."

Nina slid the pie in the oven. With her back turned, she said, "Elaine, you haven't played the piano for four days."

Her daughter turned at the door. "I haven't forgotten how, Mother."

Nina sighed. "I miss the sound, that's all. Go and rest."

"I'm going to read."

"As soon as this pie is baked, I'm walking over to get Polly. She didn't take her boots this morning. If you go back to sleep, that's where I'll be."

"I'll be awake reading."

"I'll look in before I leave."

An hour later, she clicked off Elaine's radio but left the light burning by the bed where her daughter lay, sound asleep and beautiful, embracing *Wuthering Heights*. Nina wanted to pat her, cover her with another blanket but did not.

In the warm and spicy kitchen, she pulled on boots and wrapped a scarf around her neck. She had to push Suitor back from the door. "It's not a walk. Not a walk, baby."

The force of the wind was at her back as she plowed across the school yard. The depth of accumulation surprised her and the chill that immediately penetrated her neck. Even going a short distance, she was happy to reach the lobby and get out of it for a while. She sat on a bench opposite the office and waited for Polly. Dismissal was usually smooth at Great Forest. She came over at least once a week. Mr. Bridges called out the patrols first, then the bike riders, the walkers, and the buses one by one. Mothers picking up children could wait in the front hall or parking lot. Nina liked to chat with other parents.

This afternoon, however, there were no students marching out— only one tight knot of teachers and a couple of frantic, worried looking mothers hastily dragging children to their cars. Then Nina realized something. There had been no buses, lined up and waiting out by the tall fence.

There were no buses, and Jack was not sure when they'd arrive. Six inches of sleety snow had fallen with as much as three more predicted. At two o'clock he'd called the high school, the first pick-up spot in their area. Only half the expected number had shown up on time. When the high school buses were late, the schedule at the intermediate schools backed up. The elementary schools were let out last. Jack called the transportation office. Six regular buses served Great Forest, plus a smaller one for the special ed. kids, but the guy on the phone couldn't tell Jack where they were, let alone an approximate arrival time.

"Everything's at a crawl out there. But they *will* get there," he heard.

"We should all be home by now," Jack could not resist saying. Who was this guy, anyway? Okay. Getting mad was not effective. Procedures were all off for the day. He'd figure something out.

His plan was ready half an hour before the bell rang. He had Irene draw up a list of the close-by households where a parent or grandparent was home or the student was provided a key. These children, around 50 of them, walked every day and lived within two blocks of the school. Today, they would go in groups, organized by streets, each group led by a responsible patrol. No kid would walk alone. The patrol leader would call and report back to Irene after everyone got home.

He gathered the walkers and patrol leaders in the cafeteria before releasing them. He had told them to leave books and backpacks in their desks. Keep hands in pockets or hold hands with the younger kids. Jack got out the lost-and-found box and passed out mismatched gloves and forgotten scarves and caps. "Now, no horsing around. Get to your houses as quickly as possible. You leaders call us. Mrs. Sawyer is keeping a line open. Just tell us you made it. We know who's in your group."

Jack lined them up, so alert and eager. Not scared. God, kids were a miracle in a crisis. Tim was serious. Tim was taking a group even though the other patrols were 6th graders and he was not. The kid was tough and determined, had a sort of command presence that attached the younger ones to him. Jack shook hands with each of the patrols— six boys and five girls. "I'm counting on all of you." He gave them a thumbs-up and watched them go. He'd instructed them what to do just in case no one was at home: Get out of wet clothes; have a warm drink.

"Do they have to call?" Irene covered the phone. "We're so jammed…"

"It's better. Gives them a mission." His dad had done this. Jack remembered his calm voice. "If I don't hear by a certain time…" You weren't so alone. Someone was following you out there. He went over it again, in his mind, who was responsible. The decision guys, yes. But *he* was the one sending them out, their trusting faces, and he was trusting *them*, to be strong, to make it. Keep going, get through it. That's the only way it'll be over.

Some parents were arriving to get their children, but instead of waiting in the lobby as usual, they were scurrying through the halls and grabbing kids out of classrooms. Jack stationed an aide near the door to keep a list of those leaving.

Jack brought everyone else off the second floor and assembled the bus riders in groups. He needed one teacher to wait with each group and therefore dismissed some of the staff. Several teachers volunteered to stay; he figured he needed eight. Rowena Castle took the largest group to the library, saying it was warm there, and she could use help shelving books. Jack gave thanks for Rowena and Irene, their poise. Pure gold. He'd have to do something for them. Special leave—something.

Brody cleaned off cars in the lot. The sidewalks were hopeless. Jack organized carpools for the nervous teachers. Staying together was better. "Keep on the main roads. Call here when you get home. Do it! If you get stuck I'll … I'll come get you myself!" They knew he meant it. "If no one answers here, if it's late, call me at home. Touch base. Just say you got there."

Irene signaled him that seven patrols had called in. Jack checked the time. Twenty minutes. Good. He punched out his own number. It rang a long time. *Jesus, she's not out in this!* At last, she answered.

"Honey! Boys home yet?"

"Jack! Chris is here. Just barely. Buddy's school called. Some buses are delayed."

"Yeah. Same thing here. A zoo. I've had *all* the kids stranded."

"When will you...?"

"Can't tell. I'll call before I leave here. Probably late."

"Jack. Come now."

"Impossible."

"I need you here."

"Honey, there are almost four hundred kids and staff..."

She cut him off. "If you'd had a cold today or been sick or something you wouldn't even be there."

He let it sit a while. "I'm never sick. And I am here." Before he heard more of that nervous voice, he said, "Hey, call Irene, would you, when Buddy gets home? Just so I'll know?"

A long silence.

"Don't be mad. Keep it together."

"I always do."

Irene watched him hang up. "Everything okay?"

"She's worried."

"Aren't we all?" She rummaged in a drawer. "Except you. You seem pretty good, actually."

"An act. It's all in here." He smacked a hand on his abdomen. But he did have a flow of energy. He did feel strong and even like laughing, except it wasn't funny.

Irene was on the phone again. "It's Tim. He's finished. Wants to know if he should come back here to help."

Jack took the receiver. "Just stay put, pal. I'll call if I need you. Hey, I think I owe you one. Maybe you can come home with me again. I'll ask Mrs. Bridges what's a good day." He smiled at the response and gave the phone back to Irene. "That kid!"

"You spoil him," she said with affection.

"Maybe he needs it."

Brody tapped on the glass. First bus had arrived. An hour since closing. He asked the number and called the kids over the speaker. He threw on his parka and took them out. The driver was a good one. Steady. Years of experience. She had just finished a middle school route. He listened to her, how bad the roads were—a nightmare rush hour. The government had let out early, and all the roads were packed. He told the kids they could help Mrs. Jensen by keeping quiet. He told her softly, "Do me a favor. Call me when you finish. It's important."

Back in the lobby, Miss Finchley jabbed a finger in his chest. She had called home on the pay phone, and the power was out. Her elderly mother was sitting in the dark, terrified. "I've got to get out of here."

Jack held her elbow and spoke soothingly. "How many are left in the kindergarten?"

"Twelve. Their attention span is zero. They won't even watch TV."

"Let me think." Jack had no one to cover that room. Maybe he should scatter the children among the other groups. But they were all at a straining point as it was. His eye wandered to a corner of the lobby. Polly's mother was helping her pull on boots. They were still here? All the kids living nearby were gone. Then Betty Finchley clutched his arm, and he saw Nina Talbott coming toward him.

"Mr. Bridges, I … can I do something? I stayed to help Mrs. Metcalf, up in Polly's room? Is there…?"

Nina made herself stop talking. She pressed her hands down to quiet them and felt her old cook's apron. Was she still wearing it? Cinnamon and flour dusted over it, and Suitor's smeary paws. Elaine was right. She neglected herself. The principal was looking at her intently. She must seem very odd.

Jack studied her. Nice to see an animated face, so full of interest. It seemed he'd been looking at drained and worn-out faces forever. "How good are you with kids? The little ones."

"The smaller the better."

"Betty, go ahead and go." He dumped his parka on a bench. "C'mon, Polly. You can help too."

He stayed a few moments in the kindergarten until Nina engaged the children in a penny hiding game. As he left, he whispered, "I hope it won't be too long."

But it was forty-five minutes before the next two buses arrived. He worked at keeping up morale. The remaining staff were genuinely scared about getting home. Radio reports told of cars abandoned on the highways. No snow removal or rescue equipment was getting through. Parents were now screaming on the phone. One father was hysterical. He was stuck downtown, his wife at home with a baby, and their daughter trapped in the school. He called Jack every name for being irresponsible and threatened to sue. But he was the worst one. Even the angry ones were just anxious, not mad at Jack personally. He asked for patience.

It was dark now and seemed very late. One kid asked, "Will we have to sleep here, Mr. Bridges?" and soon they were all saying it to one another, as though they knew it would happen. Jack wanted to take them all into the gym for a rowdy game, take their minds off it. But they shouldn't be overheated when they went out into the cold.

They gathered in the cafeteria for the final waiting period. Jack unlocked the pantry, and Rowena and Nina made hot chocolate in the kitchen. He heard them, their soft voices together with the sound of spoons stirring, paper rattling. It was a nice interlude. He had always liked the sound of women in a kitchen. They passed out the cocoa and crackers. He was beginning to feel it now. Fatigue. He rested, trying to get energy back.

Lettie Myers sat on his lap, too quiet, eyes glazed. Nina held a tray in front of them. "I have apple pie at home," she said. "I'd love to run and get you some."

Jack appraised the group. "Could you slice it twenty-five ways?" He smiled. "Maybe some rainy day." What a waste. Her offer was so sweet, and he was so hungry. Hadn't eaten since breakfast.

He listened to the kids. They almost did not want to leave now. Felt safer here. He told them about school buses. How they could make it in any weather, kind of like mailmen and Saint Bernard dogs. And they were beacons in the dark with their flashing lights.

At 6:30, the special ed. bus arrived, then another regular one. The driver was inexperienced and edgy. Jack worked out an alternative route with her, one that avoided heading the bus into a narrow cul-de-sac. At seven they were still waiting for the last bus and three daycare parents. Jack had two kids in his office who could not stop crying and had to be separated from the others. At seven he called the final bus. He waved off the cheering kids, having told the driver, like all the others, "Call me. Just want to know. Call." He watched them disappear, adding it all up again. What else should he do?

Rowena stayed on the phones. Irene had left earlier. Brody could start shutting down. Jack stopped Nina and Polly in the hall. "Thanks so much. You were a brick." He patted Polly. "Two bricks."

"What does that mean?" Polly stood in front of her mother, looking up at him.

"Oh, you're square and solid."

Nina laughed. "I enjoyed it. Mr. Bridges…"

"Call me Jack, please."

"And … Nina." She gestured awkwardly at herself. "Well … Jack … I was going to say…"

"You can come to our house tonight!" Polly interrupted. "We have lots of room. My daddy's away."

"Honey…" Nina was embarrassed. But Jack laughed, easy and natural.

"Thanks. I'd better go to my own house tonight. My boys will have a lot to tell me … if I can get there."

"Will you get stuck?" Nina wished Polly did not sound anxious, would not hang on him so much, but he didn't seem to mind.

Jack dropped to Polly's eye level. He zipped her jacket.

"Nah. I won't get stuck. My Jeep eats snow." He made his jaws crunch. "And you know what else?"

"What?"

"I grew up in Michigan. You know what we call a day like this in Michigan?"

"What?" Polly's eyes were very round.

"We call it spring!" Jack winked at Nina over Polly's head.

Running in and out of the building had made him warm. His parka was knee length and bulky. Worn and serviceable, Nina thought. *Like an explorer would wear.* He threw it back on his shoulders. The drab khaki color heightened the flush on his cheeks and darkened his blue eyes. He had a fresh, excited expression. A net of snow resting on his hair melted and made damp curls around his ears. Nina tried to move. She did not want to step out of the cheerful radiant circle he'd drawn around them.

"Let me get you started." He ushered them to the door. "Follow the fence line, why don't you? Just to keep a bearing. Then cut across." He wrapped Polly's scarf one more turn on her neck, covering her mouth and tucking it in back. Solemn eyes looked at him. "Now, hold your mother's hand. Don't let her fall."

Polly nodded.

He pressed Nina's hand briefly. She felt how warm he was, even through the big ski mittens she wore. "Thanks," he said again, his voice deep and raspy.

They left. There was not much wind now, but the snow continued to fall densely. It was quiet and very cold. Polly turned and waved. "Do you think he saw me?"

"Yes."

"Are you scared, Mommy?"

"No."

"You're not talking."

"It's hard to talk, honey."

"Mommy, do you like Mr. Bridges?"

"Yes."

Do you think he likes me?"

"Yes."

"Do you think he's nice?"

"I think he's romantic." She spoke softly but recklessly and too quickly. The word was warm but hung like an icicle, frozen between them. Nina walked faster, jamming her boots in the snow ahead of Polly. "I'm making footprints for you, baby."

"I don't know that 'ro' word."

Nina ignored it.

"What's ro-thing?"

"You'll learn it when you're grown up, honey."

"Does Elaine know it?"

"Yes. I think she does."

"I want to."

"Honey, don't talk. It's too cold. Let's take big steps and count them. Starting ... now!"

Jack put down the phone as Greta came into the bedroom.

"Which one was that?"

"Rowena. I called her."

"Was she the last one?"

"I think."

"She's the only one I really like."

"Yeah. She's great. She was..."

"What? Finish it."

"She was ... unwinding. Said some nice things about me."

"I'm sure."

"Geez, I hope we stay closed for a couple of days. We all need a rest." He set a drink, his second, on the night table.

"To sleep it off."

"It was a long day, honey." His voice was whispery deep, almost gone.

"You let them intrude. Why did they all have to call?"

"For me. So I can relax."

He watched her stomp around the room, pulling a sweatshirt over her flannel gown and tugging on thick socks. "What are you doing?"

"Sam is definitely coming down with something. I should sleep out on the couch where I can hear him better. I'm freezing."

"Maybe he'll sleep through."

"And maybe it's Christmas again!" she snapped.

Jack slid under the cover. "Let me warm you up." He sighed hugely. "I've been thinking about this since noon. Wondering if I'd ever get here."

Greta lay against him. "They'll have to close for at least a couple of days now. Jack, will you stay home?"

"Except for trying to get that furnace fixed." He was so tired. He hadn't been able to listen to the boys, kept nodding off while they talked. It was bad with Chris. The boy was getting away from him. He'd do better tomorrow. A long slow day. "I thought at one point I'd have to bring a couple of kids home with me. Thought those last parents would never arrive. Kids were about nuts."

"Don't ever do that to me. Just drop them off at the superintendent's house."

He laughed drowsily. "Yeah. God, I'd hate to be that guy tonight."

"So, he made a mistake."

"Guys like him aren't supposed to."

"So. When you're sup..."

"Never, baby. Never."

She was quiet.

"You smiling?" he asked.

"Uh-uh."

"You know I don't want that. I'm fine with what I've got."

"Superintendents don't shovel snow and have kids throw up in their office."

"They miss a lot."

"Jack..."

"Greta, it's late."

She was still. "I just wanted to say ... I was so happy to see those headlights turning into the drive."

He reached for her. "Jack, I can't."

"I can't either," he whispered, his eyes closed. He pulled her over to lie full length on top of him. He pressed her close, ran his hands along her spine and covered himself with her, her hair spread over his face and long legs drifting between his. And he went to sleep feeling buried—sweetly buried under a woman and not the cold snow that was still falling outside.

Chapter Five

I've Never Had Lonely Nights

One Monday morning in mid-April, Jack arrived at Great Forest to see the row of pink dogwoods blooming in front of the school. The woods behind had lost the rusty tint of March, and popcorn buds burst shiny green in the clear light. He stood looking at all of it. He'd forgotten the colors coming out together. It bothered him that he did not remember.

It was the first day back after spring break. He was early, but Irene was ahead of him. The baggy gray cardigan hung on the back of her chair. Her uniform. Maybe someday he'd surprise her with a new sweater—yellow like the forsythia outside the window. A spray of lilacs in his office were from her. Once he said how much he liked them and how they grew all over town when he was a boy.

He poked his head out to smile thanks at her. "It's behind us, isn't it?"

"Why, Mr. Bridges. I thought you liked the cold. Brings out the child in you!" Irene teased him when no one else was around. He liked her motherly affection, protective and respectful.

"Right. But you move south, you get soft. Or maybe I'm getting old." She laughed. "You?"

It was good, this morning solitude. He didn't want to start working.

Leaning on her desk, he played with the blossoms. "When you have nothing you want to do anymore, then you're old, right?"

"Sometimes."

"Listen. Have I ever told you about my granddad? This wonderful guy, lived up north his whole life, one place or another. Freezing. And when he was, oh, late sixties, my grandma was dead by then, he moved to New Orleans. More or less just like that. Decided and went. Never came back."

"What happened to him?"

"Hard to tell. He wrote often enough. We got lots of postcards, things like that. No real letters. And he sounded so jubilant. He always wrote down the temperature next to the date. 2 December 72F." Jack looked down. "Hey, Irene. You deserve a raise, listening to this stuff."

He gestured toward the dogwoods. "I've been impatient for it. I don't know. Maybe it's the kids. Cooped up too long. Need to be let out."

"Today, you get your wish."

"Maybe extra-long recess. Kind of to make up for winter."

The long inclement days were tricky, Jack's least favorite time of the school year. Tensions grew in the staff, and it seemed his office was full of complaints all day. He planned programs and tried to give teachers longer breaks. They should be okay now, all downhill and sliding into summer.

Jack worked in his office most of the morning. All the windows in the school were open, and breezes ruffled papers on his desk. He usually felt recharged after a break in the routine, could clear a mountain of work from his in-box. This morning he sat, reading sentences several times. Not physically tired but drowsy. The scent of lilacs perfumed his thoughts, disturbed his concentration, and kept him aware of the season. Spring. You're not trapped anymore. Spring. And he was looking at four walls.

He called Neal Bannerman. "About time we had lunch!"

"Perfect! I was wondering why I should stick around!"

"I'll bring sandwiches. And a couple of beers."

"Hell, I wish!"

Jack lounged back in his chair. His mood soared. Neal would be tonic.

He listened to voices through open classroom doors. Scraping chairs, the music class singing. It was all subdued, nice after a vacation. *Hysterical before and then, something spent, they come back gentle.* PE was out. All going well today. No tears, no fights, not one kid sent down from class. But the lack of interruptions made him restless. He had dressed too warmly and stripped off his tie. He needed connection.

In the teachers' lounge he pulled a Coke from the machine. Rowena and Amy Ellen were taking an early lunch, and he sat down with them. Amy Ellen had charge of the student council, and he wanted to set a date for the spring cleanup of the grounds and woods. Everything was littered, now that the snow was gone. What a waste to have Brody do it. The kids liked it, liked being out of class, anyway.

The visiting reading teacher came in, and he waved her over. Ms. Amanda Tinker was assigned to them twice a week. Jack could use her permanently. So many kids with special needs. He wanted to meet with her to discuss specific cases. "We need to get together," he told her.

Amanda removed her glasses. "Anytime," she said, touching his arm. Amanda's manner of speech was slightly suggestive, even with her students, as though they shared secrets. Jack liked the way she sounded with him.

He caught Amy Ellen's glance at Rowena. He kidded easily with most of them, but maybe he was getting too loose. The last two faculty parties, Amy Ellen had been more than friendly after a few drinks. He hadn't particularly noticed, but Greta had.

He rose to leave, smiling at each of them, keeping it even.

Amanda watched him go and sighed.

Rowena smiled. "Don't forget about that ring. Almost half an inch wide."

"All the good ones are married." Amanda sighed. "Is he always so nice?"

"Yes." Amy Ellen picked up Jack's soda can and placed it on her Styrofoam lunch tray.

Amanda dug Tic Tacs from her purse, offered them. "I love that guy, warts and all."

"He doesn't have any warts," Amy Ellen clipped.

"Oh, it's just an expression." Amanda freshened her lipstick. "But he must have something. Is there anything wrong with that guy? I mean it. Any observable flaws?"

Amy Ellen was silent. Rowena drawled, "You could say he doesn't delegate very well. As an administrator he does too much himself. That's what some..."

Amy Ellen jumped in. "It's because he likes doing all the little things. It's not a fault; it's the way he is." She looked reproachfully at Rowena.

Amanda leaned toward them, speaking confidentially. "You don't have to defend him to me. I couldn't say this to some of my friends ... have to keep that men-are-rats edge." She paused. "But him—whatever he wanted. Homemade anything—orange juice freshly squeezed." She gestured airily. "His socks washed by hand."

"Oh, no. You wouldn't. Not that." Rowena feigned shock.

The three women laughed intimately then were quiet.

"He'd never ask," Rowena said.

When Amanda left, Amy Ellen whispered, "I'm glad she's not here every day."

Jack arrived at Neal's school annoyed with traffic. The building sat in a neighborhood once residential but now heavily commercial. Several years ago, three hundred feet were lopped from the front of the property to widen the street. Perfect location for a strip mall or fast food alley, Jack thought, but not a school.

As usual, his distaste was mixed with vast admiration. The place was thriving. Neal Bannerman had been principal here for twenty years, a lengthy and atypical tenure in the county.

The outer office was swarming. Jack pushed open Neal's door. "Hey! Just once I'd like to catch you with your feet up!"

"You never will, kid. We work around here—unlike that country club you run!" He shouted at his frail but stoic secretary, "Turn off my phone, Sally! I'm not here!"

"Someday, Neal, you'll drive her away."

"A lot you know. She runs this place and she knows it."

Neal closed the door and pawed through the bags of sandwiches Jack threw on the desk. "Great! They wrapped the pickles separately. Real uptown, boy."

Jack was glad he'd come. The office took up a lot of space, like Neal himself. The L-shaped room wrapped around a corner of the building because Neal had kept them knocking out walls until he got what he wanted. Jack had spent hours in this homey place, furnished almost like

77

a living room. Stacks of papers, books, and thick county reports leaned against art projects, models, and stuffed animals the kids brought him. Drawings. Gag presents from teachers.

On all the walls hung pictures of Neal and kids, some casual, some posed. Safety patrol captains, fitness award winners. Field days, class picnics. The kids ganged up to him, pushing to be close. And Neal towered over them, his arms spread like a scarecrow's, the wide homely jack-o'-lantern grin never changing under a gradually whitening crew cut. One of the first things he'd ever told Jack about the work was, "It helps if you're big and ugly."

Jack gestured. "You ever get rid of any of these?"

"Can't. Even after they leave, years go by, kid comes back for a visit. He wants to see himself still here."

"Do you really remember them all?"

"Kind of. I work at it. I get to know them, say their names. If you call a kid by name, that's power over him."

"Yeah. I remember you telling me that. Seems centuries ago."

"This work ages you." Neal looked closely at Jack. "You look good, man. What is it? No one giving you any shit?"

"Every day. No let up."

"Kids? Teachers?"

"Everyone! No, it's mostly good." Jack was enjoying the lunch. Good not to be eating bland cafeteria food. "I still sort of fake it at times. That's all."

"'Simple problems, easily solved.'"

"Geez, you have to throw that back at me."

"Listen, Jack. You get your school running pretty well, you have your routine. Then the big questions take aim at you. You ask yourself if you're doing the right things with them. And what does it all add up to."

Jack sighed. You could say anything to Neal. So relaxing. "Uh, yeah. Sometimes there's a lot of action—but is it progress? I don't know how to measure if we're getting anywhere. We pass them along the line..."

Neal rocked, staring thoughtfully at the ceiling.

"I have a certain ... style, I guess you'd call it. But so what? Do I accomplish anything?" Jack laughed self-consciously. Neal did not speak. Jack spoke rapidly. "The teachers are key, right? You get a good one up there and the kids learn. Right?"

"Usually."

"So that should be my top priority. Staff selection and development. *The* objective. But it's elusive. How can you...?"

"Something you'll never know. Hell, all these years, and I still don't know. If I did I'd write a book." He slapped the desk.

Jack snorted. "Isn't it a matter of training?"

"Not exactly." Neal's big hands wadded all the paper on the desk, crushed the cans. He pitched the debris behind his head into the wastebasket, sneaked a look over the shoulder. "Two out of three. Not bad."

"I want to know what I'm doing. Not rules exactly, but maybe some kind of formula."

"Not in this business. You can make it if you can make it. Probably why I've lasted this long."

"But what's the most important thing?"

Neal put his feet up.

"Gotcha!"

"You're a bad influence." Neal stretched his arms to rest his head. "That's a good question, though. Most important. Maybe nothing. For me, I guess, being an adapter. I don't know how I got here, but here I am."

Jack loved to hear Neal's stories. How as a young man, he'd traveled from Kansas to Alaska, figuring his size and strength would earn him a fortune. The only job he could get paid for was teaching in a one-room school. He lived and taught there, practically in wilderness. Alone, he maintained the building and chopped wood to keep fires going. He discovered a challenge to his body and mind.

"You're still adapting. I can't think what this place would be without you."

"Lot of changes, Jack. The neighborhood going low rent. Then they redrew the boundaries and took some of our population."

"That's what I don't see—how you keep it alive."

"You find kids, mostly the ones no one wants. We got the Head Start, the severe learning problems. All kinds of special ed. for physical handicaps. There are kids out there to fill empty rooms, if you go after them. Some dopes call them the dregs. But I'm happy to have them. Of course I need help. That senior citizen program is going strong. They tutor a few kids, and we give them a hot lunch. You pull in your community."

"You make it sound easy."

"It's not. Come over after school someday. The kids have the option of staying for clubs, sports, or study halls. They'd rather be here than home. Last time I checked, we had the highest test scores for minority students in the county."

"Fantastic."

"I can take anything they throw at me. Even this new computer shit."

"Yeah. I'm wondering about that. You think I should requisition one for the school?"

"One? Hell, you'll need one for every class and pretty soon one for every kid."

"Geez, I can't imagine I have enough teachers who know how to work one."

"Look. You gotta keep up. I'm getting a lab going here to train teachers."

Jack shook his head. "Most of mine will resist anything like that. They've got enough to do as it is."

"So get two or three, probably the younger ones, and persuade them to take the training. Then they can train others. It's all headed that way, Jack. That horse is out of the barn."

"How do you know this stuff? Have there been directives I've missed?"

"Nah. I just read a lot of science and tech magazines. They're full of it. The future is approaching. You cannot imagine the world your boys will live in—or their boys."

"I'll have to squeeze money for it. But I think you're right. Some of our parents are pushing."

"Where you are they push for lots of stuff. Think they know everything. They make more money than you do and look down on you for it. I know the type."

"They're not all like that. Hey, some of them thanked me after that crazy snowstorm. Couple of fathers, even."

"Just my ornery old age talking."

"Well, heck, you could probably retire."

Neal gave him an ugly look.

"You know, write that book or something."

"Yeah. I could. Take this early retirement plan they dangle now. Gives you more money. Hell, what do I need it for? The longer I stay in, the older I'll be when I get out, and the less I'll need."

"Lighten up. I wasn't serious. Someone leaning on you? They'd be stupid to let you retire. I only meant you might want to quit and do something else."

"Sure."

"Look at you. Always something new. You see into the future, Neal. Honest. I always think about the past. That's what I can see most clearly. You're into another century already. You make me feel old."

"Well, what's so great about the past? "

"Lots."

"Name me one thing. Having no refrigeration? No air conditioning?" Neal sounded belligerent.

"Not that stuff. No. But just better. I like remembering things."

He could not tell Neal then what he meant, but later, driving back to Great Forest, he started thinking about the days before cars had seat belts, and you could pull a girl close to you, driving one-armed, and she would lean against your shoulder and whisper in your ear. Driving was no longer romantic. Nothing used to improve your mind like a long drive with a girl. *To Hell with seat belts! Or maybe I just miss being young.*

"I knew you couldn't come up with anything, so let's change the subject. How's Greta? We can't talk shop all the time."

Jack relaxed. "She's good. She'll be glad you asked."

"She perked up any? Last time I was over, she seemed so down."

"When winter finally took over, Sammy was sick a lot. Next year he'll be in school all day and maybe..." He turned up his hands. "I should help her more. I know it."

"Women and kids. We sure get it, don't we? Front and back."

"Some talk from an old bachelor/celibate."

"As usual, kid, you're about half right. I keep all the women happy around here. Can't do it at home too!"

Jack laughed. Neal looked thoughtful. "You get a lot of that? Some of them get too personal?"

Jack didn't answer.

"Well, don't be embarrassed. I get it, and look at me!"

"Most of them are older than me."

"Age has nothing to do with it."

"I'm practically the only guy around." He paused. "It's always there, Neal."

"Yes. And you like them."

"Yeah. I sure have always liked women."

Neal leaned back and spoke casually. "I like working with them. I can admit my mistakes and act like I'm not perfect when things go wrong. They try to cheer me up."

"At faculty meetings, they sit like a class in front of me, raising their hands when they want to talk," Jack said, as if to a brother.

Neal interrupted. He made a fist, pounded his knee. He spoke to the floor. "The only thing you can't do is..." He stopped. "You can't do that one thing."

"And what's that?"

"Play favorites. If you get my drift. They'll find out and then all turn against you."

"Man, you speaking from experience?"

"Don't ask me how I know. I know."

"Sounds like you should read me another chapter of your colorful past." Jack liked needling Neal.

"Nope. You're too young." Neal looked straight at him. "Don't let them come too close."

"I never think about it."

Neal stared at him.

"Well, not all the time." Jack grinned. "Not constantly. Hey, I can handle it."

"Don't bullshit me." Neal grinned back.

"Let me fix you up, Neal. I got a bunch of them over there."

"Yeah, I got a bunch here, too. Ah, the hell with it. Let's go outside."

The men walked down long hallways and out to the rear of the school. The play area was divided into two surfaces—asphalt and cement. Tall, mesh fences surrounded the property. Spring was having difficulty showing itself with not one tree, not a blade of grass.

They need dirt here, true black earth. Well, maybe not. Jack pictured the mud tracked into Great Forest, clinging to rough sneaker treads and shaken off in thick clods in the halls. One good thing was no traffic noise back here. Small girls in jelly bean colors clustered nearby. Spring was on the kids' faces. They couldn't move fast enough or shout loud enough. Jack leaned on the fence, watching.

"Always interesting," Neal said.

Jack had his eye on a group of boys forming teams for basketball. All the tall kids wound up on the same team. The shorter kids were outsmarted. Jack pointed out the situation to Neal. He shrugged, would not interfere. "You don't force that in this neighborhood. They have to get it on their own."

Jack closed his eyes. He felt drowsy and heavy. He'd eaten too much. Something settled on him—not unpleasant but sad. That morning lethargy again. A kid slammed a ball into the fence, jarring him. "What do you call it, Neal? When we spend a couple of hours like this?"

"Professional development."

Jack watched the game. "I feel like I've been teaching forever. But not so long ago, I was out there, playing ball. Samuel would get me after practice. We'd fix supper, and he'd smoke, listen to me. It's so fresh in my head, like yesterday. I went to bed—woke up here. All the time in between is ancient."

"Talking about your wild youth up in Mooseville?"

"Bear. Bear, Michigan. Have respect, man."

"I thought you and I would get up there sometime."

"Maybe. I was thinking this morning, how my two best buddies, this time of year, we always had great plans for summer, and they were always the same. We were going to get a boat, a big one, and cruise the St. Lawrence Seaway. It was our big dream, going all the way through to the ocean."

"You ever make it?"

"Nah. Samuel always took us on a canoe trip to Canada. Which was not bad."

"Do you still have them?"

"What?"

"The friends."

"Sure. Mack and Dunk. Still up there. The old hometown guys." He stopped. "I don't see them. Haven't been there in, oh, five years now. Since Dad died."

"A long time, Jack."

"There's been no need."

"So, what's your point?"

"No point, I guess. Just thinking how I was always looking forward to summer." He watched more of the game and saw it was slowing down. The short team wasn't doing so hot. "Used to be come April you had something to shoot for. Now it's way back. My springs are all past."

Neal slapped him on the back, hard. "It's the cruelest month, kid.

Mixing memory and desire."

"Where's that from?"

"Eliot. 'The Waste Land.'"

"Sorry I asked."

"You should've known that one."

"I don't read enough. Not like that."

"Some people learn by doing."

"God, you know a lot." Jack spoke with real admiration.

"I had long lonely nights in Alaska, that's all. Nothing to do but read." Neal frowned. "Thought I was a goddam Hemingway or something."

Jack waited a minute. "That's it, then. I've never had lonely nights."

Neal exploded, laughing. "Bet that's right! Hell, you have time. If you don't read young, you do it old. What are you—not forty yet?"

Jack turned back to the game. "This summer. The big four-oh."

"Lucky S.O.B. Worlds still to conquer."

"Sure doesn't feel like it." He grabbed Neal's arm, pointing to the basketball court. "Want to get in that? C'mon. One of us for each team."

"You go. I'll watch. I sink all mine in the office."

Jack threw his coat and tie on the fence where all the kids had piled jackets and sweaters. "Okay. I'm going to help the little guys." He leaped into the group and received the ball at once, dribbled up for a shot and missed. Groans. Jeers. "I'm just warming up!" he shouted.

The next time he had the ball, he made his shot good. He felt looser, lighter, even though he was sweating. Both teams played harder, and everyone was having more fun.

Jack fell out for a minute, trotted over to the fence and leaned back, keeping an eye on the court. "Gotta pace myself," he gasped.

"Don't talk. Save it." Neal paused. "I've been thinking about that earlier thing. When we were talking about what's most important."

"What have you got?"

"Two things. You have to care about them. The kids. Not love them, but care what happens to them."

"And?"

"And be an optimist. Otherwise you'd never go in to work."

The boys were waving Jack over. "I'm going back in. We've got a chance." He jogged backwards toward the game. "You may be right. You *are* right!"

"Think about it!" Neal saw a big kid, sixth grade but should have been tenth, push into Jack and almost knock him over. "Before you break your..."

"Hey, Neal!" Jack yelled. "Hey, Bannerman!"

Neal was smiling hugely.

Jack ran and panted, bouncing the ball. "I just decided what I'm doing this summer!"

Neal cupped a hand to his ear.

"I'm gonna go back home! It's time!"

Chapter Six

You Once Offered Me Pie

Nina pulled off her gloves and dug her bare hands into the flower bed, grabbing and breaking clods of red dirt. No matter how many times she added topsoil, unyielding Virginia clay persistently invaded her garden. It was there every spring, waiting for her. She yanked out tulip bulbs and threw them on a heap. The daffodils she left in, cutting back the dry stems lying in limp beige streaks. She was preparing a patch for the annuals that sat in flats and plastic pots scattered around the yard in a cluttered, jolly mess.

A flock of clouds grazed like fat sheep on the treetops over the school. A breeze, light but insistent, stirred the air softly, tempting Nina to rest her cheek on it. She leaned back on her heels and let it play on her closed eyes. It was May, the month of promise, the month she'd been born. She almost didn't mind growing older, she loved a May morning so. She listened to the rise of voices in the distance as the children came out for lunch recess. She worked along the bed on her knees, stopping only to massage her legs when they grew numb. Suitor was behaving, not digging and spraying dirt. He'd had a shot that morning and lay on the warm brick patio.

Whistles blew, and lines of children formed to go back to class. Nina looked at her watch. She lifted several fragile plants and placed them in the soil, patting and mounding gently. She looked at her watch again and threw down her trowel. She had promised to assist Polly's teacher with an ecology project that afternoon. The children were dyeing shirts with natural vegetable colors to wear on the final class picnic. Nina had helped them gather leaves and bark on an early spring outing in the woods. She had spent hours boiling concoctions with vinegar for concentrates and testing dyes on old rags. Today the class would mix or dilute them into individual colors for their shirts.

She brushed off her tan gardening pants and wiggled her toes inside her old crushed loafers. She wore no socks. Sensing a change, the dog came to rub against her.

"What do you think? Can I go like this?" She shaded her eyes and looked over at the school parking lot. Her eyes moved along the rows of cars, back and forth. "I don't want to be late." Shrugging, she gathered four cans and two laundry basins from the garage, latched the gate against Suitor, and walked across the field. It was quiet now, the early afternoon lull.

Nina pushed open the classroom door with her foot, balancing her load. She stumbled, nearly dropping everything. Jack stood at the front of the room, turning pages in Mrs. Metcalf's planning book. He smiled and immediately took the cans from her.

"This is great! All Mary had written in today's square was 'shirts' in capitals. I was just going to ask the kids. Now you can tell me." He peered into one of the cans, sniffed, and made a face. "Pickled something?"

"Sort of. Isn't she here?"

"Who? Mary? I let her go. Terrible attack of allergies. So now you're stuck with me!"

The class cheered.

Nina felt off balance and indecisive. Helpless, wanting to disappear in her crumpled clothes.

"Perhaps we should wait..." Her voice was silenced by shouts from the children.

Jack quieted them "We'll go ahead. Someone needs to explain the project to me." He had first one and then another student describe the ecology unit to him, what they had studied and why. It was a review for them all, and he asked good questions. Nina relaxed as he talked. If she did not look at him, she felt almost invisible. She smiled and sneaked a wave to Polly. Polly was not like some kids who would rather die than have their mother help at school. Elaine, for instance.

Nina poured the concentrates into clear plastic cups and asked the class to identify them. Almost everyone guessed the blueberry. Nina had used frozen berries, and the color was not deep but distinctive enough. They loved the next dark purple color but didn't know it was beets. Nina had worked on a green dye from the leaves the children had picked. She'd had to add a lot of parsley to make it come out. The final one they couldn't guess at all. A pale tan, she passed it around, let them smell it. Nina finally had to tell. Onion skins. Jack pinched his nose to make them laugh.

Each child had brought a clean white T-shirt. Nina had Jack go up and down the rows, making sure they had all printed their names on them. He acted as though she was in charge, and he was taking directions from her. She was confused then too busy to think about it.

Almost every kid wanted to use blue or purple. Only two wanted to try the onion color. Some made designs first with indelible markers. Polly kept changing her mind until her rainbow-turtle-butterfly was a blob in the center of her shirt. Several boys cut off the sleeves and made holes in theirs. Jack liked this. The dyeing took a long time. After a while, Nina didn't mind her old clothes. She was a mess, stains all over her slacks where she had wiped her hands. The children dressed Jack in a large smock from the art room.

"Now what?" he asked Nina, smiling with wonder at the dripping clumps of wrung-out shirts.

"Mrs. Metcalf decided to dry them on the low fence outside." She dumped the leftover liquid from the two basins in the corner sink, rinsed them, and filled them with the balled-up shirts. "Let me have a couple of kids to carry these downstairs."

He named two who accompanied Nina proudly out of the room. They were all shaking and hanging when Nina heard Jack behind them. "You guys get down to the gym." He watched them go to the far entrance. "Sorry. I hadn't checked their schedule. They were already late for PE."

"It's okay." She frowned at a green shirt with a black spider web across the back. "This isn't going to work anyway. The fence is all rusty."

"Shall we take them around to the dumpster?"

Nina laughed. "They're not exactly high fashion, are they? Ah, well.

I'll take them to my yard. They'll dry fast today, and I'll press and bring them back tomorrow."

"Let me." He took the basins from her.

"No, really. I can manage."

"They'll be tied up at least 45 minutes." He carried the two basins before him like pans of hot bread.

"They'll look better once they dry." Nina walked beside him, her head down, keeping about three feet between them.

"Haven't seen you lately."

"I'm there all the time."

"No. You're not."

Nina was quiet.

"Something bothering you?"

"Me? No."

They walked several yards. "You were upset or surprised or something when you came in the room."

"I wasn't expecting ... your car wasn't..." *Don't, Nina. Don't say things.* "I just didn't think you were there. In school."

"My car?"

"I didn't see it."

"It's parked around back." He slowed down. "You checking up on me?" His voice teased her.

Nina did not look but knew his eyes were alert, engaging.

C'mon, they suggested, I'm your pal. If only she were a child, like Polly, she could play along.

"I just notice things."

He laughed, delighted. Nina thought they would never reach her gate. "Okay. Thanks."

"Hey. Invite me in."

"It's not..."

"I'm kind of into this now. Let's hang 'em."

Suitor jumped up and ran around Jack, barking. Nina pushed him toward the house, but Jack said, "Don't put him away. Sounds like welcome to me."

Nina brought clothesline from the garage and fussed with the bulky coil until he took it from her and strung a V from the house, looping a fence post and back again. They worked along the separate lines. "I like this," Jack called. "Mindless, rhythmic tasks." He slapped a shirt over the rope. "Getting to the end of the row. My only goal."

The sun felt terrific on his back. He had wanted out of the school so badly today. A long morning. Endless. The Nellis couple. Just would not accept his recommendation that their son see the school psychologist. The boy had real learning problems, not solved by a tutor. This issue dragged on. And Allison Pastor. He had to get her out of the classroom before she cracked, or the kids did. Nasty. A lot of wounded pride there. Sticky. But she had to be reassigned. This summer. Not start another year. Around and around in his brain.

What a break taking over a class. And a lucky break with Mrs. … Nina. He liked her. Her face. The way she looked at him that snowy day. Too busy at the time, but afterward, remembering. Curious, admiring. No demands on him. Her face full of unanswered questions. He had wanted to see that face again.

Not quite as friendly today. Was he making her nervous? He watched her bending, stretching the last shirt, repositioning a few others to make room. Absorbed. He thought about the time her husband came home, and he'd seen her greeting him. He held that picture of her.

"I've wanted to come in here."

"You have?"

"Sure. You know. When I'm out chasing kids at this end of the yard. I'd like to … hide out or something. Lie on the grass." He grinned.

"Well, you're welcome to." She didn't know what to say or if he was serious or not. "Go ahead now, if you want to."

He did not hesitate but flopped on his side, propping up his head. After a minute, she sat a little apart from him, her knees drawn up, her shoes neatly together. His eyes were level with the dark ovals pressed into her slacks where she had knelt in the dirt. Her bare ankles looked clean and tidy and sweet. He wanted to see her relaxed, almost asleep, the way she was that time with her husband. He was absurdly happy, could sit here forever.

"You're not the only one. Checking things out. I see you over here sometimes. Doing stuff."

Could she really do this? Strange talk with a man. Not knowing what he might say. What she might. She shook her head, smiling. "Not much to see."

"Yeah. There is." He sat up, cross-legged, intent. "God, I hate to waste a day like this."

"Are you?"

"Definitely not."

Suitor padded over to Jack, presenting himself for petting and scratching. The dog rolled over, flailing, giving into pleasure. There was something almost obscene about the dog's belly. Too pink. Nina watched Jack's hands, square and capable, sift over the pliant skin. She fixed her eyes there.

She wished he were small and adorable, and she could look at all of him, the way you stared at a baby animal. The charming and unexpected movements. He was like that to her. A creature, natural and easy. You did not want to startle or make him aware. She would be more comfortable if he were not a man, not lying on her grass under her tree in his yellow shirt, clean, untouched by the grubby activity of his day. The shirt so pale, yet gathering in all the air and light of this beautiful afternoon and reflecting a brighter sunshine back to her. She turned away, as if her eyes hurt.

"It's almost over. For this year."

"Hmm? Oh, less than a month to go."

"They're eager to leave."

"Be close this time, who's more antsy—me or the kids."

"You like it."

"Yeah. It's ridiculous but I do."

"It shows."

He liked the way she said that. He let Suitor push him onto his back. "I usually do summer school just to keep at it. But not this year. Getting away this time."

"Somewhere nice?"

"Kind of. Taking my two boys back home. Well, I have three but only two are old enough."

Nina had gathered half a dozen dandelions into her lap, and now she began to braid and twist the long stems together. Familiar ground. The way you talk to men. About their children or yours. Easier and safe. "I guess I don't know your boys. They don't go here, do they?" *This is better, Nina. You sound almost normal.*

"Nah. It's better not. Anyway, one's fourteen. Chris. Started high school. Sammy's not quite five. Named him for my dad. Hoping he'd turn out that way. What a pain." He laughed. Nina kept herself very still, not to spoil it. His naked affection. "And Buddy. Eleven and a ...

well, he's a neat kid."

"Buddy? That's his name?"

"He's named for me. But it was always hard to know what to call him. So we stuck with Buddy."

"Maybe when he grows up he'll want to be John or whatever. Everyone will call him that but you. Parents can't help it."

Jack roughed the dog some more. Kids. Every conversation he had with a woman ended up about kids. Every single one. He had so much in him, but ... it was constant. And with Greta. Especially with her. The web of their lives, even the most intimate moments—what about the boys?"

He sat up, looked at the school. The afternoon sun made blanks of the windows. He could not see anyone moving inside. "Actually, I know it's what most people think. But it's not John. Jacques. My name is Jacques."

She laughed as though she'd received a compliment. "But it's perfect. A perfect little boy's name." There was a boy she thought about sometimes. The boy she did not have. Would never. He would come in from play, smudged and tousled and hungry, drinking milk right from the carton, pasting thumbprints all over the refrigerator. Jacques. Her mind snapped out the name. Round and stubby. Sleeping in his clothes and never taking a bath. Coming up behind her and knocking her over with a hug. "What's the whole thing?" she said softly.

"Jacques deGranville Bridges."

Jacques deGranville. The name slid into many syllables. The way he pronounced it. Large and open. Not a boy. A prince.

Jack stared at her, trying but not getting her thoughts. "Okay. Tell me something about you." His voice was deep, pushing.

"There's nothing about me. Nothing like that." She rose, had to move. "You said ... I'll show you my garden."

"Yeah. Okay."

"It's such a mess today."

"Hey, don't apologize. I'm not some neat freak."

She ran to the corner of the yard where the roses grew on the fence. "This is the only part I left—when we bought the place. It was all so drab. Last year we put in the pond and the fish. A garden should have water permanently, don't you think?"

He ambled across the grass and peered into the pool, counting the bright orange ovals. "Big guys. They eat a lot?"

"From the plants. It's all scientific." She laughed. "I'm not supposed to, but I feed them extra."

He looked interested. "Yeah?"

"I could use more trees. More tall trees. These two aren't … I'd love an arbor. Do you like arbors?"

"I guess."

"And the patio. We did that right away. I'm trying to get flowers planted now, for color. I'm not doing it quite right." She dropped down before a flat of bedding plants. He leaned on one knee beside her. She spoke rapidly, gesturing widely. "This will be all pansies over here. It's stubborn of me. People say they're unfashionable and silly. But I like them. All the little faces looking up at you."

"Like the kindergarten. Only quiet." He turned and her eyes, smiling, drifted in his for a long moment. What he had wanted, waited for.

He glanced toward the house, imagined her again on the patio, her arm reaching lazily. "I remember you once offered me pie. Apple, was it?"

Nina jumped up. "I don't have anything like that today."

"I almost called you about it."

"I don't..." she whispered.

"I was hungry, and I thought that would be good. So I almost called you."

"But..."

"Got interrupted or something. Story of my life."

Was he going? Surely he would go but still he lingered, casual, in no hurry. "Sorry," Nina said.

"What?"

"About the pie." *Like an idiot, Nina, that's what you sound like.*

"Another day. I'll bug you about it." He wandered across the grass. There was something ... he had hold of something and he couldn't let go. "Now this..."

He stood before the iris, the only one in bloom, a giant flower on a tall stalk, almost to Nina's waist. Jack cupped the blossom, pale pink on the outside and yellow fuzz in the center deepening to burgundy on the drooping petals. "These should always stand alone. Like a queen. Then you can see how beautiful just one is."

"They're pretty all together, too."

"I don't know. Maybe. Anything you see over and over—loses something."

"Oh, not in nature. It multiplies, the profusion just fills you up. It's ... when you can't look fast enough."

"You..." A bell rang, cutting the afternoon. He glanced at his watch. "Time's up. Gotta go." He moved toward the gate, and she followed. He put one hand on the post, hung there. He looked at her, then out over the garden. "I'd like to see this in full bloom. In ... profusion."

"You'll be away, I think." *Enough, Nina. No more.* She dropped her head to one side. Her hair fell back. She saw his eyes light eagerly, his hand come toward her, felt him lean over her. It was so fast. He was looking at her earring.

He held it gently, a delicate lattice globe with a ruby drop in the center. "Beautiful," he said. "Shouldn't cover it up."

He was so close she felt his warm breath on her cheek, but inside, deep inside as though he touched her in a hidden and secret place. "It was a gift," she whispered.

He released the jewel, and it swung a little on her ear, heavy, and it never was before. He smiled.

"Both of them, I mean."

He shrugged, laughing, opened the gate. "Duty calls." He gave her a brief farewell salute and then walked back to the school. His stride was sure, confident, elated, speaking to her.

Nina's hands found the warm fence boards and held on. If she closed her eyes, he would disappear. *He didn't put a hand on you, Nina. He did not.*

She did close her eyes. She pictured her garden, how it would look in June. And when she got the fountain working, the pleasing sound of trickling water. She imagined her legs standing in the cool water. Only it was warm, thick and swirling slowly. The golden fish swam around her feet, tickling her ankles. One leaping between her thighs, swimming in lazy circles of honey, then upwards, going upwards, the fanning tail swishing, inside her, swishing.

She opened her eyes to make it stop, to anchor herself. *You cannot have him.*

She was not standing, had no legs. The feathery caress was sweetly insistent.

Jack reached the flagpole, the school. Nina saw him turn and in one movement raise his arm, waving in a grand circling overhead arc without hesitation, knowing, absolutely knowing she would be there still, watching him.

Chapter Seven

Not a Parting But a Return

"Too much stuff, guys."

Jack and the two older boys piled gear by the Jeep while Greta sat on the deck, cradling Sammy in her lap. It was almost ten o'clock. They should have been on the road two hours ago, not starting in the heat of the day. Jack threw a canvas bag between the seats and mashed it down.

"Jack, I'm nervous." Greta had come up behind him.

"It'll be okay."

"Sammy should stay with me."

Jack leaned on the hood, drumming his fingers. "Honey, listen. I can't even discuss this again."

"He's too little."

"He's five. He'll be less trouble with us than taking him to your mother's. The whole point is for you to help her recover from the surgery."

"It's not life threatening or anything."

"Think what he'd be like with her trying to rest."

Greta looked over his shoulder at the boys wrestling in the dirt. "Now don't get all messed up before you even get in the car!"

"He'd have a tantrum if we left him here. Buddy has him so worked up." Jack put an arm around her. He squeezed her hard, his voice too loud and confident. "It's settled, babe. Trust me, will you?"

"You always talk like that when you don't know what you're doing."

"Hey! I could use some help!" he shouted.

Buddy ran at once, Chris more slowly.

"What's all this?" Jack kicked at odd-shaped bundles. "I thought we agreed. One small duffle apiece. Trunks, sweat jacket, jeans."

Greta spoke softly. "I put in socks and underwear. Sweaters."

"What for? We don't need all that."

"How will you keep clean? Where will you do the laundry?"

"We're not doing laundry."

"What if it rains? Things get wet, Jack."

"We'll just hang stuff around 'til it dries."

"If..."

"Honey, this is no fancy deal. They wear swim trunks all day, pull on jeans at night. That's the way to do it."

"You'll have to go into town."

"Okay. One pair of shorts."

"Socks."

"Guys don't wear socks in Michigan!" he sang out. Buddy laughed. Jack was impatient to get moving. The day was slipping away. He stowed bags quickly. The boys would ride with their feet up.

"You can't all be comfortable in that."

"It's perfect."

"The sides are coming apart."

"Sweetheart, I went all the way out west in one of these without even a top!"

"You need a grown-up car."

He really wanted to go now. The talking made him tired. "You need your car to get to Maryland. Why are you bugging me about this?"

"You're so eager to get away. Why are you in such a hurry?"

Jack did not look at her. "Lotta hot, noisy miles out there."

"You seem impatient to get to them."

"Waiting's not my long suit."

She left him and went into the house.

"C'mon, guys. Let's saddle up."

He strapped Sam into the back seat. Greta brought the small cooler with their lunch packed in it. Jack shoved it on the floor. Sam's legs stuck out straight across the top. "If we don't get moving, we might as well eat it here!" He grabbed Greta, hugging her, swaying with her.

"If Sammy won't eat..." she began.

"He will."

"You know how..."

"Everyone eats in Michigan!" Jack crowed. "It's the law!"

"I still don't see how you'll manage the food."

"I come from a long line of cooks. Or we go into town. There's Thunder's, there's..."

"Jack. Don't take them there."

"What is it, Dad?" Chris was interested.

"It's a bar," Greta said.

"More like a tavern. Kind of a restaurant," Jack said. "They have cheeseburgers and fresh fish, I'm telling you ... best in the whole world."

Chris and Buddy were arguing about who would get the front seat.

"I thought no headphones." Jack was looking at Chris. The boy did not answer. "Chris!"

"C'mon, Dad! I gotta have something to do."

"You'll have plenty to do."

"Not in the car." He looked at his mother.

"Jack, he did buy it himself, after all. It really belongs to him."

"That's not the point. We were going to have a break from electronic noise." Jack sighed. *Not worth a showdown. Drop it.* He turned to Greta. "Are we set?"

"I have things to do here. Then the bank. I probably won't leave until one or so. I'm going by the hospital first then over to the house."

"Tell Mom we love her."

"Yes. Call me."

"Tomorrow or the day after." Jack had his lips against Greta's ear. "I'm not very good at this."

"We don't get much practice."

Jack nuzzled her. Last night had been bad. She was jumpy, and he hadn't the energy to calm her. Finally he'd burst out, only half joking, "You worry so much about the kids. Aren't you concerned about me and all those lonely women in Bear?"

"With three kids, what could you do?"

"Anything. How did they get here?"

"Do you have to joke about this?"

"Do you trust me that much?"

"I just don't think you're the type."

He'd slept badly, Greta way over on her side, but at dawn he'd pulled her to the center.

He did not want to leave it like that. The boys were calling to her now. "A nice goodbye," Jack whispered.

"You had it earlier."

"Make me remember it." He kissed her.

She moved over to the Jeep and hugged Sam and patted Chris through the open door then around to the other side for Buddy. "Be good, be good," she said to each of them. "Don't fight and be nice to each other. Do what Dad says."

"You don't have to tell them that."

"Don't stay the whole three weeks if they get bored."

"They won't."

Jack started the engine, reached out to her for a final hug. She clung to him a little, and he felt clumsy, unable to say anything comforting or significant. He just wanted to be away. "You gonna be okay?"

"Yes. You be a good boy, too. *Please*, Jack, and set a good example."

"Is that the same as a role model?"

"It means for your own kids—not everyone else's."

"Always, honey."

He started down the driveway, and Greta ran up to the deck to wave. "Jack!" she cried. "Jack! You forgot Sam's medicine!"

"Nobody has allergies in Michigan!" he shouted and kept going.

Jack liked to drive and let his mind travel along. You might have worries at either end but the road between was a place to forget or dream. Some of his best ideas came on the move.

The boys' low chatter didn't bother him too much. Through the mountains of Pennsylvania, trees shadowed the narrow turnpike, keeping them cool. Then the whole country seemed to broaden as the road descended and flattened into Ohio. Going west, they faced the level stare of the afternoon sun until Jack turned north to Michigan. It was a solid feeling, clocking the miles after the tedious morning and wondering if he'd ever get them out of Virginia.

At the motel everything came apart. Sam whined for Greta at bedtime then screamed. Buddy said he never wanted to come in the first place.

Why didn't they just go home? "Can we, Dad?" Chris cried. "This is stupid." Jack held Sam until the wailing stopped, and he fell into wet and sticky sleep. The crying went on in Jack's head for a long time plus the road was still under him. If the kid did this every night, three weeks would seem very long. It seemed long already. He shifted, trying not to jostle Sam and get it started again. He was filthy, exhausted, trapped.

In the morning, Sam was fine, no traces on him. Jack felt hung over and said that aloud. "What's hung over, Dad?" Bud had to ask.

"Never mind."

His mood improved as he drove, the day gorgeous and alluring, and they did not have far to go.

"We almost there, Dad?" Buddy had started asking this ten miles down the road. The boys talked constantly, shouting above the trucks and rushing wind.

"Are we staying in that motel on the way home?" Chris lifted his headphones and leaned forward.

"Geez, how would I know? We're not even to Bear yet."

"I didn't like that place."

"I thought it was okay."

"It was boring."

"A motel is boring?"

"No game room. The pool was..."

"Okay, okay. That's enough. I didn't put a lot of thought into it. You know, Chris, when I was your age, I don't ever remember feeling bored. I don't think I even knew the word."

The boy plugged his ears and looked out the window.

"Are we almost there?"

"Buddy!"

"Well, where are we?"

"All right. We're, let's see, we're about half way up the big mitten. Hold up your right hand." Sam held up a hand, Buddy did not. "Look. Here we are. We go straight to the top, turn and drive along the lake. Wiggle your index finger." He reached over to Sam. "This one."

"He calls it pointer," said Buddy.

"Wiggle your pointer. That's Grandpa's house on the tip. Our house."

"Where are the bears?"

"No bears, Sam. The house is a few miles north of this town they call Bear. You can call a town anything. They don't have bears. Not anymore, anyway."

"Who lives in Grandpa's house now?"

"No one, Bud. It's just there. My friend goes out and looks after it for me. Duncan Tyler. You guys remember him?"

"Sort of."

"No."

"He's going to meet us there."

"What do we call him?"

"You used to call him uncle."

"Uncle Duncan?" Buddy giggled.

"Or, just call him Dunk. That's what everybody does."

"Is he a teacher too?"

"God, no. He works for Bridges and Bird, Grandpa's old lumberyard. Only it's Mitchell Bird's now. Mostly a hardware business."

"I've never gotten why it's a mitten. I just don't get that." Buddy had been staring out the window. He leaned over and pounded Jack's shoulder.

"Watch it! It's that way because ... because ... this is what my dad told me. He got the story from an old Indian. So God the Great Spirit was finishing up the world, and He'd put in all the rivers and mountains and deserts and stuff. The oceans. And He wanted to leave a signature somewhere so that everyone would see the world and know He'd been the cause of it all. So He put His big hand down on the most beautiful place and decorated all the edges with blue, blue water so it would stand out for everyone to see clearly. And it was Michigan. Hand of God."

Buddy turned back to the billboards lining the road.

"Dad, every other car is hauling a boat."

"That's right, Chris."

"Do we still have one?"

"Not anymore."

Jack looked back at his youngest son. "You believe me, Sam. Don't you?"

The boy took Jack's hand and tugged on it. He pressed his left palm down on Jack's right and stared up at him. Jack gently squeezed the small hand. "You know, sometimes I almost like you. Even though I never know what you're doing."

He drove a while holding Sam's hand. "I want you kids to notice the air," he called out. "You get this far north, cross the palm and into the fingers we say, it smells pure. No pollution. Take a deep breath."

Chris and Buddy collapsed, gagging and choking. "We've entered the Pure Air Zone, Captain. The men need smog and carbon dioxide! They can't take pure. Anything but pure!" The boys punched each other, shouting. The Jeep rocked.

"I can't drive with you guys doing that!" Jack roared.

"Dad, we didn't come all this way for air. What are we gonna do? They have a mall?"

"No malls, Chris. You do what you always do. You swim. You don't remember any of it?" Jack was mildly annoyed.

"I remember going in the boat with Grandpa."

Jack pictured his sons, small, wadded in orange life preservers, fifty yards offshore with Samuel. The old rowboat and Samuel in his tan fishing hat, an arm around Buddy, holding his line steady. The flip out of the water and a perch dangling. Happy shouts and he and Greta waving from the beach. They shouldn't forget. He hoped it would come back.

"It's about an hour. Do we stop for lunch or keep going?"

"Keep going!" Buddy shouted. "I want to get there!"

"Me, too. You know what? I'm having a good time!" Jack pushed against the steering wheel. "I want you guys to know that!"

He shouldn't have stayed away this long. It was too much work to get it back. And for the boys. This ought to be in their vocabularies. He hadn't made it real for them, and now he didn't know where to start. Once his entire world was this tiny insignificant corner, his bright childhood here and everything he loved. Samuel Bridges' boy—knew everyone in town. He didn't know why he'd let it go so long. It just hurt so bad when his father went. He still did not like to think about it. Samuel's death was the first time in his life that he felt real pain. Greta had said that, holding him when he cried. It's okay, she told him. You've never really known before.

She was so sweet to him. She adored Samuel. And Jack thought she had liked Bear. Before he'd had to work every summer, and Chris and Buddy were small, they'd brought them here for a couple of weeks or whatever they could manage. Samuel showed them off all over town while Jack and Greta stayed up in the old bedroom with its golden pine ceiling slanted under the eaves. Knocked his head climbing over her.

He focused on the road. Log cabin restaurants, trailer parks, pine tourist cabins. There seemed to be more of everything—more signs with grinning faces, breezy and unsophisticated, a hearty welcome to the north, luring the trade. At night a neon alley. He hadn't remembered how it all looked homemade.

"I think I remember this part, Dad."

"Good, Chris. Hang on." He drove faster, the lake appearing and disappearing, flashing blue and gold between vertical bars of silver birches. He would take a good look at it later. He would have plenty of time.

Now they passed large board signs, gaudy and proud, marking driveways leading to cottages, announcements of ownership. The final quarter mile was nothing but pine woods. Blindfolded he could find the turn into a narrow, unassuming track with a small rectangle, weathered gray, hanging neatly on two chains, the name carved precisely into the wood. BRIDGES.

Here. The Jeep crept away from the highway and along the packed sandy drive that wound through pine trees into the clearing to lasso the house. Jack drove around front, almost ramming a beat-up truck.

"Don't scratch the paint, man!" Dunk was sitting on the steps.

"Hey, have we got a pair here or what? Both of 'em junk." Jack peeled himself off the seat and jumped down. He unbuckled Sammy, pulled him out, and rubbed his bottom. "Your rear's still here. You win a prize, gang."

"What do we get?"

"Just an expression, Bud. Everyone say hi to Dunk and then you can run around. Chris, watch Sam. Please."

Dunk ambled over to the group. "Man, it's almost two. Been waitin' around."

"Yeah, well. It takes a while to get going with this crowd. You got something else to do?" Jack slapped Dunk on his skinny and sunburned back. "God, man, you never change. Still a reject from the Salvation Army!"

"Who've I got to impress?"

"The place looks good, anyway." No matter how many years slipped by, with Dunk there was no stilted how-you-been, just an easy slide into talk.

"Been workin' on it."

"Dad, can we go in the water?"

"I guess. Just wade, though. And watch Sam."

They ran through the few trees on this side to the beach curving in a generous horseshoe around the private cove. Jack wanted to go with them. Chris tried to take Sam wading, but the little boy pulled back, so Chris, being nice, stayed with him. Buddy pulled off his T-shirt and plunged in. "I guess they're all right," Jack said, turning to Dunk.

"Three years ago wasn't any beach at all. Water line came up to here."

"I remember you telling me."

"Came back, though. Last summer I had to clear a bunch of debris."

"I owe you."

"Hell."

Jack's eyes scanned the front of the house. "Maybe I'll take a look inside." He did not move. "Ah, I can't ... I gotta..." He gestured toward the boys.

"You planning on staying here, right?"

"That was the idea."

"Then the bad news is your pump."

"What..."

"I can't get it going. There's no water. Just the old hand pump out back by the shed."

"Couldn't you get it fixed? Replaced even?"

"Didn't know how much you wanted to put into it."

"I thought we agreed..." Jack stopped.

"It's been doin' nothing for five years," Dunk said. "Just sitting here, Jack."

"I know."

"Well, don't sound so mean about it."

"Hey, no. I'm not. Just wasn't supposed to happen, is all."

"I might could fix it if I had the right parts."

Jack laughed. He sat down, liking the warm boards under him. "Welcome home," he said softly.

"What's funny?"

"You remind me of someone. Dunk, if you ever decide to leave here, I think I've got work for you." He smiled warmly at his old friend. "So, we've got electricity and that's about it."

Dunk shook his head. "The generator works all right, but the refrigerator's shot. Same with the stove."

The boys came back. "We're hungry, Dad. Starved."

"See if there's anything left in the car."

"I gotta pee, Daddy. Sammy too." Buddy bounced up and down.

Jack gestured toward the woods. "Lotta trees out there."

"I think Sammy's got more."

"So pick up a stick and bury it." Jack looked at Dunk. "How long to get a new pump you think?"

"Oh," Dunk thought. "You'd have to get Craigs over in Lebeau. Nobody in Bear could." He tossed his head. "Maybe a week for them to order it, install it."

"Dad, can we call Mom?"

"No phone, Chris. Took it out long ago."

"How come?"

Jack said nothing. Chris leaned on the railing. "This is a neat deck. You see the whole lake from here."

"We call it a porch. A covered porch."

"You want me to bring in the stuff?"

Jack was silent.

"Dad?"

"Leave it for now."

"Aren't we gonna stay here?"

"Maybe. There's no plumbing is all."

"Can I go inside?"

"Later."

"We going to another motel?"

"Not a chance."

"I don't think I like this, Dad."

"I don't either, Chris. But there's nothing I can do about it."

"You sound mad."

"I'm thinking." He slapped his knees. "Okay. Camping out. I'm thinking that would work."

"Where?"

"Here, of course."

Buddy and Sam returned. "You okay?" Jack said to them.

Buddy shrugged.

Jack turned to Dunk. "Where's all the tents and stuff? Dad's gear?"

"Gone, man. You said to clear it out."

"Right. I forgot. Jesus! I was thinking with my ass."

The older boys looked at him. At each other.

"Don't tell your mother." Jack said to Dunk, "I'm supposed to set a good example." He laughed. He felt good again. And hungry. "Let's go eat."

"If you're going into town, you can get tents at the store. Mitchell's got all that stuff."

"I'll talk to him." Jack turned to his sons. "How about it? We set up camp. Right here or down on the beach."

"How do we eat?"

"Like always. With your fingers."

"Dad, there's no bathroom?"

"Chris, you're really bugging me." Jack did not connect with the boy's emerging fastidiousness. Petty objections and some overly nice, careful habits. "There's the lake, there's the woods. Who's gonna look at you? Okay, we dig a deep hole and stick a shovel in the sand pile. We're all guys, f' chrissake."

Chris stared at him then sang out, "Nobody *craps* in Michigan!"

Jack faked a punch at him. "C'mon. Give me a hand. We unload, go in to Bear, cat, get set up. Let's go!"

"Where's the thunder place?" Buddy pulled on Jack.

"In town." Jack was throwing bags out of the Jeep.

"Why doesn't Mom like that place?"

"She saw two guys in a fight there once."

"Were they killed?"

"Nah. They were just drunk."

"Let's go there."

"Yeah, let's!" Jack yelled. "Okay! Pile in!"

"Can we ride in the truck?" Chris asked Dunk. "In back?"

"If your dad says."

"Sure. Get in. Sam better go with me."

But Sam climbed into the cab next to Dunk, and that was that. Jack waved them off. "I'm right behind you!"

He climbed behind the wheel, turned the ignition on then off. He walked toward the lake and kicked off his shoes. His tender soles leaped away from the hot layer of sand, baked in the sun of mid-afternoon. Jamming his feet deep into the sand, he plowed to the water's edge and sat. Clear and green, no waves, just an occasional ripple slopping his toes. He leaned back, blurred his eyes.

It was better Greta wasn't here, for her sake. She'd worry about Chris and Buddy in the back of an open truck. Well, she'd never let them. Or Sam, practically on his own. And Jack would worry about her—the lack of facilities. But he would make this good for all of them. Simple and clean. He'd give the boys a long rope. Learn some things. They were far away from Virginia. The lake had its old restful effect on him. He emptied his mind into it, letting everything drain away.

He rose stretching and turned to face the house. Standing back in a sturdy and satisfying way, protected in the embrace of green pines, his boyhood home remained the same, looking absolutely right to him. Grand in a way and yet unpretentious, it belonged there, like the man who built it.

Every time Jack left home, going back to school and even after he was married and working, the very last thing he'd do was come down to the water. In whitest winter also, in boots crunching over rough peaked ice. Looking out on the vast level space, he'd take some of that open feeling into himself; store it for whenever he would need it. And when he climbed back to the house, Samuel was always standing on the porch or in the big window. He had this way of leaving you alone, not disturbing your privacy. He and Jack would wave to one another in a friendly yet solemn way. Later, they would shake hands and part, their official goodbye. But the real farewell was in that shared salute, that moment before going, which spoke not of parting, but of return.

Jack was glad he could think about that as he walked toward the house.

Chapter Eight

Child and Man

Sometime during the night, Sam had crawled into Jack's sleeping bag. His mouth, sweetly ringed with red juice stain, puckered against Jack's chest. Jack lay still and listened to crows fighting gulls for scraps around the campsite and wings paddling the air outside the nylon walls. He reached out one arm and opened the tent flap, breathing sharp pine breezes mixed with the slightly fishy smell of water.

Jack wanted to get up but would wait for Sam. Sam was a new kid; he did not cry and fed himself. He had a charming habit of putting his hands on his dad's cheeks when he had something to say. Whispered words. Jack was in love with Sam. He was Jack's boy and mornings were a good time.

Jack peered through the mesh opening. The already bright sun had burned mist off the lake. More than any memory of childhood, one he took everywhere with him, was waking in July, waking by water—fresh, clear, hot and dazzling—every sense touched and scrubbed by the air of a Michigan morning.

He could not wait. Gently, he rubbed Sam's cheek and the tip of his nose. The boy squirmed then popped his eyes. Jack covered Sam's mouth and put a finger to his lips. The two sat up and crawled onto the sand.

Jack's trunks were spread on top of the tent. He felt them. Still damp. He left them and followed Sam down to the water's edge. There was no sound in the other tent. He might not see Buddy for another hour and longer for Chris.

Sam plopped down and threw sand over his legs. Jack kept going into the lake. The water did not feel cold, the sun having warmed it for a while, and was perfectly calm, not blue but a golden green. His feet stirred clouds in the sandy bottom. He plunged and swam straight out, heading for the sandbar. He'd been a powerful young swimmer and was almost back to full strength since arriving ten days ago.

At the sandbar, he stood in water waist deep and marked off two spots along the shore. He began swimming laps between these points, alternating freestyle and backstroke. When he had done thirty he stopped and floated. He was trying to work up to fifty. Another week and a half, he might make it. He would figure how many more to do each day. He had lost track and wasn't even sure what day of the week it was. His watch hung on the turn signal in the Jeep. He didn't look at it now.

He swam a slow breaststroke back to shore, beaver-like, his chin resting calmly on the water. He loved their camp, loved coming into it like this. The two four-man tents—one green, one yellow—were placed about five yards apart on the south end of the cove; on the north end stood the old pine picnic table Chris had helped him drag off the porch. All their supplies were there, food and the Coleman stove, the fresh water they carried from the pump. A taut line was strung for towels and sleeping bags needing air.

In the center of the beach was the fire circle. Dunk had helped Jack roll four logs about five feet each from the woods. They squared an area and made a shallow depression in the center. Two cinder blocks, sunk deep in the sand, anchored a grill for cooking. The boys had stacked a neat woodpile between two trees and protected this with a tarp. They had found cut and split wood at the house, Samuel's work, still there. With a campfire every night they were running low. Replenishing the pile would be good exercise for him this afternoon.

The camp was definitely a good one. The only thing missing was a boat, moored out in the cove. He and Samuel always had a boat.

Buddy had joined Sam. Their naked bodies, brown all over, pleased him. Sam's hair was bleached white, and he looked tougher, more solid. He would not try swimming yet. The kid's reluctance bothered Jack. Buddy splashed out to intercept him, grabbing Jack underwater and pulling him down. He liked to horse around with Buddy; the boy was fearless.

He crawled on his hands almost out of the water and lay with his chin in the sand, the water covering and draining off the backs of his legs. There was more breeze now and the lake rolled. Bud and Sam dug holes, let the lake fill them and dug more. Jack watched them.

"Daddy, why does the water have spots?"

"What, Sam? Where?" Jack turned and sat up.

"All over."

Jack gazed at the lake, the sun catching the swells, dappling the water. "What's it look like to you, Bud?"

Buddy considered. "Like money."

"Hey, you're right," Jack said. "It is money. Golden coins."

Buddy stared at him and Sam crept to his side. Jack's voice took on a dreamy tone. "I'll tell you a story I heard years ago. I got it from my dad and I give it to you." He paused. "Of course you know the first folks around these parts were Indians. And they were proud. They had all the woods, the animals, and the water. And then the French came and started to take some things, mostly animals but some of the rivers also.

"Well, one old chief, uh..." he closed his eyes, "...uh, Chipahoo. Chief Chipahoo didn't have a lot of what you'd call cold cash. And this flunky of the French king handed him a bag of gold coins. He didn't exactly hand him the coins. Kind of waved the bag around and shook it in old Chipahoo's face, making a clinking noise.

"Well, that old chief took the bag and dipped his hand in. He pulled out a fistful of coins and threw them into the lake. Just tossed them as far as he could, in a great glittering splash. He kept doing this until the coins were gone. And then he picked up the king's messenger and threw him in too. The king never knew what happened.

"Old Chipahoo knew there was stuff you just can't buy. Those coins were worth nothing. And that's what we see reflecting out there, even today, to remind us." Jack laughed. "And that's why this is still Michigan and not the French Riviera."

Buddy looked down at the sand. "Chief Chipahoo?"

110

"That was his name. Meant Lean Panther." Buddy snorted. "Hey, it's true. And every time you swim in the morning, some of that stays on you. You come out dripping gold."

Buddy jumped up and ran back to the picnic table.

Jack grinned at Sam. "Maybe I didn't tell it right."

The boy smoothed the hair on Jack's arm. He fluffed Jack's chest. "There, Daddy."

Jack laughed hugely and pawed through the tangle. "Bit of silver mixed in!" He rubbed Sam's head. "Smartest one in the bunch!" He looked seriously into his son's eyes. "I desperately need coffee," he whispered.

He jogged back to the tent and pulled on his trunks. Buddy poked in the food. Jack put a small pot of water to boil on the stove. When it was ready, he scalded a plastic mug and made double strength instant coffee. He only drank it once a day now, and he liked it black and strong. He sat on the table facing the water eating chunks of dry cereal with his fingers and a small box of raisins. He fished peanuts from a burlap sack and ate a dozen, rolling them in his hands and picking out the meat. Sam played around the water's edge, his head shining. Buddy munched behind Jack. It was quiet, no boats yet on the lake and the birds finished with their morning racket. Jack sat still. He could not be interrupted because there was no schedule. Nothing could go wrong. There was no plan.

His beard had passed the rough, stubbly stage and was silky. He did not comb his hair. He never brushed his teeth and told the boys they didn't have to either if they ate an apple or carrot every day. The boys were ecstatic. Every three or four days he tossed a bar of Ivory to Chris and Buddy while they swam. He scrubbed Sam in the shallow water. Sam and Buddy had thick hair like Jack, and they all looked overgrown.

Lazy and crude. No, dammit, carefree and honest. Everyone on his own. There were boxes of granola, chips, and pretzels. Peanut butter, bread, some cheese, fresh fruits, tomatoes. The boys mixed powdered drinks. There were also cans of juice in the tub, sunk in the lake, where Jack kept his beer. There were no mealtimes, except for supper. They could eat what they wanted and when as long as they cleaned up afterward. At night Jack usually cooked over the fire, something easy, and about every third day they went into town and stayed for dinner.

He tried to explain it to Greta on the phone.

"But are they drinking milk?" she'd asked.

"In town. Mostly shakes and ice cream."

"They won't..."

"Yes, they will. You'll see. They're doing great."

"You sound so far away."

"Don't worry about us. Everything's fine." He was shouting over traffic noise passing the phone booth at the gas station. He loved being in charge of all this, taking the boys shopping, and they could pick what they wanted but no complaints afterward.

The idea had come to him the first day when he'd finally caught up with them at Thunder's. Dunk had everyone tucked in the big round booth and platters ordered. The only patrons beside themselves were a couple of old guys at the bar. The juke box and pinball lights faded in the dim interior shade of afternoon. Evan Thunder sat with them and Jack introduced the boys.

Buddy, noticing the trophies, asked in his curiously deep voice, "Did you kill all these animals, Mr. Thunder?"

Sammy, squeezed onto Jack's lap, couldn't take his eyes off the silent stags, elk, two bears and the wildcat, the dull gaze of chocolate marble eyes.

Chris looked around expectantly. "Does anyone else ever come here?"

"It's livelier at night," Jack told him.

"Is this lunch we're eating?"

Jack was tired of questions, weary of explanations. "What does it matter, what you call it? You're hungry, you eat." Sam ate three steak fries off Jack's plate. Jack watched him nibble a burger.

Dunk demonstrated pinball to Chris, couldn't believe he'd never played it. "You're behind on your life, kid." Jack fed quarters into the jukebox. He and Dunk finished a few beers.

"Mack's coming over after he closes up," Dunk said. "We stopped by on the way here." Mack Savage worked at his dad's garage and body shop and sold used cars on the side.

"He pretty busy?"

"This time of year, sure. They hustle that summer trade, same's everyone else." Dunk opened another bottle. "Only time of year this crummy town gets busy."

"Looks good to me," Jack said softly.

"I didn't mean anything."

And then Mack burst in, big and loud, dark glasses falling off, a baby riding high on his neck and trailing a crowd of chattering girls, looked like all ages. He grabbed Jack. "So you finally came back! Brought the troops over soon's I could." He set the baby on the wooden floor, and she stumbled off with her big sister. "Can you believe it? Five and not one boy."

"Giving up, Mack? Gettin' too old?"

"Hell! Not my fault only Patty won't let me come near her." He laughed. "All she does is feed me. Directs my attention elsewhere." He slapped his huge gut, counted bottles. "How many you guys ahead? Evan!" he shouted.

Jack sank back into the booth. The children gravitated to one another at the front of the room, Chris sharing his Walkman. "Geez, you guys. Geez." Jack grinned at his old friends. "Too *long!*"

They sat for an hour and then some, drinking, the old fifties music Evan Thunder kept playing, the children back and forth filching food off the table, the bar slowly populating and people stopping by. Old friends, happy to see Jack, see the boys and guess their ages, apparently doing nothing for years but waiting for him to come back, say how much they missed him—and Samuel. This was the best part, that eager hometown interest, where people love you because you do come back and it's the same as always until the falling off when there's not much to say, because you've let it go and maybe been away too long.

Mack talked the most. He had a girl about the same age as Chris. "Those two. There's definite attraction."

"Lay off, Mack. He's not even..."

"Look at him. The kid's a killer." Mack would not give up.

Jack stared at his son. Chris was talking to Mack's daughter, the really pretty one who had lost her baby fat, the boy's fine silky hair, Greta's hair, falling in his eyes and his standard shrug to flip it back. He said something, looking right at the girl with his mother's dark gray eyes, and the girl looking away and then back at him, and him smiling at her. Jack was uncomfortable yet fascinated. "Hey, how old were we when we...?"

"Doesn't matter. They do everything sooner now." Mack dismissed it. He had married Patty the day after their high school graduation.

Dunk had a memory, recounting years, times, actual parties they'd all been to. And he knew where everyone had gone, what they were doing now. Slyly, to Jack, "Lucinda's back. Divorced. You could give her a thrill, dropping in."

"Man, I've forgotten what she even looks like."

"She looks all different now."

"Tell us, Duncan." Mack had his eye on the kids.

Jack's eyes volleyed between his friends. "What is it I don't know?"

Dunk dipped his head under the table. "Think I dropped..."

Mack winked.

"Geez, Dunk, Lucinda?" Jack was laughing helplessly.

"Last winter," Dunk spoke precisely, "we had six weeks...in a row... and it never got above ten below."

"Hey, don't apologize to *me!*"

The bar was cloudy with smoke by then, and people were eating supper. Jack saw the kids go out the door. He rose, signaling.

"What's the matter?"

"I don't want them to get lost."

"You're lost, man!" Mack roared. "If we couldn't find them in this place!"

Jack sat down, slapping his head. Lost! In Bear! One street, two rows of stores and the lake for a back yard. Then the houses scattered here and there, picket fences and summer porches. He had to come home and his friends helped him, shedding skin, starting to get it back as they exploded with laughter—intimate, insulting male laughter—knowing each other too well from days when they had nothing and nowhere to hide.

"So!" Mack boomed. "You going to be back regular now? Not be such a stranger?"

"I don't know. I'm just...seeing how it is."

"You still thinking of selling the place?" Mack asked.

"Don't know. Back then, Dunk and I..." Jack slapped Dunk on the back. "We threw out some things. Sold some. To get it ready." Jack stopped. "That was a pretty confusing time for me. All in all. There was a lot going on. I wasn't thinking, and now I just don't know."

"Well, I don't think he'd mind. Whatever you wanted. That's the way he was."

"I don't think he expected I'd ever make a life back here. He didn't leave me his business. Just the property." Jack tossed a glass back and forth across the table, catching it in his hands.

114

After a minute, Mack rumbled, "Whatever he did, it was after a lot of thought." He sighed. "I never saw that man do a dumb thing."

"Two packs a day." Jack spoke softly.

"Shit. What did anyone know?"

"He could be here."

"None of that talk." Mack was sweating. "You sound like shit saying that."

"Yeah. Tell me about it." Jack drained his glass. "I miss him, is all."

"You know what I always think about—really think about." Dunk seemed sober now. "Those trips to Canada, Jack. Those were the best. Nothing better."

Mack chuckled. "Oh, man, your dad's old Ford pickup, the hood like a hill you could slide on. One of us in the cab with Samuel and the other two in the back. All the gear. Us going under the tarp in the rain."

"The miles we went in that thing." Dunk rarely laughed but he did now.

"Good miles."

They weren't looking at one another but at the table. Dunk cleared his throat. "He gave me lots to do; made me feel like a man." He paused. "But we were kids, 'cause we had nothing to worry about. Nothing."

Jack's glass was empty. "Guys..." he started.

Mack interrupted. "Jack, there's something we gotta do. We should have, last time you were home."

Last time meant Samuel's funeral.

"Let's clear out this shit." Mack piled up all the plates and glasses on a tray and carried them to the bar. "Thunder!" he shouted, but Evan wasn't there. Mack walked behind the bar, selected a bottle and three clean glasses; brought them to the table. "I think this is worthy." He poured.

The music had stopped, and the kids were still outside somewhere.

"Okay, here we go." Mack raised his glass. He waited, thoughtful.

"You want me to?" Dunk said.

"Nope."

Jack raised his glass, Dunk his.

"Samuel Bridges," Mack said, firmly, and the three touched glasses and drank.

All three stumbled outside, rounding up the kids and over to Bridges and Bird Lumber, now hardware. And Dunk backing his pickup to the rear loading platform and Jack tossing in tents, sleeping bags, large cooler, propane stove, rope, water jugs, rubber rafts, a battery lantern, flashlights, and insect repellant. Chris, dancing, "Dad, we're getting so much stuff!" Buddy saying over and over could they keep it all. Mitchell Bird hugging Jack, waving off any payment. "Just come and see me later. Next week or when you can."

Next to the Food Mart and Dairy with Dunk still crowding the pickup. Plastic utensils, paper plates and paper towels, cans and jars of everything, and cases of beer. Out to the house, just Dunk and Jack and the boys. Mack and the girls had to "report home," he called it. Setting up camp in the twilight, arranging quarters, stowing gear and at last sleep, long absorbing sleep with Sam not crying. That had been the first day and a fine beginning.

Every day since, Jack had refined the operation to simplify or improve the camp. On this morning, he thought it was finally perfect. Another hot day ahead. No clouds and less sparkle but the lake that deep peaceful blue. They'd had rain one afternoon—penny drops on the sand and then all blowing away—and sat on the porch watching the misty dark column move over the lake. Twice in the night Jack awakened to spattering on the tent. The beautiful sound blended with his sleep and carried over into the morning.

Chris staggered out of the yellow tent and sat beside Jack, eating a banana slowly, slumped over in a dopey way. Jack didn't talk. Chris took a long time to wake up. After he disposed of the peel, he stretched and yawned. "Think I'll drive a little now." He flipped his hand and strolled casually to the Jeep, parked where he'd left it yesterday, nosed into a tree.

Jack watched him with amusement and pride. The boy had Greta's long legs and a strong upper body. A swimmer's body. He should go out for some sport. And a handsome face—almost pretty. The eyes especially. Maybe too aware of himself. But aren't they all, just a shave before fifteen? So much to be aware of. Jack looked away. *Don't crowd him. The kid is doing fine, not screwing up and having a ball. If Greta gets mad, blame it on Dunk.*

Dunk came out most evenings to sit around the fire with them, and he and Jack talked too much about their early attempts to drive. Jack had started at twelve. Chris could not believe it. "Didn't they have laws? Weren't you arrested?"

"Oh, they had laws. It's just that no one paid much attention to them." Dunk was evasive. "We all drove inboards on the lake and then whatever was around the lumberyard. Samuel let us."

"Yeah," Jack recalled. "One time he got stuck with a delivery and no one to make it so he told Dunk and me to get into the flatbed and take off."

They laughed. "We were thirteen," said Dunk. "Not even scared. We knew everything. Just took it on down the highway."

"I was scared," said Jack. "That load kept shifting. Geez."

Chris kicked at the sand. "I bet I know how."

The next morning Jack tossed him the keys and said, "See how you do."

"Is it legal?"

"On our property, sure. Go on."

"What if I wreck it?"

"What? That?! What could you do to it? Want me to show you?"

"No."

Every day, sometimes for more than two hours, Chris drove. The same route. Out to the road, back it up, circle, down the track through the trees, loop around the house, out to the road again. Jack hadn't had a cross word with him since the driving began. Jack listened to him grind the gears.

"Dad, you said you started driving when you were twelve, right?"

"About that, Bud."

"I'm almost..."

Jack clamped a hand on Buddy's mouth. "Don't even think about it, kid. Your mother would kill me."

He checked on Sam, eating oatmeal cookies and grapes. "Anyone want to help me?"

"Do what?"

"Up at the house."

"Yeah!" The two boys scrambled after him. They loved going into the house.

Jack had left the house alone until he felt childish, avoiding it. One afternoon he took a couple of cans of beer, cold from the lake and opened it up. He removed storm windows and installed screens, propped open doors. He sat in the big room, about thirty feet long, sipping beer. A stone fireplace rose two stories to the rafters. The walls were dark knotty pine, the pine floors stained even darker. Jack thought it was stuffy and they did not stay long.

But today the place was clean—rid of creeping mouse trails and cloudy, moss-like spider webs, the sills free of the broken, powdered bodies of ancient insects. Their work had produced satisfying results. They had done the big room first. Chris and Jack had lugged the furniture, what was left, onto the porch. Then they'd scrubbed the floor and brushed the fireplace, carried out the ashes, and fixed the grate properly. The room looked spare. One couch covered with a plaid wool blanket and Samuel's old leather chair plus a few good tables, solid maple. No rugs and the lamps not working. No curtains at the windows.

The boys lost interest after that project, except for Buddy. Jack and his middle son kept on, cleaning: the kitchen, the bathroom, and Samuel's bedroom. Jack's old room sat above a pull-down ladder in the hallway ceiling. Summers, he'd sleep toward the front to get the breeze off the lake, and winters he'd move his bed to the back over the kitchen. Sometimes, when it was so hot in August, he'd go downstairs and sleep in the old hammock that Samuel kept slung crosswise on the covered porch. It was hard to remember that sweaty heat in January when frost seeped in despite the two small space heaters, and he'd wake to see white triangular patches in the corners where the eaves joined. He'd drag his clothes into bed to warm them before he dressed under the covers. He loved it. Always, all seasons, he loved it.

Nothing was left now but his bed frame with the mattress rolled on it, his empty dresser, and the pole, about four feet long, where he used to hang his clothes. What would it look like with one of today's kids, one of his own, living there? Thing-crazy, their crammed spaces, their walls plastered with posters, pictures torn from magazines, plastic everything.

Samuel's room was Spartan also and much smaller. In the closet hung flannel shirts, a blue one in particular Jack remembered, his suede jacket and an old parka with reindeer fur lining. The cedar chest remained, filled with blankets, quilts, and some pictures. Jack had not known what to do with them five years ago. He still didn't.

His father had few possessions. Jack knew this was a legacy from Samuel's nineteenth-century roots. Life was adventure and sailing; things only added weight. You could travel farther and faster with light personal cargo. The family's fortunes for decades had alternately prospered and declined in merchant sailing on the Great Lakes. Samuel Bridges, born in 1900 on hard times, a century child, never had formal schooling. But, impressionable and quick, he learned early the thrill and hardship of life on the water. Samuel's father had little money but rich experience, and all his life Samuel recited the songs, Indian stories, and tales of disaster absorbed in his childhood.

When he arrived in Bear at the age of twenty to start a lumber business, he brought with him a remarkable judgment of men and the random poetry of his youth—good and necessary qualities for acceptance and survival in the generally male culture of this small, cold town. Jack had heard his dad say success was all hard work and putting your profit back in the business. But he hadn't always followed his own principles. Even when his business suffered with everyone else in the Depression, he bought property, this acreage along the lake.

Almost everything Jack knew about Samuel's marriage, he learned from his maternal grandfather, Jacques deGranville. Old Jacques struggled in Bear to support his wife and daughter but, bookish and vague, he was a dreamy throwback to the days of gentlemen living leisurely lives on inherited income. When he was a boy, Jack liked to hear about Anny, the tiny daughter of Jacques and Janet, guarded and protected by her parents. It always seemed he was hearing about people in a story.

Anny was still in her teens when Samuel Bridges began to call on her. Jacques and his wife were suspicious. They liked Samuel but didn't think anyone deserved Anny. Samuel took his time. Being attractive and dependable, he had friends of both sexes. Most of his spare time was spent in the dark friendly male bars of which there were as many in Bear as churches. And the whole town watched this courtship for two years, with Samuel growing into his later thirties, steady and deliberate. When Jacques finally gave in, Samuel couldn't wait and insisted on being married in a week.

Anny returned from the honeymoon in Quebec pregnant. Samuel started building a proper home on the lake. He drove the crew hard, in his way, and did most of the finishing work himself. He moved Anny in six weeks before the home birth of Jacques deGranville Bridges. His grandfather always told Jack that Samuel wasn't overly fond of the fancy name, but she wanted it so.

Jack did not know if he truly remembered his mother or just the picture of her in Samuel's room, the braids wound around her head and the lace collar. She was beautiful. Old Jacques loved to talk about her but Samuel seldom did. There was a day, Jack thought he must have been about Buddy's age, when the blue-and-white checked curtains that hung at the windows of Samuel's bedroom came apart in his hands. There was special stitching all over them, but Samuel pulled them down and threw them away. "Dad, are you putting up new ones? Dad?" Jack could hear himself asking. "I guess not. No one to see in. No, I don't need them. But they were so pretty." That was how Samuel talked about her.

"What are we doing today?" Sam had climbed the wooden ladder to the loft, and Buddy was trailing Jack. "Dad, what are we doing?"

"Not much. There's a small storage off the back porch. I want to look through that and then we're about done."

Jack knocked open the latch on the storage doors, ducked his head, and stepped in. He heaved boxes out to Buddy who shoved them away from the door and started sorting. The boxes held cracked dishes and old utensils, half empty paint cans, dried and useless. Jack was still in the cabinet. He found shapeless stiff boots and his old skates, completely rusted.

"Dad, what do we do with it?"

"Haul it to the dump in Dunk's truck. All that garbage from camp too."

He grabbed one last object covered with taped yellow newspaper. He slit the paper then tore it off. "Hey! Now this!" He gently carried a glass box into the house and set it on a low table by the hearth.

"Wow! Dad! Where'd you get it?"

"Let's clean it up." Jack found a rag and polished the glass case, two feet long, one foot high and deep. In it two stuffed fawns were posed in a naturalistic setting of mossy rocks and twig-like trees with small leaves and pebbles scattered over the artificial forest floor.

"Are they real?"

"They were. Get Sammy."

The boys knelt on the floor. Jack sat cross-legged behind them. They all stared at the little animals, tiny fawns facing each other as though sharing secrets, their eyes soft and trusting, a moment still and eternal.

"It's like something in a museum." Buddy was whispering.

Sam patted the case. "Can they come out?"

"No, little guy. They have to stay in. That's where they live now."

"How did they get there?" Buddy asked.

"See, when Grandpa first moved up here to Bear he was pretty young. A few years older than Chris. And hunting was a big deal—still is. Grandpa used to go out with some guys and bag squirrels and other small stuff. Rabbits. And one time, not even in season, he shot at a noise in the bushes. He shot real low. When he parted the branches, he found a mama deer, just about to have these twin babies. They were never even born."

"They look born."

"This friend of Grandpa's did most of the heads down at Thunder's. He made this kind of special, just for Grandpa. The little fellows have some sort of life that way."

"Daddy," Buddy was looking at the fawns. "Did you ever kill anything?"

Jack looked right into his son's eyes. "No. And after this, neither did Grandpa. Never hunted again. I guess he packed this away a long time ago. But I remember it from when I was about your age."

"When you fish, is that killing?"

Jack considered. "That's hard to say. The fish is taking the bait. So in a way, he's the one who's doing it."

"But you make him want it. You're putting it there."

"Like I say, it's a big subject." He tapped Buddy on the head. "C'mon. I want to go eat."

"Can we leave it here?"

"Sure. Chris'll want to see it." He hoisted Sam and started toward camp. The Jeep was parked again. He looked around. "Where's your brother?" he called to Buddy.

Buddy pointed to the headland at the north end of the cove. Chris was scrambling over the rocks, disappearing up the beach. "That's two days in a row!" Jack shouted and ran to catch up with Buddy by the food. "Where does he go?"

"Oh. Up a ways. There's people up there."

"People?" Jack tried to think who they knew with cottages along that stretch.

"You know. Girls."

"Oh," Jack slid Sam down his back. "Why doesn't he bring them here?"

"He wouldn't do that," Buddy said. "We're here."

"Oh," Jack said again. He hated it when the kids knew more than he did.

"Besides they have a boat, and Chris gets to ski. He won't let me go with him. There's nothing to do here. Nothing for girls anyway."

"Yeah? They could go for a ride. Chris could drive them all the way to the road and back."

"Dad." Buddy broke open a bag of chips. Jack didn't answer right away. He swigged beer, thinking about taking a swim, he was so hot sweaty. But he was too hungry. Big decision, he'd swim later. "Dad!"

"What!" He came to attention, spread peanut butter, peeled oranges, and dug in the cooler for pickles.

Buddy munched, dipped into cheese spread. "Do you have to like girls?"

Jack poured beer slowly down his throat. "It's not a law."

"Chris does and no one makes him."

"They probably like him first, and then it goes back and forth. Kind of like..." Jack stopped. He couldn't think what it was like.

"I'm never. They're disgusting."

"That bad, huh?" Jack was working on a second beer, his mouth full.

"They're gross. Fat like pumpkins."

"That part gets better."

"But do you like them?"

"Sure. I like Mom." *And some others. Sort of.*

"I can't stand it."

Jack looked at Buddy's face, confused and furious. "You miss your brother?"

Buddy kicked sand. "I don't care what he does."

"Think of it like he's going someplace. And someday you'll want to go there, maybe, and he'll be able to show you around."

"I'm never. I told you."

"Tell you what, Bud. Don't worry about it. Sometimes, the greatest relief is not to think about girls." He touched Buddy's arm, man to

122

man. "This trip, for days at a time, I just don't think about them at all. And it's kind of peaceful. That's the real truth." He lay back in the sand. Sam walked on him and rolled a can on his chest. "Yo, kid." Jack grabbed him and threw him around playfully. "Don't sneak up on your old man like that."

"I'm going to be like Grandpa and never get married."

"What? Hey, Bud. Listen." Jack crossed his legs and held Sam in the crow's nest, feeding him orange sections by hand. "Grandpa was married."

"But you never had a mother."

"I sure did have a mother."

"You never talk about her."

"I didn't know her. Not very well."

"Did she run away?"

"She died." Jack kept his voice neutral. Sam ate bread from Jack's paper plate, unconcerned. "Okay. There's not much to say. She was young, a lot younger than Grandpa. I was her first child. And after she had me, she got some kind of infection that never really went away. Of course, back then, there weren't all the medicines we have now. She went on a while and then she just...died."

"How old were you?"

"I was..." He held Sam. "I was young." He'd been five.

"Do you remember her?"

"There's a picture of her in the house. In one of the drawers. Very pretty. French."

"What's French?"

"That's how we got our funny name." The heat and beer made him drowsy. He was finding it hard to talk, but he wasn't going to start sleeping in the daytime. Like some old man.

"But, Dad, who took care of you?" Buddy was insistent.

"You know—Grandpa. And her parents were in town. I had grandparents. They were good to me."

"I don't see..."

Jack stood up. "Hey, Bud. Let's do this some other time. Promise. I'll tell you all about it." The relentless questions tired him. He wished he could be more patient when he was sleepy. If Greta were here, he would have her take over. "I'm going for a swim. You guys be okay or want to come?"

"I want to fish." Buddy fished off the rocks.

"Take Sam. He won't bother you."

"Do I have to?" Buddy's whine was pitiful.

"Just this once. Be a good sport."

"It's not once, Dad. I do it all the time. He throws rocks in the water and scares the fish. That's why I can't get any!"

Jack picked up Sam. "Make a big pile of rocks, okay? The nice flat ones. Like this, see?" He showed him a piece of shale. "We'll skip them."

"It's not fair!" Buddy accused him.

And then Jack really did escape. "You catch 'em, I'll clean 'em!" He ran into the lake. "I won't be long," he called, waving.

He swam past the sandbar, farther than he had that morning. The water was deep blue and choppy. Waves slapped against his face, and he swam hard, fighting back. The groggy buzz from the food and beer left his head He felt masterful and in control. Two hundred yards out, he stopped and floated, riding the swell.

Jack's eyes traveled along the sand to the north. The beach there was wide and patterned with blankets and umbrellas and moving bodies. On the water, a couple of small sailfish bobbed, one with a purple sail. Cheerful and crowded, young people busy with play. A powerful ski boat, loaded, pulled a skier parallel to shore. Jack squinted, trying to distinguish Chris.

Should he walk down that way? See who lived there now and what was going on? Maybe go for a run; do it casually. But he liked to run late, just before supper, going the other direction and turning back to see the blue sand and the lake begin to burn in the low sun. Chris would know it was the wrong time, would despise him for checking up.

Leave him alone. He's experimenting.

If Greta were here, it would be different. She'd never stand for it. There'd be discussion, an accounting of his time—for his own good. Then an endless sorting out, a difference of opinion and something between Greta and me, not about Chris. Am I a good father? It's only girls, after all.

Girls. My son and girls. I'm not ready for this. Doesn't matter—if he is. Buddy says they're disgusting. Not forever, kid.

But what he told Bud was true. It is good not to think about it. Not any of them. Not Greta. Not...anyone. He would swim to shore and stand in the breeze to dry. He would take Sam for a walk in the woods. They would gather sticks and pine cones and cut wood. He would do

124

useful work and keep that hard edge. His body was conditioned now, his legs taut from running, and his arms strengthened from lifting.

He dove, down and down until the water held him under and everything was quiet. He kicked, moving toward shore, counting seconds, testing himself until he felt it in his chest. Taking a great gulp of water, he angled upwards and shot out, his whole upper body rising, breaking the surface, shaking and spraying like a huge beast, a fountain gushing from his mouth. He made a clownish, scattering commotion so the boys would see him and laugh.

Dunk didn't come that evening for supper. Jack made stew over the fire, dumping cans of soup and vegetables into a pot. The boys ate it on buns.

"I thought we were having fish." Chris dished up seconds.

Buddy looked down. "They weren't biting."

"Yeah, sure."

"I got some but they weren't keepers."

"We need a boat, Dad. You can't do anything without a boat."

"Right, Chris."

"We need drinks, Dad."

"We'll go in tomorrow."

"Can we go in tonight?"

"Tomorrow, Chris."

"You just want to see Julie," Buddy teased.

"Shut up, stupid."

"You're stupid."

Jack faced the lake, his head resting against a log. The sand was cooling now. He pulled a sweatshirt over Sam's head.

"Dad!" Chris tried to draw him in.

"When I turn around, I want to see the camp clean. I don't care who does what."

He closed his eyes, heard paper rustling and metal cans chinked into the trash then the muttering retreat to the pump for washing the pot. Maybe he should take them to town tonight, buy ice cream and see some people. The crankiness could be an overdose of togetherness. Jack was a little lonely himself. No company for two days. He listened for the truck, twisting his head. The woods were dusky and the boys shadowy up by the old shed. It was still light in the cove and beautiful in the lingering twilight of a northern summer, looking up through lacy tree boughs inked on opal silk, Venus punching her diamond fist through pale tissue sky. The lake had turned a rosy pewter color, shiny not flat, all one shade with the sky and no line on the horizon. He looked out with lazy, relaxed eyes. They could go to town another evening.

Then Dunk did come, just as they were building up the campfire, carrying a sack of popcorn and chocolate bars that he handed to Chris. The boys shouted hello, glad he was there. He usually played Frisbee with them, in and out of the water before it grew too dark to see. And most evenings he sang, country-rock in a mournful, quavering voice, sneaking dirty words into the lyrics. He treated Buddy and Chris like peers. Tonight he winked at Jack and pulled a sack from inside his shirt. "Interested?"

"Mind reader."

"Thought you might need a change of diet."

"Fantastic. I'm low on beer."

The two men sprawled by the fire. Sam was still skipping stones into the lake. "Come up when I call you," Jack told him.

Buddy fed the fire. "Go easy," Jack said. "It's warm."

"Gonna get warmer," Dunk said quietly. He opened the bottle, swigged and passed it to Jack.

Jack drank and then looked at the label. "Not too shabby. Only thing I like about the south." He parked the bottle in the sand between them.

"Man, what does this remind you of?" Dunk asked.

"Everything."

"No. Something real."

"The trip west."

Dunk sighed. "Was that about perfect?"

Jack didn't answer.

"Remember Vegas?"

"Oh, yeah." Jack sounded wary. "Let's not get too specific now." Chris was sitting by with a blank expression, but Jack was sure the antenna was raised.

This is the way we do it now, indirectly, back to back but listening cautiously, you trying to find out things about me and me doing the same with you.

"Those days driving into nowhere. Come upon a road and just … take it or not. All through the Rockies. We didn't know shit. Never looked at a map. Stop when you're ready and throw down your bedroll."

"The old Jeep. The true Jeep. How many nights'd we sleep under that thing?"

"Never kept us dry, either."

"Was Mack with you?" Cris asked.

Dunk snorted. "Are you kidding? Married with a kid and another on the way. Patty wouldn't let him—even if his dad would've given him the time off." The bottle was in Dunk's hand again. "Come back here and live, Jack. We'll do it all again."

"We'd kill ourselves for sure."

"How old were you, Dad?" Chris moved closer. Buddy was down at the water, plunking rocks into the lake with Sam.

"You guys about done?" Jack called softly.

"Were you in college?"

Dunk sighed. "We weren't in anything then. Not even jobs. I was bumming and your dad…" He paused for a healthy swallow.

Jack shoved a foot at Dunk. Chris hugged his knees in the bright circle of firelight, looking inattentive and therefore curious.

"It was after college, Chris. I'd been in D.C. a while. Gone there with a guy in my fraternity. We thought, I don't know, we were serving mankind in the Department of the Interior." He stopped, picked up the bottle. "Best thing I ever did—quit that job." He swallowed. "He's still there, my friend. We have lunch once a year or so."

Sam and Buddy arrived into the light. "I got five skips on one," Buddy boasted.

Chris picked up the poker stick and began lifting logs to aerate the fire. He added wood. Jack watched him, his careful deliberate movements. Like his mother.

Jack was starting to feel the liquor. He suspected Dunk had had a few in town. It was so pleasant. His body warm from the day and where the fire stroked him. But the sand was cool.

The boys moved in the light except Chris, who sat still. From the back or side, he could be Greta. Who could tell what he was thinking? Like her, he kept private. Just before supper, his stroll back into camp. How was your day? Okay, I guess. His surprising, dammit, sense of humor. Didn't she used to have that? That sweet, shy smile when he met her.

The one good thing about the lousy government job. Only she wouldn't half look at him at first. Women didn't take him seriously then.

He could not understand it. He was developed, experienced. But in Washington, no one gave him a chance. He finally stood by Greta Larsen's desk and practically begged her to go out with him. She agreed but made it plain; made sure he understood that she wasn't interested in having a boyfriend. That was fine with Jack. He needed someone to talk to occasionally.

He thought her porcelain prettiness was marred in some way by her nervous concern for "getting ahead." She listened thoughtfully to his complaints about women and then said—he remembered her exact words: "But, Jack, why would they want to date you? You have no drive or ambition. People think you lack focus." It was the same way she said now, "You're not the type."

At the time, rather than offended, Jack was mildly flattered by her attention, like that of a kind and wiser sister. She became a good friend, wanting Jack to try harder at work, not be so immature. She said he looked like a boy. He thought she worried too much about office politics and correct procedures. He wanted her to loosen up and have more fun. She wanted him to be serious. After a struggle, aware that his skills had no value in the Washington bureaucracy, that nothing about him showed off and tired of thinking about what people thought, he left.

"Dunk!" he called, suddenly. "What year was that? When we took off?"

The words came out of Dunk deep and slow. "Summer of '63. The one before Kennedy was shot." Dunk spoke dreamily into the fire. "The last really good one before I went to Nam. I never wasted so much time and money, met so many good people I never saw again. I thought, I really thought ... life could be like that."

Jack sighed. "I never did." Sam sat between his legs. "Sleepy, fella?" Sam shook his head stubbornly.

"Well, your heart wasn't in it. You were already thinking pretty hard about Greta." Dunk sang out her name.

Jack laughed. "It wasn't that way. Not then."

"You must of wanted to see her real bad. Called her from Chicago." He winked at Chris.

"I wanted to see how she was doing." Buddy and Chris were like bookends on either side of him. "Uh, Dunk. This is all ancient stuff.

How did we get into this?"

"As I recall..." Dunk started.

"Let me tell it. We hit Chicago and were out one night acting kind of crazy. It was almost the end of our trip and the summer. And I got this notion to call your mom. I wanted to see if she remembered me. Or I guess I was tired of the company I had!"

"Right!"

"So I, you know, called her and somehow invited her to come up here. If she would fly out to Detroit, we'd get her and bring her along." Jack paused. "I thought she'd like to meet Samuel." He'd been a little drunk and was shocked when she said yes. He and Dunk met her at Detroit Metro, looking like the bums they had become. She hadn't spoken to Dunk the whole time on that raucous ride up to Bear. But he did not want to go into all that in front of the boys. For a rare instance, he had their solid attention. All three of them at once.

"So, let's talk about something else."

"Samuel sure saved your ass with old Greta!" Dunk cackled. He stood, weaving, walked out of the light and down toward the water.

"Where's he going?" Buddy asked.

"Oh, he just..."

"What did he mean, Dad? The part about your ass."

Jack looked at Chris.

"I'm just repeating what he said, Dad. Just quoting."

Jack brushed sand from Sam's legs. The boy was limp. He wanted to end this. "Your mom didn't think too much of me at that point. I was a clown—and unemployed. Grandpa made quite an impression on people. He made them feel important. He had a thing."

"Did Mom like him?"

"Oh, yes," Jack said, gently. "I wish…"

"What?"

"That he … knew you guys now. That he knew Sam."

They were all quiet. Jack roused himself. "Hey, did I ever tell you about Grandpa's first job? Dunk!" he called. "Dunk! You out there?"

Silence.

"I guess he's taking a walk. Well, anyway, Grandpa started young. He was about ten when he went out with his dad to work on a sailing barge—one of the last to sail the Great Lakes. His family had all been sailors, captains some of 'em, who had their own ships.

"But this one hauled lumber, called a 'timber drover.' You'd've liked this, Bud. They carried horses and mules right on the forecastle deck and used them to haul aboard the timber or pull the boat along a canal. Grandpa helped care for the animals."

"When did he go to school?"

"Didn't. He never did. But he was smart and quick. He had a good memory, which he kind of passed on to me."

Just then, Dunk slouched back into the circle, dripping wet. "Lake's a bathtub."

"Hey, Dunk. Why didn't we ever make that trip? The one through the Seaway."

"Dunno, man."

"But why not? We talked about it so much."

"Got too old, I guess. Got too smart." Dunk sat cross-legged in his ragged denims, his skinny torso shining and bent. "Even the best of 'em, it's tough out there. Just making it across the Lakes, the tides, the wind, direction always changing. Hard to gauge."

"We were pretty good."

"Thought so, anyway." He added softly, "It's a graveyard, man."

"I think somehow Samuel kept us from it. But I can't figure how."

Jack passed the bottle, but Dunk turned it down. He began to sing, an old chant that Jack dimly recalled. The words told of the golden age of sailing on the Lakes, the cargoes of wealth, prosperity bought by a hazardous life and then disaster, failure, and decline. Jack felt his boys relax beside him, slumped, crowding bodies spent on the day, the vast world reduced to this tiny glow, time forgotten and pictures in the fire. He sang the final verse with his friend, their voices low:

"And far before her foaming bows the fiery waves did fling

With every stitch of canvas set and her coursers wing to wing.

Now in the deep their bodies sleep, their earthly trials o'er

And on the beach their bodies bleach along the patient shore."

No one moved. Sam was asleep. Jack carried him, heavy and lumpish to the tent, staggering a bit. He patted the other boys, dragging on them. "C'mon. Before you fall asleep out here. Move while you can." They did not argue but disappeared groggily.

Dunk lay prone by the fire, his face turned sideways on his rolled Tshirt. Jack picked up the bottle. An inch of liquor remained in the pint bottle. He drank some of it. He knocked the fire apart and spread out the glowing chunks, not burying it, but turning up the bright bellies of coals, letting them burn. There was no wind.

Dunk wasn't moving. Jack stowed the food and secured the trash. He brushed crumbs with a bough of white pine and poured water on spilled juice so the table would not crawl with ants in the morning.

He wandered down to the water, waded in to his knees and washed his hands. He was warm from the drinking and the air basting him because there was no breeze, even on the lake. The moon hung, a pale sliver, overpowered by the glow of the stars.

Something drifted on the lake not far from shore, something bright and fuzzy. Jack blinked and cleared his eyes. The creak and dip of oars, a slowly moving boat gliding past, a lantern hung on the stern, swaying dimly. Jack watched the red light. It reminded him of something but he could not think what. Something pretty and feminine.

He was feeling soft and dreamy and a little sad. He began to walk around the cove, back and forth, pulling his legs through the water, enjoying how it felt in the dark. He thought about Greta, couldn't put her away now. If she were here, and the boys asleep, would she come out with him on this wet ramble? He didn't want to be alone tonight.

Jack dragged his feet over the liquid sand. He wasn't cooling off. He splashed water on his face and chest. He shouldn't drink the hard stuff—not straight. He sank into the lake, keeping his head out. He spotted the pebbles of fire on the beach and marked the place. He floated. His body felt covered with fur. He was filled with a vivid and powerful affection for his wife, fixed in place, not moving, not talking. Nothing shifted to disturb the image.

In his memories, he had her.

He enjoyed thinking about bringing her to Bear that first time, her shy dismay on that awful loud ride north, awkward hours of punishing wind in the open Jeep and two filthy guys who shouted and sang to her. It was Samuel who made her feel welcome. He was enchanted that Jack had, at last, brought a girl home. Even if she was, as Jack made clear, just a good friend.

She didn't resist and spent more time with Samuel than with Jack. Jack watched her unbend and lose the prudish insecurity that hung over her in Washington. She dressed casually, not striving to maintain her business-like appearance. They swam every day. And even in her extremely modest bathing suit, her round bustiness showed off in a way she kept hidden in ruffles and cardigans at work. Jack thought about her constantly, physically, and became dumb and inexpressive, hardly talking to her at all.

Then it was almost over. Jack still had made no decision about his future. His life was not in Bear anymore. He planned to drive Greta back to D.C. and then … what to do?

One morning, Samuel took Greta out in the power boat. Jack had to get the Jeep serviced for the trip back east and spent the day in town with Mack, working on it and feeling vaguely left out. When he returned to the house, they weren't back. He waited, out of sorts and impatient. They arrived around seven, having gone all the way to the Mackinac Bridge. Samuel was fascinated by this engineering link of the two peninsulas. He'd had a wonderful time showing Greta the beautiful shoreline. They were in a good mood, oblivious to Jack's withdrawn, sulky manner. He had built a fire to grill steaks on the beach. Greta swam and then went up to change. Samuel and Jack drank bourbon, and when Greta returned she had a couple even though she didn't like to drink. It was all so amiable between Samuel and her.

And it was a perfect evening, the lake on sunset fire. Jack finally felt good because he couldn't help it. Samuel lingered, Jack knowing he didn't want it to end, how his dad hated to admit he was tired. Greta was stretched out, but she jumped up and ran to him when he started to leave. She kissed him, said "Oh, Samuel, thank you for the lovely day." And Samuel, who rarely did, hugged Jack, pulled him aside and said, shyly, "That's a good girl."

Jack, floating now on black water, his sons asleep close by, laughed at himself, his foolish temper, his youth, his mixed-up and inexplicable jealousy of Samuel. It was only natural she'd prefer his company. He had wanted so many things then, to be a man, be strong and good and take care of people. His desire concentrated in this one girl, in having her, winning her. And he could feel the wanting just as strongly now. It never went away, how he had wanted her then.

That evening had been warm, just like tonight. Samuel had turned in, and Jack built up the fire. He liked the glow as night came on. They didn't need the heat, but it gave him something to do with his hands. Greta sensed none of his restless mood, was not aware of him. She lay by the fire, relaxed and almost asleep. "I feel like I'm still out on the boat," she murmured. "I'm rocking on water."

"There's a cure for that. Take a swim." The innocuous words sounded harsh. He tried to control his voice.

"My suit is still wet," she whispered without opening her eyes. "I don't like to put it on when it's clammy."

He laughed so loudly that it roused her, the rough tone. She looked at him with innocent surprise.

"For God's sake, Greta, how do you think people swim around here at night?" Wanting to shock her, he stripped off his shorts and T-shirt. He didn't care; he wanted attention.

She was not smiling. "Turn your back."

"No."

She turned around and, sitting, wriggled out of her slacks. Hunched over, she unbuttoned her shirt and folded it over her naked front. Sedately, she said to him, "Let me go in first." She walked stiffly to the lake, keeping her back to him.

In the water, she wouldn't let him come near her but paddled in a stately fashion. He was playful and excited but didn't know how to break through her reserve. He got out and went up to the blanket. "Jack," she cried. "Jack, bring me a towel. I'm cold." She was kneeling in shallow water.

"Come over here," he called. "I'll dry you off."

"Don't make me wait. Please."

He tossed her a towel and stomped back to the fire. It burned faintly. He grabbed some logs and threw them on, smothering the flame. Mad at her and disgusted with himself, he pulled off the wood and blew on the coals, getting a little blaze going again. Then he fed it slowly. His impatience ebbed. He had lost a moment and didn't know how to proceed. But he did not blame her, only his boorish behavior.

She came out of the lake and stood waiting, the towel wrapped around her waist and her hair dripping from her bowed head like a shy pony. He couldn't move. She had to walk to him, let him know she was saying yes, completely yes, and not showing how scared she was until he touched her. He became wonderful, never so aware and proud, loving a woman. Something shifted in him and, sure of his own pleasure, he thought only of hers. Tenderness and manly confidence blended in him, and he wanted to give her everything. He remembered her eyes losing control in the firelight. Unskilled, thank you, she whispered. He knew the best part of it then, the way you could make a woman feel.

The layers of life that smother fresh experience had never buried that moment. "Oh, baby," he said now, moaning to the soft, empty night, "we started out so good. Baby, we did."

He left the water, his body cool at last but his mind unsettled, aching loneliness for everything past. Dunk was still by the fire, but it was out now, and so was he. Jack peeled off his wet trunks and hung them on the line. He tucked the old beach robe around his friend. In the tent, he rubbed repellent on Sam's exposed arms and face. He smeared some on his own neck and wrists. He lay back, trying to relax, rid his mind of the insistent noise of mosquitoes whining. His head was full of images and voices singing in his ear. He was sweating again and knew sleep was far away. He wanted to be with a woman so badly that he knew he had to be alone.

He crawled from the tent, dragging the sleeping bag with him. He closed down and secured all the flaps. Bunching the bag in his arms, he walked quietly away from the camp, back toward the woods.

He stepped lightly, unable to see the path. He kept his eyes on the bulky shape of the house. Circling the corner, he stopped at the back just outside the screened porch. The woods hung around him like a curtain. He'd have to find the right opening in the solid black wall of tree boughs.

The door slams behind me, he thought. I don't go straight ahead but turn a hair to the left, across the drive. At the biggest cedar should be a narrow trail.

He bundled the bag against his chest and thrust his right arm in front to prevent branches snapping in his face. His arm was scraped as he walked, and he couldn't tell if he bled or not. Batty insects knocked his ears like feathers. He did not stop.

He was looking for the small clearing, about fifteen feet across, where Samuel cleaned fish. Although nothing particular marked the place, he had walked the distance hundreds of times. The sense of it came to him. The ground was firmer, packed with pine needles. He stumbled, knelt to see what tripped him, and ran his hands over what seemed to be a flat box. It was the table Samuel had made, now collapsed, the legs gone or sunk in the sandy soil. Only the top remained. He'd found the right place.

Jack spread the sleeping bag in the center of the clearing. Before sliding in, he brushed sand from his feet and stood a minute to dry the sweat from his body. The ground was spongy under him and comfortable lying flat on his back. Rising tall here, the trees left but a small hole to see the sky. Jack looked through the dark telescope to the stars. Around him, he heard the crisp snap and scurrying noise of woods.

It was usually dark when they came here. Twice a week, more often at times, Samuel fished after work. He stayed late into twilight, liking the evening calm. By the time he beached his old rowboat and carried up his tackle, daylight was gone. Jack lugged the pails for him from the cove all the way to the clearing and lit the lantern.

When he was an adolescent, no, younger than Buddy, he'd asked his father why they didn't do it at the house. Samuel had thought a minute. "Your mama never liked it. Makes a mess, and the blood attracts flies. Also, it just plain stinks."

It hadn't made sense to Jack, his mama being long absent from the kitchen, but he was glad they did it in the woods. This was a man's job and a place for a man. He never remembered women coming into the woods. Only later, they took girls and tried to scare them as a coarse prelude to necking. But it wasn't a place for women to work, to think. As a boy, he was sure of that.

Samuel had kept this an orderly place. Brought his lake bass and pike, scaled them neatly. He showed Jack how to hold them properly so they weren't hacked to bits. And then peg the fish to the board with an ice pick. Take your sharp knife. A dull knife is a dangerous weapon, son. A precision slit from the vent behind the head, across the belly and pry it open. Don't waste the insides and everything goes into the gut bucket. Keep it neat. We're not worried about the darn fish at this point, but it shows your respect for the work, to do it right. A man's got to respect what he does.

Jack had his second wind and wasn't sleepy. The camp seemed far away, and the trees extending for miles. He stared straight up to the blanket of stars and watched them come closer. He could be looking down instead of up, into a well with the stars behind him reflecting on the surface. And if he raised his arm, he could dip into it, like a pool. He could take whatever he wanted from the night. In his complex life filled with events and duty, solitude was a luxury he would not squander. A thrilling awareness replaced his restless fatigue and earlier boozy sorrow. He was alone.

The pattern of stars shifted. The trees were moving far above, catching a breath of stirring wind. The woods swayed. He loved a pine wood in a stiff breeze. No racket of leaves but a brushing lulling music. And the natural scent, never a decayed moldy smell.

He was really awake. The tossing boughs swept the sky, the stars blinking and bouncing like a light being turned on and off in his face, forcing his eyes open. The stillness was gone, only his body was still in this showy night where everything danced around him. The wind sneaked under the edge of his sleeping bag, wanting to lift him off the ground.

O why sleep? Night is a poor time for sleeping; sleep takes you from life. Only how to rest from life's demands? When did Samuel sleep? No matter how late, Jack would go first, climbing the ladder, leaving Samuel in his chair, a lingering cigarette in his hand. And in the morning, hearing him awake, front door creaking as he took coffee on the porch. Even in winter, still dark, the pickup coughing and Samuel dragging chains over the snow, gaining traction to get out to the road. Jack, racing to dress and help him, would meet his dad in the kitchen— stomping his boots, beating his gloves, the motor still running outside— would be too late. But he would be in time for his father's glad smile and, "Sleep well, son?"

Jack pressed his palms against his eyelids. His eyes were sore. He was looking too hard and seeing how real it was. He had never wanted to leave. Sometimes he could feel the torn place in him, the old wound, a seam marking the before and after in his life. He could run his hand on it yet never reconcile the fragmentation.

Why did I have to go? Why did you make me?

Jack rubbed his forehead and all over his hair. He breathed heavily. Anger was coming. He recognized it, the familiar silent rage against which he was helpless. He hated this morbid and petty train of thought that visited him not often but defiantly. He should be a king, alone with his noble mind. Instead he was this too-tired child writhing on a forest floor in a whining tantrum. Frustration unmanned him.

Why did you make me go?

People should see you, just as you are. Infantile, Jack. What do you want? What more do you want?

I want this to go away.

Growing up, Jack had expected to go into the business with Samuel. He never thought of anything else. Bridges and Son. He didn't even plan to go to college, but Samuel made him. Failing to take it seriously, he was a mediocre student, just putting in the time, enjoying the social life and having Samuel down to football games. Senior year, he came home for spring break to find the new sign up at the yard. Bridges and Bird. Jack thought Samuel was kidding. But it was true. He'd made Mitchell Bird a full partner. The man had no capital but worked hard, had a brain for figures and, most important Samuel said, he was honest. There was no place for Jack.

Heat rippled Jack's body. He had not questioned his father. You must choose, son. Choose your life. He still heard the words. Gently spoken but insistent, like someone opening a door and escorting you cordially into the night then shutting the door behind you. It had never made sense. There were many wasted, experimental years, years of loss before he made any gains. He didn't like asking questions he knew would never be answered. But he kept asking.

Jack twisted on his side. The ground felt harder this way. He rotated onto his stomach, and that was better. The lights turned off. He was warm, down in the bag. Maybe he would sleep a little. He wondered how heavy the dew would be and if he'd wake soaked.

Rest. You need it. Jack drifted into the wet mornings in Canada when the dew rose from the ground like cold steam. Samuel would be up making the fire when the boys stumbled from the sack. He made them break camp and load the canoes—all the work except for the breakfast fire.

Rest. An old trick. Think about a river. One summer, no it was Indian summer and after school had started, Samuel got the itch for a short trip. He and Jack, just the two of them this time, packed their gear and headed south, not north into Canada. They put in at Grayling on the AuSable River and canoed down for several days, stopping at stores along the bank for supplies and camping at small parks. Jack was thirteen and loved going with his dad. Samuel was popular, welcome in every inch of the county. Jack could sit for hours among company and listen to his father, never crude but lively, his gifts so great, being a good talker and a listener, too.

But the best was sliding along that tamed river with his dad occasionally nipping whiskey, laughing and slouching over the gear in the bow, letting Jack paddle the canoe. Treat your old man; I deserve a rest. He loved having his dad all to himself.

The third morning, Jack woke to a gentle shaking. Samuel was sitting, rocking him and facing a copse at the edge of the meadow. Dawn trembled, damp and neutral. Nothing was visible but mist and the outline of trees. A tremendous crash and breaking of branches made Jack's heart beat fast. Samuel said nothing, just stared at the noise. Jack thought it must be a bear. He was excited and afraid and would have run but for Samuel's calm, cautioning hand. They had no gun.

Then silence except for an eerie snuffling. Toward them, slowly, came the biggest moose Jack had ever seen, prancing with comic delicacy as if concentrating on balancing the load of his antlers and being careful of his bashed in nose. The beast kept coming, larger and darker, but Samuel didn't move. Jack thought it would run over them like a train. But the animal stopped a few yards from the tarp and turned, presenting its behind and proceeding to create a most impressive pile of moose dung. Jack counted as the tower grew. He counted to thirty-two. The moose dipped its head, looking back at them over its haunches then disappearing into the trees with the ballctic tip-toe of a great performer leaving the stage.

Samuel and Jack shared a look of wonder and said simultaneously, "Shit!" Then they shouted it, making it last awhile and adding a few embellishments. Jack had never heard his dad swear. They sang a chorus, shrill and raspy.

Jack lay in the star-filled night. And his age then, this ageless man? His late fifties. Fifty was older then. Handsome and flowing with life and rugged fun. The best man. Mack's words and true.

Jack flopped onto his back. His feet were sweating. He spread the bag flat and lay on the diagonal. One star, centered in the circle of violent treetops, escaped the branches' reach. Jack fixed on its steady eye. It calmed and cooled him. He wanted to sleep now.

He clasped his hands behind his head. If he didn't move he would relax into sleep. The breeze was nice on his body. There was a youthful, almost pre-sexual mystery to the night. His mind had wandered into his boyhood, the good place he had lived and all the things he knew there—clean breath and water and winters so harsh you were in love with summer all your life.

Why did I leave? Why did you make me?

Jack tried to imagine himself now if he still lived among his friends. He'd have his family but not like Mack, lashed to the ground with kids and under his dad's thumb.

The old man will never give it up and let Mack run it. Would not have happened with you, Samuel. We could have been equals, me right up there with you. Maybe Dunk in there also. Dunk never had a chance, his dad walking out and his mom's drinking. This town has cared about him, whatever decent life he has. But something broke in him long ago.

It's hard being men together, so we don't try. We join hands and reach back to our childhood. My whole life among children.

Jack let his mind journey from Bear to Great Forest and back, from his world within to his complicated outer existence. He made no claim that his life was important in any way. But it gave him joy, yes, and strength. He needed work to do. He wanted to remember this, that alone in the night he found his life to be useful. He valued and was unashamed of what he did. He had a powerful yearning to tell Samuel how he'd found good work and that it made him happy.

Jack stretched his arms straight up and held them for a long time. Lying in this dark circle, cut out of a bight northern night, he was naked, small, and alone. It thrilled him to be so absolutely alone and his mind free. He was infant and old man, the weight of life luring him back to his rich past, flinging him out to the blinking stars, knowing nothing. Weak and helpless yet powerful. He was ignorant; he was filled with ancient wisdom.

You are lucky, Jack. Someone bought and left alone and therefore preserved a piece of this country for you so that you could bring your children to it and say this is my past. This is not a picture of it or a re-creation but the thing itself, the landscape of your father's youth.

Samuel's last summer, they had brought the two boys for a long weekend in August after Jack finished his courses. Several rainy days then a morning like June. Samuel took the boys on a fishing picnic, and Jack and Greta had spent the entire golden afternoon making love. He figured later that they'd made Sam that day. Greta thought he was nuts, but he knew.

That night at the beach fire, he and Samuel sat late. They drank bourbon and Jack, flushed and curious, sexually sated, asked his dad why he'd never remarried. The town's best perennial crop was blooming widows.

Samuel had laughed his slow chuckle and said "I didn't let myself get too lonely, son." After a pause, "Truth is I got used to being bossed once. I'm not about to try it again." And Jack knew how much he missed her and how alone he was without her. Rosy and in love, and a little drunk, he boasted. "I guess if you've got the right woman, once is all you need."

His dad, waiting, looking at him. "You were a lot of company for me, son. I didn't want to risk you, Jack."

He heard himself laughing, a faraway hollow sound, not like himself at all. His cheeks were cool and wet. A few months after that day, Samuel died in his office. He put down the phone and stubbed out his cigarette. The stroke was massive. Jack had to hear it from Mitchell Bird, how no one had left this world with less fuss. Jack didn't blame his dad. It was just hard; he thought he'd always have Samuel.

Jack and his father shared physical comfort being together. They did not embrace. Samuel never said, "I love you." Never the words. But in his life and in his voice, that fierce yet soft voice, there was a throb. In the night, out of the watchful dark, Jack heard it now, the way his father spoke his name, calling him "Jock," the only one who did. Samuel's flat Midwestern tongue worked hard around that queer French name, the one she chose, ever trying to pronounce it the way he'd heard her say it.

The trees stood as individuals while the day opened, and the night was no longer black. Jack took the corner of the sleeping bag and rolled in it, drawing his knees to this chest, hugging himself. There was no sadness in him, no pain. Child and man, feeling loved, he slept.

Chapter Nine

I liked It All

Jack sat at the drugstore counter eating a piece of black cherry pie. He heard Mack's big voice over his shoulder.

"Wish I had nothing better to do than loaf! Where're the boys?"

Jack spread his arm along a trail of empty plates. "Finished up and gone. Park yourself. You here to eat?"

"Just coffee."

"Then I'll treat."

"Big spender. I'll have some of that … whatever kind it is…pie." He winked at the waitress. "How come you guys're in town?"

"Cloudy day. Had things to do. Coming to see you for one."

"Yeah?"

"The Jeep needs something. Not sure what."

"Bring 'er over and we'll check it out." He and Jack looked at each other in the mirror behind the soft-drink syrups. "Got a little beauty on the lot has your name on it."

"I'm not even tempted."

"Been saving it for you. Two years old and only nine thousand miles."

Jack shook his head. "I don't want to hear it."

"I thought teaching paid better where you are."

"Better than here, for sure."

Mack tapped his cup for a refill. "Duncan told me you're head man now."

"Yep. I get to sweep up after everyone's left."

"Man, I never figured you'd go into that line. I was frankly astonished."

"I guess a lot of people were."

"Takes all kinds." Mack grabbed Jack's arm. "You got a good football team? D'you go to practice?"

Jack turned and stared at him, then smiled. "Mack, it's an elementary school. You knew that, didn't you?"

"You mean … the grammar school? You run the grammar school?" Mack's jaw was open. "We have Elsie Pierce doing that."

"She still hide in the closet just to hear what the kids say about her?" Jack laughed. "Maybe I'll stop by for a visit."

"Better take an aspirin along. She'll never believe it."

"Oh, I wasn't that bad."

"Hell, I was there, buddy. We were in it together." Mack shifted his large frame on the stool. "So. You got the easy life. Not much to do and long summers off."

"That sounds like it, all right."

"I could do with some of that."

"We all could." Jack stood up. "I gotta go see Mitchell. I never settled with him for all the gear. Hope my wallet's thick enough."

"Old Mitchell don't need it. He's doing okay. Takes Visa and MasterCard even."

Jack grinned. "The town has finally moved into the twentieth century."

"Listen, can you wait a minute? I wanted to … well, I don't know if you decided anything yet about the property."

"I…"

"Jack, the county's rezoning a lot of parcels of land, especially those larger ones north of town. The developers have pushed along the lake all south of here. There's hardly a foot of frontage left. Now they're licking their chops over that stretch where you are."

"Geez. My taxes going up?"

"Could be. Or you could do something about it."

Jack was silent a minute. "I decided not to sell."

142

"Well, of course, not the whole thing. But, what have you got—ten acres?"

"Closer to twelve."

"Then subdivide. You'd keep an acre or two around the house."

"But then they'd all have access to the cove."

"Well, sure. You could limit the number of houses, though."

"Nah. Doesn't interest me."

"Nothing personal, Jack, but you have no imagination." Mack threw up his hands. "Stop by the garage and I'll fix you up."

"It shouldn't take long with Mitchell."

Jack ambled down the street to the end of town and across the tracks to Bridges and Bird. Mitchell waved him in, finished with a customer, and flipped the open sign on the door to closed.

"I told the boys to come here when they finish in the five and dime."

"That's okay. If they rattle, we'll let 'em in."

Mitchell motioned Jack into the office at the rear. The room was eight feet square with one window, the shade always down. One wall was covered with shelves and pigeon holes that Samuel had built, containing old orders, the pink and yellow copies rolled in tubes and poking out. In the center stood a heavy desk with more stacks of papers, a telephone, and an upright typewriter. When he had no practice or game to attend, Jack had come here after school to type homework assignments, bouncing and swirling in his dad's chair, the dark red swivel still there, the leather cracked. Mitchell sat in the chair now and looked at Jack fondly.

"It's good to see you."

"Good to be back." Jack reached in his back pocket.

"Now, now put that away. We won't have any of that."

"I've got to pay you, Mitchell."

Mitchell Bird was not a small man, but he always seemed so to Jack. His manner was quiet, unassuming. It was hard for Jack to spend time with the man because of his nervous, fluttering hands. Even knowing Mitchell had a medical problem, it was still difficult. He tried again. "You can't give it away."

"Well, now. It's not exactly that. There's some things we ought to get straight here." Mitchell steadied his hands on his knees. "I should have called you, Jack. But I can't do some things over the phone. And you were in and out of here so fast when Samuel ... passed."

"It's not…"

"This won't take but a minute. You know he left me this business outright. And I put nothing into it but some effort. Now, that takes explaining."

"Not…"

Mitchell held up a hand and then lowered it to his knee. "Your dad was making the change about the time I came on. Lumber was a lot like farming. Big investment in equipment and depending too much on conditions of nature. The profit margin was pretty darn narrow. He did all right because he knew his markets."

"You don't have to tell me this."

"Maybe I do. Samuel was smart to think about getting into a line with rapid turnover and a high mark-up on the ticket. This hardware was perfect, with a little lumber as a side business. But, Jack, he had to take out a big loan to get his inventory, just to get started. He didn't want to mortgage the property."

"I thought he raised the money by selling most of his machinery." Jack sat on the edge of the desk, swinging his leg.

"Wasn't enough. He had to go to the building and loan."

Jack was silent.

"Of course he didn't want you to have to take on that kind of responsibility. It was his debt."

"I wouldn't have minded."

"He wouldn't saddle a man with it."

Jack went to the window. He zipped up the shade and stood looking into the alley.

"Here's the thing, Jack. Right as rain, soon's I stock up, stuff disappears off the shelves. Two years ago, I paid 'er off."

"That's wonderful, Mitchell." Jack's voice was kind. "I think Dad was lucky to have you."

Mitchell ducked his head. "It was all on my side. I've got my retirement, everything provided. In a few years, I hope to give it up, not stay forever."

"Sell it or what? A chain? Would some chain buy it?"

Mitchell stared. "That's what we're talking about. I'd let it come back to you. It's what your dad wanted, if we ever got clear. My girl won't have anything to do with it, and it wouldn't be proper anyway. No, Jack. That's why I wanted to go over this face to face. At some point, this is yours if you want it." He hesitated. "Or even if you don't."

Jack stopped moving. Everything stopped.

"You got some time to think about it now. It's not a gold mine but, like I said, it's steady."

"Yes, but..."

"Oh, and here's another thing. I've started to put something into the old account. There's been extra these past couple of years over and above what I take in salary and keep for reinvestment. You couldn't live on it but it's not mine, properly speaking, and the business doesn't need it." He fumbled in a cubby behind him and pulled out a stack of dark blue bank books. His hands trembled unwrapping the rubber band that bound them together. He handed Jack one of the volumes.

Jack flipped it open and stared at the figures, not fully comprehending.

"What does it say?" Mitchell ran a wobbly finger down a column. "Should be seven-fifty a quarter. What's that add up to now? They need to add some interest there. Must be about six, seven, ninety."

"Six thousand seven hundred ninety dollars?"

"Maybe a hair more by this time."

"Mitchell. I don't..."

"Now you take that. I'll just go on making the deposits, and they can mail you the slips. It might not always be that much, but sometimes more. Take it."

Jack heard knocking on the front window. Mitchell sprang up. "Looks like those boys found you." He ran out to unlock the door and turn the sign around. "Come in! Come in!" Jack heard him call. He sat unmoving until the boys burst into the little office. Jack took Mitchell's hand and shook it hard. "Mitchell," he said.

"It's good to see you, Jack. I'll be in touch."

"I'll be calling you. I will."

"That would be fine."

They walked outside. The sun was out, and a breeze whipped the flag in front of the post office. Jack carried Sam on his back. He tossed a set of keys to Chris. "Bring the Jeep."

"In town? They won't care?"

"It's just down the block to Mack's. Meet us." Jack mouthed to Buddy, "Walk slowly. He wants to drag Main Street alone and see if anyone notices."

At the garage, Jack had Chris pull the Jeep into an empty bay. Mack brought over a young man, about nineteen, in greasy overalls. "Randy here's gonna do his best."

"There's a leak I can't find, and she won't go easily into reverse."

"That smell, Dad. The burning smell when you start."

Jack walked off with Mack. "What'll it cost you think?"

"More'n it's worth. Maybe twenty-five bucks."

"You got anything we can drive the rest of the day? An old mule cart or something?"

Mack waved an arm. "Come on over to the north end."

Mack's father kept a couple of rows of used cars that never seemed to change from year to year, like the strings of red, blue, and yellow plastic triangles crisscrossed above. Mack led them down the center aisle and stopped by the newest vehicle there. "Here she is with your name on it."

Jack couldn't help laughing. "Well, Mack. Yeah. It is something."

The Jeep was black and shiny like new. Buddy ran his hands along the stripes painted on the sides, sundown colors of burnt orange and yellow. He traced the bold white letters spelling Renegade. "I like this, Dad."

Jack opened the door and put Sam in the driver's seat. "How does it feel?" It had the soft sides and top he liked and the clean familiar dash. The inside was immaculate. "How'd you come to get hold of this?"

"Long story. A widow. This'd been her husband's. She moved south and had no use for it."

"Anyone I know?"

"Nope. They were kind of new folks. Here about ten years. Samuel could have known them." Mack hung an arm around Chris. "Tell your dad he needs this heap."

"Dad, are you…?" His eyes were shining.

"No."

Mack threw up the hood. "Now, look at this engine."

"Look at it, Dad."

"You look."

"This is a classic." Mack motioned to Chris. "Get in. Get the feel of it. Your dad says that's the way to go—riding high and free."

"I never said that."

"Man, I could call a witness."

Jack scraped a foot over the gravel. He made a pile of rocks by his toe.

"How come there's no price on it?" The others on the lot were smeared with whitewash numerals.

"Didn't want to scare anyone off."

"How scary?"

"Eighty-four."

Jack shook his head.

"Take it for a drive. Keep it all afternoon."

Jack thought a minute. "Let's put the top down." Chris helped him. Jack looked at the odometer. "You said nine thousand. This reads closer to twelve."

Mack shrugged. "I forgot."

Jack shut his eyes. "Sixty-five," he said to Mack.

"Seventy-five."

Jack said nothing. He could feel the shape of the bank book Mitchell had given him against his left hip.

Three kids. Buddy needs braces. Every time you buy a round of sneakers, there goes a hundred bucks. The old house needs a thing or two.

"Dad?" Chris was trying to hold back.

"Let's try it. If it's okay, Mack can come out to dinner with us. To celebrate."

"We're getting it? Dad! We're getting it?!"

Jack was knocked over by Chris' face, the joy, pride, excitement. And he was the cause of it. It was only money after all. And worth it, when you had the power to connect, to make your son so happy. You were the greatest guy in the world.

"Are we going home tomorrow? Do we have to?"

"We have to start."

"Why?"

"I have to go back to work, Bud."

"Can we come again?"

"Sure."

"When?"

"Next summer."

"That's too long."

The preparations for leaving were made but Jack's mind lingered, dawdling. He could not force it to move out onto the road. Yet they were ready and would go in the morning.

The old Jeep was put to rest in the shed. He hoped it would hibernate well. The picnic table was back on the porch; the house was clean. Dunk would break camp after work, fold and pack the tents and store the gear. Give him an excuse, he said. Might even stay out here a few nights. But he declined to come this evening. Have that last campfire for yourselves, he told Jack.

And Jack was glad it happened that way. He wanted to be with them, hear only their voices. The silver plate moon rose, drawing a broad highway across the lake. "It looks like you could walk on it," Buddy said.

"I've sure tried enough times," Jack said softly. "You swim and break it up. You can feel it breaking on your body. Want to try it?"

"Looks cold," Chris mumbled.

"Let's just watch it from here." Buddy drew a blanket over his legs.

Jack built a neat log cabin fire. The night was cool, a little wind. The flames swayed vertically, like plants underwater. "Here, move closer."

"Dad." Buddy's face was painted white in the moonlight. The fire did not heat up that pale moon. "Is it very cold here in winter?"

"Yes."

"Could we come?"

"I don't know. Maybe." Jack stretched his legs to make a lap for Sam. "I'd have to fix the house first."

Chris pitched a pine cone into the fire. Sparks shot up and the cone popped. "They have snowmobiles and go out on trails. All the kids do it. Could we get one?"

"Uh…"

"Have you ever done it?"

"We didn't have those when I was a kid."

"Why not?"

"They didn't exist. We didn't do all that … recreation. It was more like work and you had to get through it."

"What work?"

"Moving the snow around. Keeping your trucks going, your house warm. Staying dry. Well, we had some fun. We skated on the lake."

"Could you go across?"

"Some years. Way out anyway. I never went far."

"Were you scared to?"

148

"It's nice on land. You walk in the woods, and the snow weights the branches and makes caves under the trees. It's quiet; every sound gets your attention. Driving at night, the snow's so deep beside the road it's like you're in a tunnel. If you're lucky more snow will be falling, and it all rushes toward you in the lights and all around you. That fresh powder, before it gets plowed and iced over, it all looks like diamonds."

"We have it like that."

"It's deeper and prettier here. And longer. Sometimes winter went on so long you'd forget there's anything else. And then one day you go down to the lake, and you're standing on the ice and it kind of bounces under you. A trickle of water squeezes under the edge." Jack hugged Sam. "It's over. Everything goes soft again."

"Want a drink," Sam whispered.

Jack stood. "I'll see what's in the old tub." He waded into the lake and hauled the tub onto the beach, turning it on its side to drain. "We got two beers and one soda. You'll have to share."

"That's it?!"

"I was trying to come out even."

Buddy found three paper cups and carefully divided the drink. Jack watched him. "Clean sweep. We eat breakfast on our way out of town."

"I don't want to go."

"I know, Bud." Jack opened a beer. "Finish up, guys. We're not staying up late."

Chris tossed more pine cones and sparks flew. Sam followed the bright balls as they streaked upward then wavered and disappeared in the dark. "Do they go upstairs and be stars?" he asked.

His brothers hooted. "The stars are already there, dummy!"

"Who hangs them up?"

The boys laughed again. Sam buried his head in Jack's sweatshirt.

"Hey, little guy." Jack cuddled him. "You could be right." He frowned at the others. "You two are so smart? I'm putting on one more log. This is absolutely the last one."

Chris stared into the flame. "We've had a different fire every night."

"My favorite thing here is a fire," said Buddy.

"Not me."

"Okay, Chris," Jack said. "What's yours?"

"The water skiing, driving, and buying the new car."

"Okay, and Buddy's is the fires."

"And the day I caught two fish."

"Right. Sammy, you gotta say something too. What have you liked best?"

The little boy was silent.

"He doesn't know," said Buddy.

"No, c'mon now. Give him a chance. What did you like, Sam?"

"Nothing."

Chris and Buddy hooted again. Jack turned Sam's head back and looked at him upside down. "Nothing?"

"Not one thing." The face tilted, smiling. "I liked it all, Daddy."

Jack cleared his throat. "Me too. I liked it all too." He finished a beer. "That sounds like a good way to end."

"No!" Buddy wailed. "Not yet."

"What are we doing next summer, Dad?" Chris jumped in fast. "Are we getting a boat? Could we?"

Jack popped the last beer. "Geez, I don't know. Maybe rent one."

"Could we do like you and Grandpa? Go out in canoes?"

"Maybe, Bud. Yeah, we could do that." Jack drew some lines in the sand. "I wonder if that would work. If Dunk came we'd have two men in each canoe." He sneaked a look at their faces registering that he'd called them men.

"Where would we go?" Chris' voice was eager.

"Probably not way up in Canada at first. We'll work up to that."

"And Mom will come here and stay with Sam. Or he can stay home with her," Buddy shouted.

"We don't have to decide that tonight."

"He can't come, Dad. He's too little."

"I want to come."

"You're a baby!"

"Tell you what." Jack picked up Sam and carried him to a tall birch tree where the table had stood. He propped Sam against the trunk, pulled out his pocket knife, and made a mark over the boy's head. "Here's where you are now. If you grow…," he notched the tree about two inches up, "this much, you can come. Fair?"

Sam nodded vigorously, his eyes wide.

"You'll have to eat a lot. And play outside where you have room to stretch."

More determined nodding.

"And you must try to learn to swim."

"I will."

"*Try.* That's all."

"Yes."

"All right! Shake, pal." Jack led him back to the fire. "Let's all shake on it. Like an oath. Next summer! To the river!"

They all shook except Buddy. "What is it?" Jack asked.

"If it's a pact we should do something more than that."

"Like what?"

Buddy pinched his lips, thinking. "It's gotta be with blood. We take the knife and each cut…"

Sam's head burrowed in Jack's shirt again. "Uh, Bud, I don't think so. That's kind of unsanitary, rusty knife and all."

"We sterilize it in the fire."

"No, Bud."

"Well, if it means anything, it hurts. They always…"

"Think up another ritual."

They were all quiet. Buddy sulked.

"We could drink something."

"That's good, Chris."

"We put something in our cups. Like sand."

Buddy made a face. "Yuk!"

"You wanted something to hurt, creep!"

"Ashes." Jack spoke quickly. "Ashes from our last campfire."

"Yeah." Buddy's face glowed. "That's disgusting."

"Mix it in your soda so it goes down okay." Jack raked ashes away from the coals. "Hold out your cups." Buddy and Sam each had about an inch left in theirs. Jack sprinkled ash over the top. "Stick in a finger and stir it around. Chris."

Chris handed Jack his cup. "I drank it all."

Jack dumped in the ash. "Doesn't look too palatable."

Chris shrugged and flipped his hair back. Jack poured in about two inches of beer. "Here. Drink that." Chris was grinning. "Don't tell your mother."

"You think I'm crazy?" He looked Jack in the eye.

"What are you standing on?" Jack looked down.

"Nothing, Dad."

Jack thought he'd stumbled but of course he hadn't. It just felt like a shock when he realized in woozy awareness—surprising and humorous and, yes, sad—the absolute unquestionable fact that his son, standing next to him, was the same height as he. The son was as tall as the father.

The first one slips by you like this. The others, if you're very careful, you can catch them at it.

He's probably known it for a while. I'm the one who had to find out all of a sudden. I should have seen it coming. They sneak up on you. Like the girl thing, and you're not leading anymore but stumbling along their trail, trying to keep sight of them. The first one is gone.

Jack put an arm around him. "Hey, Chris. Next summer, you grow a beard too." Jack loved the smile.

And they drank their pledge, warm and close. Jack stayed by the fire with his children. "Let's sit here," he said, "until we can't see a bit of flame. Not even one red dot."

Just before eight, Jack turned on the headlights. They were off the turn-pike and tearing down the last corner of Pennsylvania, then across Maryland and into Virginia and home. Jack could see it all before him, driving toward a navy-blue dusk. Behind him as he watched in the mirror through the open back of the Jeep, the sky was golden peach, reflecting the vanished sun. He grabbed the knee bedside him and squeezed it. "We're going to make it, Bud!"

"How long?"

"Couple of hours. Maybe. Check out the back seat."

Buddy twisted. "Sam's asleep. Chris has his eyes closed."

"Is he plugged in?"

"Yes."

"Then he's in a trance."

"Can I turn on the radio?"

"Keep it soft."

Buddy punched buttons until he found country rock.

"That's good. Stop there. Keeps me awake."

"Are you tired?"

"Nope." He knew he should be, but he felt charged with energy. A day when everything worked right, the miles unwinding, making good time. They'd stopped to eat, and he couldn't face the night in a motel.

152

At that point, figuring they had five hours to go, he'd decided to push on.

"Does Morn know we're corning?"

"Uh-uh. She thinks we'll be there tomorrow."

"Is she still at Grandma's?"

"She's been home about a week."

"Did you tell her about the new car?"

"Uh, no. I thought we'd surprise her."

Buddy yawned.

"Try to stay awake. You be my co-pilot."

Buddy nodded. "Is it hard to drive at night?"

"Nah. I like it. Less distracting. Not so much traffic. Gives you time to think."

The radio voices grew scratchy. "I think we're losing it." Buddy fiddled with the knob. "There's nothing."

"We're still blocked in the mountains. At night…"

Beautiful music poured into the car. Jack touched Buddy's hair. "Leave it." Jack didn't know what it was. Classical, opera maybe, and somewhat familiar, vibrant and suggestive. They drove a while.

"I know this sounds stupid, but I kind of like it."

Jack smiled at his son. "Surprised?"

Before them now all was dark. Buddy twisted on the seat and gazed out the back. Jack glanced in the mirror. The road sliced through a black vee of mountain and in the gap the sky burned red, as though the mountains were cut of black velvet and arranged in curved hands, making it impossible to ignore that cup of fire framed in their grasp. The music swam in Jack, sweet yet filled with longing.

"The music matches the sky." Buddy said in his frog-deep voice.

Jack was quiet, playing it over and over in his head. Buddy cuddled against him.

"I won't go to sleep, Dad."

"It's okay. Rest. I'm fine."

That one thing could make the whole trip worth it. The music matches the sky. If you just wait, it comes to you like a gift. Only your own kids can give it to you. Sam, by the fire, I liked it all, Daddy. Chris. One night, idly whittling a marshmallow stick, he'd heard Chris telling Dunk what he was doing after high school. Travel. Manage a rock group. Live in California. Drive a Porsche. Dunk, lazy, answering that he'd better

153

enjoy being a kid because when you get older, that's all you wish, is you were a kid again. Right, Jack? Isn't that right? Tell him. And Jack had said, you got it, that's the truth.

He turned off the radio when nothing but static emerged. He liked the sleeping bodies around him and the quiet. He could drive all night if he had to, he felt that strong. He was bursting with life. He had everything. The trip was almost over, and he had done it well. The simplicity, the accomplishment. And no, friend, he did not want to be a kid again. He was just fine. He liked having some life behind him, all the years, the experience and knowledge. Gives you confidence, manhood. Don't make me start again.

As a boy he'd fall asleep at night listening to Samuel moving in the house below him. So peaceful to fall asleep with your father, alive and awake in the house. You were safe. The feeling was in him now; seventeen and he'd never left home. He was a man who kept the youth he was with him.

Young friend, traveling companion, stay with me. Be a brother to my sons, and I'll be the father. I'll take care of you all.

Now, he was glad to be driving toward a woman. It was all he thought about the last hundred miles.

He cut the lights when he turned in the driveway. Chris woke at once. "Can I drive up to the house?"

"You don't get to practice on this one. Plus … we should break it to Mom slowly."

Greta did not appear. "Chris, knock gently. It might scare her if she's asleep and we walk in."

The curtain moved and the door flew open. She stood on the deck, hands on her hips.

Jack let Chris go first. She hugged him, happy but something else. He should have called her. He ran up and put his arms around her. "We drove all the way. Fifteen hours' drive time. Glad to see me?"

"Jack. That was foolish."

"I know. Aren't you glad to see me?"

Chris dragged her to the Jeep. "Do you love it? Dad bought it from Mack."

Greta stood, bewildered. Jack slid Sammy out and carried him up the steps. "Shake Bud and see if he'll walk. I'll try to ease Sam in without waking him." They were all whispering. Jack kicked open the door. The house was cool. He didn't turn on the light in Sam's room but lowered him to the bed in the dark. He found a quilt and tucked it all around the limp body. "As good as your bag," he said.

Greta sat on the sofa, one boy glued to each side of her, both talking at once. She held their hands in her lap.

"How about we unpack in the morning. It's late, you guys."

They groaned.

"You can talk all day tomorrow."

"Are the clothes awful?" said Greta. "I can't even think."

"Not the socks. The socks are intact."

Jack went out to get his keys and lock up. He stood a minute getting used to the fragrant, humid air. When he entered the house Greta was in their room, sitting at the foot of the bed. The covers were smooth.

"You're not overjoyed to see us."

"I wasn't expecting it."

"I'm glad you weren't asleep." He sat next to her.

"I've been staying up late."

"Good. So've I." He pushed her back and began to kiss her. He pulled kisses out of her. "God, I've thought about you. All day. I hoped you'd be in a good mood. I couldn't wait."

She sat up. "Take it easy."

"What for?" He rolled on his back. "Look at me."

"I am. That's what I'm doing."

"Let me show you my tan line."

"You don't have one."

"D'you like that?"

She tugged on his beard.

"Hey, I'm proud of this."

She was peering intently into the whiskers, separating hairs. "Jack, there's so much white. Have you seen this?"

"I haven't been looking in mirrors."

"It can't stay."

He sat up, breathing hard. "Honey, what's the matter?"

"I have to get used to you again. Talk or something."

He marched to the sliding door and pushed it open. "It's suffocating in here. I feel funny being in rooms again. We have any cold beer?"

"No."

"Any at all?"

She shook her head.

He frowned.

"I was going to shop tomorrow, Jack. Tomorrow I was going to buy beer and miss you and wait for you."

He smiled at her.

"What was Chris talking about, that he drives now?"

"Oh, that's … it was something for him to do."

"He's fourteen."

"He was okay."

"They look … you let them run wild."

"They're great."

"You all look like you've been living in a tree."

"We have, sort of." He knelt in front of her. "Honey, there's so much. I gotta tell you about Sam. It was absolutely amazing, the kid…"

"Jack!"

"What?"

"I don't like people to tell me about my own children."

"Well, I'm not…"

"You fall in here, all powerful and outdoorsy and expect me to … to…" She stopped. "You have the boys for a couple of weeks and act like a hero."

He sat next to her again, taking her hand. It was soft and her nails were polished pink. "You look pretty, Greta. Your hair looks nice that way." He kissed her ear. "Is this new?" She wore a long ruffled shirt.

"Yes."

He kissed her neck.

"Don't you want to shower?"

"I swam in the lake this morning before we left. That's cleaner than our tap water."

"Jack, I have things to tell you."

"Me too. Can't they wait?"

"Can't you wait? Jack, it's so impersonal. You don't want me, you want *it*."

"Shit!"

156

"Well, honestly." She pushed him away.

"Baby, don't think I'm some kind of animal, but…"

"Oh, all right."

"Not like this. Not letting me. Wanting me." He walked onto the deck and breathed deeply. He gave it five minutes. The light went out in the bedroom. He stood by the door, undressing. Greta was in bed. He slid in beside her. The sheets were very cold on him.

"I have missed you, Jack."

"Oh, honey."

He made love to her, but it was too rough. He couldn't slow down enough for her. He held her to him, back to front, said in her hair, "We'll do it again."

"Good luck."

"I'm good for it. I'm in terrific shape."

"I don't want to until you're you again."

"What does that mean?"

"The beard goes. First thing in the morning."

"Not first."

"Before anything."

"You're a hard woman." He wanted to tell her how it felt to have his arms around her again, and how soft she was, and he was tired of everything hard and flat. Then he was cool. He was swimming underwater and trying to get to the surface. He could see Greta's legs dangling there, and he was going to grab her and tease her. But it got all dark, and he thought he must be turned around, and he started swimming the other way. He was sinking, and he fell until he jerked and woke up. His heart was pounding. "Put your legs around me," he growled. "Wrap me in your legs."

Was it ever enough, was he ever the hero? They could still get there, but the obstacles were larger and less clear. It was such effort, and he liked things to be easy. While she slept he lay awake for a while.

Chapter Ten

He Has to Stay Over

From her porch, Nina Talbott had been watching the games children play on a summer evening. Small bodies darted in and out of shadows cast by street lights. Tonight was warm, and the children gradually returned to houses hidden in leafiness. Nina sighed and paced the walk. There was no traffic in the street.

Elaine opened the door and stood behind the screen. "I couldn't find you."

"Come out, sweetie, and shut the door. Daddy won't like the air conditioning bill."

"What time will he be here?"

"He has to stay over. I just finished talking to him."

"Mom!"

"He couldn't help it. There was a terrible overrun. Someone is flying in to inspect and he has to be there."

"Will he come for my performance class? I've been practicing *four* hours a day all summer!"

"Oh, I'm sure. That's still a week off."

Elaine stomped onto the porch and sat down. "Did he say if he bought me anything?"

"He'd just walked out of a meeting."

"This late?"

"It's three hours earlier out there."

Elaine pounded her fists on her knees.

Nina laughed. "I think he'll be here."

"He missed the last one."

"You can play the program here."

"It's not the same thing, Mom. I get up for the performance. I'm much better."

"It'll keep." Nina sat beside her daughter. "Unlike the special supper I made for him."

She picked up the long wave of Elaine's hair and let it fall over her wrist. She twisted it into a knot high on the girl's head. "I admire you, your confidence."

"Mom, why don't you have a wig made that looks exactly like my hair, and you can play with that."

Nina stood. "I'm taking Suitor out."

"I'm sorry."

"You needn't be rude, Elaine. I'm only being affectionate."

"I'm mad about Daddy."

"So am I. But let's not take it out on each other."

"I don't like to be fussed with. Sometimes I don't like to be touched."

"I'll try to remember." Nina opened the door. "What's Polly doing?"

"TV."

"When that show's over, have her go up."

"She won't mind me."

"I'll tell her. I won't be long. Lock the door."

"Which way are you going?"

"Down the street and back."

In a few minutes, Nina was strolling in the scattered night shade with Suitor. The heat had been intense for a week, and Suitor spent most days lying panting on the tiles in the kitchen. Dark was some relief. The dog pulled hard at the leash, but Nina didn't want to release him. He was too eager.

They walked one block, crossed the street and came back on the opposite side. Nina stood looking at her house. It seemed every light was on in contrast with the other, mostly dark, houses. Let them burn. Tom's voice on the phone was tired and distant. Hers, so hopeful. "Oh,

Tom, when?" "Three, four days. I'll let you know."

"Another turn?" she said to the dog. They walked in the opposite direction, down two blocks and into a curving side street, a long cul-de-sac that came to a dead end where a large black-and-white barrier blocked entry to the woods. A narrow path, starting behind the barrier, was a shortcut to the school. If you followed it for a hundred yards, you'd come out behind Great Forest. The kids on this block used it often. The path was overgrown until it met the mulched trail laid by the county. This was a frequent walk for Nina and Suitor. She especially liked it early in the morning or late afternoon when it felt cooler under the trees.

Suitor tugged at the leash. "Not now, baby. I didn't bring the flashlight."

The dog ran in a circle around Nina, the leather strap binding her legs. "You, you puppy!" She dropped the leash and tried to step out of the coil. Suitor got away, crashing into the trees. Nina stayed at the barrier calling and whistling. Then she stopped. She could hear rustling. Suitor liked poking in the ground-covering ferns.

She took a few steps along the path. "Here, boy," she called. The pale sky reflecting the city lights and the street lamps had made it easy to see on the sidewalk. But in the woods, blackness closed around her like a cloak. Cicadas buzzed, drowning the softer, closer noises. The woods were so noisy and the air so black that she saw and heard nothing specific. The very anonymity of the night was protective, and her heart beat solidly but not with fear.

She moved through the forest with the excitement and bravura of a child playing a daring and dangerous game. She slowed her pace as she turned on the wider path. Her eyes adjusted, and the trees were distinct and less dense at the edge of the wood. She easily found the planks in the embankment and climbed up, keeping her head down, not to slip her footing.

"Hello, Nina."

She reached the top and heard his voice. She looked for him, jerking like a startled sparrow. Polly had run in yesterday, her face red and sweaty. "Mommy, Mr. Bridges is back. I think." Nina had looked over and seen a Jeep alone in the lot. "Can we go see him?"

"Not today. I'm sure he's very busy."

"Didn't mean to scare you." Jack sat on a tree stump near the edge of the embankment.

"You didn't. Hello. Hi."

Nina stumbled a little, walking toward him. He stood and offered his seat. He was holding two cans against his chest and gesturing.

Nina braced one foot and then the other against the stump and removed her shoes. "I'm sorry. They're filled with wood chips and pebbles."

He watched her shake them out then strap them on. They were delicate sandals—soft tan, the color of her legs—and blended into her skin.

"Do you always walk in the woods this late?"

"I lost my dog. Did he come by?"

Jack shook his head. "You don't seem dressed for it."

"I guess not." Nina laughed and fluffed her sundress, a deep coral. She felt pretty when she wore it. She had put on her gold hoop earrings and a bracelet because they were loose and casual and made her feel young.

"You look nice. Party?"

"Just Tom coming home. But he didn't. I was listening for the cab but the phone rang instead." She tapped her toe. "Aren't these ridiculous? I put them on to serve lobster salad and pour wine." Nina looked up at him. "I'm surprised to see you."

He sat on the ground, hugging his knees. "Getting a jump on things. Only a couple of weeks to Labor Day. I was over in the afternoon and couldn't concentrate. Too hot."

"Isn't your office cool?"

"Supposed to be, but it isn't very. It's better at night. I just came out for a break." He crumpled one can and popped open the other, offering it to her.

"Oh, no. No thanks."

"It's not very cold anyway."

He drank, looking out at the trees. "Isn't it something—this sound of it? August."

She was quiet.

"See that old giant there?" He gestured toward the fallen sycamore. "I've been keeping track. Every year the few leaves it puts out wither and die earlier. They're starting already. I bet next spring there just won't be any."

She frowned. "That would be a shame. Maybe it's partly the heat. I'm trying to keep the garden going. It's so dry. I water twice a day, but the afternoons are punishing."

"I thought of dropping by."

She looked at him quickly. "When?"

"Today. To say hi and ... how are you?"

"Why didn't you?"

He shrugged. "So. Tell me about your summer. What did you do?"

"I had almost all my relatives to visit but not at the same time. My in-laws have a house at Rehoboth so we spent a week there. My sister came too. I ... let's see ... I entertained a lot for my husband and took the girls to the pool and down to the District twice a week for music lessons and ... oh, I finished a long book I've been reading forever."

"Was it any good?"

"Not at first, but then I liked it." She clasped her hands. "I make a wish and tell myself if I finish a disagreeable task, it will come true."

"And did it?" His voice had a teasing intimacy she remembered.

"Almost," she whispered. He finished his beer. She could see him clearly in the light from the school. His hair seemed more golden than brown, but maybe it was the light shining behind him. "Did you take your trip?"

"Oh, yeah. Took all the boys. We camped and fished and swam. Everything. A real summer." He leaned back. "Went all out. Robinson Crusoe. I grew a beard."

Nina laughed. "Oh, I'd like to see that."

"Yeah? You have a thing for beards?"

"On some people. If they're not too dignified."

"That about describes it."

"You must hate coming back."

"Nope. This is my best time of year. Everything new, fresh start. I get my best ideas."

"Like ... name one."

Jack slapped the ground. "Nah. It's boring. Just little things."

"Tell me. Really."

He hunched around to face her. "I want to clean up this woods and create a habitat. Establish an eco-system and use it as an outdoor lab. Find out which plants attract birds and insects."

162

"That's lovely. I wonder…" She spread her arms toward the trees. "I've thought of planting daffodils here. This man down in Prince Edward County sells bulbs by the bushel. The small English jonquils. You can practically throw them on the ground, and they'll take root. I'd like to put hundreds all down the bank and into the trees. They'd bloom early in the spring before the shade becomes dense."

He liked looking at her sitting on that tree stump. As though it were a velvet pillow, her ankles neatly crossed.

"They don't require maintenance. You don't do anything once they're in. Would I need a permit, do you think?"

"No permit. No rules for nature." Jack patted the ground, very near her sandals. He might have touched her. "I feel great about this year. This is going to be my best one. I just know it. I think I'm finally getting the hang of this!"

"Finally?"

"And…"

"Jack." Nina stood suddenly. "It's nice to see you again. But I … there's Suitor. I don't know where he is. And the girls are alone."

"Sure. I was just blabbing." Jack stood also.

"No. I like to hear you talk." Nina moved slowly back toward the steps. "I think I should try one more time. Perhaps he'll listen now."

"You think he's still playing in there?"

"He must be."

"Won't he come home on his own?"

"I don't know. He doesn't often get free."

"I'll come with you."

"You don't…"

"Go on. You go first."

She descended and started along the path, calling weakly for the dog. The blackness enveloping her was familiar this time and friendlier. The locust buzz was louder and overpowered her voice, every sound. She thought Jack said something to her and turned. He put a hand on the back of her neck and moved her forward.

"I want to show you something," he said, close to her ear. His hand was warm and definite.

He guided her onto a side path, brushing through ferns. "Look down."

She could see nothing, felt dizzy and leaned back against his hand.

She was cool and reckless. He would not let her fall.

"Look." He swished a foot through the frothy leaves and she saw a faint dusty light down near the forest floor.

"What is it?"

"Fireflies." He was standing close to her or she wouldn't hear him. "They are tired this time of year, clinging under the ferns. But they'll glow if you touch them gently."

She stared at his feet. The milky light was almost lavender.

"Aren't they pretty?"

She nodded. His hand moved down to rest on her bare back. She turned so his arm would be around her. "Jack."

"Oh, yes. When you say it like that."

"Would you kiss me? I'd like it so much." She put her hands on his shoulders. She couldn't see his face. It was wrong, to say it. He was silent only a bit, but it was too long. She was still then and afraid, a terrible moment, but he was so warm and she did not move away.

His voice emptied onto her. "Nina. I'm not going to … just kiss you, Nina."

He dropped kisses on her, and she moved her face to catch them, all of them. He was seeking her in the dark, brushing his lips in her hair, softening her. His hands didn't move. She whispered to him, how sweet, he smelled so sweet of soap and beer. His laugh was wonderful. It was wonderful to have your arms around a man and feel his laughter, the echo of it rumbling against your ear. How could they do this? Please.

"Jack, Jack … there's no place…" she cried.

"I'll find one."

She loved his voice, so deep and breaking, not controlled.

"I don't see how."

"I do."

He led her somewhere and leaned back, pulling her against him. Now his hands moved, to show her, guide her a little. "Should I…?" she murmured.

"Don't. Don't say anything." He touched her lips.

And then he talked all through it. He was the one, telling her he needed her, describing his need, exclaiming beauty that he couldn't see but only feel, she was so warm, come to me. More. Yes. Both of us. And she was there and had to stop but trembled and held him while he went on and finished with her name, almost singing Ninaninaninanina … his

164

voice rushing and covering her like water with his raspy song.

She opened her eyes. She could see shapes now and the faint checks in his shirt where she rested on him.

"Say something," he said.

"I feel like I'm hugging you *and* this tree."

"Are you very uncomfortable?"

"No."

"Then stay. Stay where you are."

"Jack. Jack, why did you wait so long—when I said kiss me?"

"I didn't want to jump on you too fast and have you run away from me."

She opened his shirt a little and put her cheek on his chest. "I was so scared. I thought you didn't want me."

"Not a chance. It's all I could think of."

"About me?"

"I've been thinking about you for a long time. Nina, Nina, did you know this would happen?"

"No. But I thought if you ever … I would not be … a fool."

They were quiet.

Nina moved slightly. "Did you … you're still so…"

"I'm like that sometimes. When I want to do it again."

"I don't think I can."

"Please."

She could see his face now, the way he leaned back, closing his eyes. Helpless and still wanting. Please.

"Give me a minute." She giggled. "I still have my dress on. Maybe I should take it off this time."

"If you do, I'll stay out all night with you."

She stopped breathing. "Could you?" She spoke softly.

"No."

"I'll do it anyway."

They walked along the path, embracing, her right leg moving with his left, their hips touching. When they climbed the steps, he went ahead, and she followed, her hand hooking his waistband.

"I can't let go of you."

"Don't."

"Well, I must go." They were standing behind the school.

"I'll walk you."

She shook her head. "Better not."

He pulled her into the dark well by the gym and kissed her. "Can you call me? I'll go in the office and wait. Please?"

"Of course."

"I won't leave until you call. I want to hear your voice."

"Tuck your shirt in."

He stood watching until she turned the corner. He went in the back door of the school and across the hall to his office. He turned out the light, wanting it to be dark when she called. It was almost fifteen minutes before the phone rang.

"Hi."

"Oh, Jack, I'm sorry it took so long."

"I would've waited a lot longer."

"The girls were asleep. Lucky me."

"The blessings of sin."

She paused. "Is that what you think?"

"Hey, no. I feel so great!"

"Not guilty?"

"Only about one thing."

She was quiet.

"I want to see you again."

"I'm smiling. I can't stop."

"Don't.

"Oh, Jack, Suitor did come home. He was out on the front lawn, unrepentant but docile."

"I hope you forgave him."

"I did."

"And thank him. For me."

"I'll bring him next time. You can give him a pat."

"Nina. I'm so ... so ... happy."

Chapter Eleven

The Perfection of Her Beside Him

Jack stuck his hands in his pockets. He wanted his hands to be warm when he touched her. He should have worn gloves, but he'd left in a hurry after dinner, telling Greta and the boys he had to work on a report. It was a month since he'd gone out in the evening, and he felt safe using that excuse. All day he'd been on edge, thinking something would go wrong. But now here he was calm, waiting for Nina.

He had chosen a large poplar to stand against. There was a certain danger in the naked woods now, the protecting leaves were on the ground and crackled in this dying season. Any slight breeze and the leaves ran like mice on the forest floor. They could not do this again. Jack felt exposed even where he stood back in the trees. A livid brightness penetrated the woods, reflecting the cloudy white sky. He had turned off the school's rear spotlights to make it as dark as possible. He stamped his feet, breathed deeply, and his breath frosted. He would have been cold if there was any wind. But the night was quiet, and he was excited and kept warm because she was coming.

Jack looked at his watch. Still early.

They had so little time. All the hours they'd been together in the past months wouldn't add up to half a day. Well, maybe. It wasn't enough. That first time, the next, and then another. The third time she hadn't worn a thing under her loose shift, to make it easy for him.

That short block of time expanded all out of proportion in his mind. It exploded into importance, vital and alive beyond reason. There was nothing but her, going to her, touching her, thinking about her. It had to last. He didn't see how they could stop. But her husband returned and they'd quit abruptly. Then waiting. The quick phone calls, not frustrating but joyous, patient because she was as eager as he and would help him, would be there.

They'd had luck; everything worked. Even the screams from the playground one painfully bright day, end of September. Not the usual boisterous screaming he was used to and could go on working when he heard it. He'd run out of the school to see a crowd of kids gathered, stooping over Polly. Her leg was twisted in a cruel way from a fall off the parallel bars. Jack had quieted her and sent two boys running for Nina. A few minutes later, packing them both into the ambulance, he'd squeezed Nina's hand. The break was not threatening to Polly's young bones, but the cast was enormous. She was home for ten days, and the teachers sent work over and kids visited. The music class stood under her window to serenade. And twice, in broad daylight, Jack walked across the yard and made a cheering call, sitting with Polly in her room, telling her stories. Afterward, downstairs, Nina gave him coffee once and lunch once and something else, very fast but wonderful. He went back to his office, ran back, he couldn't contain himself. And no one thought anything about it. He was just being a nice guy.

Every day, driving to work, autumn flared before him, consuming itself. He would hang around after school, sometimes walking into the woods with Tim. This was the boy's last year at Great Forest, and it had not started well. Tim was defensive and rude. The kid lived in constant fear of being dumped in a home. Jack put him in Enid Lacey's class. He had doubts about Enid's skills, but she'd been around a long time and was friendly and tolerant with the kids. Tim tested her patience every day. Jack heard plenty about it. He was determined to see Tim through, but he couldn't stand to talk to the stepmother. The woman's life was chaos and communication was worthless.

Jack concentrated on some good moments with Tim, trying to encourage him. The boy was so bright; even if he never did homework he was years ahead of his classmates. Jack liked to hear the tough, sometimes profane, talk coming from this dark angel with his small body and knowing eyes. Jack knew he'd be okay, somewhere out in the world, if he could just make it through a few more years of book reports and report cards, teacher reports and specialist reports. Jack walked when possible with his arm around Tim, wanting him to be aware of his emotional and physical support.

Jack found him behind the school one day. The kid had scooted out on the old dying tree and shinnied up an extreme branch. He hung by his knees, upside down. C'mon, Tim, Jack had called. It's against the rules. I hate rules. C'mon. You worry me. Don't worry about me! People worry 'bout me then I gotta worry 'bout them! C'mon, Tim. I'm waiting.

A couple of times, Nina had seen him with Tim and waved. They'd stood together, and she'd made conversation with the boy but gazing at Jack, the way he loved best, respecting and adoring. You care about them, you wonderful man. You're so good. And he was, would be magnificent.

Do everything right, take care of everyone. Only let me have her. Just this one thing. Don't take her away.

One morning, after a heavy frost, the landscape blurred with colors more neutral, less distinctly painted. Jack couldn't stand to see it fade. He'd closed his office door and called Nina.

"I'm just on my way out," she said.

"Damn. Where?"

"It's my day in the country. I drive out toward the Blue Ridge apple orchards and buy a few bushels."

He looked at a large square on his desk calendar. It would take two phone calls to be free. "Want company?"

"Don't tease me."

"Which way d'you go?"

"Out route 50 toward Middleburg."

"Okay. There's an Amoco station just after the turn to the county airport. Park there and wait for me."

"How long should I wait?"

"Forever."

She laughed. "Seriously."

"I'll *be* there!"

That was the longest stretch of time they'd had together, and they had not made love. But if he could repeat any time with her, those five hours would be it—the perfection of her beside him. They drove an hour until she found the farmers' market. He loaded boxes of Romes, Staymen and Delicious into the Jeep for her. What do you do with them all? Give some away, make stuff for the freezer. They last a long time. The smell was tangy as they drove again. He was so hungry. They ate terrible fast food, not caring. Oh, I should have brought a picnic but there wasn't time. Sweet Nina. Don't worry about it.

It was a warm day and they were far from Courtland County. He put the top down. I've never had a ride in an open Jeep, she said. They're not very romantic. Watch, he said and drove past horse farms until he found a lane to turn in and went cross-country, one hand on the wheel and one around her until he stopped under an ancient beech tree, its yellow leaves a gorgeous inferno, and kissed her.

She sat with her back against the trunk, and he lay with his head in her lap looking up at a tree that was here before George Washington. He reached for her blouse. No.

She kissed his hands. I can't. Do you mind? I'd die if anyone saw us. Not refusing totally. He raised his head. There was no one, not a house or cow anywhere. It's different in the forest. I know we're alone there. Her modesty touched him and made him protective. It was nice, to show her this; how much he liked her, that it wasn't only physical.

He had done nothing but kiss her. Even so, his memory played back a tantalizing, sexy afternoon. She asked questions, curious and intimate, so he would tell about himself, all about how he grew up. She murmured responses, caressing his lips as he talked. He almost went to sleep, and she said it was all right, go ahead I'll wake you when it's time to go. But he stayed awake. She played with his hair. I love your hair. I put my hands on it and almost feel it growing. You're so natural. Why do you smell so good? What do you use? And he told her nothing. Just soap. Nothing else? Nah. I hate junk on me. Then her face dropping and kissing him upside down, her hair falling in two dark commas along his cheeks, making the kiss so private.

He drove slowly on the way back, stretching time. They went through a small village, one street. I'm starving. Pull over. She ran into the drugstore, and he sat idly watching a young couple strolling. The boy had a hand in the rear pocket of the girl's jeans. They both looked younger than Chris.

Nina brought him a double dip hot fudge sundae. Laughing. I had to buy the dish and spoon, too. They didn't have any plastic. She fed it to him, cool and rich, while he drove. One golden beech leaf stuck in the windshield. He watched it flutter. He would keep it, put it in his wallet. Just before they arrived at her car, it snapped away in the wind. He was glad in a way; it saved him from being too silly and romantic. And he didn't need it. Nothing was more clearly drawn in his mind than the color of that day. It was so good just being with her.

And it was good he could remember that because tonight the prospects for anything but hand-holding were dim. He jumped up and down, looked at his watch. He could stand one more minute.

He saw her bulky shadow up on the ledge and then climbing down. He waited, knowing she would find him.

"Am I late? Are you freezing?" She stood in front of him, bouncing, hugging her coat across a huge, pregnant-looking stomach.

"What have you got in there?"

"A blanket. I thought we might be able to sit on it a little. And something else."

"For me?"

"Kiss me first." She dropped some things on the ground and flew into him, spreading open their coats and pressing her body to his, her arms going around him, under his jacket.

"This isn't nearly warm enough for you," she said, tugging gently at his windbreaker.

"I know that now."

"You should have worn that dear old parka."

"I wanted to look nice."

"Here, put your hands in my pockets."

"What is this?" He touched the deep silkiness of her coat, excited by its ruddy color. He brushed his cheek on her collar, buried his nose. "You have such pretty things." He tried not to think where she got them.

"It's rabbit."

"Can't be. No bunny ever looked this good."

"Then okay it's fox. I just wore it because I thought we wouldn't be moving around, keeping warm."

He kissed her, holding her tight. "I love it. It makes me want to pet you. No, don't move."

"I want to give you this. Jack, here." She stooped and poured from a thermos. She gave him a steaming cup and something wrapped in a cloth napkin.

"Oh, baby." He ate and drank. "How did you know?"

"You're always hungry."

"No, but I can always eat. What is this?"

"Hot chocolate, made the right way, and gingerbread."

"Great stuff."

She put her arms around him and listened to him swallow. "I've been making that for twenty years and never had a batch not turn out. My mother's recipe."

"Twenty years?" He finished and leaned back on the poplar, putting his hands on her shoulders.

"Want some more?"

"Maybe later. Twenty years?"

"I started young in the kitchen."

"Nina, how old are you?"

She frowned, thinking. "Does thirty-three sound a lot younger than thirty-four?"

"Much."

"Then that's what I am."

"You don't look either one."

"Well, I am. Besides, I'd rather tell you my age than my weight."

He pulled her close, stroking her hair and then down her furry back. "What is it?"

"I hate to hear you put yourself down."

"Is that what I'm doing?"

"Sometimes. When you say you're fat."

"I don't say that."

"Well, plump. And you're not. You're…"

"What? Think of a good word."

"Compact."

"Not good enough."

"I can't describe it," he growled. "I just love to have my arms around you. A perfect armful."

"Oh, God, Jack. Don't talk to me like that." She was laughing.

172

"Why?"

"It's wickedly seductive. You like me the way I am."

"But I do." He kissed the top of her head. It felt natural to him now, resting his chin this way. With Greta he was ear to ear and both ways of holding them had felt strange to him for a while.

"I look at myself all the time. I expect to see … oh, what … horrid depravity. But I feel beautiful. I really do."

"Yes."

"Jack, sometimes I … panic. Can we do this?"

"Why not?!" He was almost shaking her. "*This* … you make it all… Listen. I wasn't some jerk going around looking for this. But now it makes everything, my life, more … just *more*! Does that make sense? D'you see?"

"Oh, I don't care! Let's not think about it."

"Great. That way it won't get complicated. Here." He took the blanket she brought and folded it in fourths. "Let's try this." They cuddled together, his hands inside her sleeves. "I'll keep kissing you so your lips won't freeze."

"It's not that cold, Jack."

"I know. But I want to."

"How much time do we have?"

"Another half hour."

"I think I'll make it."

"I'm sorry we never have a good place to go."

"This is more original."

"Than what?"

She recited, as though he'd heard it many times, "Than driving around where you might be recognized, than motels that you can't afford, than parking where someone might see us, than restaurants ditto."

He smiled.

"Besides, this way the girls think I'm out walking Suitor. If it's very long I say I stopped to see Mrs. Cooley. She's old and they never talk to her. If I left them for long, it would look odd. I know they'd tell Tom."

"Where is he?"

"West coast."

"No, the dog."

"Tied up by the school." She kissed him. "It is warmer like this."

"Nina, do you know how to type?"

"Not … what a question. Why do you ask? A little."

"I have this crazy idea."

"I'll listen to anything." She fed him more gingerbread as he talked, so his hands could stay in her coat.

"This guy, Jules Coker—do you know him?"

"I know Maryann Coker."

"He's her father. He brought me this plan to redesign the playground. He's trying to start a construction business. I hate to get involved with a parent's personal agenda, but you know it's kind of rundown."

"It could definitely use something."

"I've tried to get the superintendent to upgrade it, but there's always no money or the money has to be spent elsewhere."

"Poor baby."

"Coker thinks we can raise the money ourselves. The design is basically just moving some of the equipment we have and laying a softer base. The expensive part would be one new structure—one multi-purpose climbing, swinging, sliding unit guaranteed to keep every kid in school happy and occupied constructively."

"All at once?"

"It would service about thirty to forty at a time."

"You sound like a talking brochure."

"Jules has been flooding my inbox."

"Typing? Me?" She prodded him.

"Oh, yeah. Jules wants to form a separate ad hoc PTA committee to look into this. I figured I could recommend you because of Polly's accident and your vast concern with playground safety and all."

"Did I ever say that?"

"If you were secretary of this thing, we could see each other at meetings, and then there'd be all these papers to pass back and forth and stuff like that. I could see you, look at you. Something might … happen for us."

"I've never been the PTA type. I hate committees." She giggled. "I never joined anything in the Navy. I was not a good Navy wife."

"I thought they took points off for that."

"I was young and Tom didn't care." She sighed. "He wanted to make it all on his own anyway."

"It would get us through winter."

"Will it last that long?"

"Sure. There's money to raise. It may all fall through because of the money."

"Is it a lot?"

"Five thousand. At least."

Nina shrugged. "I thought you were going to do that eco-thing. That seems cheaper and more—educational."

"This is where the push is. If these power guys get behind it, we might just raise the money."

"I hate fund raising."

"Actually, I'm not sure I approve of a completely structured play environment for kids." He sighed. "If it were strictly my choice…"

"Tell me."

"I'll bore you."

"No."

He took a deep breath. "I think kids like a messy play area—something to get their imaginations going. They're too boxed in. You know what I'd like? If I could turn this whole forest into the playground—untracked and wild. Let them explore, build hideouts, climb. That's what I think would be really healthy, not this other."

Nina put her arms around him.

"But this would look solid. It's something that shows. And if we have the community behind it…" Then, against her ear, "And, oh, Nina, I'd see you. And maybe work something out."

"Do you *want* to do this? It sounds like it would take up a lot of time."

"Everything I do is time. I suppose there are more … I don't know … instructional things. But I want to see you." He pulled her to her feet. "Let me, here, let me be against you. Hold me."

He pressed her to him and felt the coat fling around him as she rubbed the backs of his thighs. "I'm so frightened." He held her fiercely. "I'm frightened of what I feel for you. My life, there was a circumference to it. I could name its features. Now I can't describe it. There are no boundaries. I can't say anymore what I might do … think … say." His voice was gasping. "It's so big, and I feel like I'm holding you every minute. There's something turning in me all the time. I'm scared and I love it." He shook her. "I love feeling this way. I must have this!"

Nina covered his lips with hers. She wanted his words inside her. His powerful need. I'm scared and I love it. She had to keep it inside. Last week, when Tom was home, she sat on his lap in the sunroom and Elaine was at the piano. The music was French, Debussy perhaps. She held herself very still as the notes played inside her. The piece was showy, brittle runs and arpeggios, glassy and shattering. Then warm and smooth, moving to a lower octave, deep and peaceful. She didn't understand music, how it was made or even where it came from. But when it entered her, something in her had no name but her lover's name. His name. She embraced her body to keep it from escaping. She was afraid of it ever getting out.

"Nina. Nina, I can't think anymore. Say you'll do this with me, and we'll be together any way we can."

"Yes. I don't know anything about it. Yes. I'll do anything."

"You're shivering. Are you too cold? Do you think we could? Now?"

"Anything."

Chapter Twelve

A Dangerous Animal

Rowena Castle stopped by Jack's office one morning before school but it was empty. At the library door, she detached a large purple satin heart from the glass. February was over and thank goodness. From the shopping bag at her feet she took a large object, a lion face with blazing eyes and a mass of curly yellow hair. She had made a mature lion with a droopy angry mouth and a protruding fierce nose. If you turned the face over, a round baby lamb appeared, wooly and blue-eyed. The children flipped the face back and forth according to the weather. Sometimes it changed several times a day.

Rowena held the heart, studying it. She had designed it years ago, a heart as big as a turkey platter and trimmed all around with real lace. She'd fussed over it, hating to finish it, adding embroidery in silver thread and velvet ribbons trailing down. She tried fluffing it but it remained flat. Tired and dusty. Too romantic and not like the month at all. Rowena stuffed it in her bag. She would get rid of it. Make something about presidents. Or snow and ice. That was more symbolic. She'd make a glacier buried in snow, icicles, and blue glitter. Wet and cold. You'd shiver just to see it.

She left the lion face showing—appropriate for the first of March—and went back to her office. She plugged in the coffee maker and sat down to do paper work. She saw cars pull into the parking lot and teachers struggle into the building against the wind, most of them lugging satchels and bundles. *We are always carrying. We take the job home and bring it back. And people make fun of our sensible shoes.* She picked up her coffee mug. Jack's sat there, undisturbed and collecting grime from disuse.

Rowena poured a cup and lit a cigarette. She saw the Jeep pull in. Jack got out and, instead of jogging into the school, leaned on the fender. Rowena watched him. Various staff members arrived and greeted him, but he didn't follow when they hurried to the entrance. He stood in the wind, hunched over, his collar turned up. Was he waiting for Tim? Rowena knew he sometimes sneaked the boy into the cafeteria for a makeshift breakfast. But it was at least half an hour before any kids, except patrols, would arrive. Maybe he was trying to decide whether to come to work. Rowena allowed herself a private, grim smile. Many days, he seemed absent anyway, and half the time his door was closed, even when he had no one in conference. Rowena smoked and drank her coffee, looking at him. Jack still seemed to be waiting.

Amanda Tinker knocked on her open door. "Busy?"

Rowena turned. "Come in."

Amanda wandered to the window. "What's he doing? Thinking of a reason to cut?"

"Who knows? It's none of my business." Rowena moved to her desk so Amanda would face her and not outside.

"Dammit, Ro, we have to talk to him. This reading incentive program can't go any further without his input and help. We've done all we can."

"We should…"

"No. I'm not doing one more thing until he meets with us and goes over this proposal."

"Have some coffee."

Amanda poured. "Did you get on his calendar for this morning?"

"I haven't yet. Let's try after opening announcements."

"I have my first group."

"Then I'll try. What are your free times?"

"Between ten-thirty and eleven and right after lunch."

"Okay. I'll lean on him."

"I mean it, Rowena. He asked us to take this on, and I haven't time to waste if he's not…"

Amy Ellen Webber walked in. "If he's not what?"

"If he's not going to give us the support we need," Amanda fumed.

"It'll be all right," Rowena spoke quickly.

"How? How can it? If we don't start in about two weeks, it'll be pointless."

Amy Ellen interrupted. "Is this about the reading program? Is he dragging his feet?"

"His feet are not even moving!"

"Amanda, let's drop it for now. I'll pin him down for a time and then come by and let you know."

"Sure. And if he puts us off, I'm dropping it for good." She left.

"Well!" Amy Ellen pulled a mug from her tote and filled it. "She's certainly…"

"Yes, she is. And with good reason."

"Maybe he's just sick of her, Rowena. The way she's always hanging on him."

"I don't think so."

"There must be a reason."

"Perhaps. But he was the one pressuring her to organize a school-wide read-a-thon. Something substantive, not just showy and fun. I said I'd help, of course, since I knew the library would be involved anyway. He was really pushy about it—hey let's do it, get it all ready to go, do it the last couple of months. Big flourish and then carry it into the summer."

"So, just do it."

"Amy, we can't. We need his approval on a lot of materials to be printed. We have to do a workshop for the faculty so they know what's expected. He has to enlist parental involvement. You know he has to be the one to do that."

Amy Ellen started taking out the metal clips pressing waves in her hair. "I still think he's just sick of Amanda. He gives me all the time I need. I'm organizing the kids to help clean the playground."

Rowena sighed. "The playground is all he's interested in, Amy."

"It's a big thing."

"It's only one thing. There are others."

"But it'll be so nice, Rowena, once it's done. I love the plans."

Drawings of the "new" playground and a scale model of the new structure were displayed in the lobby. Rowena saw them a half dozen times every day. Children stood in groups, gazing at them.

Amy giggled. "He's been wonderful at the fundraisers. Didn't you think it was darling, the way he let kids throw wet sponges at him for a quarter?"

"No. I thought it was undignified and silly." And not very profitable, she'd heard.

"It was so cute."

"It wasn't so cute the way he blasted us at the last faculty meeting. And he nearly took Brody's head off yesterday."

"Things have gotten kind of slack."

"Alice submitted the paperwork to him three weeks ago for approval of her life science unit. She needs the money for an incubator and two field trips. Yesterday morning, the papers were still on his desk."

"Rowena, you know you always say we talk about him too much."

"Goodbye, Amy. I really have work to do."

She hugged Rowena. "We're all going to feel better when spring arrives. It's always a little hard to get through." She walked away, patting her hair. Rowena watched the back of Amy Ellen's stretch pants and high-heeled mules. *I take it back about the sensible shoes. There's always an exception.*

Rowena moved a stack of review books from her desk. She was mad at herself for showing publicly how irked she was with Jack. After all, he was just acting distracted, worried maybe. *He's under pressure. He has a lot on his mind. He's human.* She didn't want him to be merely human.

The morning announcements and pledge to the flag squawked out of the box. She didn't care about the playground.

Let him do it. Let it be his main focus. The reading program can wait. There will always be a reading program. Or they could do a half-baked job. But he shouldn't dump on Amanda. We're professional. We're adults. We can take the ups and downs and moods and lack of direction, forethought and hindsight.

But a child? Tim? Tim was the one thing she could not forgive.

You just don't take a child and buddy-buddy with him for almost three-and-a-half years and then start jerking him around. Not a child whose whole life is instability and insecurity. A child who has no one to fall back on.

Rowena lit another cigarette. *Honey, you are getting old and cranky. Where's the joy? You have become what you feared—a bossy, know-it-all, old maid school-teacher librarian. So tend to your books and mind your own business.*

She glanced over the schedule. No regular activities until a video at ten for the second grade. A volunteer was checking in books at the main desk, so Rowena slipped down to the office and tapped on Jack's door, not bothering to ask Irene if he was free. "I need five minutes."

Jack looked up and smiled. Not the dazzling smile of welcome he used to give her, but at least he didn't frown and say, "Later." Rowena walked in and sat down. "It's about the read-a-thon."

"Ah, yes. How's that coming along?"

"It's gone as far as possible without your help."

"Okay, Rowena. Have Amanda drop off the paperwork."

"I think we all need to sit down for about an hour, go over the materials and set some deadlines."

"Things are tight. I'd better read it on my own."

Rowena shook her head. "We want to make a presentation. It might take you forever to get back to us on your own."

Jack looked at his desk.

"After school?" Rowena pressed.

"I'm talking to some people about the playground. We're trying to get financial support from the local business community. Let them use it in their advertising."

"Okay, when?"

He looked at his watch. "Let's make it before school tomorrow. Seven-thirty here."

"I'll tell Amanda."

Jack looked directly at her. "Rowena, I appreciate all you two've done for this."

"Tell Amanda. She needs a stroke." Rowena stood.

"Sure."

"Jack, while I'm here." Rowena sat down again. "Tim is not good."

"He's fine."

"I don't like to say anything."

His eyes were neutral.

"He's confused, Jack. You encourage him to come to your office and do his work. He doesn't like coming to me anymore. Then you cut him off. You're not here."

"We get together once a week or so."

"I'm sure he's too proud to show how it hurts him."

Jack was quiet a minute. "I think I know him pretty well by now. He's cheerful when I see him."

"Yes. He wants you to keep liking him."

"I will."

"He doesn't know that. And it's more than instructional. He needs…"

Jack slapped a hand on his knee. "He needs. What more can I do?"

Rowena stood quickly. "I went too far."

"No." Jack stood also. "It's okay. We're all concerned."

"I sounded critical. Don't…"

"I try with all of them. But I'm not his parent, Rowena. I run things, but I'm not a parent around here."

"Of course not. I said I overstepped."

"I'm not his father."

Rowena shook her head. They were standing close. Jack had to look up to see her face. He touched her arm awkwardly. "Tomorrow morning. Bring coffee."

Jack closed the door after her, glad to have it over. He'd been avoiding Rowena. There was a question in her eyes lately. He was relieved it was only Tim. It could have been about Nina. He thought Rowena had heard them.

Nina. Dear Nina, she couldn't help it. She was giddy seeing him, even when others were around. She told him she had to shove her hands into pockets or grab something to keep from touching him. He liked watching her try. She hung around the school more. Once he'd heard her in the outer office with Irene. "Oh, Mrs. Sawyer, I've been thinking I should take a course or something. How about fourth grade? Do you think they'd let me? I missed so much—never can remember long division." And Irene didn't get it, that she was talking to him, telling him she wanted to be there every day.

He'd called her, laughing. Don't be so obvious. I don't know what else to be. Be subtle. Don't stare at me. I'm watching your hair grow. Is that subtle? Nina, try. Try composure. But he had to admit to himself that it was wonderful to have her so crazy about him.

He walked out of the office one afternoon, and she was there in the lobby waiting for Polly. Am I composed, Jack? Is this how you do it? She was perfectly still but her voice throbbed intimately. He was sure Rowena had noticed. She was behind him entering the teachers' lounge. She must have heard and had given him thoughtful looks ever since.

It was probably her interest in Tim all along. He wanted to call Nina and tell her they were safe and he wasn't so worried. But he didn't want to chance it during school hours. It was too easy for someone to punch in on the line. It was difficult also if Tim was hanging around. Better to send him off to help Brody. He would try calling later and hope her teenager was off the phone. Some days, he sat late in the office, dialing for an hour. It was a letdown to leave work not having heard her voice. It relieved the pressure for him; he could escape into it.

Talking helped but he needed her too. Last month they'd managed twice. Maybe things would get better now. It was almost spring. This morning, standing in that wind, waiting for her to come to the gate with Polly, just to see her, he'd noticed something brown in the wind, of earth and not the gray smell of winter. But it wasn't satisfying somehow. He was like one of those bears awakened too early from hibernation. He was roaring hungry but still a little sleepy too. A dangerous animal. Careless. He would tell Nina. Jack smiled. He liked thinking he was a bear.

"Dad, why is it a lion?"

"Were you outside today? Do I have to explain?"

"I don't associate lions with wind."

"It's just an expression, Bud. Don't you have homework?"

"I did it on the bus."

"That's ridiculous. If you can do it all on the bus, you're not getting enough."

"Jack, butt out." Greta sat across the coffee table from him, folding laundry and matching socks.

"The kid is going to junior high next year. What kind of preparation is ten minutes of homework?"

"Do you want to work with him? Give him assignments?"

"That's what his teachers are supposed to do."

Greta shrugged.

Jack looked around. "Where'd he go?"

"He left when you started yelling."

"I wasn't yelling. I was annoyed." Jack stared at his newspaper. He reached for the amber drink on the table at his side. "Is Sam starting another show?"

Greta squinted at the TV. "I think it's the same one."

"How many hours is that?"

Greta stacked clothes in a basket at her feet. "You're home one evening and all you do is pick on us."

"Don't start on me."

"I didn't say anything."

Chris slumped through the room. They sat quietly and listened to doors slamming in the kitchen. He came back with a glass, a sandwich and a large bag of chips.

"I don't want you eating in your room."

"Sure, Mom." He flopped easily on the sofa beside Greta. She patted his knee.

Jack watched the shape of Chris' mouth chewing. He heard every sound. "Let's see. You ate two meals at dinner and now here's another?"

"So?" Chris answered with his mouth full.

"So you tell me. You going for a record?"

"I was hungry, Dad."

"Doing a lot of heavy studying?"

"I did some. Most of what I had."

"Do it all. Isn't that what you're supposed to do?"

Chris hesitated. "I need help with the rest."

"Well, bring it out here. Let's see it."

Chris shook his head. "I'm gonna ask Mr. Reasoner tomorrow in study hall."

"I'm sure I can..."

"It's math, Dad. Algebra 2 Trig."

Jack rattled and sorted his paper. Chris gulped and swallowed. "We didn't have trig in my high school. You should be grateful you have a choice of subjects instead of complaining about it."

"I wasn't complaining, Dad. I just said..."

"Look. Do your work and everything's okay."

"All *right!*" Chris stormed out.

"Chris!"

"Why are you calling him?"

"I want him to take those dishes to the kitchen."

184

"I'll do it."

"No. It's his responsibility."

"Jack!" Greta moved to a small stool and sat by him. "Jack, it's like you're trying to pick a fight with him."

He finished his drink.

"Was it get-the-principal day?"

"Geez. Everyone's after me. My ass is chewed in twenty places."

"Bad?"

"Maybe not that bad."

"Who?"

He gestured. "Oh … all down the ranks. Jules. Three calls today. He squeezed a hundred bucks out of the trophy shop. Has another list of names for me to call."

Greta shook her head.

"And Rowena…"

Greta turned sideways, distracted. "Can this keep a second?"

"You want to hear my problems or not?"

"Just put it on hold. Okay, Sam. Time to turn it off."

The boy climbed onto Jack's lap, leaving the set on. Jack hugged him, wrinkling his nose. "What stinks?"

"Turpentine," Greta said.

"He get into some paint?"

"Gum in the hair."

Jack nuzzled his son, breathing deeply. "I want to remember this. How easy they are to fix at this age. No trouble. Are you, Sam? No trouble."

Greta took him away. "Bath and shampoo," she said. "Yes!"

Jack rose and turned off the TV. He took his glass to the kitchen, dumped cubes in the sink and started fresh. He opened the front door and closed it again quickly. A small gale was blowing. He turned off most of the lights and stood looking out the window, watching the trees battle the wind. It made him ache. He was so tired. And yet he was tight inside. He wanted the liquor to untie knots in him.

He saw Greta's smoky reflection in the glass. She had put on her white terry robe and large green slippers. The boys had given her the slippers last Christmas, and she wore them loyally, even though they had orange noses on the toes and little eyes that clicked and rolled and looked up at you. She stood behind him and put her hands on his shoulders. He did not turn around. "I'm on hold."

"I had to get Sam done. If he goes too long he gets a second wind."

"If I go too long, I…"

She forced him around. "Jack. Buddy says goodnight." She noticed his drink. "Again?"

"Last one."

"I don't think it's good for you." She squeezed him. "Not good for your waistline."

He batted her hand away. "Lay off, will you?"

He went over to his chair and stretched out, putting his feet on the stool. Greta stood by him a minute, then sat on his lap. He moved a little until he was comfortable.

"Is this okay?"

"Yeah. Fine."

"Now. Tell me everything."

"It's nothing. Just stuff I have to work through. Just work."

"Work is everything to you."

"A pile of shit."

"Jack!"

"Sorry. It's … okay, one thing. This playground. The money is trickling in, but we only have about half. Most parents are behind it. But some have kids that are graduating. Or they're moving, and they don't want to contribute to anything they won't reap the benefit of. So it's slow."

"When do you think you'll be done with it?"

He shook his head.

"A good guess then."

"Maybe into next year."

"Next year? Oh, no, Jack. No!"

"What can I do? There's special insurance. School board approval. It's not an exact science."

"That sounds like Neal."

"He called me today. That's why."

"I don't think I can stand it."

"You can't! What's it to you?"

"You're home late or out evenings. When you are here your mind isn't."

"What do you want from me!"

186

"Keep your voice down." She put her arms around him. His face was crushed on her shoulder. "Let's not fight," she whispered.

"It feels good. I didn't think I had the strength."

Greta giggled. "I bet you have plenty of strength."

Jack shifted. "My leg's asleep."

"I'll get off." She picked up his legs and put them on the floor. Then she sat on the foot stool facing him. "I know I'm heavy on you."

He could see that she was hurt. "No. It's that … that robe or something. It's rough on my face."

She patted his cheeks. "Are you sore? Cut yourself?"

"I was out in the wind today. I guess I'm chapped."

"I'll get lotion."

"No." He took her hand. "No. Hey, don't worry about me. I don't want you to be concerned about me, okay?"

She was quiet, not looking at him.

"I sound like Tim." Jack snorted. "'I don't want people to worry about me, man.'"

"I haven't seen him lately."

"Nah. It was too cozy. I'm lightening up."

"Is that good for him?"

Jack drank and didn't answer.

"He depends on you, Jack."

"He's gotta cut loose sometime. He's out of there next year."

She sighed. "Maybe."

"I give him plenty of time. More than anyone else."

"You mean so much to him."

"Greta, that kid is a survivor. He's going to make it."

"He's little."

"He's tough."

"Don't let him down, Jack."

"I really appreciate this, Greta. I have now heard from everyone on this subject, and I thank you for adding your opinion."

"Everyone?"

"Rowena," he mumbled. "Bitching at me."

"That doesn't sound like…"

"Well, for her it was bitching."

"What does she think?"

"That I let him get too dependent on me."

"That's right."

"Then that's why I need to put a little distance there. Can anybody see that but me?"

"Don't be stubborn about it. Keep an open mind."

He leaned back and closed his eyes. "My mind is shutting down for the night."

"Jack." She grabbed his knee. "Bud was asking about that canoe deal. This summer. Are you still planning to take them?"

"I hadn't thought about it. Sure. Why'd he ask you and not me?"

"Guess."

"I haven't been that crabby."

She didn't answer, but she did smile at him. "I think it will be good for all of you. Sam, I'm not sure."

"I'll watch him."

"I want Chris to be away from those girls."

Jack drank. "Which ones?"

"The ones in the letters. There must be two or three sending them. He gets several a week. And the girls from school call here all the time."

"Girls do that."

"I don't like it. Doesn't it bother you that he's so young and starting this?"

"No."

She stood. "You coming?"

"A minute." He toasted her.

Greta frowned "Don't fall asleep in your chair."

"You can come rescue me."

"I'll be sleeping. I won't notice."

He watched her walk down the hall, her feet clumsy in the slippers. He wanted to see those graceful legs, but they were hidden all winter. He could shout at her, hey, show me your legs. He finished his drink all at once and started to get up. But he sank back in the chair. Everything was quiet in the house, but outside the oceanic wind swept the night. He closed his eyes. If he were on a ship's deck and out at sea, he would be riding and falling with the swells. The wind pounding the windows excited him. The house lifted, rocked and settled again. And inside him also. Maybe he could go into his den and call Nina. Would she answer quickly, the first ring? She was probably awake, thinking about him. Don't call. It's dangerous.

188

He began to feel calm inside. A river, not churning waves. He would move with that river, let the wind blow him downstream. He would rest and let it take him. Don't fight it. The wind outside but he is the river. Keep flowing. Remember that.

And then he did get up and go to his room and undress completely and get in bed with his wife. But she was right. She was asleep and didn't know he was there.

Chapter Thirteen

Can You Last a Summer?

At eleven o'clock in the morning the temperature in the second floor classrooms reached ninety-two degrees. It was the last day of school, and the county's official time for dismissal was noon for students. Teachers were supposed to stay until the scheduled three-thirty closing.

Usually, Jack liked closing day; smiles on all the faces, musical voices and that cheerful explosion like fireworks when they hit the door at dismissal. Today, the heat and humidity had sapped them. He half expected them to limp away.

A small fan worked along with the feeble air conditioning in his office. Papers covered his desk. He'd placed weights on various piles so the fan's faint breeze would not float and mix them together. He wished he could bury them all under one giant rock. Just get to the bottom, get them all into their proper folders, cubbyholes, boxes. *Work your way through the paper. It's almost over.*

Jack went to the outer office and turned on the PA. "This is the final announcement of the year, students. I know how much you miss me during the lonely days of summer vacation." He smiled at the cheering, laughter, and loud booing. "I know your teachers have supplied you with lists of books to read and suggestions for scientific experiments.

They want you to keep a journal if you go on a trip and do a work-book of math problems. You're supposed to learn a new sport or start a new collection. Spend time in the library. All that is good. It helps you grow—not that you need help with that!" He paused. "I want you to do one more thing. Every day I want you to go to your room or go outside and do nothing. Just lie on your back or sit under a tree and do nothing. Try not to think about anything. Do it for at least fifteen minutes. And if your mom or someone asks what you're doing, say it's an assignment for Mr. Bridges. Everybody got that? Okay!

"And, teachers, this is for you. County regulations allow me to release personnel when temperatures reach an abusive level. I think we passed that point an hour ago. Most of you have turned in your classroom inventories and book lists. For those of you who have further work, the building will open at eight tomorrow. I urge you to leave this punishing heat and get a head start on your summer break." He pushed the off button and turned to Irene. "Was that a popular announcement?"

"Very."

"Unfortunately, I need you here."

"Well, of course."

"I've got to do that PE inventory for Selma and the accounts are…"

"I know."

"Was there something?"

"I was going to ask … some of us are going to lunch and…"

Jack looked at her perspiring face. "Go. Go somewhere cool. You and I can finish up tomorrow and Friday. We'll get more done in less time."

"I can stay."

"Listen, it's fine." He waved his hand, dismissing her protests, looked at the clock. "In five minutes, start the countdown."

On the final day, instead of an orderly dismissal, Irene got on the PA and shouted, "Let's do it, kids!" And the whole school chanted, "Ten… nine…eight…seven…" until they blasted into the hallways and down the stairs, a joyous force scattering papers, carrying leftover social studies projects, plants, animal cages, tearing open report card envelopes and the teachers all the while calling, "Walk, people! Remember to walk! Slow down!"

Many of the teachers and Jack also gathered in front to wave and shout goodbye as the buses rolled away with kids hanging out the windows, the teachers calling, "Keep your hands in! Hands inside!" Then they all hugged one another in spite of the heat because it was over, and they were grateful to be leaving, grateful Jack had let them out, too.

"Come with us. Come out to lunch," they urged him.

He declined, saying he had work, he had calls to make. He went back to his office and left the door open for anyone to stop by on the way out. He felt good. He'd made them happy with this early release. And they all vacated, even the daycare group. He was pleased that Lorimae, every year, planned a picnic and trip to a pool on the last day, so her kids weren't left behind but rode off with everyone else. For a while heels clicked or squished along the halls, doors slammed, voices called back and forth. Then it was quiet, the fans turned off, and all the cars gone from the lot.

Good. He had managed a nice upbeat order to end the year.

The phone rang. The administration office had not received an essential report on numbers. He'd have it there in the morning. Another call from a parent. They were moving, and she wanted to know if she could pick up her child's records. Have the new school make a request and we'll send them. Thank you, Mr. Bridges. We hate to leave you. We hate to have you go. We'll miss Chip.

Jack wandered the littered hall and upstairs, checking doors, all properly locked. He wanted Brody to start sweeping, but Brody was gone. Jack hadn't meant to include him in the de-staff announcement. Perhaps he would return after lunch. Jack stirred a foot through an arrangement of loose-leaf and construction paper. He didn't care. He didn't want to engage in conversation or make a decision.

He walked downstairs, pausing on the landing to look out at the playground. It was the same, nothing changed. Jack closed his eyes, trying to picture the plan. It was gone. Last week Jules had come and taken the model from the lobby to store it over the summer. They would try again in the fall to raise the rest of the money. They'd stalled at two-thirds the amount needed, and the PTA was somewhat splintered over this issue. Some people wanted to abandon the playground since it proved unpopular and spend the money on computers. Others were adamant about keeping to the original goal. Jack wanted nothing more than never to hear about it again, but this was not possible. He owned this mistake. But he would give it a rest. He would not think about it all summer. Put it on the list of things he would not think about.

Jack grabbed a diet soda in the faculty lounge. It was tepid. He slapped the machine. He left the can on the table. The office phone was ringing. Finances. He hadn't sent in the final report. What is this? Do you guys have any idea what it's like, an actual closing with little bodies around? He dropped the phone. Why did everyone sound so hostile?

Was he the one? Like with Buddy. Could we drop this, Bud? Why are we arguing? Well, you started it, Dad. Was it all his fault? Did he start that business with Tim?

Enid Lacey had come to him in May saying she had to retain Timoko Wells. Jack had not seen it coming. "If this was a possibility, Enid, you should have let me know before now. The kid has to be informed early so he has a chance to make up the work."

Enid spread her large comfortable self in the chair. "Mr. Bridges, I have been teaching for eighteen years. In all that time I have retained only two children. I have never retained a child in sixth grade and prevented him from graduating."

Jack had started to speak but Enid held the floor. "I have thought about this deeply. I even asked my mother for an opinion."

Jack smiled. He had met Enid's mother, a retired teacher after thirty-five years in the system. Perky and bright, he wished he had her on staff. "This is serious business, Enid."

"I realize that. As far as I'm concerned, this boy has failed to turn in enough work or complete the number of assignments to pass the grade. He just hasn't done the work."

"What about giving him extra credit?"

Enid rolled her eyes. "I do not believe in extra credit."

"His ability tests put him at ninth grade."

Enid snorted. "Then why have class? We'll give them all tests and let them move on. Those *tests* say nothing of day-to-day achievement."

Jack thought. "All right. I'll set up the committee, and we'll go over the data. I'll inform the, uh, parent and the area psychologist who's worked with him. We'll have to meet right away."

"I'm ready."

"It's a terrible emotional blow to fail a child, Enid. I don't like to do it. Their friends are so hard on them."

"In all fairness, it is difficult for an entire class to see a boy fritter away the whole year and yet pass the same as everyone. I have some students who struggle for Ds."

"I see your point, Enid. Perhaps if you worked with him."

"I have worked and worked with him, Mr. Bridges."

He didn't want it to happen but he was caught in the process. After that chat with Enid, the committee met three times. Tim's stepmother was indifferent and Jack, patience depleted, became angry. Do you *want* him to fail? And she, drifting away: Do what you have to.

Jack wrote the letter and signed it. Timoko Wells would repeat sixth grade at Great Forest. As compensation, he brought Tim home for dinner, and Greta had been so nice. It surprised him, how nice she was. Later, driving Tim home, the boy said, "Buddy told me about that trip you're doing."

"Which one is that?"

"The one in canoes."

"Yeah. He told you, huh?"

"Could I go too?"

Jack turned to Tim who stared straight ahead. The kid was wearing shorts and rubber sandals. His hair was long in back and dropped in bangs in front of his eyes. He looked very small and hard. Jack rested a hand on Tim's head as he drove. "Did Bud tell you where we have to go for this?"

"Uh-huh."

"Did he ask you to go?"

"Just told me about it."

"Tim. Hey, Tim. What do you do in the summer?"

"Nothing. I hang around. Watch TV."

"See, in the summer is when I spend time with my family. The boys, they don't see much of me sometimes. They kind of look forward..."

"I wouldn't make trouble."

"No. Not that. Of course you're no trouble. But it's a long time." Jack waved an arm. "It's for a month—at least. Your mother probably..."

"Please take me."

Jack pulled up in front of Tim's house. Daylight was almost gone. There was no car in the drive. "Anyone at home?"

Tim shrugged. "I have a key."

"Tim..."

"*Please* take me with you!" The eyes naked and dark, the body earnest and begging, hands folded on his knees. "I'm no trouble, man!"

"Tim, I know this has been a rough year for you. Mrs. Lacey..."

194

"I don't give a shit about that stuff. Damn Mrs. Lacey!" He opened the door and left it hanging while he ran toward the house. Jack slid out and followed him. He tried to grab Tim, but the boy jerked away giving Jack's arm an angry lashing. "Don't touch me! You got no right to touch me!"

"I was trying to hug you. I'd never hurt you, Tim. You know that."

The boy stared down, his slight body rigid yet trembling.

"Listen. I want you and me to be friends," Jack coaxed him.

"Sure."

"Will you look at me?"

Tim shot his eyes up and then down again.

"You going to be okay?"

"Sure. Why not?"

"I'll talk to you tomorrow. You come and see me every day."

Jack had waited for Tim to go in the house but he wouldn't. Finally, Jack had left him there. He drove a block and then turned and cruised slowly by the house. It was dark. Tim's house was the only one without lights, but Jack could see him sitting hunched over on the steps. He knocked on the horn twice, a friendly signal, but Tim never raised his head.

At home, Greta said, "I think he tried to fail. He did it on purpose."

"Why?"

"To hang on. So he wouldn't have to go. It's familiar."

"It's sad he's smart enough to put all that together."

"Yes."

"He needs help—more than any of our people can give him."

"You're talking about professional help? Would the mother pay for it?"

Jack shook his head. "Never."

"So what will you do?"

"I'm fresh out of suggestions."

"There must be something."

He looked past her. "I'll put it away and see if an idea comes up and bites me."

"You don't have to get rude."

"Sorry. I'll come up with a recommendation. No one has to take my advice. But there's only so much ... I can only go so far with a kid."

Tim had stopped by every day. He had not mentioned the canoe trip again. Jack didn't think it was forgotten, but he was glad not to talk about it anymore. He was trying to figure out how he could stand the summer, not seeing or talking to Nina. They'd agreed they wouldn't until August again. They had none of that busy camouflage now, the schedule of activities they hid in. And he must go away. The minutes and days of separation already seemed long. He had counted them.

He thought about it all the time. If they were smart, if *he* were, they'd use the time to forget each other, to do without. He'd never breathed the idea to her. He wanted everything to go on and be the same and never change. But the only way to keep it the same was to stop. Then he would be safe. He was very close to losing control of it. He felt the danger of it, either way. They must stop but not yet, not this summer. It was crazy and he thought about her all the time.

Jack wiped sweat on his sleeve. The equipment room was windowless and airless. He should have brought a fan but now was so close to finishing it wasn't worth it to stop and drag one in. He shoved the vaulting horse into a corner and draped it with a plastic cover. He pushed rolling barrels of basketballs in front of it. Soccer balls and red rubber kick balls were bagged in huge cocoons of webbing. Coiled jump ropes hung on the wall. Jack flipped pages over the clipboard. Some stuff missing but not much. He'd have Brody check classrooms when he did the final cleaning.

Jack cleared a space for the crash mats. The first one he examined had a large tear on the underside; dried foam crumbs sifted onto his hand. He dragged it out to the gymnasium. Any intact or properly taped pads he left in storage, but all those needing repair he wrestled into a stack against the gym wall. His hands left damp prints when he lifted them from the mats, but he liked the heavy work. When he finished, the pile was three feet high, and he sat down on it. It was cooler in the large room and he enjoyed the quiet.

"Jack? Hi!"

"Nina." He smiled.

She walked toward him hesitantly. She was carrying a loose bundle. "It's ghostly out there."

"Yeah. I let them all go. It's about a hundred upstairs by now."

"How long have you been in here?"

"What time is it?"

"Two-thirty."

"About an hour and a half." He stood up. "How'd you get in?"

"The front was locked so I came around back. I saw the Jeep."

He took everything from her arms. "What's this?"

"The lost and found box in the lobby. That's what I came over for anyway. To get all the stuff Polly leaves behind. Look." She held up a green windbreaker. "From two years ago. I thought it was gone forever, and now here it is and she's outgrown it."

"Nasty of her. Growing."

"Hi." She smiled.

"Were you looking for me?"

"I'm always looking for you."

"You ... I'm glad you..." She was so clean, not a touch of makeup. She wore white sneakers and white socks rolled into fat cuffs. Her blouse was white with short sleeves and a little round collar. She had on navy blue shorts, and her arms were brown and her legs, too, and so smooth they were shiny. She seemed about ten years old. "You look like you're going to camp."

She leaned toward him. "Kiss me goodbye."

"Better not get too close. I'm so dusty and sweaty."

She hugged him. "Are we really all alone here?"

"Nina. Not here, Nina." He pulled her down, and they sat together on the crash mats, dangling their legs over the side. "I'm beat. Missed lunch."

"Why are you doing this?" She squirmed back and sat cross-legged.

He made a face. "Selma Jean sprained her wrist at field day. I'm just helping her out."

She inched toward him. She put her hand on his chest.

"I'm so warm." He stroked her hair and neck and under her chin. "I was sitting in my office after everyone was gone. I was thinking..."

"About me, I hope."

He kissed her and didn't say anything.

"Jack..."

"Nina. Nina. I keep thinking—could I give you up? If we didn't..."

She jerked away and jumped to the floor. "Is there some reason you're saying that?"

"Don't be scared. I didn't mean to scare you. I meant ... I guess I meant that I scare myself when I think of it."

She melted onto him. "I don't care if you are warm." She put her arms around him. "I don't care if you boil. Don't say that. Listen to my heart bumping. Don't say that. We don't have to decide anything. Nothing has to change." She put her hands flat on his back, pressed him to her. "I'll never ask you for a thing. Hold me. I'm still scared."

He held her fiercely. "Sometimes I want to say everything I'm thinking. Geez, if I've ruined this."

"No. Never." She rubbed his back soothingly. "God, you are tense."

"This has not been a five-star week."

She pushed him back. She lifted his legs and made him lie down full length on the mats then crawled around him, placing his hands across his chest.

"What are you doing? Preparing me for burial?"

"That's not funny." She slapped his thigh. "Going to massage you."

"Sure you are."

"It's not like that. This is therapeutic. I'm going to loosen your belt. Here. Now help me get your shoes off. Release your foot."

He lay like a lazy patient, amused. She was brisk and clinical. "Should I roll over?"

"Not at first. We start with you on your back." She patted him.

"I need to drop a few pounds."

"You look fine. Now relax. You can close your eyes if you like."

"Not a chance. I want to see all of this."

She positioned herself on her knees behind his head. She reached her arms under his shoulder blades and began to stroke toward his neck. Almost at once, he breathed in a more relaxed rhythm. Her hands were small but strong.

"Does it feel like floating? It should start out that way."

"Yes."

"Good. We're on the right track."

She worked. "I won't ask you questions. It's better if you don't talk. Not the slightest effort."

"What if I get aroused? How will I let you know?"

"You won't. You absolutely won't." She massaged the back of his neck lightly and then his head began to float. "I couldn't anyway. It's the wrong time."

198

He loved these shared intimacies. She planned for him. He wanted to say is it very bad, how are you, but his tongue seemed to be asleep. She kneaded his shoulders and rested a fist on some spot near his collar bone. He didn't know why but it felt terrific, that gentle pressure. She moved to his right side and began working on his upper arm. His arm rested on her knees. He had lost the ability to raise it himself. She massaged each finger slowly, carefully then placed the arm at his side. It lay limp, palm up, not a part of him. She was taking him apart. Each limb she worked on seemed to separate from his body. He was in pieces. Wonderful.

She talked softly. "I'm going to do the other side now. Just relax. You're being so good. So good." When she finished his left arm, she spread his legs into a vee and knelt between them, stroking his torso along the sides. Not pounding, not slapping, just the continuous circular motion, pulling something out of him. He could hear her panting and felt her warmth.

She did his legs, each in turn, just the tops and sides. All around his knees until they felt soupy. He couldn't remember anyone really touching his knees. And then his feet. She pulled off his socks and did each toe, pulling it, shaking it, taking everything away, all the people, the voices.

"Can you roll over now?"

She helped him, turned his cheek to the mat and put something soft under his face so he wouldn't feel the plastic. And she started again, the back of his neck and his shoulders, leaning up and pressing harder this time. She worked on muscles, her fingers searching, walking along his back until she found the right spot. Each knob along his spine, the small of his back. Wonderful there. Warm but never too warm. And each rear cheek, round and round. The backs of his thighs. She stroked with her fists and then pummeled him lightly. His body slowly became whole again. He was aware of his blood circulating. She was right. There was no sex in this. No thought. His feet. The bottoms of his feet. He floated, complete and weightless into nothing.

Nina slid his leg off her lap. "Jack," she whispered. She ran a fingernail across the sole of his bare foot. He didn't move. She smiled.

In slow motion, she rose from the mat. She stood a minute, looking at his sleeping face, flexing her hands. Then she walked quietly out of the gym, down the deserted hall and across the playground, so hot and still.

She was wearing the sun. It was nice to duck into her cool house. Suitor lay on the wood floor and raised his head to greet her.

"That's okay, baby. Don't get up." She filled his water dish.

Nina looked at the clock. She had to pick up the girls from the pool at five. She rotated her shoulders and stretched. Her arms were a little sore, but she didn't mind because she had liked doing it, and this made her remember how nice it was. Upstairs, she did a few things to make herself fresher.

In the kitchen again, she removed jars and containers and set them on the counter. On the breadboard, she placed a loaf of oversized whole wheat. She sliced two pieces, each one three-eighths inch thick, with a practiced eye and a sharp knife. She spread them with mayonnaise, evenly to the edges and placed lettuce leaves on one, dark ruffled leaves from her garden that would peek out of the sandwich. Then she piled shavings of crisp head lettuce all over the leaves, a light yellowy green bed. Quickly she overlapped slices of ham and thin, lacy Swiss cheese. She made it very tall. She dabbed a taste of hot mustard on the top slice of bread, then cut the sandwich in half, diagonally, being careful not to flatten it. She stuck a toothpick through each triangle, one with an olive and one stabbing a sweet gherkin. She put this on a plate along with three sections of an orange.

Nina pulled two bottles of cold German beer from the refrigerator. Tom had brought it home ages ago. She put them into a squashy vinyl insulated pouch Tom had picked up in Scandinavia. She draped a cloth napkin over the plate and walked back to the school. She didn't look around to the other yards. *I'm invisible. No one can see me.*

She found him still asleep. He had rolled onto his back, one arm across his chest and the other curving over his head as if he was holding it on.

Nina sat on the floor watching him. His expression was calm and serious, as though this sleeping business was important, and he must do it correctly. She was quiet and wanted him to sleep for a long time. His eyelids fluttered and opened. He stared blankly at the ceiling then scrubbed his hands all over his face like a little boy. Then the smile. She could bathe in that smile. "Hi. Have you been here all along?" The voice husky.

She offered him the plate. "I thought you might..."

"Sweet!"

They sat on the mats, their backs against the wall. She opened the beer, watching him eat. He ate the oranges first. "This is the most beautiful ham sandwich I've ever seen. It should be in a museum."

"I like the way you hold it."

His eyes questioned her.

"With respect."

"I love drinking beer in a green bottle but I never do."

"I'm glad you are now."

He talked with his mouth full. "How long was I asleep?"

"Half an hour."

"Felt like a year."

"It's supposed to."

"Where'd you learn that?"

"My mother had to be in a rest home. They were nice but just didn't have enough staff for all the ... you know. She was so sore from lying there. A physical therapist taught me."

"You have a career." He patted her hand.

She giggled. "There's more to it than that, I hope."

"I could get up and tap dance."

"Do."

"I don't know how."

"I love to dance."

"I'll take you. I will."

Her expression changed. A faint sadness. "Do you want the other one?" She pointed to the silver pouch.

"In a minute." He took her hand. "I like this. I like it when you're such a pal to me."

"I wish you'd tell me everything in your life."

He said nothing. *I can't tell you everything.* He traced a line along her eyebrow, down her cheek and around her ear. He did it over and over. She had tiny gold dots in her ears. *Just you and me. Nothing else. The only way I can keep you. Nothing else can come in.*

"Think about how lucky we are."

"I do." Nina hesitated. "I won't see you again after this, will I?"

"No. Not for a while."

"When are you leaving?"

"The boys and I..."

"No, don't tell me." She put a finger on his lips and then kissed him.

"I love to kiss you when you've been drinking beer. You're so sweet."

"Nina ... somebody might…"

"No one can see us. I looked through the window when I came back and you can't see along this wall."

"Still…" He jogged over to the double doors and pulled them tightly shut. Then he yanked up the handle bar door lock. "That's better." He flopped back on the mat. "I always think someone's watching me."

"You're getting cautious."

"Don't make fun of me. Sometimes I want to get caught. A real mess, you know? Then I'd have to make a move, decide…" He was shaking his head. "This way I don't, I mean, it's all up to me. If I want it to change."

"Shh. You're getting all tense again. Don't." Nina knelt between his legs, hugging him. "You don't have to do anything. No one's asking you for anything."

"You're right. This is good. I'm going to kiss my girl and neck and not worry." He was filled with the mystery of her, how she could make everything go into place. He sat as close to her as he could without sitting on her. "Does any of this bother you?" he murmured.

"Only that I don't have enough of you." She nuzzled him. "Such a waste. This is so close to a real bed."

"Don't talk about it."

"Why?"

"Because you can't. You said."

"Mm." She unbuttoned his shirt and kissed his chest. "Lie back," she whispered. Her hands moved swiftly, spreading his shirt open, loosening his trousers. "Let me look at you. I never get to look at you."

"Don't do this to me." He felt exposed, uncomfortable. He wasn't even aroused, wasn't letting himself. Instinctively, he tried to cover himself.

"No. Don't take it away."

She leaned over him, kissing him. She put a hand on his forehead, stared into his eyes. Her eyes were sad, mysterious, pleading. He couldn't understand her. He kissed and kissed her. "What can I give you?" His voice sounded muffled and far away.

She put her mouth on his ear. "Let me have you. Just be mine. Be in my kingdom."

She placed her hands on his chest, different hands now, not impersonal and healing. She caressed him, allowing her fingers to drag slowly, insinuatingly. "You are so clean," she said. "I like it that you have light body hair." Her hand trailed the line of his belly. "I need to see you."

She pulled his khakis down to his thighs, running her hands smoothly on his hips. He raised his buttocks to help her. "Thank you," she said. She didn't touch him at first. It was so nice to see. The hair silky and not too dark, growing in and down and toward his member in reaching, curling tufts. So neat. As though it had been swept. She made him open his legs a little.

She sat cross-legged on his left side. Jack saw her arm move across his groin and felt his testicles cupped in her hand. Her hair fell on the side of her face.

"Look at me, Nina."

She turned, smiling. "They like the nest I put them in."

"What are you doing?"

"I like your body, that's all." She stroked his penis, a non-color now, almost gray, pointing modestly down. She liked holding these soft organs. "You were never circumcised." She seemed to be talking to herself, and he didn't answer. She smiled sweetly at him and then back at her hands. "So covered up and ... shy."

Jack stretched. He was always the aggressor. This was different. Passive now, he didn't know what to do. He knew he was pleasing her. "Do you want me to get aroused? Would you like that?"

She nodded.

He leaned up on his elbows. "We'll both watch."

She framed her fingers around the dusky triangle. When he began to fill and rise, she stripped back the foreskin to help him emerge. He could do it fast. He had always liked how fast he could get it up. He made it move to see if that would make her happy. "Is it enough?"

She laughed. "This is what feels so good." She circled her thumb and middle fingers, but they wouldn't close around him. "In me. So thick."

A drop appeared at the tip. She touched it and brought the pearled effluence to his lips, glistening them. She bent over him. Jack lay back and closed his eyes. He would do nothing. He was free. There was only that one part of him that she wanted. There was nothing on his body, and he was falling but so hot and swimming in a hot sea, not friendly, making him hurt, trying to get air and being thrown against rock, bruising stone, then the soapy white foam of a gentle wave carrying him, bringing him to rest on soft, warm sand. He opened his eyes.

He was curled on his side. Nina was sitting against the wall, her head thrown back. Her knees were drawn up, and her eyes were closed. Jack reached a hand over and grabbed her ankle, shaking it, growling.

She smiled. "I thought you might sleep."

"I slept enough." He rolled on his back and made a noise that sounded like purring and ended in laughter. He shouted with laughter. "Damn! Damn!" He stood and hopped, squishing the mats while he pulled his clothes together. He pawed into the bag and twisted open the remaining beer, drinking thirstily.

He hunkered down beside Nina. She opened one button of her blouse and fanned herself. He brushed her damp hair away from her face. "I must do something for you."

"You just did."

He offered her the beer, but she kissed the mouth of the green bottle and pushed it back to him. "I don't want to ... dilute what's in me."

He thrilled when she spoke, satisfaction on her lovely face. She rested, feeling him inside her, becoming part of her that would not go away. She closed her eyes and took his hand, kissing his fingers then moving down, holding his hand against her breast, her body flooding womanhood and love.

"Beautiful man," she whispered.

He sat very close, not leaving an inch between them. He cared about nothing but her.

"Must go," she murmured.

Angry, proud, sad thoughts invaded him. Everything confused. He gathered her things and stuffed them in the vinyl sack. They walked across the floor silently, along the foul lines of the basketball court. Jack kicked open the door with his knee. "I think we got away with it." He kept his arm around her all the way down the silent hallway. In the lobby, he stopped before opening the outside door and said, "I'm still holding you. Remember."

They took the short route, through the play equipment. "I'm sorry it didn't work out, Jack."

"Next year."

"Maybe you were right. The kids should have a freer place. Fewer restrictions."

204

"We'll get it done, Nina."

"I know you will."

"I'm not turning back with over half the money raised." They passed beyond the play yard to the open field.

"Don't talk about it."

The heat was desert-like and punishing. Jack thought he would explode, wished he would. It was an effort to walk, like moving awkwardly on stilts. He forced himself not to touch her. He wanted them to be somewhere green and cool, where he could say some things, calm down and get it right. It was too hot to think and everything in his head was too red or too white to see clearly. He was glad he was holding the silver bag and the child's clothing, because it soothed him to be touching something of Nina's. He didn't know they had reached her gate until he heard her say, "I'd better not invite you in."

"Oh, no. I wouldn't anyway." He hooked the bag over her shoulder and the jacket over the fence.

"I hate this, Jack." She shaded her eyes. "You know how I want to say goodbye and this isn't it."

He moved around so his body made a shadow on her face. "I'm going to figure out a plan for us." He laughed a little, his voice catching. "How much of me can you take?"

"Nina was quiet. "I'm not asking..."

"No! I am. I'm asking, Nina." And he was. He knew what he wanted, if not how to get it. He sounded stronger and his voice deeper, pushing. "If I can think how to do it."

She didn't answer. He felt dizzy, as though he might pass out.

God, this is crude. The wrong way, confusing to her. She'll get scared and back off, think you're doing this because you got laid. No. There's no part of anything you want that's not her. It's not worth it, any of it, without Nina.

"I'm not leaning on you. Forget what I..."

"Jack." She whispered his name. "Jack." She held her hand on her throat. Her eyes were clear, direct, not as dazed as his were but then she wasn't looking into the sun. "I'd do anything. Anything."

"We're lucky, Nina. You said we have that." He wanted to take her hands and jump up and down. "Can you last a summer?"

"Much longer."

"I have to do this thing with the boys."

"Yes."

"I don't want anything to spoil that."

"No."

"Think about kissing me."

"I am right now."

"Keep thinking about it. I'll call you. I'll call you every day before I go."

"I'll be here."

"And when I get back…"

"I'll still be here."

He looked and looked at her." It's true. All of it."

She backed into her yard and pulled long stalks of snapdragons and daisies and columbine to make a spindly, frothy bouquet. "Take them." She shoved them into his hand. "Go away before I give you every flower." She ran into the house, and he saw her dark shadow moving through the interior.

He walked slowly. He was not frightened by any of it. He would never be frightened again. He was almost back to the school when he looked down and saw the shattered blossoms. With every step he had slapped the loose bunch against his thigh. and they had come apart. He was sorry he had destroyed Nina's flowers, but he couldn't help it. You could gather more flowers. He had broken them simply because he was happy. He was so happy, and he had to do something foolish and hard and definite.

Chapter Fourteen

I Was So Scared

"Dad. What are we doing today? Dad!"

Jack nearly spilled off the couch. His legs were twisted in a scratchy plaid blanket, and his feet were hot. He heard the rain washing over the roof, a steady flow in the downspout, splashing onto a pile of rocks outside where it ran away from the house. It was the fourth morning of rain.

"What time is it?"

"Seven-thirty."

"Go back to bed."

"But I'm already up."

"Look out the window. Can you see the lake?"

"No. It's all streaky."

"Where's Sam?"

"Sleeping."

"Then forget it." Jack rolled over, pulling the blanket off his feet and over his head.

"Dad."

"Later, Bud. I mean it."

"This is no fun."

"Pretend you're living under a waterfall. Then it's more fun."

"How long is it going to rain?" Jack did not answer. "If it rains all day, are we just going to do nothing again?"

"I'm asking you to shut up, Bud."

Jack heard a deep sigh of disgust and frustration. *Join the club.* Buddy crossed the floor and climbed the ladder. The older boys were sleeping in bags on air mattresses in the loft. Sam was in Samuel's old room. They hadn't started out this way.

The first day had been fine, a perfect Michigan day. They set up the camp, built a fire, and made plans for the canoe trip. Sammy stood under the blade mark from last summer. Jack said, "Stand on your toes. How about that, you made it!" They crawled into the tents under stars and crawled out in the morning under a sky dirty and pale. "Something's passing through," Jack said. They went into Bear, bought supplies for the trip and a poncho for each of them. When the rain began he said, "Let's tough it out. If this is the worst thing that happens, so what? Don't let it spoil the fun. Are we men or what?"

They slept in the tents, water pouring down the sides. Don't touch the nylon. They won't leak if you don't touch them. Try telling Sam. Or Chris, with his long wacky limbs. This stinks, Dad. It isn't working. Everything wet.

The next day they moved into the house. This front sure is persistent. Let's hang in there. They set up the small stove on the back porch. The house had not improved with vacancy. Yesterday, Jack had called about getting the plumbing working again. No one was starving, but they could all use a shower. The boys hated to bring in water, never carried enough, and were soaked doing it. Clothes and gear were everywhere, drying. Jack had them haul in wood, and that, too, was stacked to dry in teepee formations. Last night they had a fire, and the wood smoked and hissed. No one stayed up late.

Except Jack. He sat a long time, lifting and stirring logs, keeping it going. A bottle stood on the hearth, and when the boys were asleep he poured some in his mug from time to time, sipping. Later, he hadn't bothered, drinking straight from the bottle. He needed strength if he was going to do it. And he would.

He would have her. She would be wonderful.

You just have to get over the bad time and the hurt and the rearranging. Find out what the laws are. What do I want, if it were only my choice? I want Nina. For a long time just her. Her kids, of course. Greta will never give me Sam or Chris. Maybe Buddy. But would Buddy want that? The kid finally likes his school. I like the house, but Greta should have that, be generous. Great Forest. There'll be bad feeling. Loss of face. People will hate it; think we've been fooling around. We have. Hell with it, I'll go. Leave teaching. Damn problems all the time. Make a change.

I'll take over Bridges and Bird. Mitchell can go. Leave the name, what the hell. Or keep Mitchell and move him out gradually. He'll go for it. He'll have to. Move back up here for good. Nina here. He couldn't stand it. They'd be so happy. Sometimes she was the only person he wanted to be with. Like right now. Keep a picture of the two of us. She'll love it, I think. I know. And the girls. But the older one, her music. Nothing like that around here. Nowhere to study. She'd have to stay with the father. And then it would be Jack, Nina, Polly, and Buddy. I always wanted a daughter. I'll teach her to row a boat. And I'll go to work in jeans. Sell rope and hammers. A challenge. Learn the prices of everything. A clean business. Know your inventory and when to restock. And once it leaves the store you don't have to worry about it. You read your success on a piece of paper at the bottom right corner at the end of a column of figures.

Jack opened his eyes. He hadn't banked the fire last night or put the screen back over the grate. Careless. He vaguely remembered lumbering to the couch and falling down fully dressed. He felt on the floor, and the bottle rolled when he touched it. He knew he'd had a lot, but he couldn't remember killing it. He hauled it up and set it on his chest, rubbing his eyes and staring at it. Definitely empty.

Coughing, trying to clear his throat, he rose and stretched his cramped muscles. He could smell himself, and it was bad. He walked toward the kitchen carefully, feeling dizzy and mad at himself. Soft footsteps behind him. "Is it okay to come down now?"

"Yes, Bud."

"I was listening for you." Buddy picked up the bottle Jack had set on the counter.

"We call that a dead soldier."

"I don't get it."

"Throw it in the trash for me."

Buddy stood at the bag in the corner, held the bottle high over his head then dropped it like a bomb. He smiled at the splintering crash when it hit the empty peanut butter jar. "Bullseye."

Jack held his head. "Bud," he croaked. "Be a good kid and fill the bucket."

"It's not my turn."

"C'mon. I need to wash up, and there's no water. None for coffee even."

"I've already been out once to pee."

"You went to the latrine?"

"No. I did it off the porch."

"Then it doesn't count."

"Dad!"

"Bud, if you don't do this one of us is going to die. Now!" Jack winced, talking.

Buddy stomped onto the back porch, pulled a poncho off the pile, picked up the bucket and left, slamming the screen door. Jack looked at his watch. Eight-fifteen. He wanted to be far away from here. Sam staggered into the room and jumped onto Jack.

"Hey! Not ready for you, kid." The boy curled his legs around Jack's waist and rested his head on Jack's shoulder. Holding him with one arm, Jack poked in the supplies. He opened the cooler. The milk was still good. Sam was not so baby-soft now, and Jack felt how hard and bony he was. He rubbed his cheek on Sam's but the boy pulled away. "That's okay. I know it scratches." He smoothed the pink skin with his knuckles. "You hungry, tough guy? Ready to eat?"

Buddy dragged the bucket in with both hands, water splashing and dripping all over the floor from his poncho.

"Couldn't you take that off outside?" Jack hated how testy he sounded. Buddy had set the pail on his foot.

"It was heavy and I didn't want to stop."

"Well, go shake it on the porch."

"God! I'm just doing what you said! God!"

"Watch it."

"You watch it!"

Jack took a step toward him then said softly, "Watch your mouth, Bud." He rattled boxes. "We have a little of this, a little of that."

"I'm not hungry."

"Dry off then see how you feel." Jack didn't look at him.

Chris leaned in the doorway, in sweatpants with feet and chest bare. He stretched. His face wore a distant waking expression. Jack thought he looked clean and handsome. This irked him. "I could use some help. Why don't you light the stove?"

210

"I need a shirt. All mine are damp."

"I think there's one of mine hanging on a chair someplace."

Chris didn't move.

"Go on. It's okay."

"I can't wear yours anymore, Dad. They're tight across the back."

Jack stared at him a full minute. *And too tight across my stomach.* "Try your granddad's closet. There's stuff in there."

Chris returned wearing a soft chamois shirt the color of caramels. He was patting his chest and flexing his shoulders. "Can I keep it?"

"Sure."

"It's cold again."

"It'll warm up."

"Didn't yesterday."

"What kind of cereal do you want?"

"Is that all we have?"

Jack didn't answer.

"I don't like cold food on a cold day."

"I'm making coffee."

"I don't do caffeine."

"You're on your own, guys." Jack dipped a pan of water, stepped onto the porch, and lit the stove. The woods looked dreary and uninviting; gulleys all along the driveway and pebbles washing away. The Jeep had made ugly tracks where he'd driven in the mud yesterday and spun the tires hard. He didn't have to, but he'd felt like it. The water boiled. He made coffee and felt slightly better. *It's not the weather, it's the company. If it were like this and I had Nina, it would be okay. I wouldn't care.* The boys came out and sat on boxes next to him. Sam made a poncho tent and crawled under.

"What is it? You took a vote, and we have to be in the smallest possible space all together all the time?"

"There's nothing to do, Dad." Buddy shrugged.

"Are we doing anything today, Dad?"

Buddy already asked me that, Chris."

"Well, are we?"

"You got any ideas?"

"Can I get out the old Jeep and drive?"

"It won't start."

"Can't someone come out and do it?"

"Mack will when he gets time."

Chris sighed. "Everyone's working. Even Julie's got a job."

"The kids around here usually do that. Have you maybe thought…?"

"It's so boring. The only reason I came was for the canoe trip."

"We're going."

"But *when?*"

Jack gestured to the outdoors. "You tell me."

"I'm sick of this place. I don't want to be cooped up here."

"It's called cabin fever."

"Are you having a good time, Dad?"

"Not the way you guys are acting."

"It's not my fault."

"You're right, Bud. It's bad luck, bad timing." Jack finished his coffee. "Let's clean up the place then go into town. Get a weather report, have lunch." The boys didn't move. Jack clapped his hands. "Let's go! The sooner we finish, the sooner we…"

"What? The sooner we what?" Chris said.

"We get out of here." Jack looked at his watch. Nine thirty-five. The day was already a rainy week long.

Jack stared out the picture window. The porch overhang protected this one so you could see something besides a sheet of running water. The pine trees, branches dark green and heavy, seemed every day to stoop lower, waterlogged, to the ground. Trails of water ran down the path to the beach. He saw bits of the lake, its charcoal gray surface the texture of steel wool. Forbidding, but at least you could see it now. Four o'clock in the afternoon. The sky showed faint patterns of clouds, white on gray or mud, like smoke drifting in the wind.

"I think it's breaking up. A new front pushing out the low."

"You said that two days ago."

"Come look, Bud."

"The weather report said no change."

"You think those guys know more than I do? Don't answer that."

"We should have stayed in Bear."

"What for?"

"We could've stayed at Thunder's. Watched TV."

"We'd had enough. Place was nothing but summer people. People with nothing to do in the rain."

"We're summer people."

"Not in Bear we're not."

"Feels like it."

"You want to go outside?"

Buddy shook his head. "Too cold."

Jack was happier to stay inside also. The wood had finally dried enough for a decent fire. The house was warm. "Where's Chris?"

Buddy pointed upstairs. "The new tape."

Jack had let them buy a lot of junk. "Why don't you read your comics?"

"I did."

"All of them? How about reading them to Sam?"

"He's busy."

Jack heard boxes toppling on the porch. "I guess I'll leave him alone." He dropped to the floor and did pushups, panting on fifteen and giving up after twenty-five. "I need more exercise. If we're going on that trip."

"We're not going."

"We'll get there, Bud."

"No, we won't. You never keep promises anymore."

"What are you talking about? When?"

"Before this. For a long time. You're always mad about something."

"Don't change the subject. Give me an example. Name one thing."

"I don't want to."

"You can't."

The boy screamed. "You didn't come to my basketball games, only three times, you didn't take me to the museum for my social studies project. Teddy's father had to, and you don't even know what I want for my birthday!"

Jack grabbed him by the shoulders. Buddy twisted away, but Jack held on. "How can I know if you don't tell me?"

"I can't tell you because you never come home and talk to me."

"I think the word never is unfair."

"Not much."

"I went to more than three games. More like half."

Buddy wouldn't look at him.

"I was your coach for two years."

"But now I'm good. We win sometimes."

Jack went into the kitchen and got a Coke for Buddy. He also opened a new bottle of whiskey and poured an inch into his mug. He returned and handed Buddy the can, tipping his mug to it. "Pals."

"What are you having?"

"Tea."

"No. You're not."

"If you know so much, why'd you ask?"

"Why don't you have a Coke?"

"I'm trying to lose weight."

"You don't really lose weight. You lose mass. Mr. Ellis said so."

"Thank you," Jack said sarcastically. "Thank you, Buddy Bridges, for the sixth grade science lesson."

"I'm finally interested in learning something, and you make fun of me."

"Don't push me. I could easily be in a foul mood again." Jack lay on the couch. It was warm and somewhat steamy in the room even with the low fire. He was drowsy.

"Why are you letting Sammy on the trip?"

"I said he could."

"You said if he grew and if he swam."

"He did grow."

"Not the whole amount. You cheated."

"I let him stretch."

"You don't even know if he can swim yet."

"I bet he can."

"You don't know! You wouldn't let me. I always had to do everything the way you said. You let Chris drive, and you let Sam do everything we do."

Jack closed his eyes. "I do what I think is fair."

"But it's not fair!"

"Bud. It's not written down somewhere. I told Sam that stuff so he'd have something to shoot for. He was such a baby chick."

"You said he had to learn to swim."

"He'll have a life jacket on. And I'll keep him with me."

"I don't care. We're not going anyway."

"Hey, Bud. Drop it. I'm going to close my eyes for a few minutes.

214

Keep an ear out."

"They're already closed."

Jack didn't answer. He wanted to be alone, be away, and not think about kids. What he'd do with Nina some night up here with the wind blowing. The rain was light now, he almost couldn't hear it. Maybe it was really over. They would hit the river. He wanted to do it. Get it behind him and then not make any promises ever again. Except the big one to Nina.

But you've already made that one. And you're safe on that one. You'll make good. The rain is stopping. I can't hear it. Slide the canoe into the water. Step in the center and hands on both sides. Lower yourself then pick up the paddle. Sam in the bottom, sitting on a flotation cushion. Don't let him up on a seat. No seat belts. Push away, don't rock the canoe. Samuel says stroke and hold. Dip and stroke and hold. Twice on each side. Arms sore. Let Samuel rest.

Jack opened his eyes abruptly. The silence startled him awake. He heard no rain, only a steady drip in the downspout. Gloomy yellowish light was in the air like dust, and the room was stuffy. Jack drank water in the darker kitchen. He couldn't see too well. He looked into the downstairs bedroom then climbed the ladder stairs. Chris lay on a sleeping bag, head back and eyes closed. The mouth hung open. Jack removed the headphone.

"Where are the boys?"

"I don't know." Chris shrugged, blinking.

"It's six o'clock. They're not downstairs."

"I was asleep."

"And running down the battery." Jack dropped the Walkman.

"You didn't tell me to watch them."

Jack backed down the ladder. On the front porch, he saw Buddy sitting, hunched over. Something familiar in the shape of the figure made him feel protective. Kids sitting outside houses.

"Hey, Bud. Thought I'd lost you!" Jack slapped Buddy on the back and sat down. He gestured toward the sky. "Our luck is changing."

Buddy was silent. Jack looked around. "So where's Sam?"

Buddy shrugged.

"He's not inside. Where'd he go?"

"I don't know. He went out."

"What? To the latrine?" Jack walked to the end of the house and looked around the side. "Didn't you go with him?"

"Am I supposed to do that?"

"C'mon, Bud. Lighten up. Everything's getting better now." He continued looking toward the trees, back up behind the pump. "How long's he been gone?"

"I don't know."

"Guess. About how long?"

"Twenty minutes."

"Geez," Jack hissed. He walked up the slope to the place where he'd dug a latrine. His boots dragged in the soft sand. "Sam!" he called. There was no one at the trench. He picked up the shovel they used for policing the area and cleared away some muddy clumps of earth, filling in the hole a bit. He dug deep for drier sand and shoveled that around the pit, making it more presentable.

He returned to the front of the house, waving to Buddy as he rounded the corner. "He back yet?"

"No."

"Well, shit, Bud, get off your butt and go look for him!" He saw the boy go away from him, toward the other side of the house to the pine trees where he parked the Jeep. Jack turned to the shed. It was empty. He went a way into the woods calling "Sam! Sammy, where are you?" The woods were empty and silent and frightening with no rain and no sunshine. His arms were soaked from brushing aside dripping limbs. Water seeped down the back of his neck. "Dammit! This is not funny, Sam!" He stopped and listened.

He giggles sometimes when he wants you to find him. He wants you to find him and tickle him and pretend to get angry and then swing him around. He does this stuff. All the time.

He ran back to the house. Chris was out now and talking to Buddy. Jack grabbed Buddy's shoulders. "Think! Where would he go?"

"Maybe down to the water."

"That's the *last* place he'd go. He *knows*. He knows the rule." Jack ran toward the lake, shouting back, "Keep looking!" He slipped on the path and almost went down. It was getting darker. It shouldn't be so dark in midsummer, purple clouds blocking the horizon.

He spotted him. There he was, coming out of the water. Jack stumbled, his boots kicking through the weight of wet sand. He's okay. He's gonna get it, I'm so mad, but he's okay. Why in his bathing suit? Then Jack saw how oddly Sam was walking. He was out of the lake now

216

and dragging something along. But smiling.

"Hi, Daddy. A fish bit me."

And Jack saw the left foot. A neat cut almost precisely halfway, starting from the outside and slicing not quite to the instep. Jack dropped to his knees. Sam's foot opened in a red vee and flapped as though held together by one fragile hinge. One foot, so tiny. How could one tiny foot bleed so much?

Jack made Sam lie on the wet sand. He pulled off his shirt and rolled it under the boy's head. He was yanking off a boot and shouting, hoarsely, "Chris! Buddy! Chris! Buddy!" His sock, even damp. He pressed the two sections of the foot together and wrapped the sock around it. He didn't hear the other boys' pounding feet until they were stopped behind him. Sam looked up and said, in the same cheery voice, "A fish bit me!"

Chris laughed. Then he looked at Jack's hand. The blood was trickling out between Jack's fingers where he held the white tube sock, now red. "Daddy!" he gasped.

Jack did not move and spoke calmly. "I want you to take the Jeep. The keys are here in my rear pocket. Go call the doctor. The pay phone at Myers' gas—two miles about. I think that's the closest one."

"Daddy!" Chris was trembling. "Daddy, I've never driven it. I've never driven at night or on the highway."

Jack continued to speak, almost in monotone. "You'll be okay. It's the same as the other one. Just stay to the right of the painted line. We need a doctor here. That's the important thing."

"Which doctor?"

"There's only one. Peterson."

"Shouldn't you…?"

"He can't be moved. I need to stay here. Go now, Chris. Please, go." He didn't turn. He listened, and after a while he heard a door slam. The engine started, died. Started, died. Jack raised Sam's leg carefully and held it across his lap. The Jeep started and made a great noise as Chris circled the house then grew fainter.

There's still plenty of light. Don't go off the track, you'll get stuck. Before you pull onto the road, watch that curve to the left. Sometimes they come at you so fast. Take it easy. Hurry. It's okay if you're scared. When you're scared, you're careful. Hurry.

Buddy was staring where they couldn't hear the Jeep anymore.

"I need some things from the house, Buddy."

Buddy nodded, not looking at him.

"Make two trips if you have to. We need a couple of blankets. And stuff to pack around this foot. Anything. I can't think what. Towels or something like that. Clean if you can find them."

Buddy started to leave.

"First, can you take off this other boot for me? I need the sock."

Buddy yanked hard. It was awkward. Jack didn't want to disturb Sam. "Easy. There, now can you peel it off and hand it to me?" He wrapped the other sock on top of the first and kept pressing his hands around the foot. "Okay, that's good. Go!"

Buddy ran. Jack kept staring at Sam. His color was funny, and he wasn't talking. "Was it a big fish, Sam? Did you see it?"

The boy nodded weakly. "Big."

"Then it must have been a whale." Why was he whispering? He had to talk louder, so Sam could hear him. "Gosh, think of seeing a whale."

Sam smiled sweetly. He closed his eyes. His hand rested on the sand. Jack saw the stiff fingers jerk a little.

"You can tell all your friends." Jack's voice was breaking. "Who you gonna tell?"

Sam didn't respond.

"And of course Mommy. What shall we tell Mommy?"

Jack stopped. Buddy returned, arms piled. "Where does it go?"

"Just drop it." Jack couldn't move his hands so he instructed Buddy to fold one blanket in fourths and place it next to Sam. Then Buddy took Sam's shoulders with Jack still holding the foot, and, moving it as little as possible, they slid the small body onto the blanket. "Now the other one goes on top."

Buddy covered Sam. "I brought a pillow for his head."

Jack could feel his face smile. "What do we have for bandages?"

Buddy shook out material that shone white, almost blue-white in the dim evening.

"What?" Jack strained to see.

"I found them in Grandpa's room. In a drawer."

They were pillow cases. Jack's mother had made them of fine cotton and trimmed them with her handmade lace and embroidered flowers of silk thread.

"Is it okay?"

"Perfect. Fold them the long way. We might have to tear them." Jack wrapped a long, thick strip around the foot without removing the bright red socks. Even in the weak light, they could see how wet the blood was. The clean white cloth turned pink and then dark.

"Why is there so much blood?"

"There's a lot of blood in the body, son."

"But he's just bleeding in his foot, right? It's coming out of the foot."

"Sam has big feet," Jack said softly. "Can you run up there again? Bring some water and a spoon. I'm going to see if he can take liquids."

Buddy spurted off. Jack counted a minute by seconds.

He's at the station. He's made the call. There's no rescue equipment in Bear but surely at the county hospital. Or the fire station in Lebeau, that's closer. They must have it there. Doc will come. He'll stop this and get him in the ambulance. He's on the way. They're always prepared up here for any disaster.

Jack listened, twisting his head. Buddy was coming back, carrying a styrofoam cup, staring into it. He lowered himself next to Sam.

"Try to raise his head. Slip an arm under his neck. See if he'll take the spoon."

Buddy tried. Jack folded and tied another cloth around the foot. The foot was now the size of a melon. "Hold this and let me try," he said to Buddy. "You gotta press hard." He placed the pillow under Sam's leg and gently backed away. He cradled Sam's head and attempted to insert the spoon between the boy's tight lips. Stroking Sam's jaws, he softened the mouth and dripped water in.

"Is he sleeping?"

"He's in shock."

"What's that? Is it like dying?" Buddy's deep voice shaking.

"No!" Jack said sharply. "It's not like dying." He pressed two fingers to Sam's neck. "See? I'm taking his pulse. It's right here."

"What if you weren't here? Would he die?"

"I am here."

"Do kids die if..."

"Stop talking about dying!"

"Are you mad at him for going into the water?"

"Not anymore."

"Would you be mad if someone made him?"

Jack was absorbed in trying to see change in Sam's face. "Need a flashlight. Once more, Bud." Anyway, who could make him? He never went in alone."

"I dared him."

Jack looked into the round dark eyes.

"You were sleeping and I got mad at him and told him you said he was a baby, and he had to swim or not go. I told him and then he left and you woke up and I was scared to tell you and…"

"Buddy! This was an accident. You must hold that foot, and I will keep him warm. It was an accident. We are taking care of him. Hold that bandage. Don't let go, and I won't either."

Buddy was sobbing. "But I didn't want to kill him!"

"You didn't. I need you to help with this, Bud."

Why don't I hear the siren? Why is it so quiet? The red light. I'll see a red light flashing in the trees. It's going on too long.

"Take deep breaths. C'mon, we'll do it together. You gotta keep it together. Look how you're helping me. Of course you didn't want to kill him."

And then it was the light and so much noise and search beams and the men found them on that wet, gray beach. It seemed to Jack that in two minutes, Sam had been carried on a stretcher and packed into the ambulance. One young man took his arm. "You riding with us? Doc Peterson went ahead to the hospital."

"I'll come behind and bring the boys."

"Right." And they were gone.

The first thing Jack did when he let go of Sam was grab his second son who was still sobbing. A rough hug, lifting him. "Thanks, Buddy. Thanks, Buddy." He opened an arm to Chris. "You guys," he said, bound up with them. He pounded Chris' back. "How was it?"

Chris whispered. "The pay phone was out so I had to drive into town, and Doc was at dinner so I found him. He knew who to call. I was so scared."

"We're all scared."

"Is he all right?"

"Let's go find out."

They waited a long time at the hospital while Sam's foot was set and stitched. Then they waited for him to wake up. Jack bought the boys hamburgers, but he didn't eat anything. They tiptoed into the room to see Sam's foot now wrapped as big as a white football. Buddy gazed in awe at the bottle of fluid dripping into his brother.

"Say what you want 'cause I'm putting him out in about two minutes," Peterson told them.

"I better stay with him," said Jack.

"If you want to. But you might as well save your strength, and he won't know the difference."

"There's no phone at the house if…"

"He's not in that kind of danger."

"What, then?"

"We'll see. This cast is just temporary. We'll put on a stronger one later. Then a heavy boot. The doctor sighed. "I can't tell right now about recovering full use."

Jack wrote down a number. "If he needs me."

"He needs sleep now. And we'll watch him, be sure of that."

Jack drove the boys back to Bear. "Aren't we going home?"

"I'm letting you sleep at Dunk's tonight. He's got a room and not much more. But I think you'll be better all there. He'd like the company too."

"Where will you be?"

Jack looked into Buddy's face, his moon face and still too intense.

"I'm going to call your mom."

"Mitchell! It's Jack!"

"I heard you got trouble."

"How'd you…?

"It gets around fast."

"Yeah. I always forget. Say, I'm at the store."

"Key came in handy, then."

"Yeah. I need to call Greta and the drug store's shut. It's late to bother anyone, so…"

"I understand. No problem."

"I didn't want you to worry if you saw the light."

"I did and I didn't."

"Well. It'll be on the bill, but I'll take care of it."

"You will not."

"Mitchell…"

"You call her, Jack. It'll make you feel better."

"Thanks."

"I'll pray for him."

"Thank you, Mitchell." Jack hung up the phone. He had called Mitchell to stall and think of what to tell Greta. But it was nice, that paternal tone. The concern of someone telling him what to do. Call your wife.

He'd thought of doing it at the hospital, but he was in such bad shape there. He still didn't know, wanting to wait until morning. But she'd be angry not to know right away. Maybe she'd be mad at even this delay. A quick call now then again tomorrow when he had more information.

"Greta, it's me."

"Jack?" The voice distant, fumbling. Then snapping, "What's wrong? Something's…"

"Sam was hurt. He cut his foot."

"Oh. His foot." He heard her breath let out.

"He's in the hospital."

"Oh, Jack. Tell me all of it. The whole thing." He heard the fright again. Impatience too, with him.

"He … he stepped on something in the lake. Doc thinks it was a broken bottle or a sharp object like that. The cut went across the foot and just about … just about took it off." He stopped and waited, but she didn't say anything. "Dunk's going to help me rake the cove tomorrow and find what did it. Probably something pitched off a boat."

"Is it…?"

"He's mostly put back together. He's … he lost a lot of blood, honey. They had to give him some."

"But he's okay."

"Yes."

"You can talk to him and everything."

"Yes."

"How long…?"

222

"He has to be in at least a week. They have to get it set right, and he has to be kept quiet. Then ... I don't know. He'll need therapy." Jack stopped talking. Greta was silent a long time. When she spoke it was in a whisper and he had to ask her to repeat it.

"How are you, Jack? Are you all right?"

"I don't know. I'm hanging in there." He was surprised, the way she said it. How are *you*? He couldn't tell her how he really was.

"Jack, you sound funny. Are you truly okay? Tell me the details."

"Can it wait? This was a long shitty day. Sam could've…" he choked.

"But he didn't." Her voice was calm. "We've been through…"

"It always seems like the first time to me."

"Okay. I'll hear it later." She waited then said, "It's never the times you think. You could watch them every second."

"What is this? You don't even sound upset!" Jack was now worked up. "I expected you to be so mad, call me a bastard for neglecting the kid, not taking good enough care of him. I had my defenses ready. C'mon. Accuse me of something."

Dead silence. Jack changed the phone to his right ear. He put his head down and lay the phone next to it. "Say something."

"I would never call you that. What you said."

"No."

"Is that what I'm like?"

"No. Sometimes maybe."

"But that's your basic image of me."

"I was scared, Greta. And very sorry. That was guilt talking. Guilt and fear."

"You said it was an accident."

"Yeah. Well. Everything is. You can call everything an accident."

"Jack, where are you calling from? Where are you right now?"

"Dad's office."

"Oh. I thought maybe the bar."

"Why'd you think that?"

She ignored the question. "You rarely call him 'Dad.' I always hear you say Samuel."

"Mitchell keeps it pretty much the same."

"All those peculiar papers?"

"Yeah."

"The swivel chair?"

"I'm sitting in it now."

"Leaning back? Feet on the desk?"

"This is a serious call. I'm sitting at attention."

"I'm relieved. You sound more like yourself."

"Greta, this has been a terrible day."

"I know."

Neither one spoke. Jack opened the middle drawer in the desk and pushed around rubber bands and broken pencils. "It was nice the way you said that. About how I was doing. Was I all right."

"I know how you are about Sam."

"How?"

"Better than me."

"No."

"Much better. More patient. He doesn't fuss at you." He could hear her moving. "I'm thinking that if he had to get hurt, it was lucky you were the one. For him, I mean." She was quiet again. "Maybe it's selfish. I'm glad I didn't have to see it. Three boys. So many emergency rooms."

"Bud's kind of messed up."

Her breath quick again. "He was…?"

"Not physically. No, he's okay. He just … he's been thinking some things." *Like I don't…I'm no fun anymore. He takes it out on Sam.*

"Have you talked to him? What is it?"

Jack sighed. "We talked. I don't know if we're connecting."

"I think that's going to get harder. You two're so much alike."

"Buddy?"

"You don't see it."

"I'm intense like that? Talk your head off?" She laughed and he smiled. "I haven't heard much of that lately. Hey. We must cut this off. This is Mitchell's dime."

"Okay," she said. "Sure."

He squeezed his eyes shut, trying to read her. Loneliness there and disappointment. He usually called her from the pay phone, one leg hanging out and shouting over traffic noise, hearing about every other word, quarters on the ledge. "Call me back," he said.

"You want me to? You sound tired."

"Yes. Right now." He gave her the number. "I won't move."

He kept his hand on the receiver. He really owed her more than he'd given so far. And they needed to be on good terms, for all that was coming. The phone didn't ring. Okay. He could use a minute. Jack rolled his head in a circular motion and rotated his arms, flexing his shoulders. He unlaced his boots. Having pulled them on over his bare feet they were filled with sand that he hadn't noticed until now. He emptied them into Mitchell's wastebasket.

Remembering something, he rummaged in a bottom drawer. Samuel had a stash for his bourbon in case of a special occasion. Jack searched clumsily, found nothing. *Mitchell, you're a good man in spite of this.*

It was quiet. He turned on a small desk lamp and snapped off the overhead to make it easier on his eyes. The lamp was shaded green and left the room in shadows. Jack picked up the phone and listened to the tone for a second. *Any time, Greta. I'm waiting.* This is so typical. She has no idea what he needs. He buried his head in his arms and shut out all the light. *I should leave, go home and crash and tell her I just couldn't hang around.*

The phone rang. "Okay. What did you want?"

"What do you mean?"

"I asked you to call an hour ago. I forgot."

"It was ten minutes, Jack."

"I'm sitting here stinking like a pig, almost passing out, and you're…" He stopped. He heard a faint clinking. "Are you eating or something? Where are you? The kitchen?"

"I'm in the bedroom. I made a pot a tea, and I'm drinking out of an actual cup and saucer and stirring it with a spoon. When you all go away, I treat myself with some respect."

"Are you eating something?"

"No. Why?"

"I'm hungry."

"Gee. Something new."

He took a pencil stub from the drawer and began making long, intersecting lines on the back of an order form. "You sitting up or on the bed?"

She hesitated. "I'm lying on the bed."

"You wearing that shirt I like? The one that doesn't quite cover your…"

"I'm wearing one of your tank tops."

"That's it?"

"It's been very hot here."

He closed his eyes and tried to feel the heat of Virginia's summer. It seemed like he'd been cold and wet for a year. Greta in just a top. "Do you have that pink polish on your toenails?"

"Jack, stop it."

"Why?"

"What good can it do?"

He said nothing. *None. No good.*

"So, what's the status on the canoe trip?"

"It's over. Nothing doing for this year."

"I'm sorry."

"Yeah. I can't wait to tell them, of course."

"I've been thinking. What's going to happen?"

His heart shifted. "When?"

"This week. With Sam and all. How will you manage?"

"I don't know. I have to figure that out." He tore the paper off the pad and began another drawing. He made lines and triangles and shaded in certain areas gray and some black.

"I'm coming up."

He slashed a line across his doodling.

"You want me to. Don't you?"

"Sure." His voice was flat, tired.

"Is there some problem?"

"How will you get here? I can't come down to Detroit for you."

"I'll figure it out. They must have a commuter flight to Alpena or someplace."

"You're different. You don't sound like you."

"I've had a nice, relaxed week."

"Doing what?"

"Thinking, mostly."

He didn't ask her.

"I think about myself too much."

"Greta, thanks."

"It'll take both of us to hold him. When he discovers he has to stay in bed for a week."

"I don't think so. Honey, he's pretty weak."

"There's stuff you haven't told me."

"Just … the degree of the thing." He heard that little clink again and the bed creak. "What are you doing?"

226

"Getting under the covers."

"Geez."

"Jack. I want to hear all the things when I get there. I don't want to hear them over the phone. Day after tomorrow."

"Sure, honey."

"And you're going to go over to the beach and find what it was? Buddy and Chris won't…"

"Frankly, I don't care if I never see that particular beach again."

"I always liked it," she said softly.

"Some of the magic has gone out of it for me."

"It was magic, wasn't it?" she whispered.

"There were moments."

"Like making Sam."

"That was the house. You wouldn't on the beach again."

"Well, I meant the whole place."

Jack pulled the phone into his lap and leaned back, throwing his feet on the desk. He was disgusted with himself and sympathetic to his wife. *I'm usually shouting at her when we talk long distance. It's because it's so quiet. I can hear her so clearly and it's dark. This is no good. It won't work if you go soft.* He had to keep things straight in his mind and be hard.

"Why didn't you want Sam?"

He heard her gasp and his own harsh breath in the phone. The question repeated itself, louder in her silence.

"Jack. What's wrong with you?"

"I'm in a go-to-hell mood. I could chew on a baby kitten. Why didn't you want him?"

"I did."

He let her listen to herself.

"It was a surprise, and I had to get used to it, is all."

"How many years?"

"What are you saying, that I don't love him?"

He breathed deeply and said in a gentler tone, "No. Not that."

"I was not at my best, Jack."

"Ah."

"What's that supposed to mean? What do you know about it? I wanted something and another baby wasn't it. But you never saw that. It was all for you. 'Don't make me use it, Greta. It's not the same. It'll be okay. I need you.'"

He let her yell at him, old words; he'd heard them before. Her anger was gratifying somehow. "It wasn't always like that."

"I let you talk me into things. I wanted to make you happy. I thought that's what I was supposed to do."

"You liked it too. I'm not wrong about that."

"When I wasn't scared about getting pregnant."

"Well, you took care of that. Didn't you?"

"I had to protect myself, Jack. I told the doctor I didn't want any more, and he fixed it for me. What's so terrible?"

"I should have been in on that!" He'd never told her how angry he'd been.

"You were still upset about losing Samuel. I didn't want to cause more…"

"I was fine by the time the baby…"

"Right. Sure."

He was quiet, breathing hard. He drew a series of circles, interconnecting.

"Jack, we shouldn't be doing this."

"Why not? Why the hell not?!"

"Wait 'til I get there. Then you can tell me everything."

Jack started putting question marks in all the circles, some large, some tiny.

"What did you want, Greta?"

"When?"

"You said you wanted something. Not Sam."

"Oh, well. It was a long time ago."

"What?"

"It's not important."

"What, dammit!"

"How much do you want to spend on this?"

"Whatever it takes." He was being nasty, and he didn't care. Anger was clean. "I thought that summer was happy. That's how I remember it. Easy time."

"Yes. And I was happy. But I … there was Buddy starting first grade in the fall, and I was thinking…"

"Keep going."

"I was feeling kind of finished with that phase of it. In my mind I had some freedom. And it was, what I wanted was … I had this idea of

228

going back to work."

"The whole clash was about a job?"

"Not everything. But at the time I was thinking I'd make the move. It meant a lot to me."

"And you blame me."

"No."

"I gave you a kid, and you have to punish me for it."

"Punish you?"

"I'm just trying to understand this."

"It's not that difficult. I liked working. The routine of it. There's order. You always know when things are due and what to do about it. The kids are ... were chaotic. I was so good in the office, and I wasn't always a good mother, Jack."

He closed his eyes. "Yes, you were," he whispered.

"I'm better now. But not when they were little."

She was crying. He heard the sniffling, and now he felt rotten that he made her cry.

"Greta…"

"Wait a minute." She put down the phone. He wrote numbers on a fresh sheet of paper, getting up to twenty-three. The phone clunked, and he heard her blowing her nose. "I had to get Kleenex."

"I'm sorry."

She blew again.

"So, Sam's gone all day if you…"

"Jack, do you know what I did last summer? After I finished helping mother? I applied for work at a temp office."

"You never said."

"It was embarrassing, Jack. I was humiliated. They had a whole list of machines you were supposed to check off that you knew how to use. Guess what? I couldn't make one mark."

"You just take training. That's what everyone does."

"I have no confidence. I was depressed, and then you came home early before I was really okay—bursting in with the boys all over the place and you hot and horny and…" She stopped. "Sometimes you don't even look at me."

They were both quiet.

"Sometimes I'm not a sensitive guy. You should've told me."

"I can't talk the way you do."

He listened to that sentence again. "What way?"

"Just ... you. Open. The thing people love you for."

"Do you? Is that why you married me?"

"You're making fun of me."

"Why did you want to marry me?"

"I didn't! I didn't even want to go out with you!"

"So, why did you?"

"I don't remember."

"Yes, you do."

It was so quiet in the office and out in the town that everything he heard was in his own house hundreds of miles away in Virginia. He heard Greta shifting in the bed.

"I ... you were unexpected, Jack. The way you would look at me, as though you knew you were irresistible."

"I don't think that about myself."

"Okay. Maybe it was just me. And, anyway, after a while it didn't matter because it was true. I couldn't resist you." Her voice was small, and he could not tell if she was still crying. "After we, well, you know, started making love, I felt like I was giving up. And I was so caught up with you. Men had never been ... I never thought anyone would want me like that. But I didn't like the control ... the way you're in charge of everything."

"I don't control…"

"I guess that's how a man looks at it."

"Name something I have control over!"

"This house!" she snapped.

"Aren't we beyond that one? Will that one ever be finished?"

"You never even asked me."

"You want to move? Shall we just move and end this?"

"It's the *way* you did it."

He didn't speak for a while. "I wish I were there—looking at you."

"If you were, we wouldn't be talking like this."

"Yeah? Why not?"

"We just don't."

"I'm going to think about that. If it's my fault."

"Don't. I wasn't accusing you or anything."

"I think you should. Tell me I'm an ass."

"Don't talk like that."

230

"I am. That's exactly what I am."

"Okay. You are."

"You smiling?"

"Yes."

He drew three circles, small to large, stacked up like a snowman figure. He put breasts on it, small perfectly round breasts with tiny dots in the center. He gave her dark hair, sweeping over the face in bangs, and a sweet smile. He drew a heart around her.

"So you want to go back to work."

"I don't think so."

"I thought that's what we were talking about."

"That was sort of ... the past. I've kind of changed my mind."

"Are you going to tell me?"

"You'll laugh maybe."

"I won't."

"You must be so tired."

"I'm so tired I'm wide awake."

"I don't think this is the time."

"I'm interested." He drew a stick figure, next to the plump lady. It was neutral, just lines for arms and legs. Between the legs he put two short lines with an oval connecting them.

"Jack, it's crazy. I've been thinking about whether we should have another kid."

"You fixed yourself on that one, lady."

"Okay. Forget it." Her voice was frigid.

"Well, what are you, nuts?"

"I didn't mean a baby. I meant ... Tim."

Jack rubbed his eyes. His head was pounding and he felt warm.

"Are you there?"

"I had to switch ears. This phone is about a hundred years old and the receiver's like lead."

"Did you hear me?"

"I can't..."

"Timoko, Jack. He's been on my mind. I can't stop thinking about how pathetic he is. It just seems we should have him."

"Greta, this is…"

"Don't say anything."

"You don't even like kids that much."

"Not in masses, the way you do. But one by one I do."

"My head is not working."

"Don't think about it."

"It's just not possible."

"Perhaps." She paused. "I thought you'd like it. I was mostly thinking about you."

"I can't go around adopting all the hard luck kids I meet."

"I said, don't think about it now."

"I'm not promising to think about it ever."

"It's just wrong, Jack."

"This is not how I see my life."

She was quiet.

"Greta." He poured his voice into the phone. "Honey, it's wonderful that you ... I don't know how to ... but don't..."

"Shh. I shouldn't have brought it up."

"I made you."

"Listen. Do you still want me to come up?"

"Yes. Call here and tell Mitchell when you're coming. The house is a little, uh, primitive. Don't expect much."

"Don't tell me about primitive. I live with four boys."

"Hey. Not yet, you don't."

"You didn't get it. You *are* out of it."

"Okay, you can include me among the boys. But don't get your hopes up about Tim."

"How's Chris? You didn't tell me about him."

"He called me Daddy three times when he saw the blood. That's the only thing I've liked this whole stinking week."

"You two getting along?"

"He used his head about getting Peterson. Mostly he ignores me."

"Why does this bother you so much?"

"He doesn't *do* anything, Greta."

"Those girls still hanging around him?"

"Not so far."

"Well, that's a relief."

"He needs more to.do. I'll see if Mitchell can't find something for him here. Be good experience."

"I don't want him to end up in a store."

"Back off, Mommy."

"Don't tell me, Jack. I think he has something. I do."

"Rock music."

"I want them all to be something."

"They'll be what they are. Leave it alone, Greta. You've never liked what I do."

"Jack. Oh, Jack."

"Scratch that. That was very low."

"I was only talking about Chris."

"Hey. You know what he'll say when he hears you're coming? He'll say: 'All *right!*'"

He heard her smile.

"Kiss Sam for me."

"Yes."

"And Buddy."

"If he'll let me."

"I want to see you, Jack."

"Not the way I look now, you don't."

"Even that."

"Greta, get on the plane."

The line clicked. His ear throbbed. His neck hurt and his rear and everything in between. He took a clean sheet of paper and drew another stick figure, making the legs very long. He made large, U-shaped breasts, covering the whole chest area and softly shaded ovals at the curvy bottoms. He stared at his picture for a long time. Then he crumpled all the papers on the desk and pitched them into the wastebasket. *Don't read your trash, Mitchell.* He turned off the lamp and put his head down on his arms. He felt comfortable and slept for over an hour without moving, and when he woke, he was relaxed and not worried or confused.

Jack walked barefoot out of the store, carrying his boots, locking the door behind him. It was almost five in the morning and dark under the lingering cloud cover. He walked along the street, seeing no one. The lights were on in the coffee shop, and he tapped at the window. A young girl came to let him in.

"Coffee hot?"

"Just brewed. You want it here or to go?"

"To go, I guess. What else you got?"

"Truck's not here yet. No donuts."

"Rolls? Anything?"

"There's half an apple pie left."

"I'll take that."

"Slice?"

"The whole thing."

She smiled at Jack and put a plastic fork and a napkin in the empty half of the aluminum tin. He tied his boot laces together and hung them over his shoulder the way he used to carry his skates. The coffee was warm in one hand and the pie cold in the other.

"All set?" The girl opened the door for him.

It was still gray when he stepped on the sidewalk, but there was more feeling of life in the town. He heard car engines and someone whistling. At the one intersection, he turned left toward the lake. The town maintained a beach area, but nobody used it. A weathered dock about sixty feet long snaked out over the water. Some people referred to it as a wharf, but Jack knew you could not upgrade it from a crooked dock no matter what you called it. He walked to the end, stepping carefully, and sat with his back against the pilings and his feet dangling over the side.

He ate the pie first, with his fingers, then drank the coffee. He liked the way it smelled here and the way the coffee taste mingled with the fishy rotting wood. When he was a kid, he would drive his boat to town and tie it here. Sometimes he and Samuel would race each other home, the truck and boat on either side of the shore line. He grinned, thinking about it. The sun was coming up on him; he felt it behind the clouds. The breeze was offshore, still dampness in it but warmer and giving out hope for a change in the weather. He faced the water and let the breeze push on his back.

He made Nina come and sit with him so he would not feel so alone. She was quiet, but he felt her there, her leg against his and her arm around his waist, so peaceful and complete. He let himself think it would be this way. He'd been lucky his whole life, to add new people and still carry with him everyone he loved. He had everything he really wanted. Even the distinct loss of Samuel was not final. He had Samuel; the guy never left him. He was there and always had been.

How can I keep this woman?

Women had been good to him. And he thought about that. A boy without a mother is an orphan to women. He was cared for. Growing up, they fed him, so kind and interested, those lovely mothers and widows in the town. Perhaps it was really Samuel, a way to get to him. But that wasn't all of it. There's something in him, Jack, that liked and trusted women.

Why this one? If it were only physical, if I only wanted her body, I could stand it. What is in her is everything I've ever desired in women, the joy that rises when she greets me, the secrets she keeps about life, about me. I want her, God help me, I want her. If I could name what she is to me, I could take it apart and destroy it. I can't name it, and I cannot have it. Not a question of adding on this time. I would have to break and destroy, pretend, say I don't love Greta. And I can't do that because it isn't true.

And if I run away, they will not disappear. It's too strong, and looking at their faces would burn me slowly to powder. You allowed them to need you. You wanted them. Say no to yourself but not to them. If you can't say no, you deserve to have it yanked, all of it, every shining face and wonderful piece of your bright life.

Nina was still there. He wanted her to know about Greta. He tried to explain. How he would help Greta let go of Chris and how Chris needed that.

I'm just getting started with them, and things are never finished. And you understand that she's difficult sometimes, and I struggle with it because there are things between us that have nothing to do with the boys. And she has a great heart. You always have to remember that, the way she cuts through a tangle and sees what is truly important. I admire her, and I'm proud of her for what nobody can see.

But it's not easy, not the way it is with Nina. And he knows this about himself, that he likes things to be easy.

The town was really moving behind him now. Everyone checking up on the day. People would see him and come to ask about Sam. He didn't turn around. There was so much he had to do, this day and for many more. He sat with his feet down in the water. He wanted to be by himself awhile longer, sitting and staring at the colorless morning, utterly alone and feeling nothing.

Chapter Fifteen

It's Not the Whole Story

Jack enjoyed a moment of listening to the school, the quiet along the corridors and Irene's typing and calm voice in the outer office. Three weeks into the semester and things were settling down. No parents lined up requesting class changes for their child, the stack of yellow phone messages dwindling. A meeting was scheduled for this afternoon with Porter and all the principals in this section. Jack had his report ready and felt good, knowing he had a grip on it.

"Knock, knock." Rowena Castle stood in the doorway, holding his mug with steam rising from it.

"Hey! Aren't you nice." He motioned her in. "This is service."

"I'm afraid I have an ulterior motive."

"No problem. I've got the time."

Rowena sighed. "It's our boy again." She gave him the coffee and sat down. "This is the second day in a row he's cut. He stayed out once last week. I asked him if he was sick, and he said no. Now twice."

"Not good."

"Before, even when he didn't do any work, he at least came to school."

Jack drank the coffee, thinking. "I'll alert the attendance office. Get on his case a little."

"I called the house last night, but no one answered."

Jack fiddled with a few things on his desk. Rowena was looking at him in a way that was somehow significant. "I'll call," he said. "Or drop by."

"It's just that it's so early in the year for things to go bad."

"Right."

"I think he feels out of it, being older than the rest of the class. Not having any friends."

Jack twisted in his chair. "The boy could not be promoted, Rowena. I'll stand on that one."

She nodded. "It was the right decision. And I didn't mean that anyway. I'm trying to analyze the problem. That's all I'm trying to do."

He smiled at her. "I think you've crossed that line. That invisible line from teacher to friend."

"I am too involved. Old and crabby too. I can't take it anymore. Burnout."

"Ms. Castle, you will never burn out. I can tell. Never."

"I don't know, Jack. It happens to all of us."

"Not you."

Rowena laughed. She stood. "Okay. I've had my pep talk. I'll leave before you get out the pom-poms."

"This was it? No more problems?"

"Oh, sure. Lots. But I'm going to lob them at you one at a time. More fun that way."

"You're sadistic, Rowena."

"Is that why I keep doing this?"

"I'm glad you came down." He saluted her with the coffee mug. "Thanks."

Jack thought how nice it was, being on the right side of Rowena again. He picked up a stack of papers and started to read. He put them down, flipped through the school directory, and called Tim's house. No answer. The kid was probably hanging around the strip shopping center he went to almost every day after school. Jack had spotted him there on his way home. He had talked more with Greta about the situation. She still wanted him, wanted to try it. Jack thought there would be trouble. The mother must get something out of it—money, control of a trust fund something. It would likely be a mess. They hadn't discussed it with their boys.

Jack leaned back in his chair. He'd spent a lot of time making things right with his family after Greta had come to Bear. Jack had given Chris some difficult but satisfying jobs around the lake house. Greta said he should take the two older boys on the canoe trip, and she'd stay with Sam. Buddy was the one who didn't want to go. Said he just wouldn't until Sammy was ready. So they'd all stayed together, and the summer ended well. It surprised him. They had worried about Sam. He was walking now with a light cast. It might be a complete recovery, but they wouldn't know for months yet.

He and Greta had made plans to fix up the Michigan house and use it more. It had been nice, having her there. And he had been good, waiting with Greta until it was straight, just her and not both of them in his mind. He could do it up there. They had stayed in Bear until the day before he absolutely had to report to work.

He kept himself busy at Great Forest. One teacher was a beginner, and two others were new to the school. The training sessions went well. He organized a faculty family picnic to build team spirit and was pleased with its success. The year began with a solid, unified vigor. Jules Coker was after him immediately about the playground, but Jack told him it was on hold. They would get to it later, after he took care of more pressing business. Jules was annoyed. He didn't want to sit on the money, wanted to build momentum, enthusiasm, get it going again. But Jack put him off.

He did not go walking in the woods, and he did not wander to the far end of the school yard. He saw Nina but not alone. She and her husband sat in the last row at welcome back night for parents, and he smiled at them in a neutral, pleasant way. He would talk to her when he was ready. There was some way to do this. He was working on it. He wanted it to be clean. He didn't want anyone to be hurt, and as soon as he had complete control, he would see her. He was waiting for that time. Dialing her number, he'd hang up, his hand shaking. Every day he spent time not calling Nina. He would see her once more, and since it would be only one time, he wanted to keep it before him awhile.

He was waiting with Tim, also. It would be awkward to begin some process at present, with the boy still attending Great Forest. Jack was trying to get it right. Maybe he should take the whole school year and think about it. There was plenty of time. He would stop by Tim's house at the end of today and get him back in harness. He'd assess the situation with the stepmother; see what problems they might have with her.

Her elusive manner regarding Tim, there's some story there. She's young and didn't ask for this responsibility. It was given her. Think kindly, she's human; try for some real contact this time.

Jack stood and put on his navy blazer, headed toward a third grade room on the second floor. The teacher was having difficulty with the new math text, explaining an atrocity called the ink-blot page. Jack told her he'd help and had written his name in her planning book. Along the way he noticed art work appearing on the walls and in the glass showcases. By winter, he would be tripping over science and social studies projects and students crawling around on their knees, painting murals on sheets of brown paper.

Just before he entered the classroom, he remembered his meeting that afternoon at the superintendent's office and his plan to go straight home afterward. If he wanted to check on Tim, he'd have to double back here, then home again. And there was some reason, something about Buddy, why he told Greta he'd be home early. He'd call and get a reminder and then decide. If he stopped by Tim's tomorrow, on the way to school, that might be better.

The next morning, shortly after Jack finished the announcements, two policemen arrived at Great Forest. The school frequently hosted policemen for assemblies on seat belt and traffic safety. There was something friendly and comforting about the presence of officers patiently explaining statistics to the children. This morning, Jack showed the two men into his office, which they filled with their massive bodies and police paraphernalia—the boots, hats, belts clipped all around with leather cases holding more objects. Guns. This space was fine for little people but not comfortable for large men with serious business to conduct.

"We're looking for information on one of your pupils." One of the men spread a notebook. "Timoko Wells."

"Yes. Tim."

"You know him?"

"Yes. Quite well. I went to his house this morning but no one was…"

"He's been reported missing."

Jack asked the men to sit, but they continued to stand, and he admired and was afraid of their purposeful manner.

"Mr. Bridges, we need to establish when the boy was last seen. And where. There is no clear consensus on that."

"He last attended school three days ago."

The younger man made a note. "That was on the sixteenth."

"Yes."

"Would it be possible to talk to some of the boy's friends?"

Jack thought. "What are you…what suspicions do you have?"

"None right now. This is being treated as a runaway. If we find any reason to think otherwise, detectives will go to work on it."

"I see."

"How well did you know the boy?"

"Quite well, as I said."

"Uh-huh. And did you know the family? The mother?"

"Not in a social or personal way."

The older man, the one not taking notes, looked at Jack. "Are you aware of the situation last summer when this boy was left on his own for some weeks?"

"Weeks?"

"A neighbor reported that the parent was away for two weeks, perhaps three, and Timoko was alone for that period of time."

Jack swallowed hard. He sat on the edge of his desk. "I didn't know that."

"This neighbor said there were older boys who hung around there at that time. This Timoko is…twelve, right?"

"Twelve. Yes." His mind was spinning. "Didn't anyone call child protective services?"

The more mature cop cleared his throat. "People generally don't like to get involved. That's our experience." After a pause, he said, "Would you be able to name or identify any older friends or companions of the boy? Former students here maybe?

"I don't know."

"How about friends here? Anyone who might know where he is?"

"I can give you some names."

"We would like to talk to these kids."

240

Jack stood. "I have been considering this. I cannot allow you to interview any children here. The parents must be the authority in this."

"It would help us out."

"I'm sorry, gentlemen. You have no idea how disruptive and how frightening this might be. And I have no jurisdiction to allow you to question students. I will call in any teachers who might be able to give you useful information, and you may talk to them here."

"Okay."

"And I will try to think just who among the student body could help. There are some who have moved up to intermediate school who might know also."

"Okay. Thanks."

"He was alone for two weeks?"

"That's what they say."

"At the house? He wasn't staying at a friend's?"

"Apparently not. According to the neighbors, he was left there alone to fend for himself."

The younger officer turned pages in his notebook. "We gather he is independent and quite mature for his age. You agree with that description?"

"He acted that way."

"Can you think of anywhere he might have gone? Might want to go?"

"I ... my mind is kind of blank on that one."

"What was his mood? Can you remember? Up? Despondent?"

"He was ... I don't know. He seemed okay."

"These questions are just to jog your memory. People get used to people and they just don't notice things. Then afterwards ... after ... everyone remembers."

"After what?"

The older man coughed. "In this case, after he comes back."

"But where would he go? How ... his bike..."

"His bike is at the house."

"I need to think about it. Let me start sending in some of the staff. Can we do this without alarming anyone?"

"Sure. There's no alarm yet. Just a missing kid."

The older man, the one Jack decided had a more reassuring manner, more protective, said, "The kid probably got honked off about

241

something. He goes somewhere, lays low for a coupla days, makes everyone miss him, then he shows up. Wants to get found. Happens all the time."

"Really? All the time?"

"In 98 percent of these cases."

"Okay. I'm going to get Enid Lacey first. She was his teacher all last year. And our janitor, Mr. Brody, has a kind of fondness for the boy. You guys want anything? Coffee?"

They both said yes.

The policemen stayed at the school all morning. Jack asked the teachers quietly and individually not to discuss the subject of Tim with the children. He thought if they could contain the problem, everything would be smoother when Tim returned. At noon he went out in the yard, and he knew by the way students were grouped that the upper grades all had the story. No matter what you did, they sensed and found out; they talked. Police looking for him. Was he in trouble? Would he get it?

Leaning back on the fence, Jack interacted casually with the kids. He tried to pick up on any gossip or false information so he could set them straight. He discovered nothing useful, but it was good to be there among them, patting heads and shoulders. Kids are a hard fact of life. Affirmative, the sheer numbers of them. They're all over the place, coming to him then running away, the little ones pulling on him to join in play, but he says no, thank you, he just wants to watch today.

The teachers came out for their duty times and he talked with them. The trees were dark green until the breeze whipped them silvery and blew playground dust into Jack's eyes. A hint of coolness in the wind, even at midday, an autumn temperature, and Jack has been thinking it is late summer.

He went back to his office, impatient, feeling the press of time. He asked the policemen to keep him informed He wouldn't expect any news right away, but please, whenever. The men have said they would visit families this evening, all the families on the list Jack had given them. Jack pictured them doing this, the child being questioned, important with big eyes, sitting on a sofa, a parent on either side, the mother's arm around her baby.

He wanted to do something now. There must be something. He must not appear nervous or anxious in front of anyone. But he did not like waiting, and all his patient waiting of the past month had been a strain. He could only wait if he had plenty of activity.

He called Greta. The relief of expressing his fears soothed him. Now he said he was afraid, and now it was not so bad.

"Jack, they'll find him, won't they?"

"Of course. You know, gosh, they send out pictures, they have all this stuff that goes out."

"He could be hitch-hiking somewhere."

"Right."

"Not that much time has gone by."

"You bet. I think they're really on top of it."

"Why did that mother wait so long to report him?"

"I think they just don't count it or start to work on it for a few days."

"Well, I guess they know. The man said ... what? They usually show up."

"Ninety-eight percent." Jack said it with authority.

"Was that an actual fact or just an expression?"

"Greta, I'm only telling you what the man said."

"Don't get mad at me."

"Honey. I know I sound kind of choppy. I feel like I should be out driving around or something. Looking."

She was silent.

"D'you think that would do any good?"

"No."

"What's wrong with people anyway?"

"Jack, call me if you hear anything."

"Of course."

"Are you coming home for dinner?"

"Sure. Unless ... no, I'll be there."

He did go home for dinner but afterward returned to the school, taking the route through Tim's neighborhood. A patrol car had been parked in front of the house, and he saw another down the block. So, it was going to be all right: Somebody would remember seeing him, would know an address, a phone number. Or, Tim would call from a turnpike plaza or a pay phone in West Virginia or New Jersey. Come and get me.

I've run out of money. It was a joke. Can somebody please come and get me? And Jack would ask to go with them and bring him back. He could talk to the mother then and try to come to an agreement. How did you do these things? Were you a foster parent first or plunge right in? He and Greta would talk to her together. It was time now. Really, they had to get started. A boy, twelve, on his own for weeks. What did he eat, for God's sake, or do? Who talked to him? Drifting. Only drifting and he could end up ... anywhere.

Jack stayed in his office doing busy work. He heard Brody knocking around upstairs, his strange affection for Tim keeping him at the school, devising a major project requiring much moving of desks. Then he heard the man's soft shuffle down the stairs and out the back door. How long would a cigar take, and maybe a shot of whiskey? Jack thought of surprising Brody and joining him in a nip. No. It would be undignified and maybe embarrassing. Let him do it alone, secretly, and worry about Tim.

The night outside was humid and warm again. Jack had several windows open, and he listened, for what he hardly knew. Distant sirens. A sudden cry. He finished looking at a stack of yellow sheets, teachers' requests for money—special projects and extra field trips. He decided to approve all of them. Everything to help kids learn something and get along was worthwhile. He began working on a schedule. The lower grade teachers were asking for an earlier lunch time and more PE hours each week. The master schedule looked tight. He could manage one but not the other. Writing notes to himself and clipping pages together, he got through another twenty minutes. It seemed warm with no breeze coming through the outer office window. He stood and rummaged in the closet for a fan.

"Mr. Bridges."

Jack turned to the familiar voice and the unfamiliar sound of his name. Brody lurched in the doorway. The man's head was bowed, and he supported himself with a hand on the frame. He often gestured or pointed to Jack, or mumbled a "you" or "he" in Jack's direction. But Brody never called Jack by name, and now he said again, "I got something to show you, Mr. Bridges."

"Certainly, Clem." His manner, so formal, made Jack want to be personal.

Jack followed him out the back and across the grass, uncut and weedy, to the steps on the embankment. At the bottom, Brody clicked on a pocket flashlight. Turning right, away from the path, he crashed through the dry undergrowth, breaking as much of a trail as he could for Jack. Jack heard heavy breathing and smelled smoke and sweat on the old man's body. With light so dim, Jack couldn't see around Brody, couldn't see up ahead, and bumped into the wide form of Brody's back when he stopped.

Jack, whispering, said, "What, Clem?" and then stepped out where he could see the light pointing on the ground. The beam was so slight in circumference, faint and smoky, that Brody had to brush it back and forth on Tim's diminutive body for Jack to see it full length. The boy lay on his side, but the head was twisted as if he'd fallen flat on his back. His eyes were closed. One arm was flung out and the other crushed under him, at a funny angle and obviously broken. His feet were bare, but the rubber sandals were close by, stuck in the brambly tangle of bush limbs. Jack squatted beside him, looking at the many cuts and scratches on the skinny legs. Ducking his head sideways, Jack read "Redskins" on Tim's T-shirt. He glanced up. This spot was directly under the old sycamore.

Jack looked at Tim again, thinking about what people say, that in death a child is sleeping. Or appears to be. There was none of that sweet peacefulness about Tim. There was something old and ugly about this dark scene, and Jack trembled, because he didn't seem to be dead, not as you imagine death, but rather thrown away, discarded.

He rose slowly and hung an arm on Brody's shoulder. "Turn off the light. Please." His voice was thick and tired. After a minute, Jack straightened his back. "I'm going to call them."

Clem Brody didn't move.

"Could you stay here with him, Clem? Would that bother you?"

"Not me."

"I'm sure it won't be long."

"Don't matter."

Jack started away.

"You need the light, Mr. Bridges?"

"You keep it." Jack took a few steps. Without turning, he said, "I'm glad you found him, Clem. I'm glad it was you."

One October afternoon, six weeks after they found Tim, Jack stood looking out the rear library window. From his first day at Great Forest, he had always liked this second story view straight into the trees. He noticed the colors had lost the bright stenciled edge of the first frost and now the muted leaves were indistinct and falling. It seemed that autumn was going quickly this year. Or perhaps he had been careful not to see it.

He listened to Rowena reading to the second grade. Bells and peasants and animals lived in the story and Rowena made her voice sound like all three. The narrative was simple, the best kind Jack thought, and the tale came out evenly with a tiny problem solved and everyone triumphant. Jack had a mad impulse to go to the group and tell them, each one, how lovely a story can be and especially when someone with a shining voice reads it to you. And they must never forget it. But he went on standing at the window, his back to the room. They would take what they could from all the offerings, remember or lose it somewhere in the years. It was their choice, after all.

Rowena stood beside him.

"Oh. They're gone. I didn't hear them leave."

"You'd better watch that. The kids'll walk all over you if they think you're not paying attention."

"That's what I have you for. To prod me."

Rowena sighed and looked toward the trees. "Are you over it yet?"

He said nothing.

"That was a stupid question."

Jack smiled at her "You're allowed one."

"Did they ever give you a complete report?"

"Yes. Just yesterday. The final is no sign of foul play, no apparent ... suicide. No signs of neglect. It's quite clean. Fall from tree. Accidental death."

After a minute, Rowena said, "And is that what you believe?"

"It's not the whole story. It never is."

"But that's basically it."

"Yes. I suppose."

"How long, you know what I'm saying, had he been there—for days?"

"No. They say about twelve to fifteen hours. So it could have been like the police said. He was hiding out in the tree, waiting for people to miss him. He could have dozed off and fallen."

"I wonder how it happens. I always think this, when I read the paper about these kids. Wasn't there anyone watching them?"

"Rowena, don't."

"Jack, shouldn't we have…?"

"Don't, Rowena." He said it gently. "Just … don't."

"All right."

"The thing is … it's kind of died down around here. The kids don't seem as jumpy, and the teachers have things … well, pretty much under control. And the county finally got rid of the damn tree. D'you think I need to say any more about it?"

Rowena looked at Jack. He wasn't as tight and angry as he'd been the first days after Tim's death. But fatigue lines lingered on his face and around his eyes. It had been exhausting, keeping control, containing emotions and yet allowing the children to express their shock, curiosity; their fears. He had gone to each class, met with the staff, the parents. Counselors had been sent. Everything had been done. And everyone had said repeatedly how wonderful Mr. Bridges was, how kind, how sensitive and patient. He'd broken down only once that Rowena had seen. After a faculty session, one new young teacher had gushed to him, intending to flatter, "Mr. Bridges, I can't tell you. It's almost as though this boy were your own." And Jack had snapped, "They are mine. All of them!" and walked away.

Now he was asking her if he needed to do more.

"This report will be in the paper, right?"

"Probably."

"Then give it a rest. Don't open it up again."

"Rowena, thanks."

"Uh, Jack. Before you go."

"Sure. What's up?"

"There's a rumor."

He sat heavily on the small library table, the one for the primary grades. "Okay. Tell me."

"It's the one about you leaving here."

"Geez. How do they hear these things?"

"So, it's a possibility."

"Porter has a school in trouble. The guy quit on him."

"You're really thinking about it."

"I'm considering it, yes. It's bigger than this. About double the size."

He hesitated. "I'd be so busy there."

"Why you?"

"Porter likes my skills with staff and community."

"I think I'll have a cigarette."

Jack followed her to her office. The shades were drawn against the afternoon sun, and he raised one. The playground was deserted, there was nothing to see. "Rowena, don't ... don't spread this around. Nothing's definite."

"Would I talk?"

He smiled. "I like to think I can tell you anything."

"When?"

"Hmm?"

"When will you go? It's a long time to June."

"They want me before that."

"When they want you, they take you."

"There's no muscle on me. No pressure." He lifted books from a stack on her desk and glanced idly at the titles. "You guys would like a new face around here."

Rowena stared at him a long time. "I think you're taking it."

"I'm considering it. That's all."

"Two weeks. You'll be gone in two weeks."

"Rowena." He smiled at her, wanting her to approve or at least to understand. "It won't be that soon." He looked out at the front school-yard and across and beyond to Nina's house. "There's so much I still have to do here."

Chapter Sixteen

Something Good and Beautiful

Nina hid behind the curtains in Polly's room and watched for Jack. He said he'd come in the afternoon, and from up here, she could see him the minute he left the school. She crouched for a while, resting her elbows on the window ledge until she felt cramped. Slate clouds piled in towers overhead, threatening rain. Oh, what if he came and was all wet! She ran downstairs and put the kettle on, staying in the kitchen and straining to see.

Last week he had asked to see her, formally, as if inviting her to the prom. Then he couldn't make it, and all the time until this morning, when he called again, she was sore from listening, waiting; not breathing her secret. He must come today. And then she saw him, walking into the wind, his head lowered and his khaki jacket puffed and fat behind him. She wanted to see his face as he came close but couldn't until she slid open the patio door. Every voice inside her argued don't touch him, let him do something first, but when he gave her a real smile she leaped and hugged him, drawing him back into the room, her arms under the jacket and glad he wasn't wearing a suit but only a soft plaid shirt and tie.

"Hello, Nina." He didn't kiss her but held her tight against him. "Can anyone see in here, d'you think?"

"No. I'll close the curtains if it makes you nervous." She ran to the wall and pulled the sheers together in a quiet swoosh, dimming the light. She did not switch on a lamp. "I thought it would rain and you'd be soaked. Winter always starts this way and then it's so dreary and wet."

"Nina, let's not talk about the weather." Jack slapped an open manila folder on her coffee table. "And we won't talk about this either. Here're all the lists and letters I have for the committee. I'm turning it all over to you. I stuffed extra paper in there, to make it look like plenty." He unzipped his jacket and threw it over a chair. "I told Irene it would take about an hour to go through these. So that's what we have. An hour."

"Yes, okay." Nina sat on the sofa, hoping he would also, but he took a single chair opposite her. "What did you..." she said as he cried, "Nina!"

"Oh, yes, tell me what to say!" she begged him. "What can I tell you?"

"Nina, Nina." Jack sat rigidly in his straight-backed chair. He leaned forward a little, resting one elbow on his knee, trying to relax. "I only want to know what you've been thinking. About us."

She sighed. "Oh, good. You said 'us.' I haven't known. I go over and over it. How you said you needed time. So I didn't want to push. And all during August, when I knew or thought you must be around and not calling, I thought, well he's being careful, and when he's ready it will happen. But then after that little boy, I ... every time I saw you, it hurt me to look at you."

She stopped. So nervous and she was talking too fast and not saying it right. It was hard when he wasn't sitting close to her. He was sweet and earnest. "When I heard about you leaving, oh, Jack, I was so low and wondering about it all, and when Polly brought home your letter to the parents it was awful. But then, I don't know, I couldn't help it, I began to hope. I thought, good, he's doing this for us, getting into another place where the difficulties won't be ... will be easier to..."

Jack's head was bowed, and he was shaking it no, no, as she spoke.

Nina jumped up. "I made tea," she cried, running to the kitchen.

Jack didn't follow her but waited patiently until she returned with a tray. She set it on the low glass table, and it shone there with china and silver and bright drops of jam on biscuits. She perched on the sofa and poured. Jack didn't want tea, but he wanted to drink from the pretty cup she touched, so he sat by her on the deep, patterned Oriental rug and let her serve him. He leaned an arm on the sofa and looked up at her. She was wearing slacks the color of dawn and a loose top, velvety and golden like honey.

"Your hair is so long and pretty now."

"I kept growing it for you. I thought you'd like it."

"Nina." His chest was tight.

"I was hoping we could go on somehow."

"Every day, Nina, I try not to think about you."

She tucked her feet under her, dropping her head back on the cushion. "There has to be some way."

"There's no way. We have to … you have to know that. I say this to you and it's … it hurts saying it. But there is no way."

The room grew darker. "I think it will storm."

"Not the weather, Nina. We don't have time."

"Is it the family? Just tell me what it is."

"I'm not going to be the one to turn my back on them." He put his cup on the table. "That's the line I've been rehearsing for this."

She was quiet. "I always knew you couldn't, but I never let it be real." She spoke in a dreamy tone. "This doesn't seem real to me right now. I've thought about it so long that it isn't happening."

"It is."

"This is not the last time I'll be with you."

"Yes. Alone, yes."

"Jack. Oh, Jack."

He slumped, his head close to her knees. "I thought I could do this better." He stretched his legs across the carpet, liking the sensation of her behind him and above on the sofa. "The thing is, I wanted you to know what I was thinking and understand it so we wouldn't even have to talk about it. I want everything, don't I?"

She didn't say anything.

He looked at his watch. "Shit." He sat up cross-legged and shook his head as though to be more alert. "I'm not sorry about anything except I never took you anywhere nice."

She smiled lazily. "The thing I always wanted to do was go to the movies and eat popcorn from the same box."

He laughed. "You're so easy."

"And then I wanted us to sleep in a bed together and get up in the morning and smooth the sheets together and put on the quilt to keep it all warm and nice."

"Nina," he whispered. "I don't do that. I really don't."

"That's okay. You can wait for me in the kitchen. I always wanted you there. A warm summer morning and your hair is damp and curly from the shower and you have on trousers but no shirt and you're reading the paper. I bring you a cup of coffee, and you don't even look up and thank me because you're so used to me, I'm just a fixture in your life. You don't have to be so polite to me."

"Don't!" he shouted, standing and reaching for his jacket. "Don't do this!"

She flew to him. She must have pressed him too hard, and what if he hates that she has thought up a life for them. She waited for her panic to go away. "I shouldn't have … I'm sorry."

He caught her hands and held them. "Don't berate yourself." He said it fiercely. "Everything you say is … exactly right."

"Please come back." She led him to the sofa. "We still have time."

He threw himself down again. "It's too difficult if you talk like that."

Threading her fingers in his hair, she petted him. "I'll be good. You mustn't get mad at me."

"Not you, Nina. The whole goddam situation."

"Shh." She was quiet a while. Now that she had him beside her, she wanted that and not to be talking. She heard the rain begin, like the sound of cloth tearing. All the months of nerves and being on a constant high and now he is here and she wants to sleep, she is so sleepy. But she won't and perhaps wake to find him gone.

"Last summer," she said, rousing herself. "I wanted to tell you what my sister said to me last summer. I was saving it for you."

Jack frowned.

"Is it okay?"

"Sure," he murmured. "Tell me." Her hands soothed him.

"She came to the beach house with us, and one night I made a huge Italian dinner for everyone. It's kind of a family tradition; my father-in-law really likes it. Tom got this authentic Chianti that strains like pudding in your teeth. I wanted to walk it off, so Anne came with me, and we stood with our feet in the ocean, and she poured out her wine and we watched it swirl away." Nina caressed Jack's face and made him close his eyes. "She said to me, 'There's life, Nina. A little color and

252

warmth, and then it disappears, and you can never tell it's been there at all.'"

"She know about us?"

"No."

"Not true." Jack was drowsy, his voice sluggish. "What she said."

"It is if you forget me."

"No."

"I'm ordinary except for you."

"Not that."

"We never existed, Jack."

"We did, Nina." He groped for her hand and held it tight. "I just want to know that you'll be okay."

"That I'll forget you and everything will be all right."

He kissed her hand. "Yes, please," he whispered.

"No. I'm not even going to try." His languor depressed her. She didn't care. She would not say only the things he wanted to hear. "It's not over, Jack. This will not stop."

"If I start thinking about you everything else goes to hell."

"Then let it and come to me."

"You can see why I shouldn't do even this much."

"What if I can't … I just can't stand it? What if I call you?"

"Please, Nina." His eyes were still closed. "I can't even let myself look at you. Don't."

She threw his hand away. "All right, I won't. I'll never call or try to see you. You'll never have me interfere in any way. But I'll be here, Jack. I'm not going anyplace, and I'm not going to change. I'll wait. I'll wait and wait. It's what I do all the time even now. I'll pray to be strong and us to stay away from each other. If that's what you want. And don't you call me. But every time the phone rings, I'll hope it's you."

He was on his knees, and she cowered in a corner of the sofa. "I didn't want to hurt you. The stupid agony of this! I meant to come here, face you, make it all right. Do it like friends."

"We're not friends, Jack."

"We're friends and everything else."

"Then, why?"

"Because!" he exploded. "Because I cannot smash lives that I helped to create. And I'm working at being what I should. I come from something, Nina. Oh, Nina, I'm weak. I'm a louse and a jerk. But I'm not cruel. I have something to give them even if it's only myself. It's work. It's such hard work I hear my bones creaking. The strain is … it feels more natural standing here yelling at you, which I've never done, than being nice to my wife!"

She watched him pace. He fell into a chair and jumped up, stomping back and forth in front of her.

"It's this crazy thing and was all clear in my mind until I came in here. I had it all straight. There's no answer to this. What I want is over. You can't shake off everything you've ever done. It leaves you with too little. And I want to keep it all. I want to keep you. God! You're the perfect girl for me! I'll always believe that."

He went to her then and put his head in her lap. He put his arms around her, burying his face, smothering himself against her. He did not want to go out into the cold November rain, and it would be easy to stay here a little longer where it was warm. No one needed him; it would be all right to keep this. He should not be feeling so good right now. He stalled, the best and worst in him raging, so torn that even in moments of ghastly sorrow, he thinks of something good and beautiful to grab onto and make his life bearable and worth living.

"Nina. Oh, Nina. I know I will be happy again. I can't help it. It's awful but true, and you should know this." He brushed his cheeks alternately across her belly, and it was wonderful, that soft fabric and her scent like wood and flowers. He sank into her, and he was happy then and filled with the joy of this woman.

She felt how heavily he relaxed on her, and she must not move but let him stay, keep him there. This time she would not let go. His arms grasped her, and he kissed her and she felt his kisses under her breasts as he dragged his head back and forth. He began to shudder all along his body with a kind of dry violent sobbing, and she held him. *He is relenting.* She pulled back on his hair and gazed lovingly on his face, his eyes staring into hers and his voice deep with struggle, his arms clinging to her, rasped, "Help me. Help me get out of here."

How did she lift him, lead him to the door. And whisper to him, urgent, longing, and frightened, dragging on his arm,

"I can only do this one time."

"Make me go. Kiss me." Pulling away, clinging to her.

The rain was serious now, and she had to push him into it. She didn't see him; she was staring so hard and blind with terror. When her eyes were clear again, she had to imagine how he had run, leaving only tracks through the grass, far apart and driven deep, where his feet had smashed into the spongy ground. She had nothing to do, so she stood there a long time, watching each indentation fill with rain and turn muddy in color.

Epilogue

Why Do Big Men Cry?

It is an early evening in March and cool. Nina opens the door for Suitor then steps back in to slip on a light jacket. Tom calls, "Want company?" and she is surprised, but not showing it says, "Sure." Then Polly clumps up from the basement where she is constructing a Greek temple out of cardboard that Nina doesn't want to look at and cries, "Can I come too?" So they all three stroll through the yard and out the gate and across the field to the school. Suitor runs ahead and then back to them.

"Where's his leash?" Tom asks.

"I'll watch him," Nina answers.

She wants to show Tom the new play structure. It is in place now. The entire playground design is almost complete. All the old equipment has been moved into a more attractive pattern. The centerpiece is the new wooden giant with ladders, turrets, a swinging bridge, slides, everything. Jules Coker has made this a memorial to Timoko Wells. People always feel sorry about tragedy involving a child, and they want to do something about it. This was Jules' idea, and he has been triumphantly right. Money has poured in. The committee will meet one more time and then disband. Nina is having the last gathering at her house and intends to make an occasion of it. She already has food prepared and in the freezer. The children have been kept from the area while all the posts are settling properly and the structure is tested for weight limits. It will be a special day when the students finally are allowed to play there again. The new principal is organizing a ceremony.

Polly climbs on and bounces in a tire swing mounted horizontally on three chains. Tom inspects the workmanship with idle curiosity. "Why the crushed rock, Nina? Isn't this a dangerous surface?"

"It's temporary for drainage. That will all be covered with mulch chips."

"So this is incomplete."

"It's still off-limits to the children. A few more days anyway."

"Then Polly should not be on it."

"Oh, I think it's okay."

Tom surveys the arrangement. "I like this configuration," he says warmly.

Nina doesn't answer. She is watching the moon rise behind the woods. It is large and yellow and appears to be on the same level as her eyes. The black spikey trees, empty still, break the face of the moon into uneven pieces. It looks cold, but Nina feels the approach of spring in the dry wind. She is ready for a change and wants the world to keep moving around her because it's hard when things are the same, day after day.

She wanders to the domed jungle gym and leans forward, curving her body on the bars. Tom comes up behind her and starts talking, but she misses the first few sentences and has to ask him to repeat what he said. He is annoyed and lets her know it, and she is sorry.

"Our first house down at Norfolk—remember? It seemed vast after the apartment. I had to go through all five rooms calling you, Nina. I never knew where you were."

"Yes?"

"I feel like that now. Where the hell are you?"

"Right here."

He slaps the metal bars and climbs a few rungs. "Are you with me?"

"Yes." She stands and looks up at him. He thinks she has some woman's thing, and it is overall, she believes, the easiest way to explain her behavior, her moods. The entire subject of female biological problems is widely recognized, yet unknown in many particulars. She smiles, encouraging him. "Say it again."

He sighs, speaks with exaggerated patience. "There's a possibility, a good one, I'll be offered a different position. Well, they did offer it. Based here or San Diego. But there's no travel. Maybe once a year or so. Twice. Mostly though, I'm at a desk."

Nina takes a breath and holds it. In all of that she has heard only "San Diego."

"So, what do you think?"

"What did you tell them?"

"Nothing yet. I said I had to talk to my wife."

"We'd have to move?"

"No, no. I said it's here or San Diego. If you want to stay here, it's fine."

"I do."

"Then, okay." He is looking at her. "But, Nina, I'd be home almost all the time. That's the big change."

"Oh, Tom!" And now she lets the words tumble. She takes his hands. "I will like that, having you around." It is true. If he is home she will have a lot to do; he is so distracting and demanding. The girls can use a stronger hand, and Elaine behaves better when he is here. She says again, "I'm so pleased."

His hard expression softens. "I'm amazed."

"But, why?" She squeezes his fingers.

"I thought you liked me absent sometimes."

"You'll see!" She laughs now. She makes him put his arms around her, and he is so solid and big that surely, surely she will feel protected. A man this fine and handsome will be enough to hide in forever.

He is patting her head, saying, "Well, I'm glad. It's what I want to do."

She murmurs. She almost hums. "It would be awful to move Polly. We can't do it."

"Really?" He looks down at her. "Now, she's the one I thought might benefit…"

"No, no. She's fine now." Nina pulls him along. "Let's walk. C'mon, double-time around the yard."

She doesn't want to talk about Polly. It always ends up making Tom angry. Of course, the way Polly carried on about Mr. Bridges was very bad. And at first Nina was understanding and shared every emotion and used her own child's grief to say it, over and over, his name and why is he leaving. Holding Polly, rocking with her, I thought he liked us, how can he go away. Nina would soothe her. You mustn't be sad, baby. He hasn't really left. Lucky for us he is just in another place, helping other children. And Tom so impatient with it all that Nina hid most of it from him. Until she was frightened of Polly's morbidity. The night she sobbed, could not sleep, please, Mommy, I want to go to that school, the one where he is now. Please let me go to Mr. Bridges' school.

But things are better now. Nina forced herself to go over and talk to Polly's teacher, and they decided that this was an "adjustment" problem and that soon, Polly would "adjust." That seems to have occurred. Polly still talks about Mr. Bridges but in ways that Nina considers appropriate.

It helps Nina to go into Great Forest again. She didn't want to at first. For weeks, the mood had been so generally dismal, the faces lost and not cheerful. The teachers slogged along, through the Christmas program without him, and everyone said it wasn't the same. It was expected, but Nina didn't want to see it and hear it so she stayed emphatically away. Recently, she has begun working in the library two mornings a week. The work is useful and quiet. She doesn't mix with the teachers or pretend she is on the staff, but Ms. Castle draws her in for coffee breaks in a nice way. So she hears things about him. They all talk about him all the time, and she never realized this.

She was surprised one day when the flashy one, the one who wears pink slacks too tight, said that he had a new car. "He drives a gray Chevrolet sedan now." At the words Nina stiffened. So she might have passed him on the road, or he could have been parked at the school, and she never knew. Nina doesn't quite believe it about the car. It seems wrong. But the teacher spoke with such authority, as though she knew all about him, that Nina has been timid about expressing herself or asking a question.

Just yesterday, she heard them say how popular he is at the new school. They all love him over there. That smart one who teaches the handicapped said, "I feel the way I did when Kennedy died." And Ms. Castle, who seldom speaks directly about him, said forcefully, "It's easier when they die." And Nina had a flash of comprehension, like she has all the time now, that, yes, death is a kind of oblivion where you can hold someone you love, but separation just puts him desperately out of reach. Nina would like to ask Ms. Castle what she meant by that remark. She thinks she would like to talk more with that woman, but it isn't good to show too much interest. She merely asked if Mr. Bridges was coming to the ceremony next week, and the one with the fancy hair said, "No, and I'll tell you why. He doesn't want to interfere."

Nina has a difficult time believing she won't see Jack again. It isn't the end, cannot be. She kept waiting for the phone to ring, for him to say, I can't do it. Or, let me see you again. Just once, Nina.

One day, she was sure he would call. He was still at Great Forest, one of his last days there, and the Jeep was parked out front long after dismissal. She had the idea that he was waiting for everyone to leave, so he'd have privacy. Tom was home, just in from a run, mixing martinis in the kitchen. Nina fussed with dinner. She listened to Elaine talking on the phone in the next room. She picked up the extension and said, "Time's up." But it went on. He might be trying even at that moment. She kept her head down, peeling carrots. She went to the door and screamed, "I mean it! Off the phone!" Tom stared at her. After a while he said, "She's done. Make your call."

"I didn't need it. It was the idea of it. She abuses the privilege."

"You're the one who worries about her not having any friends. Here she is, acting normal and you take her apart."

"She doesn't have to talk so long."

"Maybe she needs her own line."

"For god's sake, Tom." But she dropped it because he was looking at her in such a peculiar way that she was sure he suspected something. She didn't want to get into a mess about it. And after all, he probably wasn't calling anyway. And what could she have said, with everyone standing around? She made it up with Elaine later, and they have been doing well ever since. She doesn't try to treat Elaine like a child anymore; that is gone. She accepts her as a new, younger, immensely talented friend.

Tom is talking to her again, and she turns to him as they finish their circular walk and return to the central playground. Polly is dangling over the top railing of a ladder like a strand of spaghetti, and Tom is noticing how shrunken her clothes look. There must be four inches between her sock tops and her pant cuffs. Tom doesn't like this. His daughters should be well-dressed. "Nina, don't you ever shop for her?"

Nina is sorry because she really has not noticed how tall Polly is getting. Yes, it's her fault for not paying attention. She is against Polly growing up, Tom tells her; that's at the bottom of it. It's his idea of joking. He treats the girls like young adults and Nina like a child. It's one on the things she sees clearly now and that she has allowed it. It's too late to change it around. She is just glad to understand it.

This will give her something to do. She will take Polly out, and they will buy new clothes and maybe everything in a new style. It will be fun. And also some things for Elaine. But Elaine chooses most of her own clothes now with the allowance Tom has given her, and she doesn't particularly like Nina to come along. So Nina has this idea that she will plan a party for Elaine, all springtime and pretty dresses. They will have as many as Elaine wants; everyone, her entire class. They'll be all over the house, noisy and these great boys lounging in her kitchen. Yes, Elaine needs to be young and with friends.

Polly runs to them. She is fretting because they have moved the parallel bars, and she can't see the place where she broke her leg. She asks Tom to help her find it, and he goes off like a good sport to search for the exact spot. Nina tags along. Polly starts to talk about how Mr. Bridges carried her home that day, and Nina, wanting to divert her from this dangerous topic cries, "Try to catch me, sweetie!" as she ducks under the poles and bars.

Polly is in a phase where everything is alive. She eats with the same spoon every night because she thinks it knows her. She asks if the bars, the swings, the climbing poles, all remember the children who have played on them. Tom snorts. He dislikes this kind of childish nonsense and thinks Nina is wrong to encourage it. Will they remember me forever, Polly asks, even after I grow up? Nina starts to tell Polly about all the spirit children and how they come out at night when no one can see them. And there's a spirit Polly for every year she's been here because every year she's been different.

"You let her fantasize too much, Nina."

But Nina goes on. "Only when no one is watching them."

The little girl stops and thinks. "And is there a spirit for Mr. Bridges?"

"Yes. I'm sure."

"More than one?"

"No. He was always the same."

"Mommy…"

Nina catches Polly under the arms and swings her around. She swoops her like an airplane, but she has not been quick enough. The child at last stands dizzily on the ground and remembers what she wanted to say.

"Why was he so sad to go?"

"He loved all the children here."

"Then why did he go?"

"Some other children needed him." This has become rote for Nina. Tonight she has no patience for it.

"I saw him cry."

Nina is silent.

"Why do big men cry?"

Nina sighs, gestures. "Ask Daddy."

Tom gives her a look. This is his least favorite subject, and she knows it, but she is rather tired. She watches the two of them, feeling detached. He puts Polly into one of the old rubber strap swings and pushes her slowly, thoughtfully, as though giving himself a minute before an important presentation. He clears his throat.

"Your teacher, Polly ... no, let me say it another way. This was a first command for your teacher. When a man takes on a first command, it is with the highest, soaring ideals. He has such ... hope. In some ways, he can never go higher."

Nina notices he is using his most authoritative, lecturing tone, but it sounds good, and Polly is not squirming. She is glad he can do this. Oh, we need this, to have him set us straight.

"And except for perhaps his last command, a man seldom has more personal dreams about his work." He sounds less instructional now. "So, when he has to leave and go on, a man sometimes, he sometimes cries or in another way shows his feelings. But that's okay. That proves he's a true man, showing emotion when it's true. He doesn't waste it on small matters, doesn't carry it on the surface, but only deep down. And if he feels it and does not show it, he's no man."

Tom looks at Nina and shrugs. That's the best I can do. She smiles to let him know it's wonderful and that he is. She believes this. Sometimes she thinks he knows so much, is so worldly, that she could tell him about Jack and he would understand. It would make her more interesting and distinctive to him. But, of course, she will not. She still has enough sense to control that impulse.

She has told someone. She couldn't contain it one day and called Anne and talked for two hours. Then again the next day. She explained the phone bill to Tom by saying it was Anne who was upset, was having a sexual crisis. Tom thinks this is normal for Anne. Anne is not shocked that Nina behaved as she did, only tells her it was an immature affair. She can't comprehend Nina's choice and thinks it's a childish reversion to ... well, something. No matter what Nina says, she cannot make him sound wonderful enough for Anne.

Because it's all things she can't explain—looks, gestures, kisses— even to herself. What does she love about him? When she repeats the conversations, they sound juvenile or false or silly. Anne has sent her some books, and Nina reads them constantly or at least looks through them. It's strange but they do help. They help because she can stare at them blankly, thinking of other things. No one says she is idle. When she laughs suddenly or tears flow uncontrolled, she says, "This is nothing. It was something I read the other day." She also likes talking aloud to Suitor. Such a sympathetic face and he repeats nothing.

Nina knows, she has thought this for a long time, that she must control this. She used to manage, when she had him and thought about all the details and things she had to do to get to him. He stayed inside her, his name like a poem she recited endlessly. But now, lately, when and how did it happen, he has escaped and is out there, surrounding her.

She noticed once at a party, the man she was chatting with became Jack and also a man standing behind her. And one day, arranging flowers, he was the bouquet. He's there all the time. Thoughts come and go in her mind, and he is in all of them. When he was with her and she could hold him, his very self, his warm thighs, it was definite and held her in place. He is anywhere now, anything she grasps. She has never confused him with Tom, ever, until recently and it scares her. She loses her center, and one time, making love, Tom put her on top and then she felt Jack climb on her also and she called, "Anchor me!" and Tom was hurt, withered and demanded to know just what she was telling him. She couldn't say. It was shocking and outrageous that she really didn't know, and it was difficult for a while between them.

Things will be better, though, if Tom is home. He will be real to her again. She needs his presence and is glad to feel this way because she wants to be careful with him.

And if she is lonely at times, and heavy with dark dreams, she will live with it because, overall, she has come closer to life and understands more, thinks more, through knowing this one man whom she wants so much. There are days when the pain is lighter; there is an exquisite tenderness to her pain. She is high on pain and desire, and then she allows herself the pictures of him, opens her mind to seeing him, goes wild with his face bending to hers and his hands and his head thrown back and the way he was waking up. That is what she can't stand, that she will never again see him awaken. So she has to make herself relax and calm down, and she thinks of her favorite image of him, the one that brings her peace.

She is looking out her window and she sees him from above and at a distance. The children are running after him, the grass is tall and their feet lost in it. He lets them catch up so they can lead him to a game where he is all important. He moves into, wades into the swirling children, all of them taking a hand, dozens of them, and she cannot see him walk because it's smooth and they seem to be carrying him. The day is bright and happy.

Nina cannot remember if she ever saw this in fact, but it doesn't matter because it's the way she sees him now. And it brings her close to him. *He must think of me. It's too strong. I could not feel this way all alone.*

Like right now. The softness begins, which takes her to him. Nina looks up to the moon, a white feminine moon, high and bouncing, brushing clouds from its face, wanting to be seen. Jack is beside her and above her. She doesn't know what will happen, never knows. She goes out to him, wraps him around her. There is a musical presence in the night. Perhaps she will stay awake all through it, so she can think about him in the quiet.

Tom comes to her, turns her toward their house. All the lights are on as usual. He points to the large open window. Elaine is playing a Chopin waltz. Of course, Nina thinks, the music is real.

"There's nothing so romantic as a girl at a piano," Tom says.

Nina smiles radiantly. She shares this with him and understands him completely. Tom is the ground under her feet. If she can only remember this.

"Let's go home," he says.

They start toward their house, Polly between them. She wants her parents to swing her along, the way they did when she was a toddler. But now she hangs down and is heavy, awkward, and too tall, or her legs are too long to clear the ground. She twists around, looking back at the school, the play structure. Doing this, she yanks hard on her father's arm and Nina feels the pull. Tom tells her to settle down and walk right.

Nina sees that he is annoyed. She wants to stop it so that he will go on being nice to Polly, and that will make Nina happy, and then she will do nice things for Elaine, and in that way they will all go on.

So she smiles at her husband and slows her pace and leans down and whispers softly in her daughter's ear, "Don't look back, darling. Let the little ghosts come out and play."